A GAME

OF BONES

Historical Fiction Published by McBooks Press

A Game of Bones

DAVID DONACHIE

THE PRIVATEERSMAN MYSTERIES, NO 6

McBooks Press
ITHACA, NEW YORK

Published by McBooks Press 2003
Copyright © David Donachie 1997
First published in the United Kingdom in 1997
by Macmillan London, Limited

Cover painting by Geoff Hunt
Maps from *The Neptune Française* by Bellin, 1773
Detail from "Normandie. Costes du Cotentin" *page 6*
Detail from "Normandie" *page 7*

Library of Congress Cataloging-in-Publication Data

Donachie, David, 1944-
A game of bones / by David Donachie.
    p. cm. -- (The privateersman mysteries ; no. 6)
ISBN 1-59013-032-4 (alk. paper)
1. Ludlow, Harry (Fictitious character)--Fiction. 2. Great Britain--
History, Naval--18th century--Fiction. 3. Solent Channel (England)
--Fiction. 4. Privateering--Fiction. 5. Mutiny--Fiction. I. Title.
PR6053.O483 G36 2003
823'.914--dc21

                                                  2002012356

Distributed to the trade by National Book Network, Inc.,
15200 NBN Way, Blue Ridge Summit, PA 17214
800-462-6420

Additional copies of this book may be ordered from any bookstore or
directly from McBooks Press, Inc., ID Booth Building,
520 North Meadow St., Ithaca, NY 14850. Please include
$4.00 postage and handling with mail orders. New York State
residents must add sales tax. All McBooks Press publications can also
be ordered by calling toll-free 1-888-BOOKS11 (1-888-266-5711).
Please call to request a free catalog.

Visit the McBooks Press website at www.mcbooks.com.

Printed in the United States of America

9   8   7   6   5   4   3   2   1

To Helen, Bob, Donna, and Diane

AUTHOR'S NOTE

THOSE familiar with the Normandy coast will recognize the location of the Îles de St. Aubin if not the name. Dramatic imperatives required that the Marcoufs gained a dimension they lack in reality, though in their true incarnation in the days of sail they were more of a hazard.

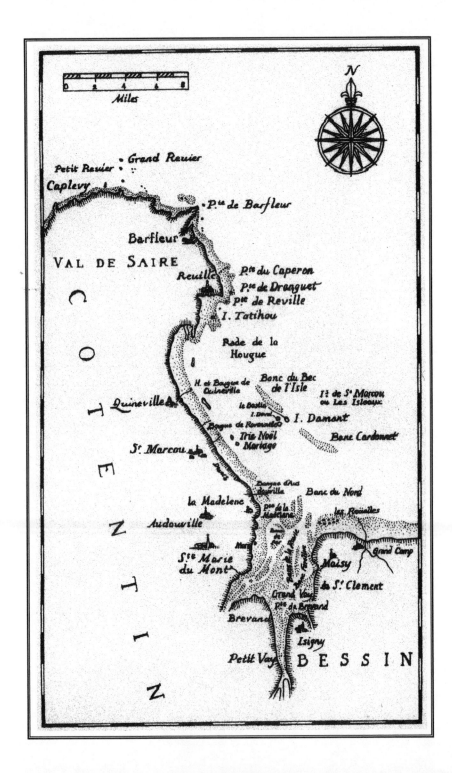

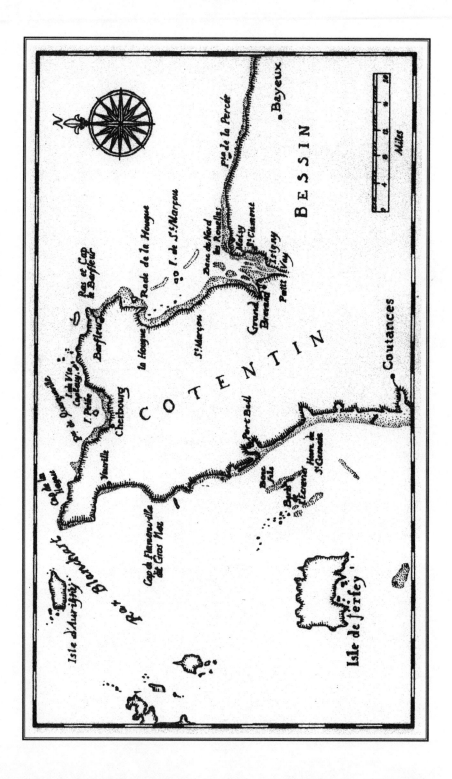

CHAPTER ONE

THE SOUND was much altered, the boom of the cannon lengthened to distant, rolling thunder. But what Harry Ludlow was hearing, as he sat high in the crosstrees, was too regular to be elemental. He knew he was in the English Channel, as certain as any sailor can be that he was in deep water, and that an action was being fought outside the limited range of his vision. But more he could not say, since the white blanket of fog seemed to press against his very eyes. And, naturally, there was little wind to move him forward. Over and over, accompanied by the sound of his own clanking pumps and the annoying rattle of Flowers playing a set of bones, he heard the dull, reverberating thud, his head twisting like that of a snake as he tried to place the source.

Looking down, the deck of *Bucephalas* was similarly invisible, conjuring up the impression that he was suspended in space, with no credible means of support. But he knew it was there, just as he was sure that every man, bar those pumping, would be on deck, like him searching vainly over the bowsprit, seeking some clue as to which course they should follow. Closing his eyes, Harry leant against the rough-grained wood of his upper mast. He suspected that he was close to a small corvette his lookouts had spied the previous night, a tub so slow he would have guaranteed a capture in clear weather. He was fairly certain that whatever vessels they were approaching, the range was shortening. But he'd been a sailor all his life; captain's servant, naval officer, and now a privateer, so he was no stranger to fog. And he knew from long experience just how much it could distort sound.

He felt the ropes moving long before Pender came to join him, but he was unaware of his identity till he spoke, his soft Hampshire burr also affected by the damp, cloying mist.

"How we doin', your honour?" His face, deep-tanned and damp, swimming into view.

"One ship is firing heavy ordnance," Harry replied, "the other something smaller. Yet they have a regularity that goes with practice. The larger cannon are more haphazard. So I think one is a substantial merchantman, lacking the crew for a proper fight."

"Could the other be a warship?"

There was a wealth of unstated concern in that question, since avoiding such vessels was of paramount importance. *Bucephalas* was in no fit state to face even a modest foe. Two years away from home had done nothing for her hull, and in one sea fight she'd sustained damage below the waterline, and subsequent leakage, that demanded constant attention. Yet even in perfect trim, the reasons for steering clear of an enemy ship of war, French, Spanish, or Dutch, were obvious. Privateers made their profits from taking and selling the ships and cargoes of the King's enemies, not from pitched battles where their only reward was glory.

And Pender was trying to remind him, without actually saying so, that here in home waters they were as much at risk from their own King's ships. With the war four years old, and the number of enemies that faced Great Britain multiplying, there was not a Royal Navy vessel at sea, from first-rate to sloop, that wasn't short of its complement. Harry Ludlow had aboard *Bucephalas* a crew of hard-bitten, fighting sailors, all blue-water men, that any King's officer would give his eye-teeth for. Legally they couldn't strip men out of Harry's ship, since he carried protections for his crew. But that very thing had happened the last time they'd been this close to home, proof that such judicial niceties were likely to result more in breach than observance. After such an absence, and in line for their fair share of the fortune Harry and the two-year cruise had earned them, his men were anxious to avoid anything that smacked of risk.

But they had in their captain a man who could never resist the sound of gunfire. They knew he'd steer towards it, even if in the fog he couldn't see that those very same cannon might threaten him. It was in his nature, and had marked his behaviour since the first day he took command of his own vessel, but recent events had exaggerated the trait. Harry Ludlow had suffered a grievous personal loss. The men who'd sailed with him from the Gulf of Mexico, via the port of New York, had learned one thing very quickly: the only thing that lifted his melancholy was action, especially that of the most desperate kind.

"Happen we won't see them," said Pender, trying to make his voice sound rational instead of hopeful. "In this pea soup we could sail right past, not a yardarm apart, and never know they was close."

"Helmsman!" Harry shouted, leaning past Pender to do so. "Steer two points to larboard, and tell that bastard Flowers to belay on the bones."

"Captain," Pender growled, as those very same instruments, made from the jawbone of a right whale, gave an angry, final crack. "We have no need of this."

"Nonsense," Harry replied, his voice as tight as the hand gripping the stay. "It could be the icing on the cake, especially if it's that wallowing tub of a corvette we saw last night."

"A cake we might lose altogether if'n it ain't."

"You're not shy, are you?" Harry hissed, using a tone of voice that he'd never before employed with this man.

Pender's voice was equally unfriendly. "I don't know what I'd do if another asked me such a question."

There was a time when Harry Ludlow would have quickly apologized. But then there had been a period, seemingly distant now, when he would never have thought such a thing, let alone said it. Too much time alone had changed him. What his brother James, now on deck and as worried as the rest of the crew, termed introspection. Pender didn't care a toss what it was in Latin, Greek, or double Dutch. To him it was a bad mood that threatened them all, an excuse for him to indulge in the very limits of the customary relationship he had with his captain, and chastise the man.

"We don't need icing. And I don't need fighting to ease my sleep."

"Go back on deck, Pender," Harry replied calmly. "And that, just in case you are in any doubt, is a direct order."

The temptation to stay and argue was overwhelming, but Pender knew it would be fruitless. Whatever bond had existed between them was no longer there. What had happened in New Orleans had changed that, just as it had altered Harry Ludlow. The man who loved life and laughter and could calculate danger to the inch was no more. Gone was the captain who cared not only for his crew's welfare but for their good opinion.

"And, Pender," Harry added, as the man who'd once been his servant, and until recently been a friend, turned to leave, "you mistake your position. You will in future remember that I am the captain of this ship. We may not be a naval vessel, but that does not deny me the right to impose discipline, to the extent of flogging someone if required."

Pender was too shocked to respond, a most unusual state for a man who prided himself on never bowing to authority. And he was hurt, something Harry Ludlow would have seen if he'd turned to look. They'd been together for nearly five years, the only break enforced by unfortunate circumstance, and in that time they'd been through all manner of exploits. The man threatening him with a flogging had sailed halfway across the world to rescue him, and a goodly portion of his crew, from the hell of a King's ship. Pender slid down the backstay, and as he descended the lump in his throat seemed to grow to match the anger that swelled in his breast.

On deck, with the heat from below thinning the fog slightly, it was easier to see both people and objects. The men had been looking over the side all right, but they turned to gaze at him in an anxious way that indicated their concerns. James Ludlow, standing by the binnacle, approached him as he landed, just as Harry, hearing another boom of cannon, louder this time, called down for a second slight alteration to the course.

"What did he say?"

"He reminded me of a captain's rights in the article of punishment, one which, if he saw fit, goes as far as letting the cat out of the bag."

James didn't gasp, a melodramatic device adopted by some members of the crew, since there was no real surprise in what Pender was saying. Sharing the great cabin with Harry these last weeks, as they'd crossed the Atlantic without the sight of so much as a fishing smack, had been an increasingly unpleasant experience, in which his normally considerate brother had turned into a waspish pest. Though in the confines of the ship his company was hard to avoid, James had done his very best, trying to reduce his presence in the cabin to that of nothing more than sleeping. Harry ate alone, stared out of the casement windows at the wake in utter silence, and banned everyone from proximity while he walked the quarterdeck. When altering sail or giving orders he generally behaved like the kind of martinet naval officer he'd often claimed to despise.

"I think he'll only be happy if we're sunk," James replied.

"If he wants he can jump from where he sits now," said Pender bitterly. Yet more booms erupted, seeming now to move the air around them, causing him to pause. "And with my blessing, as long as he takes care to find the deck."

James put a hand on Pender's shoulder, his voice low and compelling. "It is a temporary thing, an attack of melancholia brought about by his loss. It will pass, in time."

"You said that in the Gulf when we took on them two armed merchantmen," Pender replied, looking around the ship, though the scars of that engagement where hidden by the mist.

They'd had an even closer shave in the Florida Channel, crossing swords with a Spanish frigate. If the wind hadn't turned foul, so that the Dons couldn't get across their hawse, they'd not be here, talking now. James was well aware that the crew'd had to pump ever since that day just to keep a check on the water level in the well. All that labour for damage that had Harry been a little more patient could have been fixed in New York.

"It's only by God's good grace," Pender continued, "that we crossed this far without sighting a ship-of-the-line to attack. And now, when every man aboard can smell the peat of his own home fire, with a King's ransom to be shared, he's steering a course that might see us all pressed or sunk in sight of the shore."

As he spoke, making no attempt to lower his voice, the murmurings of the crew changed to growls. Flowers started to rattle the whalebones again, his sharp, staccato rhythm a perfect foil to their mood. They were edging towards the pair by the shrouds, as if by proximity they could enforce some kind of collective action. James was about to speak, to reassure them, when Harry's voice, louder now, called out.

"Two ships fine on the starboard bow. I can only see their topmasts, but they're there for certain. Take station on the larboard guns and prepare to fire as they bear."

The hesitation was minimal. But it was palpable, which made James wonder just how these men would behave if it actually came to a fight. Nor was he sure whether it was ingrained discipline, fear, or Pender's voice repeating the command which had them doing as Harry had ordered. But once the spell was broken they moved quick enough, well aware that whatever they were about to engage in, it could only be made worse by tardiness.

Aloft Harry felt his spirits lift as the fog thinned slightly. *Bucephalas* was drifting along on one of the numerous ever-changing currents of the Channel, the slight warming caused by a more southerly flow just enough to provide faint vision. The thin trace of the two ships' upper masts, hidden a moment ago, were now like spiders' webs right ahead. Peering forward to look at the pennants made him feel even happier. He recognized one as French, and the other as the flag of the East India Company. The enemy

ship's masthead was lower than the merchantman, a good indication that it must be the corvette, either a privateer like him, or
a navy ship on a speculative cruise. Whatever, it was a worthy
opponent, one that would occupy all his thoughts as he sought to
best her, so that the images that had occupied his mind these last
weeks would be blotted out.

The fog, still thick closer to sea level, made it hard to see the
state of the action. John Company ships, big ocean-going vessels,
were well armed. They had to be in order to survive the long voyage to and from India, where the threats to their security started
as soon as they weighed, and didn't diminish until they dropped
anchor in the Hooghly. But their crews, numerous by normal merchant service standards, were not of sufficient numbers to both
fight and sail the ship, and certainly too few to defend against a
determined and well-executed attempt to board by a heavily
manned enemy.

Judging by the twin sets of topmasts, edging slightly closer,
that was the objective of the Frenchman, using the lee and shallower draft of the larger, drifting vessel to reduce the gap. And in
the light airs that kept the fog in place, the Indiaman was short
on options to avoid such a fate. What sails they had aloft hung
limp in the moist air, only occasionally ruffled as a wisp of breeze
lifted the edge. And all the while the guns boomed out, the blast
thudding into Harry's ears, and the smoke adding a different hue
to the mist which obscured the decks.

Nothing in their actions indicated that they'd seen him
approach. Harry Ludlow prided himself on being tactically astute.
So in a situation where hard information was lacking he normally favoured caution. With very little wind and no idea of precisely how matters stood, he'd no way of ensuring that when he
did engage, both ships would not assume him to be an enemy
and turn their guns to face this new threat. He could find himself caught between two fires, bombarded as much by his
fellow-countrymen as his enemies. But with the exhilaration that

now suffused his whole being, he didn't care. There was a fight to engage in, with the risk of success, death, or mutilation. For a man in his mood, that was more than enough.

"Lookout aloft," he yelled, aware that he could do nothing more from up here. In any engagement his place was on deck. The man got his orders from a captain already sliding down towards the deck, simple instructions to keep an eye on the masts, and tell him if they showed any sign of becoming entangled.

Landing with a thud, he looked around, checking as much as the mist would allow that all his men were in place. The quarterdeck was empty, no one willing to risk their captain's wrath by encroaching on his preserve by so much as a strake of planking. He called to the helmsman, ordering him to steer the ship, which was crawling through the water, so as to take him to the blind side of the Frenchman. He might not make it, might not get the chance to put an unexpected broadside into her hull before they collided. So be it.

It was at that moment Harry Ludlow realized he was unarmed. Pender, normally present at his side, was nowhere to be seen. And the weapons that his servant habitually had ready were missing too. James was likewise absent, the artist brother who always had his sketch-pad ready at a time like this, so that the earliest image of the action could be recorded accurately. Those of the crew he could see, men prone to look aft on these occasions to discern in their captain's eye the state of the approaching battle, were staring fixedly forward.

He'd served on ships with unpopular captains. He knew full well what this meant. But he didn't give a toss. All his attention was taken up with the ethereal shapes which suddenly loomed up at *Bucephalas* out of the fog, the outlines of the two battling ships, now so close together that the merchantman could very well have already been boarded. He lifted a finger to feel the faint wind, and gazed aloft, doubtful that either it, or the fickle Channel current, would carry him beyond the Frenchman with any chance of maintaining surprise. Better to get off some early roundshot and force

the enemy to respond. Turning round, Harry stepped behind the
helmsman and pulled a cutlass from the rack, issuing simultaneous orders to port the helm.

"Larboard battery, fire as you bear."

"Which ship, Captain?" called one of the senior gun captains.

"Damn you, you fool!" Harry shrieked. "Can't you see that
the largest one's an Indiaman? Fire at the bastards in the corvette,
then stand by to board."

Bucephalas swung round on a southerly course, to crawl, parallel, down the Indiaman's side, guns trained right forward. The
Frenchman was half hidden behind the Company ship, set at an
angle across her stern, showing everything abaft his own mainmast to Harry's gun crews. The sound of battle, of sword on
sword, of men screaming and swearing drifted towards them
through the mist. As each gun captain saw, peering through the
port, the shadowy outline of the corvette's stern, he pulled on the
flintlocks, sending balls crashing into the other ship.

The response from the Indiaman was immediate, and devastating. Her cannon, double-shotted and square-on to *Bucephalas*,
roared out a salvo that took Harry's ship all the way forward from
amidships to the bows. The foremast, just above the cap, snapped
in two like a matchstick. As it toppled slowly over the starboard
side, with ropes snapping and blocks falling, it took the wounded
bowsprit with it, leaving Harry Ludlow with nothing forward of
the mainmast with which to control the ship.

Even in such light airs the head immediately began to fall off,
the force of the making tide swinging it round to expose his naked
bows. Harry screamed for axes, at the same time ordering his men
to man what larboard guns could still fire. Practically dead in the
water, and with little in this situation to defend himself, there were
several agonizing minutes while he lay at the mercy of his opponents. They, either French or English, he knew not which, used
the time badly. Instead of smashing through his unprotected bows
with roundshot, an action which would probably have crippled
him, they loaded their cannon with bar shot, elevated the aim,

and sent their next broadside scything through the mainmast rigging.

The range was opening, as the leeway took the two ships away from his, the fog closing in again to hide them from his gaze. He rushed forward, determined to keep them in view, ready to put boats over the side if need be to make boarding possible. Yet he was aware, as he yelled the orders that would clear the debris off his deck, that if his crew were responding they were doing so without the enthusiasm that had made every endeavour on this cruise a resounding success.

CHAPTER TWO

"MAN THE boats!" he cried, as he saw the last faint outline of the hulls disappear. This was shouted at a crew desperately engaged in clearing the ship of the existing wreckage, as well as tending to the wounded, too heavily occupied to respond with speed. The level of invective they were subjected to, when it became apparent that Harry Ludlow seemed to care nothing for his casualties, drove yet another spoke into their diminishing regard for their irascible captain.

He was beside himself, spinning this way and that, oblivious to the blood that stained the deck, cursing men individually and collectively as the boats were hauled alongside; Pender, who'd been absent from his usual station by his captain's side, was particularly exposed to it—so much so, that for the sake of his own self-respect, let alone his standing amongst the crew, he could not help but respond.

"Are you out of your head, Capt'n?"

"Don't dare address me in that manner," Harry roared.

Pender responded in kind. "I can and I will. That's the English Channel below our keel, fifty-fathom water with a swell that can make just trying to row a boat near fatal."

Harry raised his cutlass in a threatening manner. "Get on that damned rope and haul those boats in, Pender, or so help me I'll use this."

"Harry!"

He spun round. His brother James was standing there, the shock on his face extreme.

"What in the name of God are you thinking about?"

"I'm thinking about taking one or both of those ships, which

I could do easily if there was a man aboard with the stomach for a fight."

"We can't board an armed, moving vessel in deep water," Pender pleaded, more to James than to his commander. Even a self-confessed lubber like the younger Ludlow could appreciate the difficulties. It was hard enough to try and board a ship in harbour with everyone asleep. But in open water, with a ponderous channel swell and a crew that was alert and dangerous? "It's suicide."

"Is that what you want, Harry, to kill yourself?"

James had to avoid the temptation to step back when faced with the aggressive way his brother approached him. But he held his ground, and felt the heat of Harry's breath as he spoke quietly, but insistently, his voice devoid of any affection.

"You will oblige me by going to and staying in my cabin. The running of this ship is my concern, not yours."

"I have a share . . ."

Harry raised his voice once more, seemingly no longer concerned about the damage he was doing to his brother's position.

"Your share! So does every man aboard in the profits we earn. But I don't hear any of them have the damned cheek to demand explanations from me on the deck of my own ship. You presume too much, brother."

"And what about me, Captain?" asked Pender.

Harry spun round to face him. "You may go below if you wish, and skulk in the bilges where you will be safe."

"Does that go for anyone who's of the same mind?"

The voice had come from the back of the assembled crew, the fog making it even harder to discern the source. But the murmur that rippled through the ranks indicated it was not a single individual who felt that way.

"I want no man along with me who lacks courage."

"What about those who're brave enough," Pender added, "but too brainy to see the sense?"

"I think, Harry," said James, calmly, "that you have a mutiny on your hands."

"Then I'll go by myself." Harry spoke as he turned, the words uttered before he saw the pistol James was holding, aimed steadily at his head.

"This may change your mind."

"You won't use it, James," Harry replied bitterly, raising his cutlass so that the point was aimed at his brother. "And if you did, I'm not sure that I would care."

"There's not a man aboard wants that, Captain," said Pender, moving closer.

"There's one," Harry replied.

He hadn't turned towards Pender, so he didn't even catch a glimpse of the weighted sandbag with which he hit him. James did, and as the blow was struck he stepped smartly backwards so that his brother, falling forwards, wouldn't run him through. He saw first the surprise in Harry's eyes, then observed calmly the way they went out of focus, this coinciding with the first hint of a loss of the power to stay upright. Two sailors, the Pole, Jubilee, and another called Carrick, stepped forward, to take their captain under the arms. James spoke again, as soon as they had him secure.

"Take him to the cabin, Jubilee. Pender, we'd best double the party on the pumps. And would it be possible to get some kind of jury foremast rigged, so that we can steer properly?"

Seeing the way the man was looking at him, some of the confidence he'd demonstrated evaporated, to be replaced by an uncertain tone. "That is the right term, is it not?"

"It is," Pender replied, with a grin. "But I never thought to hear it from your lips."

James looked sadly at Harry, being borne away by the two sailors, his feet dragging along the planking.

"Neither did I, Pender. Neither did I."

The April sun had burnt off the fog by the time Harry came round. Light streamed into the cabin through the casements, which immediately told him the bows were pointing to the north. He tried to sit up but James put a hand on his chest, and still weakened by the blow, he had little strength to resist.

"I wasn't exaggerating about mutiny, brother," James said, as he saw Harry's eyes casting around with uncertainty. "And since you are in a position in which, temporarily, I can overawe you, I intend to take this opportunity to pass on a few unpalatable truths."

The eyes turned away from him as Harry looked at the bulkhead beside his cot.

"No one could be more saddened at your loss than I was myself. But I must tell you that since that day you have not been fit company for a human being. You have been boorish, bad-tempered, moody, and damned rude, both to me and to the crew. And in an attempt to smother your sadness, you've taken us all to the edge of perdition on more than one occasion."

"Are you finished?"

"No, Harry, I am not. You have accused men who have been loyal to you of cowardice, not least Pender. How you could do that to a man who more than once has saved both your life and mine, escapes me."

"Then in the time you've been at sea with me you have learnt nothing. A captain must be obeyed."

"Even a fool?" Harry opened his mouth to respond but James was too quick for him. "That sounds very like some of the worst kind of naval officers we have encountered, a species you purported to despise. Do you really subscribe to the values of men who will serve out a seaman a hundred lashes for no purpose other than some notion of wounded vanity? Perhaps you should have stayed in the King's service after all. Or is it merely the corrupting influence of power that all you seafarers have. I for one am very grateful that Father saw fit to send me to school, and not to sea."

That was designed to wound Harry deeply, and James could see he had succeeded. The son of a successful sailor, Harry had been listed on the books of his father's ship when he was barely breeched. His entire education had been afloat, first rated as a captain's servant, then as a midshipman, and finally as a lieutenant. While he was growing up with salt in his veins, James had benefited from their father's increasing wealth. Harry progressed from ship to ship when Thomas Ludlow had become both an admiral and a knight.

Profiting mightily from the lucrative Leeward Islands command, and too forthright in his disputes with the Admiralty to be re-employed, Thomas had retired to become a country gentleman. A widower, he'd seen his daughter married to the offspring of an earl, and his youngest son progress through school and university and private study to become a successful artist. But for all their achievements, he was most proud of his eldest boy who, with a fair wind and an absence of peril, looked set to follow him to the very pinnacle of naval rank.

James had often wondered if Harry's court martial had hastened their father's death. Having just participated in a successful battle against the French, in which Admiral Rodney had trounced an enemy fleet in the Saintes Channel, Harry had every right to expect substantial financial reward, and a step in the promotion ladder. Instead, for reasons on which he'd never elaborated, he'd fought a duel with his first lieutenant, and put a pistol ball in the man's shoulder. Called upon to apologize, he refused, leaving a court that was kindly disposed towards him no alternative but to remove his commission.

James, respecting his brother's feelings, never mentioned the matter nor enquired the cause. But several years at sea, and the odd hint dropped by his brother, had allowed him to form certain opinions. Carter, the wounded man, had been well known as a martinet. He not only liked to flog the men, he also took delight in demeaning his officers. James suspected that the argument had been about many things, but that the primary one was naval discipline, too zealously applied.

Harry was not one to condemn flogging out of hand. As he often said to James, it was a right given to all captains, in law, and there were men with whom he'd sailed who'd respond to nothing else. And the feelings of the rest of the crew required consideration, especially where the culprit stole from his mates. But he did not use it unnecessarily, and sailing in a ship manned by volunteers, each of whom had a vested interest in efficiency, he'd never had to let the cat out of the bag on the entire cruise. In happier times James had heard Harry rail against a system that dragged unwilling men to sea, in ships sometimes officered by sadists, who were fed rotten food, robbed of their meagre pay, and denied shore leave in harbour, all accompanied by regular flogging to keep them in line.

"Do I deserve that?" asked Harry, trying to subdue the harsh note of anger in his voice.

"You do, brother, and a great deal more abuse besides. The men you lead have followed you, unquestioningly, into battles that were none of their concern."

"What a collection of saints you make them sound."

The men who crewed *Bucephalas* were far from that. They were in the main hard-bitten scoundrels who welcomed a fight, and loved to take a prize then spend their share of the profits ashore. This was done with no regard for the future, in a land they called Fiddler's Green, on all the things that tars cherished: drink, gambling, women, and song. And when the money ran out they wanted to get back to sea and earn some more.

"Regardless of their personal morals they have not let you down, so it is particularly sad to see you do that very thing to them. I presume you are not anticipating a long run ashore yourself. If life on land bored you before it will do so doubly now. Once the ship is repaired, I can see you desperate to get away again. When you do, you will need a crew."

Harry sat bolt upright, before James could restrain him, his eyes blazing angrily. "There's no shortage of men willing to sail with me, brother, though there might be some that I will wish to leave ashore."

James yawned slightly before he replied, and when he did so

it was in a tone of studied languor that Harry had heard him use so often to devastating effect.

"If you're referring to me, Harry, I must tell you that persuasion or command will not be required. And if your mood does not improve with earth under your feet, I doubt I shall seek your company on terra firma either."

The hail from the masthead with the skylight closed was faint and incomprehensible. Harry pulled himself to his feet, rubbing the back of his head as he did so.

"Who hit me?" he demanded.

"Collectively, everyone on deck, including me."

"Would you have shot me, James?"

There was no avoiding Harry's stare, nor did he try to. Both knew that for all his veneer of sophistication, honed by years spent mixing with the cream of society in the salons of London, James Ludlow had a fierce temper. His languid manner covered a steely determination that surfaced rarely. But when it did he was as capable as his brother of irrationality.

"How can I tell, Harry? But let me say this. If I had pulled the trigger it would have downed neither a brother nor a friend."

"It will be good to have my cabin to myself again," said Harry, pushing past him to make his way out on to the deck.

The crew, some looking aloft and others peering over the larboard bow, knew he'd come on deck. But none turned in his direction, and lest he doubt their indifference, they went back to the tasks they'd been performing without orders. The pumps clanked on, sending a steady stream of silver water over the side. The stump of a jury mast had been rigged, with another spar acting as a temporary bowsprit. The men working in that section were occupied in reeving the ropes and blocks that would operate the small scraps of sail which was all that these makeshift timbers would sustain. Harry resisted the temptation to call aloft to the lookout. Eventually, Pender, who'd been supervising the work, came aft to report.

"Two boats in the water, due east, full of men." His voice was flat, not friendly, not servile. "One of them has waved a shirt so we reckons they're distressed."

"Position?" Harry demanded, not looking him in the eye.

Pender, if he was angered by that, kept it out of his voice. "Can't rightly say. We've drifted somewhat since the fog lifted. Even on a sea like this it makes it easier to work."

"How long?"

"Four hours. I assume we was on a course you set afore that."

Harry finally looked at him, and there was no regard either there or in his tone. "Your assumptions are unwelcome, Pender."

"They tend to go with the answers to questions, Capt'n," Pender replied, bitterly. "If you ask for one you get the other."

Harry ignored him and turned away, pulling a telescope from the rack and heading towards the side of the ship. A call to the lookout told him where to aim and soon the boats, crammed full and low in the water, swam into view. He dropped the glass to study the progress of the work forward, and reckoned that they could close the gap with what he had aloft. The commands he issued were obeyed with such alacrity that he had no cause to complain, but there were no smiles nor jokes, none of the usual banter which marked a crew at ease with their station.

Once the course had been set, with the gentle breeze playing on *Bucephalas*'s quarter, they retired as far away as possible from Harry Ludlow, leaving the windward side of the quarterdeck, the traditional preserve of the ship's captain, for him to pace alone. Once within hailing distance he took a speaking trumpet and called for the occupants of the boats to identify themselves. The man who complied, wearing a salt-streaked but well-tailored blue coat, and waving a hat trimmed with expensive ostrich feathers, made Harry suspect their provenance before the voice became distinct enough to confirm it.

"*Lothian!*" he shouted. "East Indiaman. Ten weeks out of Calcutta, bound for the Pool of London."

"We will heave to," Harry replied, dejectedly. There might be two India ships which had got into difficulties in the same day, but he doubted it. This was the one he'd encountered in the fog. "We have sustained damage that makes it hard to manoeuvre. It is safer if you close with us."

"God bless you, sir, for stopping."

"Open the gangway," he called out, his voice containing a goodly portion of the anger he felt. *Bucephalas* hadn't stopped, but had been found wallowing and drifting. "And put down some side ropes in case he has passengers. A sling in the yards and a sail rigged as a stretcher to lift out any wounded."

They rocked on the swell while the boat struggled to make up the leeway to the side of Harry's ship. If it was hard work, it was at least safe. Without anything to steer by the head, he could easily have caught a fluke of wind that, swinging his ship, would drive them under. Finally the first boat crunched into *Bucephalas* and the crew manned the side ropes to help the distressed survivors aboard. Several wounded men came up in the slings, and were immediately taken below to the cockpit, there to join those already under medical care.

The captain in the well-cut coat, having seen his crew off both boats, was the last to board, making sure before he did that his final possessions, his cutter and longboat, were securely lashed to the rescuer. He climbed up the ladder with an ease born of long usage, and as he came through the gangway he looked around at the damage which no amount of temporary repair could disguise. Finally he spotted Harry Ludlow, standing on the quarterdeck, and lifted his plumed hat in salute.

"Captain Henry Illingworth. To whom do I owe the honour, sir?"

"Providence," Harry replied, wearily. "Which as you know is exceeding fickle."

CHAPTER THREE

"HE'S A damned villain, sir," boomed Illingworth, his loud voice magnified by the low timbers of Harry's cabin, to which they'd repaired as soon as the introductions were completed.

His florid complexion, aided no doubt by his wine, gave him a colour to go with his abundant grey-tinged red hair. Thick lips, prominent teeth, and bulging eyes, on a face dominated by a thick nose, made it impossible for him to hide any emotion. He looked either very angry, very subdued, or when he smiled exceedingly self-satisfied. All three had been on display as he'd described how having set sail from Calcutta in convoy he'd run ahead of his compatriots with the aim of being first home, only to meet his nemesis in the English Channel.

"Damn me if he didn't offer to sell me back my ship if I met his price in decent coin. Goes by the name of Auguste Tressoir. Had the damn cheek to introduce himself, and give me chapter and verse about the charms of his domicile port."

"Which is?" asked James.

"Isigny-sur-Mer," Illingworth snorted, derisively. "It may have been *sur mer* in times ancient, sir. But from my knowledge of the place it's a silted-up backwater now, useless for any depth of keel without a near-flood tide. But that is where he's taken my ship. Worse than that, Tressoir's made prisoners of my passengers. He intends to hold them, as well as the *Lothian,* for ransom."

"Then they must be worthy of it," James replied, as Illingworth held out his goblet for a refill.

A large handkerchief was produced, and the thick nose, after a hearty blow, received a vigorous rub. "They are that, Mr

Ludlow. Sir William Parker and his family are exceedingly well connected. Indeed, two of his brothers are admirals, both favoured with advantageous appointments by the ministry."

Harry wasn't sure whether it was the look of enquiry he wore or his own momentum that made Illingworth continue. "It was a most unfortunate occurrence that Sir William let this be known. But he is a man of parts, one might almost say a person of a boastful persuasion, who demanded of Tressoir that he treat both him and his party with respect."

"You, I trust, would not have done so."

"Never, sir. Silence is always the best policy on these occasions. Tressoir had been gifted enough by the mere capture of my ship. *Lothian* had a cargo worth a quarter of a million sterling."

"Did that include your private ventures?" Harry asked.

"A few pearls, sir, of trifling value," Illingworth replied, coughing slightly, then suddenly reproducing the handkerchief to cover both his face and the embarrassment of dissembling. At least he hadn't insulted them with an outright lie.

James smiled, as aware as Harry of Illingworth's dissimulation. Every John Company captain carried valuables back from the East, to augment a scale of pay which was well above the norm for ships' masters. Diamonds, pearls, silks, and spices were the favoured personal cargoes, and all would be sold to professional smugglers, long before his ship made its landfall, thus avoiding the need either to pay duty or to admit officially to their presence. Five thousand pounds' profit was not uncommon on the round trip, much more if the captain had the means and experience to place private advantage ahead of Company benefit. Well aware that he was unlikely to be believed as to the value of his goods, Illingworth kept talking, if anything more loudly than before.

"Sir William may well have had some ventures of his own. Lord knows his wife's jewellery was worth a mint of money. Besides that, it is not uncommon for returning Company officials to bring back the results of their labours. In that they merely follow in the footsteps of Clive and Warren Hastings, though I doubt that Sir William was amongst the first rank of Bengal nabobs."

"If that's the case your ship could be worth as much as a million pounds," said James, enjoying the startled reaction that the figure produced.

"Nothing like that, I do assure you, sir."

"Then half, perhaps?"

"Sadly, yes," said Illingworth. But he wasn't downcast. In fact, he was looking eagerly at Harry, mouth half open and eyes alight. It soon became obvious why. Leaving the protection of a convoy might be lauded if he'd arrived safe home. But having been separated and captured, Illingworth could well be in deep trouble.

"I know she'll not become a potential prize until Tressoir's had her twenty-four hours, but she might still be worth the chase. Naturally, I would be willing to reward any man who chose to recover her before then. And I'm sure Sir William would have both the means and the inclination to do likewise. Added to that, the Company can in such circumstances be exceedingly generous."

"I cannot go in pursuit of your ship, Captain Illingworth. During your short time on the deck you will have observed that I have sustained damage that makes such a notion impossible. And no doubt you have heard the pumps clanking away."

"I observed both when I came aboard, Captain Ludlow." Illingworth lifted a thick, enquiring eyebrow. "There was a ship that tried to engage us just after we'd been taken. It was impossible to make out her true nature in the fog, of course, but I reckoned her as British. Tressoir had a man in the tops yelling out her course and speed. He showed some skill in his timing, as well as the way he employed my cannon. Indeed he removed the fellow's upper foremast, bowsprit, and goodly section of bulwark."

"That would be us," answered James.

Illingworth turned to face him, his brows now knitted in something approaching indignation. "A little more subtlety might have achieved a result. That bull at the gate approach, when you didn't know the state of affairs, was gallant enough, but exceeding hazardous. The whole advantage of the fog was tossed away."

The merchant captain's hands had begun to move, as he tried to convey the movements of the two protagonists. Busy with that, he didn't see the reaction his words had produced on Harry's face.

"Had you come up on his open side and boarded he would have had a hard job to avoid being taken, since my own crew were barely constrained. Let me say without doubt that I would have granted you his ship as your prize, something in which the Directors of the East India Company would have supported me."

"We have no need of Company rewards, Captain Illingworth," snapped Harry. "Nor of advice on the way to capture enemy vessels. This is an area in which, I think, I have somewhat more experience than you."

"I intended no slur, sir."

Harry stood up and glared at him. "Yet you have seen fit to issue one. And that to a fellow sailor who has just gone out of his way to rescue you. I suggest to you that being personally in distress does not grant you the right to question the actions of a man like myself."

"Forgive me, sir," Illingworth protested. But he spoke in vain, since Harry's back was already halfway through the cabin door. He turned his gaze on to James. "I meant no slur."

"You would not need to with a man in such a mood," James replied, sadly. "It might be best if you avoided his presence until we make our landfall."

"I have yet to ask where we're headed."

"The Downs, Captain. Our family home is no more than six miles from the very heart of the Deal anchorage."

"An excellent place to berth, sir. I had intended to shave the Goodwins myself, weather and tide permitting, having always found the offshore tradesmen in that part of the world very obliging."

The way he said "offshore tradesmen" was designed to avoid the word smuggler, while leaving James in no doubt about what he meant. James's waspish reaction, so close to the tone of his brother Harry, shocked him.

"I have had some experience of Deal smugglers, sir, and it was somewhat less than obliging. Indeed they are to me a damnable crew."

Illingworth recovered quickly from what was obviously another gaffe, returning to the safer subject of the ship and its problems.

"Deal lacks a dockyard, sir, and the Stour is a mite shallow for a ship of your draft. If I'm not mistaken your vessel badly requires such services."

"You have the right of it. The hull has gone two years without a scrape, and nearly all of that spent in warm waters. I am told we are trailing several feet of weed. And we have been in many a battle, Captain Illingworth, being hit hard below the waterline on one occasion."

James looked away, remembering Harry in the harbour at New York. With the new nation, and its trade, booming, every shipwright had been occupied. Too busy to effect repairs immediately, they'd naturally assumed that the privateer captain would wait. He did, but only long enough to trade the gold and silver he was carrying for Federal bonds guaranteeing him vast tracts of land if they couldn't be redeemed.

Several of the crew, seeing the results of their cruise turned from coin into paper, were less than happy, even though in a country desperately short of specie Harry had concluded a splendid transaction. But once that deal was done he couldn't abide the inaction and so set sail with his bottom unrepaired.

Illingworth, still talking, dragged James's thoughts back from these unpleasant recollections.

"Then I would not be surprised if you have lost some of your copper, Mr Ludlow, and that the worms are at this very minute gnawing on your hull."

"Then I bid them cease," said James, standing up, "lest we founder where we are."

"I beg you speak softly, Mr Ludlow," Illingworth replied with deep gravity. "The teredo worm has ears and an abiding hatred of the species *Homo sapiens*. Having spent time in Indian waters, and seen what damage they can do in mere weeks, I am convinced of it."

"No doubt my brother has plans to take care of that. My guess is that he will head for the dockyard at Blackwall Reach, since that is where *Bucephalas* was built."

"Then you will oblige me if you do so, sir," Illingworth added, now looking distinctly gloomy, "though I look forward with some trepidation to informing the Directors of the loss of my own vessel. I have even less desire to pass on to them the terms that villain Tressoir proposed."

James came on deck long after he'd been told of the latest hail from the masthead, time enough for those already present to have confirmed the nationality of the two frigates bearing down on them. They were closing fast, their man-of-war's pennants streaming to leeward. Pender was standing close to Harry, but it was obvious from the gap between them that no contact existed.

"Signal, Capt'n," said Dreaver, quietly, his foxy face anxious lest he inadvertently cause offence. "*Master to repair aboard.*"

"Pender, the ship's papers and log," Harry replied, "and let's get the cutter over the side."

Pender hesitated and looked set to object, entirely due to the tone Harry had used, plus the lack of the usual courtesies. But there was really no point in quibbling. Both orders had to be obeyed, as much to oblige the Royal Navy as to satisfy his captain. Illingworth, following James's advice to stay out of Harry's way, was not on deck. But he was sent for and the speed with which he appeared testified to his knowledge of what had happened, plus the possible consequences. He came to join them forward of the mainmast, hat in hand, his face wearing an extremely worried look.

"The lead ship has been identified as *Amethyst*," said James.

"The other seems new built, and is therefore a mystery."

Illingworth nodded. *Bucephalas* was manned by ex-navy men to whom the outlines and figureheads of the King's ships were as familiar as their own faces. His forehead creased with concern. "I fear we are both at risk here, Captain Ludlow. Let us hope that the officers on those ships have their full complements aboard."

"I carry exemptions for my crew, sir," replied Harry, without turning to face him, his voice showing no trace of sympathy for Illingworth's plight, nor even a hint that what he was saying, judging by past experience, could well be over-sanguine. "They are signed by a senior member of government. So I expect, close to home shores, they will suffice to protect me."

Illingworth glanced at his own men, now without even a ship to safeguard them from impressment, then opened his mouth to ask the obvious question. Harry spun round and cut him off abruptly.

"I suggest, sir, that you accompany me. I will have enough of a task pleading for my own crew without doing the same for yours."

"Are your crew named, sir, in their exemptions?"

"Yes."

"Yet you must on such a long commission have lost many of their number, to natural causes if not the bloody cost of battle."

Illingworth was right. Of the eighty men who'd set sail from Deal two years previously just under sixty were coming home, and a round dozen of them were carrying wounds that might well keep them ashore in future. The truth of the remark didn't please Harry, as was obvious from his increasing silent anger, but that didn't halt the merchant captain, to whom the fate of his own thirty crewmen was much more important than his rescuer's ire.

"Perhaps your losses are enough to cover the number of unwounded sailors I brought aboard. It would be a cruel fate that saw them taken aboard a man-of-war after a voyage to India."

"What would happen, Captain Illingworth, if, in a careful study of my log, such a manoeuvre were to be rumbled?"

Hat off, with his red-grey hair streaming straight back to lee-ward, Illingworth, even as he composed his face to plead, looked very like a man wearing a gargoyle mask. "Every captain afloat seeks to avoid the press. The navy expects subterfuge."

Harry continued as if he hadn't spoken. "I would expose my own men to the fate which awaits yours, sir, that is what would happen. Having plucked you from the sea I feel that I have done enough in the charity line."

"As you wish, sir," replied Illingworth, replacing his hat.

He stepped aside to let Pender give Harry the large oilskin pouch containing his papers. From somewhere forward the sound of playing bones, accompanied by tuneless whistling, could be heard again, a tattoo of rapid, then slow, rhythmic cracks which seemed to heighten the drama of the occasion. Harry had never liked the sound much, whether it was made with metal spoons or whale bones. The instruments Flowers was using were his pride and joy, twin nine-inch pieces of hard bone, flat and smooth on the playing face, and intricately carved with scrimshaw work on the arched back.

"Will someone tell that damn bone player to belay," snapped Harry, rubbing his forehead. "The noise drives me mad."

No one had to pass on the message, since the sound of bones and whistling ceased abruptly. The boat was already bobbing in the water and both captains climbed down in silence, which was maintained as they were rowed across to the frigate, even though Illingworth looked set to speak on several occasions. But Harry stared past him, not willing to converse in a situation he dreaded, in which he would be at the least exposed to a very high degree of condescension.

CHAPTER FOUR

THEIR reception was as frigid as Harry expected, with no hint of ceremony as they came aboard. The officers and midshipmen on deck, efficient like the crew, either ignored the pair or stared with ill-mannered curiosity, trying to guess which one was the privateer captain: Illingworth was the better dressed, so they naturally directed their extra malevolence at him. Left hanging about on deck, so that they would know the depth of the navy's disdain, they were finally ushered into the great cabin after forty minutes.

"Good God, it's you!" said the captain, his eyes nearly popping out of his head.

"Rykert," Harry replied, holding forward his papers.

The frigate captain didn't take them right away. Instead he indicated to his steward to bring forward a couple of chairs. Clearly, whatever attitude he had assumed for this meeting had been blown off course by the fact that he knew Harry Ludlow.

"How many years is it since I last saw you?" he asked. When Harry didn't reply, he kept talking, his voice betraying suppressed excitement. "It was on *Albemarle* I recall. Have you heard about St Vincent?"

Harry shook his head slowly as Rykert grinned happily, and spoke enthusiastically. "Then you'll be pleased to know that on St Valentine's Day Admiral Jervis trounced the Spanish fleet, with our old acquaintance Horatio Nelson very much to the fore. Indeed, rumour has it that without his cheek there would have been no fight to speak of. He had the *Captain* and you'll not be surprised to hear that even without the necessary orders he took her into the thick of the action. The man's the hero of the nation now. Captured two ships at once, crossing the deck of the *San Josef* to board the *Santissima Trinidad*. It's been called 'Nelson's patent bridge for capturing first-rates.' Isn't that just the finest thing?"

Rykert's voice trailed off as he picked up the look in Harry's eye, not sure if it was sadness or indifference, his own face losing the happy expression that his visitor, in receipt of such news, should have shared. No doubt he would have been intrigued at the flow of Harry's thoughts. The mention of the *Albemarle* had conjured up happy memories; Rykert and he had taken passage to America aboard her in the year '82, Harry on his way to an appointment in Admiral Hood's flagship, *Barfleur,* while Rykert was bound for Halifax. Yet it was the name of her captain that had the greater impact. Harry'd been a relatively new lieutenant when they met, perhaps more impressionable than he was now. An instant rapport formed immediately, manifested in a dozen different ways. Partly it was Nelson's directness which appealed, his way of cutting through the normal hyperbole of naval conversation to state the kernel of any truth. But the way he ran his ship impressed Harry just as much, since he was able to converse easily with everyone from his premier to the lowest waister without the least trace of condescension, while the considerate way he treated his midshipmen was an example to every officer in the service.

Others spoke of Nelson's reckless bravery, but to Harry it had been evident from the very first dinner they shared, a trait made manifest as soon as any discussion of tactics took place. Nelson had absolute faith in the quality of the British seamen and was fond of quoting his own mentor, his "sea daddy," Captain William Locker, a man who never tired of repeating that "No officer could do wrong who put his ship alongside that of the enemy." Nelson's only quibble with that remark was to enquire as to the absolute need for a ship.

In another man that might have been taken for bombast. But Nelson's past exploits, happily related to Harry by the *Albemarle*'s officers, scotched such a notion. The two became firm friends, exchanging many a letter. That lasted until Harry was dismissed the service and terminated the correspondence. Thinking now of how much he'd idolized the man, and how far he'd fallen from the standards he set himself to emulate, brought a lump to Harry's throat. And nothing served to demonstrate this more than his recent behaviour aboard his own ship.

"Are you all right, Ludlow?" Rykert asked, slowly, since his visitor had been silent for almost half a minute.

"Allow me to name Captain Illingworth, of the *Lothian*," said Harry, quickly turning to the man in question, who'd had the good grace to stay behind him. "His ship was taken by a French privateer not twelve hours ago. Mr Illingworth, this is Captain Julius Rykert."

Illingworth bowed, then followed Harry's example and sat down. "I wish I could say it was a pleasure, sir. But the villain who took my ship has robbed the day of any of that commodity."

Rykert kept his eyes on Illingworth as he took Harry's packet. "The *Lothian?*"

"East Indiaman, sir, home bound with a valuable cargo, and some important passengers. It was mere luck that had Captain Ludlow close enough to see my boat in the water."

Rykert had opened the oilskin pouch, extracting from it the log, plus the papers relating to *Bucephalas*. Details of the size of the ship and a list of her stores held little interest for him. Only one document commanded his immediate attention. That, several pages long, was stained, crumpled, and covered in the glue that had been used, along with a backing sheet, to stick it together.

"This is a pretty piece of parchment," said Rykert, holding it up between finger and thumb, then leaning forward to examine the writing. "And a rare one."

Harry didn't reply immediately, as if his mind was still elsewhere, an effect magnified by the lack of passion in his voice when he finally responded.

"I'm afraid one of your fellow officers was so ill-bred as to tear it into several pieces. It must have been the identity of the signatory that so upset him. But if you look you will see the superscription and realize that the crew of my ship are exempt from impressment."

Rykert flicked it open to reveal the last page. The heavy government seal was intact and the writing above it plain. The captain's eyebrows shot up as he identified the signature.

"Dundas, by God! I'd be interested to know how you extracted such a licence from a man like him. Especially since, strictly speaking, the granting of such things is not in his province."

"I have no objection if you wish to dispute it with him."

Rykert smiled. "Only a fool would cross swords with Dundas."

"Indeed," said Illingworth, looking at Harry Ludlow with profound respect.

Henry Dundas, as well as holding the office of Secretary of State for War, was also the senior director of the East India Company. He was William Pitt's closest friend and political ally, the man who made sure that when contentious bills reached the Commons or the Lords the Prime Minister could command a majority. To achieve this he had to be able to bribe or browbeat reluctant backbenchers, which meant that the massive patronage at the government's disposal, both at home and abroad, was in his hands. Though not an official of the Admiralty, he could make or break someone like Julius Rykert with a flick of a pen.

That officer had opened Harry's log, and was examining the latest entries, his remark that they were on course for the Downs earning a nod. The whole history of Harry's ship was in that one book, every event, trivial or important, entered assiduously, each man lost, and every wound sustained to flesh or timber, right down to a list of stores consumed. And, of course, it contained a report on each action he'd been involved in.

"My premier reported that you were pumping hard, Ludlow. Is that from harm you sustained this morning?"

"No."

Rykert looked up at this; for the first time since Harry had entered his cabin he looked angry instead of perplexed. His square head almost shook with repressed indignation.

"Do I warrant an explanation, or will I be obliged to search back through your log?"

"We fell foul of a large Spanish frigate in the Florida Channel. She managed to hole us below the waterline. Not seriously, but enough to present us with a permanent leak that my carpenter couldn't completely plug."

"Perhaps if you'd had Nelson along, he'd have taken her for you." Meant as a joke, whatever humour it generated died in Rykert's throat as he saw the look in Harry's eye, more like despair than outrage. "And now you've gone and lost your foremast."

Illingworth answered when Harry, seemingly in some kind of trance, failed to respond. "He was seeking to aid me, sir, a most noble and valiant effort."

Was Harry aware that Rykert was looking at him with something bordering on disbelief? Privateers were no more in the charity business than the Royal Navy. They acted from motives that were purely mercenary. The merchant captain, seeing the stare, continued hurriedly.

"Captain Ludlow could not know, because of the fog, that I'd already been boarded and taken. The Frenchman, a fellow called Tressoir, pretended that the fight was still in progress by creating a hullabaloo, then used my heavier guns to terrible effect. That, added to surprise . . ."

Illingworth threw up his hands and stopped speaking as his fellow visitor's head shot up, well aware that he was in danger of sparking Harry Ludlow's temper again. Rykert flicked back through the log, though he wasn't really reading it.

"You've been to the West Indies?"

"And the Gulf of Mexico, the Florida Channel, and New York," Harry replied.

"And how was the hunting?"

The question was posed in quite a friendly manner, one that Rykert had, in the main, used throughout the interview. But the response from Harry was swift, harsh, and discomfiting.

"You have the right to ask me many things, Captain Rykert, but I do believe that is a private matter."

"A glass of wine, I think," said Rykert, looking for all the world as though he hadn't noticed the tone of voice Harry had used. His steward moved without a direct order, serving the drinks as his captain perused more closely the crumpled certificate of exemption.

"How many men did you bring off the *Lothian*, Captain Illingworth?" he asked, without looking up.

Although he had been preparing for the question ever since the frigates had been sighted, Illingworth was taken off guard by the suddenness of Rykert's enquiry.

"Thirty, all told, but that includes some wounded, my cook, and my steward."

"And you mentioned passengers."

"Indeed I did. Sir William Parker and his family, plus the daughter's companion."

Rykert looked up. "Sir Peter Parker's brother?"

"Yes."

"They are aboard *Bucephalas*?"

"No, sir, they are not. I thought I had said."

"Then you must forgive me if I missed it."

Illingworth nodded to accept the apology. "They have been taken away as prisoners, to be held for ransom. Tressoir also informed me that there is nothing in France to buy my cargo other than worthless *assignats*. So he offered to sell *Lothian* back to the Company for hard coin, gold or silver, and to ransom my passengers for the same commodity."

"This will be very unwelcome news in Portsmouth, Captain Illingworth. Sir Peter Parker is the port admiral on that station."

"I wasn't sure if he still held that office."

"Tressoir, you said?"

"Aye. Cruises in a small corvette. Well armed, of course, but a tub in the sailing line from what I saw of her. He could never have got close to us in any kind of wind. But in light airs and fog, and knowing the damned Channel currents as he did, the swine had the advantage. His base is Isigny-sur-Mer. That is on the River Aure in Normandy."

Rykert's face took on an amused half smile. A man like him, who'd spent years blockading the French coast, knew where Isigny was better than Illingworth. Mentally he conjured up an image of the wide estuary, Le Baie du Grand Vey, fed by the twin rivers, the Vire and Virène. Isigny was on the River Aure, a tributary of the Vire, at the point just above where the tidal waters ceased. The Aure he didn't know, except that for the town to work as a port it had to be reasonably deep.

"He told you this?"

"Yes."

"Then you are aware that it might not be true?"

Illingworth puffed out his chest in a self-important way, his face carrying a very smug expression. "Not if he truly wants to trade. Besides, I can vouch for it, sir. Derouac, my steward, is a Guernseyman. He even understands the local Norman argot, which is more than you could say for most Frenchmen. He listened to Tressoir's crew talking, and Isigny was mentioned more than once as the place they would spend what they'd earned. I know the estuary vaguely. He will have no end of trouble in getting my ship far enough upriver to be safe from attack. He will most certainly have to wait for the height of this month's tide."

"It's a pity, then, that I am not my own master," said Rykert, clearly saddened by the idea. "I have orders and observations to take to Admiral Bridport."

"Are you finished with me?" asked Harry coldly.

"I've had enough of your manner, Ludlow," snapped Rykert, showing open emotion for the first time. "I cannot think why you suppose I would bear you any personal ill will. We were never close friends. But I do believe that in the voyage that we shared we got on tolerably well. I dare say when you came aboard you anticipated an insult at every turn. If that is the case, it gives me some pleasure to disappoint you."

"Would such an attitude be so unusual, when a naval officer quizzes a privateer?"

Rykert responded with half a smile. "No. I am no different from my fellow officers in having little love for your kind. That is why you were left on deck for so long. But it is not my practice to condescend to someone I can call something more than an acquaintance."

"Then that," Harry replied, without humour, "is singular enough in the service."

"Captain Rykert," said Illingworth, who was looking at Harry with alarm. He might have exemptions but the *Lothian*'s crew did not. No good would come of upsetting Rykert when he was about to enter a plea. "My men have returned from a long commission. They have pay outstanding and wives and children ashore who depend on them." He stopped, unsure whether the slight smile playing around Rykert's lips was the prelude to agreement or amusement at his tone of supplication. "It would be most unfortunate if they were taken up by the navy."

"Far be it from me to rob these poor creatures of their pay, sir, nor the comfort of an India ship. Never mind that the country stands in peril, and for want of hands every ship in the fleet is below its complement."

"You may refuse, sir. But to practise upon me is very cruel."

"But I am not, sir," Rykert protested, opening his hands.

"Then you will not press them?"

Rykert shook his head, then fixed his eyes on Harry, his tone brisk and businesslike. "I cannot leave you at sea in such a parlous state, Ludlow. You have a serious leak and damage to your masts and rigging. I'd never forgive myself if your ship foundered for want of my assistance."

"I can manage very well, thank you."

"I know you will not refuse a helping hand. I will send aboard a midshipman and a party of sailors so that you may put more of your men to pumping. I will also escort you into Portsmouth. Your ship needs a dockyard. Your men, Captain Illingworth, can stay aboard *Bucephalas*."

"Captain Rykert is a gentleman, sir," boomed Illingworth, as they climbed back into their cutter. His confidence, which had waned since Harry's first outburst, had now returned in full. Above them, the party that would come aboard under the orders of a midshipman was being assembled.

"You think so?" replied Harry, sourly.

Illingworth tried not to stare, but the effort was beyond him. He knew that Harry's mood had changed, that something said in the *Amethyst*'s cabin had engendered it, but was at a loss as to what it could be. Whatever, it had made his host more amenable, or at least less abrasive.

"He has left my men *in situ,* has he not?"

"He also proposes, Captain Illingworth, to land them in Portsmouth."

Illingworth's expression changed, as he realized how little chance his men would stand in a naval port. They'd be had up by the press before they'd tasted a drop of ale in Portsmouth Point.

"Then why did he not take them aboard directly?"

Harry was staring at the space between his feet. In the fifteen years since he'd seen Rykert he hadn't forgotten how clever the man was. He too had travelled as a guest of the nation's new hero, Captain Nelson. Adept at complex maths, Rykert had shone at the kind of mind games sailors play to stave off boredom. He'd added to that the ability to get on with all of his fellow officers without showing any special attachment to one in particular. Sometimes, when Harry had caught him off-guard, Rykert had worn a singular expression. It was just like the last one his two visitors had been favoured with, a look that spoke volumes for his attitude towards his peers, proclaiming a mind which held itself superior in every way.

"He doesn't want your men, Illingworth, and will be perfectly content to see them sent aboard the receiving hulk."

"Why not?"

"Because," Harry replied, without enthusiasm, "he's a cunning bastard. That certificate of exemption runs out the moment my ship is out of commission, which it will surely be in any dockyard I enter. With the greatest respect to you, would any navy man in his right mind take on sailors used to the soft life of an East Indiaman? He would not, sir, especially when he can have, when he likes, the entire battle-hardened crew of a successful privateer."

CHAPTER FIVE

"IS IT really my fault, James?" Harry accompanied the question with a penetrating look, hard to see in the failing light. In front of the stump that served as the jury foremast the great stern lantern on the *Amethyst* was beginning to glow brightly. As they turned in their pacing, the prow of her consort, *Precise,* was visible over the stern. "We could have run into those frigates regardless of Tressoir and the *Lothian.*"

James knew that to be untrue. But he was not much given to kicking a man when he was down, which Harry most certainly was at this minute. Nor, for all his curiosity, was he prepared to quiz his brother as to what had brought about this welcome change of mood. He'd set off for that frigate with an ill-tempered scowl, and returned still angry. But something had happened aboard the *Amethyst* to alter things. Whatever it was had allowed him to examine his own recent actions with something approaching objectivity, and see them for what they were.

James did wonder if he knew just how much trust he forfeited by his conduct. It wasn't that the crew were soft. Many of them had sailed with hard-horse captains, men who supposed a mere smile to be a sign of terminal weakness. Those who were ex-navy would have steered into battle with such a superior with the same level of enthusiasm as they did under Harry Ludlow, as long as they could perceive even a modicum of fairness.

His headstrong nature, which often landed them in situations not of their choosing, was taken as mere fate, any discomfort alleviated by Harry's habit of coming off best, and his genuine concern for their welfare. It had been rare, in a normal day's sailing, for him to ignore any man who crossed his path. Though he liked to run his ship navy-fashion, he'd share a joke readily, without any loss of authority, and listen carefully to ensure that no underlying grievance was being ignored. Many aboard felt they owed him their very lives. Had he not rescued them from service under a tyrannical naval officer, a man who flogged for pleasure? When danger threatened he called for an instant obedience which had always been readily given.

But he'd fallen from grace, and that had taken him below the level of other, less worthy men. He dropped so far that he was being roundly cursed for their present predicament, with one or two voices even raised to advance the opinion that his action had been deliberate, an attempt to cheat them out of their share of the spoils lying safe in his cabin by having them pressed into the King's service.

"How many times have I said to you, James, that I have the Devil's own luck?"

"Often enough, Harry. And at times, as you well know, you've tempted Providence to the limit."

"Luck is a very necessary commodity, brother, which needs to be pushed. You know the size of the oceans, how slim are the chances of meeting a ship in deep water, let alone an enemy. The men won't follow someone who is unlucky. They don't serve for love any more than I do."

"Humbug!" snapped James, who was determined to keep Harry in his present mood. "I've never met a sailor yet who was truly contented ashore."

"I think, for me, that has just become possible." James was well aware that the remark was posed almost as a question. When he failed to respond, Harry continued. "Can you mark the time when that luck of mine evaporated?"

Adept at keeping his own counsel, James was not about to be drawn, even if he knew full well what he was alluding to. Harry had known many women in his time, the transitory nature of a sailor's life generally proof against too deep an attachment. But in New Orleans he'd met Hyacinthe, a beautiful Creole, half French, half Negro. His infatuation was so quick, and so profound, that he'd promised to bring her back to England, quite prepared to cock a snook at anyone who was troubled by her dubious past. James had counselled caution himself, the memory of which provided an extra impetus for him to change the subject. But Harry beat him to it.

"Did I ever talk to you about a man called Nelson?"

"If you have, I don't recall it."

Harry was looking over the side, so James couldn't see the look in his eyes. But the voice was evidence enough that he was upset.

"It sounds strange now, but he used to be something of a hero to me."

"I never knew you had one, brother."

Harry turned round, James looking away abruptly so as not to react to the wetness around his brother's eyes. "At a certain age, doesn't everyone? He was a post-captain when I met him, with a list of exploits as long as your arm. Brave, I think, to the point of foolhardiness, the best man with a crew I've ever seen. His men adored him. He's a commodore now, top of the captain's list, soon to hoist his admiral's flag. And, guess what? He's gone and won a fleet action that's made him the hero of the nation. Whatever luck I've had, it doesn't extend to that."

This was a side of Harry new to James. All the regret for what he'd lost by leaving the navy was in his face. He didn't have to say that a kinder fate might have put him in the midst of the battle he'd just mentioned, given him a chance of the glory he'd openly craved for as a serving officer, and stifled ever since. But James knew that to indulge his brother would do nothing to solve their very pressing difficulties.

"This is no time for prattling about luck, Harry. What we need now is not wishful thinking but a clear head."

Harry looked up, giving James a wan smile, before he turned his attention towards the waist. He could still see, in the glim, the party of sailors Rykert had put aboard, sprawled on the gangways either side of the ship's boats. He'd racked his brain for a way to outwit them since they'd followed him on to the deck, but nothing presented itself short of violence, which would bring the whole weight of the Admiralty down on their heads. They would face arrest wherever they landed. Staying afloat, even in a seaworthy vessel, would make them fair game for every ship in the fleet.

"I asked Levenson to dinner, which he declined. He must be the only midshipman in the entire fleet who won't sell his soul for an extra ship's biscuit."

"You would have plied him with drink, no doubt?" asked James, happy to see that in considering the problem Harry had changed from his previous mood.

"Indeed. I would have had him insensible. But it is not to be. Rykert has chosen well. When I pointed out to him that a guard on the spirit-room might be advantageous, given that the crew, in despair, would very likely seek solace in drink, he gave me the most superior smile."

Harry's voice changed, to mimic that of young Levenson, who looked to be no more than fourteen. "Captain Rykert expressly pointed out that such a request was to be refused. That we were to take station by the boats, and stay there till daylight, without accepting hospitality or advice."

"He anticipated you."

"Don't play chess with Rykert, James. The man's a damned wizard. He's certainly checkmated me this time. Mind, Julius always was a clever cove, though one that could never quite hide his light under a bushel. That's got him into hot water on more than one occasion. If there is one thing a senior officer hates it is to be hauled up short by a junior, especially if that person has the right of it. I wouldn't say I've observed him forced to grovel, but I have seen him struck mighty low."

"It does a man no harm to have his pride dented occasionally."

"I suppose not," Harry replied, quite deliberately ignoring the irony.

"Which brings us to the subject of Pender." Harry groaned, which confirmed to James that he knew, deep down, just how much he'd offended the man. "It must be done, Harry, and I for one am prepared to tell you so. I have no idea of what will happen tomorrow. You may well return to the same bilious state in which you have subsisted for the last six weeks."

"There's no need for actual words with Pender."

"I think you might be surprised," said James, taking his arm and pulling him aft.

In the event, Harry was proved right, though the artist in James could not help but be fascinated by the silent exchange. Both faces, stiff at first, eased imperceptibly, as Pender picked up the changed mood. Harry likewise realized that he would not actually have to speak about the recent past, which relaxed him further. It seemed only minutes before their relationship was back on a normal footing.

"I had hoped to get all of you away in the boats. God knows we've got enough, what with Illingworth's as well. There are any number of places to land between Eastney, Hayling Island, and Selsey Bill."

"It can't be done without violence, Capt'n, an' it ain't just that midshipman. I suggested to some of his men, quiet like, that they partake of a bit o' rum. Would you believe that they are to a man temperance Methodists?"

"I think it's important that the men don't despair, Pender. There's many a slip betwixt cup and lip, and Rykert is as exposed to the truth of that old saw as any man."

"If'n they hear you say it, I dare say it might go some way to mollifyin' them."

Harry squirmed slightly. "Surely you can tell them, Pender."

James couldn't resist making Harry even more uncomfortable. "It's beneath a captain's dignity to apologize, Pender. I should have thought you would have known that. They are like gods upon their quarterdeck, masters of all that they survey."

"That's unfair, brother."

"I fear I must wound you further, Harry, by telling you that in your behaviour these past weeks, if not your general demeanour, it is anything but."

Pender, reminded of how he'd suffered, continued in a harsh voice. "They need to know their shares are safe, an' all, Capt'n. They like wealth they can touch. That bargain you struck in New York has got some of 'em rattled."

That actually made Harry wince, especially since he'd added to the value of their shares by what was, in effect, a loan to the struggling government of the young republic, desperately short of coin to transact necessary business. And the money had a history. Because of the way it had been acquired it might be difficult to explain away if landed in England. So much better to invest beyond the reach of a grasping British Government. And as for coin, he'd retained ten per cent of the total and promised them their shares and wages to be paid from his own resources as soon as they touched their home shore.

"They think I'd cheat them?"

Tempted to drive home the nail, Pender gave Harry a baleful look. But then he relented and softened his tone. "It's one or two, your honour. An' I've said it before, since I don't recall you hiring them for the size of their brains, that's all it takes to get the rest worked up."

"You'd best lead on, Pender." As he reached the cabin door he turned back to James. "We will need to ask Captain Illingworth to supper."

"Another apology within the same hour!" said James, with feigned surprise. "This is worthy of an underlined entry in the ship's log."

Harry frowned, finding the notion unwelcome. "The mere invitation should suffice for that. Ask Willerby to get some toasted cheese going. And tell him I want the smell of it to spread right across the deck. Levenson might be a paragon, but I've yet to meet the mid who could pass up toasted cheese for supper."

Following behind, James heard Harry's next words to Pender.

"If we can get him away, don't offer those Methodists a drink. Offer them the chance to desert, with enough money once they get ashore to pay their passage home and build a damned chapel if they so desire."

He couldn't help smiling. Though it would very probably fail, such a turn of mind, and the way he'd displayed it to Pender, was very like the Harry Ludlow of old.

The wind had hitherto favoured them, but it swung round to the north-west during the night, forcing Rykert to proceed at Harry's pace. As a naval officer he could command many things, but not the speed at which the crew of *Bucephalas* tacked and wore in a vessel that had every reason to be slow. These were men in no hurry to make a landfall, and they took a savage delight in the way their actions continually forced both frigates into extra, tiring manoeuvres, which kept the watch on duty in the rigging.

Levenson was rocklike in his determination not to disobey his commander, so that when dawn broke, he had to fight to contain the hunger which seemed to shrink his stomach. Dry biscuit washed down with water was no good to a growing lad. But his men had fared no better, and the shared deprivation seemed heroic. He felt almost saintlike in his fortitude, conjuring up images of Sisyphus and his rock. The smells that had wafted out of the galley seemed to linger in his nose. Yet he'd withstood temptation through the long night hours, refusing both coffee and toasted cheese, eventually seeing in the captain of the *Lothian,* sent to offer him hot spiced rum to ward off the cold, the image of a beguiling devil.

The youngster was frozen to the marrow, tired, and very near to being depressed. But the growing light showed land on the larboard side of the ship, and through the mist he thought he could just see the rocky shores and sandy bays of the Isle of Wight. Harry Ludlow, unable to tempt Levenson to partake of his hospitality, had nevertheless pumped him for information about the fleet and his captain. In return he was exposed to a reprise of

Jervis's action off Cape St Vincent. The breathless way the youngster spoke reminded Harry of his own previous self, which made listening to the story more bearable. He rose somewhat in the youngster's estimation when he told him that he actually knew Nelson, who was now clearly, in the eyes of the whole British navy, the only man worthy of praise.

"He disobeyed the fighting instructions by pulling out of the line," said Levenson eagerly. "Isn't that just the most amazing thing. And Old Jarvie refused to reprimand him."

"Sometimes it is the right thing to do," said Harry, faintly hopeful, "disobeying orders."

"Only to achieve a victory, Captain," replied Levenson, the enthusiasm disappearing from his demeanour, to be replaced by stiff formality. "We shall raise St Helen's soon."

"Eight line-of-battle ships!" shouted Pender from aloft, his telescope pointing north, "and three admiral's pennants. No frigates or sloops."

"Bridport's our only hope," said Harry, to Illingworth.

"You've only got that youngster's word regarding that situation," the merchant captain replied, his voice full of doubt.

Harry turned to look at him, wondering whether he would have cause to regret the way he eased in his behaviour. This act opened him up to a steady flow of unwelcome advice, with Illingworth taking it upon himself to interfere in conversations that were none of his business. But Harry, knowing he would soon be gone, resisted the temptation to check him.

"Out of the mouths of babes and sucklings," he answered, pointing to Levenson.

Rykert, it transpired, was a client officer of Lord Howe, the titular commander-in-chief of the Channel Fleet. Since Black Dick, old and gouty, spent all of his time taking the waters in Bath, Lord Bridport had the unenviable task of conducting operations without the benefit of the supreme office. Needless to say, there was little love lost between the two senior officers, something which Harry might be able to exploit, especially since he and Bridport were acquainted.

The admiral knew that Harry had the control of two parliamentary seats, would deduce that in these troubled times such an asset was highly valued by a government which often only scraped a majority. The captain of the *Amethyst* might find himself rapped over the knuckles for daring to interfere with the lawful progress of a privateer captain who appeared to have the ear of Henry Dundas. It was slim hope, but the only one Harry had available, especially since his last meeting with the admiral had been anything but friendly.

"Boat pulling towards *Amethyst*. In a hellfire hurry too."

Harry shifted his telescope to pick it up. The early morning haze was lifting slowly, giving greater definition to the seascape. And the sun, a silver orb, was beginning to show through the fog. Very faintly, Harry could see the outline of a capital ship, lying at the southern edge of the anchorage.

"Thank God the fleet is still here," he said, before turning his attention back to the approaching boat.

The officer in the stem was waving madly, and hailing the frigate with the aid of a speaking trumpet, while his men, who seemed to be marines, pulled at their oars as though they were being pursued by Lucifer. The sudden sight of *Amethyst* luffing up had Harry shouting rapid orders for *Bucephalas* to do likewise and avoid running foul of her stern. As soon as he did so, *Precise* ran alongside, cutting off the route to the open sea.

"Can anybody hear what that officer in the boat is saying?" Harry called forward.

"I think he's trying to tell him the fleet's not here, Capt'n," replied Flowers.

"His eyes will tell him that's untrue," said Pender, who'd slid down to the deck and was now pointing north to the anchored ships slowly emerging from the mist.

"Perhaps the French have invaded," said Illingworth.

"Nothing's impossible," said Harry. "Young Levenson said something about trouble in Ireland. The French got all the way to Bantry Bay last autumn without being intercepted. Bridport was seriously compromised by that. It was only luck that they didn't land and make matters worse. Practically the whole French fleet got back to Brest intact."

"Is that good for us, or bad?" asked James, who'd come up behind Harry and Pender.

Harry turned round and grinned. "I'd say good, brother. An admiral in trouble is so much more malleable than one who's just been successful."

"I think I preferred you when you were a pessimist," James replied. "The last time you met Bridport, I seem to remember you were less than entirely polite."

James was right. With half his crew pressed into a man-of-war, and their captain desperate to get them back, Harry had very nearly threatened Bridport, something which no man, high or low, enjoys.

"I'm sure he's forgotten all about it, brother."

"Captain Ludlow." Rykert's voice boomed across the water. Harry saw him, wrapped in a boatcloak, standing by the taffrail of *Amethyst,* speaking trumpet in hand. "I am required to return forthwith to my station off the Goulet."

"Brest," said Harry, for James's benefit.

"However, I intend that my midshipman should stay aboard with you till you're abreast of Southsea Castle. Their guard boats will see you through the narrows into Portsmouth harbour. I myself will escort you past the St Helen's anchorage. Mr Levenson, I will send two boats for you. As soon as that is done, please bring back with you the men from the *Lothian.* Steer straight, Ludlow. And remember I have the right to sink any vessel I consider a hazard to shipping."

"No, you don't, Rykert," said Harry under his breath.

"What have you got in mind, Captain?"

"As soon as he puts up his helm, so will we. If his orders are to take him to Brest, then he won't hang around to keep us bottled up in Portsmouth."

"What about them guard boats?"

"Manned by junior officers, Pender. I might not be able to play the high and mighty with Rykert. But I think I can ignore a mere lieutenant, especially one that has any hope of one day being a post-captain. Likewise Levenson. James, ask Dreaver to get out the charts for the Solent and the Hamble. There's a dozen dockyards between here and the Needles that will be able to mend our hull and furnish us with a new mast."

"Capt'n," said Pender, who'd put his telescope back to his eye while Harry was talking to his brother. "There's something right odd about the ships' flags. And the rigging."

"Which ship?" asked Harry.

"All of 'em. The whole fleet."

The pale, early morning sun, now well above the horizon, had turned from silver to gold affecting everything it touched. Even the black sides of the ships of the Channel Fleet were altered as the shiny paint on their massive hulls reflected the light. To a landsman's eye they might all look alike, different merely in the number of their decks, but to Harry each was familiar, and the sight of these massive vessels always moved him. He'd served in some of them and seen the rest in harbours all over the world, could pick out the differences in their figureheads and stern decoration. Had he stayed in the navy he might even have been in command of one by now.

Queen Charlotte was there, along with *Royal Sovereign*. A sweep of the glass showed him *Pompey* and *Ramillies*, both of which he'd served in. He lifted his telescope from elaborate gilt-edged carving to look at the masts, searching for the pennants that would identify the ranks of the various senior officers. The sharp intake of breath as he made sense of what he saw caused Pender to speak.

"Plain red at the mizzen, every one of them."

"What does that mean?" asked James.

"They fly that when they go into battle," said Illingworth.

"They're not even cleared for action," said Harry. "They're not going into battle."

"Yard ropes are reeved," said Pender, "and some of the ships are dressed in red bunting. One or two have nooses rigged at the main, an' all. And there seems a rate of ship visiting going on judging by the number of boats in the water."

Harry's voice rose suddenly, and he shouted towards the waist. "Mr Levenson, gather your men by the gangway, if you please. I will not be entering Portsmouth harbour, as requested. I shall of course provide you with a boat to take you back to *Amethyst*."

"I have my orders, Captain Ludlow," the youngster said, throwing back one side of his coat to reveal a sword.

"You have that. But if you hail your captain he may pass on to you the intelligence he has just received. On the other hand you may use your own eyes. But it makes no odds if you do neither. If you fail to comply, I will be compelled to use force."

"Harry, what are you about?" asked James.

"I am in the process of regaining our freedom of action, brother.

"Pender," he said loudly, "get a party of men together and disarm the Amethysts. Once that is done get them into a boat so that they can row back to where they rightfully belong."

"I warn you, sir," piped Levenson, "this is dangerous, especially with the whole fleet hard by."

"The whole fleet you refer to is no threat to me, young man, though it may well prove so to you. You should by now be able to see the line-of-battle ships with the naked eye. If you cast a glance aloft, you will see something to shock you."

Levenson had his hand capped over his eye, even though the sun was behind him. He probably would have preferred to remain silent, but in his youth he exclaimed with surprise at what he saw.

"What does it signify?" he asked after a slight pause.

"It's very simple, sir. The whole of the Channel Fleet is in a state of mutiny."

CHAPTER SIX

HARRY and Rykert stared silently at each other across the water as Levenson and his men came aboard. The King's ship let the cutter drift free, and was under way before the last man made it to the deck, signalling to *Precise* to fetch her wake. Harry, in a less frantic mood, got Illingworth and his men, less a pair too wounded to travel, back into their boats, with the suggestion that their safest landfall would be to the east of Hayling Island. He then set a course to run between the north shore of the Isle of Wight and Spit Sand, having decided to make for the Beaulieu Estuary and Buckler's Hard. Any temptation to stay around the fleet, to find out what was going on, was put to one side. Safety was paramount, and there was little of that to be had for a damaged privateering ship in Britain's premier naval base.

Strictly speaking, Buckler's Hard wasn't designed for repairs; it was a yard for new building, naval in the main, and large merchant ships since it had been extended in the previous decade. The village itself was three rows of houses running inland from the slipways, a site entirely dedicated to the shipwright's craft, laid out and constructed with that very purpose in mind by the second Duke of Montagu. There was a resident doctor, happy to take temporary charge, for a fee, of a dozen extra patients.

Sheltered from the prevailing westerly winds, it could provide Harry with new upper foremasts. And being in a tidal basin he would have little difficulty in careening *Bucephalas* then refloating her when his hull was repaired. But the prime asset of Buckler's Hard was its isolation. It took its wood from the surrounding New Forest, bringing in everything else by sea; access to the village from the interior was severely limited, a pair of rutted tracks easily guarded against the chance of intruders. And every man, woman, and child in the place depended in some way on the yard for their livelihood, so that their eyes, ears, and local knowledge were well tuned to any threats of danger.

Theoretically exempt from impressment, the owners and villagers were not inclined to take chances: by land, no press gang could get within ten miles of the place without being observed, and the long wynd of the Beaulieu was a double safeguard. With a sentinel placed inshore of Gull Island, and a boat standing by to relay any message he cared to send, Harry Ludlow was as secure as he could be outside the liberties of the Cinque Ports, none of which, in any case, had the facilities to repair *Bucephalas.*

His greatest difficulty was in persuading Balthazar Adams, son of the owner, to stop work on the ships he was building and attend to his needs. He had a 38-gun frigate, *Boadicea,* on the stocks, as well as the *Snake,* a 16-gun sloop, both under the watchful eye of an agent from the Navy Board, keen to see them completed. Fortunately, he was temporarily absent. Even more telling, the remaining gold Harry was carrying spoke loud in these times, when the new paper money, recently introduced by the Bank of England, was deeply mistrusted.

Balthazar Adams, in the way of all boatbuilders, seemed able to ally every misfortune of both the nation and her allies in his bid to talk up the necessity of charging a high price. And his face, with doleful, slanting eyes and a prominent nose, gave him the appearance of a particularly sad hound, adding an extra physical dimension to the Armageddon-like list of woes. His father, Henry Adams, was a Banquo presence during the discussions. Supposedly retired, like most fathers he couldn't abide the idea of letting go and sat silently by the window of the extension tacked on to the front of his house to give him a better view of the work in progress. Drawings of ships built and proposed, together with sketches for figureheads lined the small room which, with the exception of a large astrolabe, was simply furnished. Every so often, old Henry would peer through his telescope at the ships on the stocks, an instrument so powerful he must have been able to count his workers' every pore.

"I don't know what's to become of us, Captain Ludlow," said Balthazar, "what with our fleet no more good than an ancient coracle in the defending line. There's no Nelson or Jervis on hand to help us now. Those French dogs could be here at any minute, sailing up the Solent without so much as a frigate to bar their passage, to be received with cheers from our own tars, very likely."

He raised his hand to indicate the hulls that towered over the space between the houses, dominating the small cottages to such an extent that in some cases they cut out any sunlight from the front doors. Children, too small to work, played around the great oak baulks that held the structures in place, their high-pitched cries mingling with the crash of hammers and the sawing of wood, all overborne by the smell of hot pitch.

"I must finish these ships afore then, sir, or face ruin. And what would happen to the poor folks of this village if that came to pass. Starvation, sir, that is what would occur, with those bairns you see afrolickin' now, wrapped cold and dead in sacking, to be tossed into an open pit."

"And the men too weak to fill it in," said James, his voice as doom laden as that of Adams. "Woe unto us."

"How right you are," the master shipwright replied. He knew he was being practised on and gave James a glare. But it was fleeting, soon replaced by his more doleful countenance.

"All I asked you, Mr Adams, was how much and how quickly," said Harry. He'd been quite happy to let the man go through the whole rehearsed litany, being well accustomed to such behaviour. But James's intervention had brought matters to a head. "I have already said that I will pay you in gold. Foreign coinage, I grant you, but you may have it by weight."

It was Henry who replied to that, an older, more frail version of his son, shaking his head in a way that swung his now fleshy jowls.

"Now there's something to mull on. I don't care for paper, sir.

And neither will the nation. The stuff will go the same way as the *assignats* of those damned French Jacobins, and become worthless."

"Most of the damage to the upperworks can be left," said Harry, to Balthazar, as if old Adams hadn't spoken. "I need that hole below the waterline plugged, or better still repaired, and I'll stand as much scraping as you can manage between tides. You can see for yourself that we require new upper foremasts and bowsprit, plus any rigging, sails, and spars I can't supply myself. I reckon, at most, with my crew to clear and restow the hold, three days."

He raised his hand to spin the astrolabe, then pointed to the stacked timber outside. "Which will serve to season some of this green timber you're using in the King's ships."

Balthazar Adams opened his mouth to protest, but his father chuckled. And when the son saw the smile on Harry's face, he couldn't help but respond.

"Gold, you say?" he growled, looking out at *Bucephalas,* rocking gently on the tidal water in the middle of the river, close to the ranks of spars, masts, and poles which floated in the water. There was no doubting her trade. Not even the most myopic soul could mistake her for a merchant vessel. Just over a hundred feet long and well armed, the natural grace of her lines was somewhat spoiled by the accumulated damage. But she was still a hunter, not prey. "I take it you have enjoyed some good fortune."

Harry face clouded immediately. "And some bad."

Adams responded to that as well, his lugubrious countenance becoming sombre again. "There always is a reverse side of every coin, gold, silver, or copper, Captain Ludlow, an' no amount of prayer will ever alter that fact."

"A price, Mr Adams, if you please," said James quickly, as he saw Harry turn away, seemingly staring at the figurehead drawings pinned to the office wall. The shipwright grabbed a quill and looked at the ship before leaning over beside his father to scribble on a scrap of paper. Whispers were exchanged and repeated several times, with questions to Harry about the state of various ship's sections. Finally both seemed satisfied. The son held the paper at arm's length, looked at it hard, then grunted.

"We can see no profit in this, but as God-fearing Christians we cannot indulge in usury."

James took the paper out of Balthazar Adams's hand and shoved it under Harry's nose. Three hundred and seventy guineas seemed steep to him, but then he was no sailor. He wasn't sure if the nod in response was because his brother looked at it, or didn't care.

"I think we must insist on the time limit, sir," said Harry, after a moment's silence. He hadn't turned, and was clearly still affected by what Balthazar Adams had said about the fickle nature of fortune.

"Never fear, it will be swift," growled old Adams, spinning round to look James straight in the eye, "since I want your lads barred from every place but the village chapel, and that's not an injunction that will hold for long." He turned again, to indicate the children playing tag around the yard. "I've enough brats here as it is, without your lot getting to the womenfolk and producing a dozen more. That's not something my workers would take kindly to. We want our chisels bent to working on wood, not human flesh."

"Make it so, Mr Adams," said James. "But you must take time to tell us what in God's name has been going on at Spithead."

What followed was rumour piled on conjecture, with father and son seemingly unaware of the contradictions of what they imparted. One minute it was a peaceful revolt, another, bloody revolution, with the only absolute being that without a fleet, the nation was defenceless. It was clear that every capital ship had acted as one, then elected delegates to represent them, an unprecedented action which had the whole country awash with rumours regarding French spies, Jacobin agitators, United Irish rebels, and banned Corresponding Societies. Whatever the cause was, it brought Harry back into the conversation, pushing to the back of his mind unhappy memories.

Speculation as to what would happen next was natural, though not a subject on which any one of them could be brought to agree. The only points on which they did concur were the shocking fact that such a thing could happen, and the absolute necessity, by fair means or foul, that the mutiny should be brought to an end.

"You will most certainly need this, Pender," said Harry, handing him a folded letter, "and I still rate it a sound idea to kit you out in a servant's livery to go with it, just so there can be no mistake. The fleet might have mutinied, but that's not certain to deflect the Impressment Service from hunting out bodies. In fact they might well be toiling twice as hard."

"Portsmouth was my home, Capt'n," Pender replied, taking the letter which identified him as a gentleman's servant, and therefore theoretically inviolate. "The press never took me when I lived there, nor when I went back to fetch my nippers, an' I don't suppose they could do so now. Why, if any of my old mates were to spy me in the street in a servant's get-up I'd be a laughing stock."

"Very well," Harry replied uneasily, "get our dunnage aboard the cutter. And Pender, I want you to put this into the chest containing the residue of our specie. Put it down into the furthest reaches of the hold and chain it to the deck. Pick the men personally whom you want to guard it."

"But that's only paper, Capt'n."

"That might be so. But it has a value of a quarter of a million sterling, redeemable in America by whosoever holds it in their hand."

"Only in ten years, brother," said James.

He'd been unsure whether Harry, acting in his usual headstrong way, had done the right thing in New York. Tying funds up of that magnitude three thousand miles away seemed to him fraught with risk. Not least because of the unstable nature of the borrower. They might call themselves the United States, but nothing James had observed in his time there had convinced him that was the case. And the new President, Adams, commanded none of the affection afforded to the victor of the Revolutionary War, George Washington.

"That may very well be so. But both you and I know how much these certificates will be worth, just as we are both aware of how indiscreet our men can be. Old Henry Adams may not trust the crew with his women, but neither do I trust his men when there's something as valuable as this to steal, and a ready escape route into deep forests just waiting to be employed."

"Why don't we take that, and the balance of the coin, with us?"

"I'd rather land it at Deal, brother. It's no safer but certainly a lot more discreet. Only the fear of loss would make me deposit this at Portsmouth. And if I did every naval officer in the port would know within an hour, which will do nothing for our reception."

"The reception will be as it always is with the navy, which means we're likely to be exposed to no end of condescension. I still can't fathom why you want to go there."

"I've told you, curiosity. There's never been a whole fleet mutiny before. Single ships yes, like *Culloden* and the *Bounty*. I'm afire to see how they've managed it for one thing, as well as sort out the truth from the fiction of what the Adamses said. While we were below he told me half the Board of Admiralty is in the town, trying to sort matters out."

James smiled and gave Harry a knowing look. "Always supposing that is the truth, do you expect them to consult you?"

"No."

James slowly yawned. "So you will merely be an observer, on the periphery."

"How can you not wish to be present at such a telling thing? It's the most amazing event since the Paris mob stormed the Bastille. The whole British nation stands in peril and you yawn."

"I do not mind being present," said James, "but I have a

natural affection for being at the centre of things, which even when mutinous hardly includes Portsmouth."

With the wind still blowing north-westerly, the cutter, sails bowsed into tight triangles, flew across the Solent, eating up the ten miles between the mouth of the Beaulieu and Nettlestone Point at a spanking pace. The sun was shining, a perfect late April day. Huge voluminous clouds, black in the centre, edged with bright silver, lay to the north over the Hampshire Downs, promising rain. Harry was as happy as James had ever seen him, as though being off the ship had released him from his memories. But it was partly, he knew, his sheer love of movement. Harry hated to be still, and derived as much pleasure from racing along in a cutter as he did doing twelve knots in *Bucephalas*.

Most of the Channel Fleet still lay at St Helen's, with four of the line plus some frigates anchored at Spithead. From a distance the combined squadrons were as dangerous an armada as had ever been. Each great ship, the foremost engines of war that existed, had a destructive power that inspired awe. Guns that ranged in calibre from mere nine-pounders to a massive sixty-eight on the carronades, one broadside delivering several thousand pounds of metal into an enemy hull. No land force, even rarely a fortress battery, could match it for power.

Constantly in service, with the majority of the crews bred to the sea, this was the instrument that allowed Britain to match the great continental armies. These ships, and the dozens of others in service around the globe, were the "Wooden Walls," the bulwarks which made Britain great. It was little wonder the depth of the alarm when this protection seemed removed.

Close to, the differences from any fleet Harry had ever seen were subtle but very telling. The red flags and bunting were singular enough, but the really sinister note was struck by the nooses strung from the yardarms, as though each ship was getting ready to partake of a mass execution. There was no irregularity apart

from that: from what little they could see from their low elevation, work was being carried out in a normal fashion, with boats
loading stores and repair work to the rigging proceeding normally.
Taking a detour to sail through the St Helen's fleet, dodging the
other sightseers who'd come to witness the tumult, they discovered that each vessel was, apart from the mutinous insignia, the
very opposite of a hotbed of bloody insurrection.

There were no cheering mobs on deck, nor any sign of drunk-
enness or laxity. Indeed, even from his lowly position Harry
observed that the junior officers were at their proper stations. The
crews, at anchor, were below, and by the sounds emanating from
the open lower deck gun ports, were behaving better than they
did in normal times. Balthazar Adams had told him that the mutineers had sent the "wives" ashore, and forbidden them to return
until matters were settled. No drink, other than the normal rations,
was to be consumed. So there were no bumboats full of whores
and traders scurrying around, no hint of fiddlers and licentious-
ness, none of the normal 'tween-decks riot.

"Look, your honour," said Pender, pointing towards a boat
slicing through their wake. Harry turned, close enough to see that
it carried no officer: two men sat in the stern, both dressed in clean
scarlet kerseymere waistcoats. The crew of what was clearly a captain's barge were titivated to the nines, a riot of blue and gold,
with jaunty caps to finish off their exclusive rig. It was not uncommon for wealthy captains to dress their barge crew to impress. It
was unusual to see anyone else sitting in a place officers reserved
exclusively for themselves.

"Who are they?" asked James.

Harry shrugged, unable to answer truthfully. The way Adams
had described them, the men who'd led the mutiny sounded like
swarthy cut-throats, the dregs of the fleet. By the cut of the hair
and clothes he knew these men to be officers of petty warrant
rank. To see them, amongst the steadiest men in the fleet, sitting
in a captain's barge surprised him.

"They look something more than able seamen, Pender."

Harry pushed the tiller to bring the cutter round, while Pender leapt forward to shift the sail, forcing James to duck as the boom swung over his head. They came round in a long sweep, fetching the barge's wake. Harry had no intention of trying to overtake it, nor could he have done so with a crew rowing in such a well-disciplined way. They fairly shot across the anchorage, and as they came close to a 100-gun ship which Harry recognized as *Queen Charlotte* they raised their oars with handsome precision, gliding alongside the entry port with no risk to the paintwork.

"They could be ferrying an admiral," said Harry, as he eased the tiller to take the way off the cutter. He could see other figures by the entry port, sailors in long winter waistcoats and breeches, waiting to bid their visitors welcome. There was even the odd red marine coat. But there were no officers present. They were on the quarterdeck, leaning over the rail, observing the scene and gesticulating to each other, some angrily, others with an air of resignation.

"Let's bear up for the Sally Port, Pender," said Harry. He was tempted to try to board *Queen Charlotte,* dying to find out what was taking place, to ask the host of questions engendered by what he'd seen. But there was no guarantee that the men who controlled the ship would let him.

Closer to the harbour, they sailed past the Spithead squadron, four sail-of-the-line including *London* and *Marlborough*. Slightly further inshore lay Sir Peter Parker's flagship, *Royal William*. No hint of mutiny was apparent there and the flag that flew aloft wasn't red, but the proper pennant for a Vice-Admiral of the Blue. Marines, pipe-clayed and smart, stood to attention at the entry port, and the quarterdeck had a good quota of officers with telescopes, all of which, at the same moment, seemed to be trained on Ludlow's small craft.

Harry ignored them, his eyes ranging round the land defences. Every fort and redoubt, even the old medieval towers that guarded the narrows, seemed to be at full alert, with guns manned and run out, as though those ashore anticipated that the men of the fleet, having taken control, were about to invade their native land carrying the torch of revolution.

The crowd around the steps pressed forward as they landed, each one mouthing a different enquiry that turned the whole into an incomprehensible babble, making it difficult for the boatmen to come aboard. Eventually they managed to squeeze through the press of bodies, passing a numbered medallion to Harry bearing the inscription of their yard.

It was equally hard for Pender to find anyone interested in carrying their sea chests, once the locals found out that they were neither famous men nor mutineers. But he succeeded eventually, and with an injunction to mind their purses he led the way through the throng. The whole of the town seemed to be gathered along the Hard, the main thoroughfare that ran from the dockyard to the Gun Wharf, gossiping and creating rumours, all eager to witness the next round in the continuing fight between the government and the sailors' revolt.

They called at the Fountain, the Dolphin, and the George without success. Likewise the Vine and the Blue Posts. Every hostelry seemed full, with officials, admirals, and government ministers, representatives of bankers and newspapers, not to mention the merely curious who'd come hot-foot from London to see for themselves what was happening. Harry started to curse the latter roundly until James reminded him that their sole reason for being here was exactly the same. And here, in such a very naval place, the name Harry Ludlow, used in the hope of gaining favour, counted for nothing.

It was Pender who solved the problem of accommodation, taking them away from the better parts of the town to the narrow streets and alleys in the bustling part of the town known as Portsmouth Point. They tried the Old Ship and, once more refused, they were ushered to a house in Love Lane, property of a Mistress Blackett. The lady knew Pender, emitting a high-pitched screech when she saw him. And judging by the way she enveloped him in her ample bosom she had a soft spot for the man. It was several minutes, during which many an endearment was exchanged, before Pender could introduce James and Harry.

"Why, gents, you are most welcome," she said. "Though I doubt my 'umble 'ouse is grand enough to accommodate your like."

The strong scent wafting out of the open door, and the sounds of singing and merriment from the parlour left both brothers in no doubt as to what sort of accommodation they were being offered.

"We want somewhere private, Mary Blackett," said Pender. "And we'll move ourselves the minute a space comes in any of the proper inns."

Mary Blackett curtsied, an act which spread her already voluminous skirts beyond the confines of the doorway. "You shall be favoured, sirs, with my private quarters, which is quiet enough for a grievin' nun. But should you require a little hullabaloo, then a mere knock on the wainscoting will suffice."

Pender looked round at the glum faces of the Ludlow brothers, responding himself with a wide grin, as if to say that if they weren't in their element, he was.

"Perfection it ain't, I'll grant you. But I don't doubt if they'd had the like in Nazareth, Joseph would not have turned it down. And if you're looking for better quality in the brothel line, your honour, this one will be fuller than the Fountain, which means that anyone staying here, or at the George, and is in possession of an appetite will be coming this way. Why, I'd bet you now that the folks you hear revelling know more about what's going on in the fleet than the First Lord himself. Besides, it's this or back to Buckler's Hard."

"Lead on, Pender," said Harry, giving James a hearty shove. As they made their way through the door neither man observed that they were being watched, nor took any notice of the thickset fellow in the heavy black coat and large round hat who'd managed to follow them all the way from the Fountain without being seen.

"Here, lad," he called to a scruffy urchin, holding out a coin. The boy had looked up fearfully when he heard the gruff voice, but the lure of the sixpence was greater than his alarm. "Hop over to Mistress Blackett's and ask of her if she's really got the famous privateer captain Harry Ludlow under her gables. I'll be at the Fountain. Find out yea or nay, and this here coin will be yours."

The boy nodded and ran off, skirting round the back of the house to Mistress Blackett's kitchen, while his benefactor turned back towards the shore, mentally composing the note he would send to London, to find out if the warrant on Harry Ludlow was still in force.

CHAPTER SEVEN

HARRY and James couldn't rest at Mistress Blackett's, though they did have a glass of port, and a bit of conversation for decency's sake, which naturally included Pender. The lady herself was afire with both delight and curiosity, quizzing them about how they came to be in the town. That led to some evasive answers, and in the article of wealth taken at sea one downright lie, though the knowledge of having been in battle was hard to contain, and she'd picked up where *Bucephalas* was berthed outside her own front door. A slightly dissonant note was struck when she alluded to the services she could provide: Harry's response was so sharp in declining that it bordered on the very impertinent. But James, ever adept with the opposite sex, poured a little emollient flattery on to their hostess's surprise.

The whole of Portsmouth was gripped with the fever of the fleet mutiny and the Ludlows were no exception, catching very easily the mood that comes with being at the centre of great events. Even James, normally very deliberate in his progress, was eager to return to the Fountain to pick up on the latest gossip. Pender was unwilling to over-expose himself in the very heart of his home town. He'd been absent for five years, but the warrant for arrest that had made him run to the King's navy might well still be in force.

But he had his own visits to make, and he was just as curious as the men who employed him. Though he didn't say so to Harry Ludlow, he knew that he could find out a lot more about what was happening to the fleet in the hovels and back streets than ever they would find out in an oak-panelled taproom. So they parted company at the door, with Pender taking to alleyways so

narrow no man could pass another, while Harry and James went
back to the more open areas around where the Point looked over
the huge anchorage. The streets around the wharves and dockyard were crammed, people busy exchanging rumour and
speculation. The Fountain itself, with the proprietor's servants
ensuring that only persons of a certain quality were admitted,
seemed a haven of peace, even though the taproom was full of
serving officers, a number of whom seemed to wear a particular
expression; that of men who saw their hard-won livelihoods disappearing before their eyes.

Harry recognized several faces, but declined to acknowledge
the questioning looks that were aimed in his direction. The Ludlow brothers secured a table that gave them a good view of both
the reception rooms and the hallway, then settled down over a
steaming pot of coffee to await events. Harry knew, and James
surmised, that it wouldn't be long before some of the naval
acquaintances, ever eager to trade information, would make their
way to the table.

"I say *Culloden*, Peggy, my girl." The man's voice rose over
the buzz of conversation, this accompanied by an emphatic thump
on his own table, one that rattled the crockery and brought about
a temporary cessation in everyone else's conversation. The act
failed to startle the good-looking if rather pale young woman who
sat opposite him. She was young, slightly over-dressed, and wearing too much face powder in an attempt to increase her years. But
she was clearly attuned to her companion's temperament, since
the slightly bored expression on her face remained unchanged.
That is, until she realized that everyone in the room was looking
at her.

Her companion—if he even noticed—wasn't bothered. A big
man, with high colouring in a handsome countenance, he had a
mass of wavy hair, snow white now, though it had clearly once
been blond judging by the hint of yellow at the very tips. He continued in the same vein, his intemperate tone now magnified by
the silence.

"And that to any rascal who even dreams of disobedience. Troubridge strung up a round five of the miscreants within a fortnight of their insurrection. The yardarm, girl, is the place for a mutineer, not the comfort of a quiet chat in the commanding admiral's cabin."

"Jack Willet Payne," said Harry softly, as James leant forward with an enquiring look. "Always was of a full-blooded hue. A ladies' man, I gather, even as a shaver. Never served with him myself, but one midshipman who did said that the discomfort alluded to by his surname failed to identify the proper seat of unease."

"How many in this room have you served with?" asked James, smiling.

Harry shrugged. "One or two."

"Judging by the number of knowing looks we received when we came in, that's an understatement."

"I've met more, of course. A sailor's chief pleasure is ship-visiting when at anchor, that is if you exclude shore taverns and bawdy houses. Many of the men here were mids or junior officers when I was in the service, so I've dined or drank with them. I've even traded blows with a couple who impugned the honour of my ship."

"Well, since we have come to glean the state of affairs, would it not be a good idea to corner one?"

Harry lifted his cup, the smile on his face rather forced. "When I have finished this."

James knew very well why Harry was reluctant. For a man who normally avoided his naval contemporaries, just being here, in Portsmouth, was a strain. The idea that he might approach one of them, rather than the other way round, was making him decidedly uncomfortable. So much so that James guessed his brother was beginning to regret the impulse that had brought them here.

"Have more than one cup if you wish, brother. I'm sure that they are as curious as we are, and given the rumours that are flying about regarding Jacobins and stockjobbery, some may even see sinister purpose in our presence. I doubt you'll drain a second before we are accosted."

James proved correct. Harry had barely begun to refill his cup when a captain rose at the other side of the room and, watched covertly by three or four others, crossed to speak to them. He was a portly man, his face fleshy and weather-beaten, with a protruding stomach that showed a great deal of his white waistcoat. Harry stiffened, and concentrated on his pouring so much that the officer was upon them for several seconds before he looked up. The feigned surprise he adopted was as transparent as gossamer.

"Griffiths, is it not?"

"Harry," he replied, his round face looking perplexed.

"James," he said, definitely flustered, "allow me to name to you Captain Edward Griffiths."

"It used to be that you knew me well enough to call me Ned. Does a civilian coat change that?"

Harry shot to his feet, catching the table and spilling into his saucer some of the coffee he'd just poured, acting for all the world like a nervous youth in the presence of a stern uncle.

"Of course, Ned," he said, putting out his hand. "It's good to see you."

"So good that you walked straight past me when you came into the room."

"It's been a long time, has it not? And you have changed a bit." He looked down at Griffiths's protruding stomach. "You have an air of prosperity that I don't recall. It suits you, as well."

"A little flesh on the jowls, I grant you, Harry. But have I changed so much that you failed to know me?"

"Please join us," said James, as he saw his brother flush slightly. Harry didn't like being checked, even if it was justified, and was as likely to reply to that remark with an insult as an apology. He waved to a servant to fetch a chair as he stood himself, that followed by a slight bow to Griffiths.

"I'm happy to make your acquaintance, sir. I fear my brother is often too ashamed of me to introduce to his old naval friends."

The word ashamed broke the mutual stare between the two men, as Harry turned to refute it, and Griffiths looked for any possible cause.

"I am such a lubber," James continued smoothly, "that my own father would turn in his grave to see it."

Griffiths glanced from one to the other, as if checking the family likeness. It was there of course, though James had none of Harry's heavier build, being slim enough to look elegant rather than muscular. But the fair hair was of the same colour and texture, while the penetrating blue eyes spoke of a blood tie so strong that one face being ruddy while the other was smooth was irrelevant.

"I served as a volunteer under your father, sir. It was my first floating home. I remember him as being exceeding kind to me. More so than he was to his own flesh and blood, since he stretched Harry over a gun and birched him more times than I care to remember."

"It is my misfortune," James replied evenly, "that I did not serve with him, though I dare say the nation has good cause to be very thankful."

"Take my hand, Ned," said Harry softly, "and with it my apology."

"Readily," Griffiths replied, grasping Harry's outstretched arm just below the elbow to pull him closer. "Though I fear I cannot take up the invitation to join you. I have another officer, a guest, at my table."

"Then let him come too, sir," said James, before Harry could speak. "Indeed, if you name him, I will be happy to invite him personally."

"Patton, Captain Philip Patton. I dare say he has his eyes on my back at this very moment."

"You are more interesting than that, sir. Every sailor in the room, with the exception of that loud-mouthed hangman with the trollop, has his eyes on your back."

"Sit down," said Harry, quickly, as he observed just how right his brother was. James had already left, easing his way through the tables to where Griffiths's companion sat, an empty port bottle before him. His arrival was greeted with a glacial stare.

"Captain Patton?" The sailor nodded while he bowed. "I wonder if you would care to join my brother and me. He and Captain Griffiths are old shipmates, and will bore each other rigid with nostalgia if left to their own devices."

Patton grinned instantly, which changed his rather stern countenance dramatically. He was good-looking, with dark hair and eyebrows. The crows' feet now very evident at the corners of his eyes indicated a readiness to smile.

"With only an empty bottle before me, and a vacant chair, how can I refuse?"

"With difficulty, sir," replied James, returning the smile.

"But I must warn you that I too have served with Griffiths, so I may only compound the boredom."

James generally didn't have much time for naval officers, finding them too stiff for his taste, too ready to take offence. But this Patton was inducing a quite different feeling, mostly communicated by the directness of both his observation and his look, which was steady and held James Ludlow's eyes without the slightest trace of dissimulation. Quick, in the way of all artists, to decide on a subject's abiding trait, he reckoned Patton to be the kind of man much sought after by his contemporaries. As a commander he was no doubt adored by his men, as well as being very probably a fellow with the wit to chastise his superiors without forfeiting their regard. In fact he seemed to be that exceedingly rare creature, the ideal of the naval officer.

"Are you offended by indiscreet yawning, sir?" asked James, grinning.

Patton stood up, still amused. "If I were, sir, I'd be in a constant stew, and I would also resign my commission. Fresh air, even in the form of a gale of wind, cannot compete with naval taletelling as an aid to slumber."

Once they arrived at the table, Patton dealt with Harry in such a direct manner as to totally disarm him as well. What was normally an occasion of stiff reserve became instead an instant rapport.

"I know of you, Captain Ludlow," he said, as soon as Griffiths had performed the introductions. "And everything I have heard of you stands in the credit column. In fact, having served under Lieutenant Carter, I count myself pusillanimous for not putting a ball in him myself."

Griffiths had begun to blush. Like most people he avoided the subject of Harry's court martial, and especially the name of his fellow duellist, like the plague. But the blood drained from his face as he saw Harry respond with a look that bordered on gratitude, as if he was pleased by Patton's directness. He was, since it had removed that subject from all their minds with the speed of a surgeon's saw.

"Patton was the very first to spot trouble brewing," said Griffiths, giving his friend a look that was a mixture of admiration and concern. "Indeed, sensing that matters were serious, he took it upon himself to find out what was afoot, and wrote a report warning their Lordships several months before the event."

"You warned them of the mutiny?" asked Harry, slightly incredulous.

"Nothing so positive as that, Captain Ludlow. And how could I predict such a calamity as this? But I did tell them that feelings were running abnormally high, and that discontent was widespread. You will know of many a case where late pay or a particularly unpopular officer have caused a crew to refuse to weigh."

"Sensibly never referred to as mutiny," replied Harry.

Patton replied with a sharp nod. "And generally quickly settled to the satisfaction of all. Perhaps in what I wrote I didn't manage to convey in words strong enough the different nature of the men's grievances."

"But your report was thorough," Griffiths insisted.

"All I know for certain, Ned," Patton growled, "is that it was thoroughly ignored. Still, deafness seems to be a very necessary component of high naval rank. Even your uncle's not immune."

Harry looked perplexed until Patton added, "He's nephew to Admiral Colpoys."

"Sorry, I'd forgotten your relations."

Griffiths nodded, then his face turned sad. "I was surprised too. It wasn't just Bridport and Gardner. I have the *London,* Harry, my uncle's flagship. I saw nothing, and neither did my officers. Of course we knew there was discontent, that things were made worse by the addition to the crews of quota men. But mutiny, and on such a scale."

"I only know the bones of the thing," said Harry, unable to conceal his eagerness, as he glanced at both naval officers, "and I'm sure you've had to recount your tale dozens of times. If you could bear to repeat yourself, Captain Patton, I'd be much obliged."

"Happily, Captain Ludlow. What else is there to talk about?"

CHAPTER EIGHT

THERE WAS so much which didn't need saying, of course. About the sailors wages, nineteen shillings a lunar month for a seaman, which had been set in the Commonwealth. Of a system that, under the disguise of necessary deductions, could deprive them of up to a third of that sum. The remainder was often up to two years in arrears, and then only paid out in tickets redeemable at the port at which the ship had been commissioned.

Unable to go ashore in wartime, for fear that they'd desert, the crews usually sold their pay warrants to Jews and bumboat women at a discount, further depleting the total that they could pass on to their dependants. And that all took place at a time when they were being fed short measures of poor and sometimes completely rotten food, cheated by pursers whose avarice was legendary, under the command of officers who ranged from enlightened saints through common tyrants to quite a few who when it came to the lash were downright madmen.

So a sympathy for the sailor's plight was taken as read by Patton as he outlined the series of events that had led to the present impasse. It was as if the people involved, and the series of actions that had unfolded, had been put specially in place to frustrate the legitimate demands of the seamen; men who when they'd originally protested had taken good care to affirm their loyalty to King and Country, and their willingness to do battle with the French fleet should it emerge from Brest.

"Howe's the main culprit, if you exclude the system of abuse itself. He should have retired in '94, after the Glorious First of June. Bridport has his faults, but he's not helped by having a titular superior who never even comes to Portsmouth, let alone goes to sea. The men sent their original petitions to Black Dick well over a month ago, while he was taking the waters in Bath. He took his time about reading them, then passed them on to the Admiralty without comment. As a result, Lord Spencer didn't even look at the damn things. Bridport had taken the fleet to Brest and back in the meantime. When the men returned they must have expected some response. Finding none only made matters worse."

Patton, picking up on the rumours, had gone to visit each ship in turn. There he found men in groups, whispering, gesticulating, and clearly angry. "Yet they obeyed any order they were given, Ludlow. That was part of the plan, I think, and it was a shrewd one; to do nothing that would bring punishment down on their heads."

"It was damned embarrassing, Harry," said Griffiths. "The feeling that you were losing control. Some of my Londons even trespassed beyond the mainmast and stood yattering on the quarterdeck."

James couldn't resist a breathless, "Never." Harry and Patton spotted the irony, but not Griffiths, who was too taken with his own remembered woes. "I thought I ran a good, tight ship."

"I told Lord Bridport of my conclusions," Patton continued. "He wrote to Whitehall to warn them. Only then did they tell him of the petitions that Howe had received. I've never seen Bridport so angry, and he was right to be, having been left in ignorance of something it was his responsibility to contain. He's not as popular as Howe, few are with the men. But he is respected, and I'm sure if he'd had prior warning he could have headed things off."

Patton paused for a moment, taking a deep breath to contain his own anger at what he was now relating. "The damn fools then compounded that sin, and cut the rug from under his feet, with instructions that the best way to calm things was to get the crews back to sea. Bridport knew it to be a foolish idea, but still passed the orders on. That's when matters came to a head. The men aboard *Royal Sovereign* refused to weigh, though I believe it was touch and go till the Queen Charlottes manned the foremast shrouds to cheer. Then it was red flags at the mizzen and boats sent off round the whole anchorage. Before the day was out we had what you see now. The very first fleet mutiny the country has ever known to contend with."

"My Uncle Colpoys, who can be short-tempered, tried to stop delegates coming aboard from the other ships, but Bridport ordered him to desist. You should have heard him curse. Thank God the men didn't hold it against him."

Patton had been reasonably matter-of-fact till now, containing his own emotions well, even though what he was describing was for every naval officer a catastrophe. For the first time he showed a trace of temper.

"You know as well as I do, Ned, that the crew don't hold you or your uncle responsible. Damn it, they don't even hold their fleet commanders to account. They think the whole system is rotten."

Griffiths's face hardened, showing for the first time the kind of determination that was required to command a 100-gun ship like the *London*. "I should know if my men are conspiring to disobey me."

"Is it a conspiracy?" asked James. "We heard a rumour that there's a French involvement."

"In one sense, yes," replied Patton, avoiding Griffiths's angry look. "But I, for one, am convinced that despite that the legitimate grievances of the men are sufficient cause. They don't need Jacobins or seditious combinations to inspire them to act, even if it looks on the surface to be that way."

"Why?" demanded Harry.

"Every ship-of-the-line sent in the same petition," said Griffiths, with a deep frown. "The same list of demands, almost to the letter in the identical nature of the wording."

"That smacks of some kind of collusion, surely," said Harry.

Patton's face creased with worry. "I can't be sure that there's no outside influence. But if there is, I am certain that it's not French inspired."

"Again I must ask why," Harry persisted.

"The men are loyal," snapped Patton. "Every ship has sworn that should the enemy put to sea, so will they."

"How could anyone ever have doubted that?" Harry replied, taking care not to sound too smart. "But it still begs the question. If it's not a Jacobin plot, how, without some kind of combination, did they manage to organize it themselves? Sailors can't gather in large groups without being noticed. And I can't believe a mutiny of this magnitude was planned by conversations held through open gun ports."

Patton managed a grim smile. "No, Ludlow. This was done ashore, and not by the common seamen. The petty officers took the lead, and if there is any kind of seditious gathering, like a Corresponding Society, then that is where it lies."

"What are they demanding?" asked James.

"For themselves, nothing," replied Patton, his eyes continuing to hold Harry's steadily. "Which gives them great moral authority."

Griffiths picked up the thread as soon as Patton paused for breath, his voice full of the suspicion which, despite hints to the contrary, clearly troubled him.

"It's uncanny. Every delegate in the fleet, and there are some thirty of them, knows what to do and say, even when the case is altered in discussion. They showed a discipline from the very outset which would make you proud were it better directed. Mind, I am less convinced than Patton here that there are no French agents involved. The only thing that makes me think he might be right is the fact that there has been no bloodshed."

Patton took up the tale again, clearly intent, by the look he gave Griffiths, to lay any notion of a conspiracy directed by outside agencies.

"It's the very opposite of bloodshed. Initially, not one officer was so much as threatened with violence, even those hard-horse floggers who deserve it. Strict order was imposed to the extent that they even laid the lash to the back of one of their own for being drunk. And when the frigates tried to join the mutiny they were told to leave matters to the delegates from the capital ships, to get to sea and watch out for the enemy fleet, an injunction they only obeyed when they were actually threatened with a broadside."

Harry turned to Griffiths. "Why then, Ned, do you still have doubts?"

"Two delegates came from every ship to the first meeting, a recipe for chaos normally."

"They were the very best of the fleet before the mast," insisted Patton. "Quartermasters' mates, yeomen of the sheets and the like, though I admit even they had a self-control that astounded everyone, and stated the demands, even clarified them, without any kind of consultation."

Griffiths reacted with some anger. "It beggars belief that a group that size could agree so readily to sudden proposals without some guiding authority."

Through the arguments of these two men the details of the story unfolded, and Harry could not help but think that they'd brought it on themselves. The two men before him were good officers, Patton especially so. But they had contrived to live with a system in which the endemic abuses were tolerated. Any dissent should have come from their ranks, not those of the lower deck. The fear of losing employment, of existing on half-pay, terrified every commissioned officer.

The Admiralty, even when they'd been told that mutiny was possible, had ordered Bridport to send eight of the line down to St Helen's, the usual starting place for a cruise to blockade Brest. The Admiral had passed the order on to his second in command, Sir Alan Gardner, even if he doubted the wisdom of the instruction or that the men would obey. That said more than anything about the hierarchy that he himself had once served.

Did they not realize that the petty officers, ex-seamen and closer to the lower deck than officers, probably sympathized with their one-time comrades? Even if they didn't the sullenness produced by the conditions of service was something they lived with every day of their lives. They were allowed ashore, could meet and talk without being overheard, had ample time and good cause to lay the plans that had brought matters to a head. Did it need anyone from outside to fire them up to act?

The mighty Board of Admiralty, who should have known what was going on, had indeed been forced to leave London for Portsmouth. Patton was now describing how they offered concessions, quite naturally hedging the whole thing around with unacceptable conditions.

"Spencer refuses to meet with them," Patton continued, "so Gardner, Colpoys, and Admiral Pole took the Board's first offer to the delegates. When they were rebuffed Gardner completely lost control and threatened to hang every fifth man in the fleet."

Griffiths shook his head slowly, though whether his confusion related to the folly of the men or of the messengers, he didn't say. "Things looked set to turn nasty. The flag officers, my uncle included, were bundled off the ship. But before that happened the men restated their grievances, and added a unanimous demand, without even discussing it, for the inclusion of a Royal Pardon."

There was a moment's silence before Harry spoke. "That must have been worked out in advance, options discussed, not necessarily by one individual, but several men, a hard core who have the same aims as the mass, but a clearer view. Perhaps it's even one individual."

"If you could find him," said Griffiths, "you'd earn a dukedom. Never mind Jervis and Nelson and that folderol they had at St Vincent."

"I thought they'd won a substantial victory," James interrupted, clearly perplexed.

Harry gave him a knowing look, one that tried to convey the fact that any exploit of the Mediterranean command would receive scant praise from the Channel Fleet. And neither would praise the North Sea contingent, shivering at the Nore, the Downs, and Yarmouth, facing an enemy, the Dutch, that in quality of seamanship and fighting spirit surpassed anything that came out of

France or Spain. Griffiths, ignoring James's interruption, had kept talking, showing his confusion as he did so, unable to accept a conspiracy one minute, convinced it existed the next. Harry knew that in the end it mattered little. It was painfully obvious that this affair had to be resolved.

"If it's not stopped, Harry," Griffiths concluded, "Billy Pitt will be forced to sue for peace."

"Surely not," James said.

Patton gave him a hard look, one that was clearly intended to indicate that he, a civilian, could not comprehend the scale of the problem. But he was too polite to actually say anything. Not so Ned Griffiths, who pointed out in a harsh tone that the fleet was everything; that the mutiny could spread to the Nore, and that it would infect every fleet the country had at sea if it wasn't either checked or satisfied. As he spoke, he got more and more heated, and Harry observed that James was beginning to bridle.

"I might be tempted by a dukedom, Ned," he said, interrupting the lecture.

"Harry," James responded, a note of alarm in his voice. He was well aware of his brother's penchant for interfering in things that were none of his affair. Harry, who had a dangerous look in his eye, suddenly grinned at him.

"Never fear, brother. If I could find the hand that guided this, I'd shake it as long as it wasn't French. From what I can hear the men have asked for no more than their due."

Both officers looked confused, not willing to agree but as sure as Harry that what he was saying was nothing but the plain truth.

"And what kind of government is it," Harry added, "that can give the army, which has suffered nothing but humiliation, a rise in pay, and ignore a navy which has won two fleet actions in the last three years?"

"Hear, hear," said both Griffiths and Patton, in voices loud enough to make nearby heads turn in their direction.

They talked on, mulling over causes and effects and how they had been achieved. Partly, as Griffiths was forced to acknowledge, it was the present composition of the fleet. At the start of the war the navy had recruited or press-ganged sailors, men used to the rough ways of the sea, but that had changed when they could no longer cope with the massive expansion brought on by the nature of the conflict. The levy placed on all the inland towns, demanding a quota of men for the fleet, had changed the nature of the crews. The proportion of landsmen in each vessel had increased, so that in some newly commissioned ships they were close to being the majority.

That had brought into a strictly ordered world, through convictions in courts, debtors' gaols, and threats of transportation, men who could read and write, including the odd person with legal training. This was certainly borne out by the nature of one of the petitions, a copy of which Griffiths passed to Harry. There was none of the usual arcane wording of the common seaman's plea. These were laid out in clear, cogent English, ordered and precise.

"This could have been drawn up in Wapping by a hundred-guinea attorney," said James, after he'd read it.

Patton snorted. "And to think that Black Dick Howe read them all, and felt no cause for alarm. The wording alone should have alerted the old goat."

"And the present state of things?"

"Rumblings at the Nore, with no hint of difficulties at the Downs or Yarmouth, though rumours have come from Plymouth that Sir Roger Curtis's squadron refused to sail to anywhere but Pompey. It seems that on each station they're waiting for the Spithead delegates to earn them their demands."

"They have their Royal Pardon," Griffiths added. "Spencer might be prickly in the article of his pride, but he showed great application on that. He had it signed by the King in twenty-four hours, which at least got two-thirds of the fleet down to St Helen's. They were offered twenty-two shillings for seamen, which was acceptable until the Admiralty refused to extend it to recently recruited landsmen."

"I never heard of that rating before."

"No," Patton replied, adding a rueful smile. "The board made it up, they said to save money. But really it was an attempt to divide the men, to separate the sailors and the landsmen. Amazingly, Gardner nearly got them to accept it. But then the two delegates from the *Royal George* arrived and swung the meeting against him."

"Who just happen to be men from one of the ships where the mutiny started," said Harry.

Patton fought hard to avoid the look that said Harry Ludlow was stating the obvious, and didn't quite succeed.

"Valentine Joyce and John Morrice, they're called," said Griffiths, "and for my money they certainly hold sway over some of the other delegates. I've been told that pair are watched wherever they go."

"And?"

Patton smiled, and held up his hand to interrupt Griffiths. "I have it, on good authority, that they are no more than what they say they are, delegates from their own ship."

"The offer has been increased," said Griffiths, dolefully, "but the money parts have yet to be agreed."

Patton interrupted again. "And they have to be voted through Parliament, which takes time. That's what has made the men impatient. The ships refused to sail from St Helen's this morning."

"I saw that for myself."

"You could say," said Griffiths, shaking his head, "having settled one mutiny we now have another one, much worse, on our hands. Half the officers in this room have been ordered out of their cabins, though thankfully without a scratch to anything but their pride."

"I saw plenty of officers aboard the ships of the St Helen's squadron."

"These are the unpopular ones, Harry," whispered Griffiths.

Patton pointed a thumb at the ceiling. "The admirals are at it this very minute, right above our heads, trying to work out a form of words which will get the men back under control."

"Bayonets will do that, Patton!" All four men looked up simultaneously, into the florid face of Captain Jack Willett Payne. Behind him stood the pretty, over-powdered young girl, blushing a trifle as she contemplated her companion. "Cold steel or the wrench of rope is the remedy."

"If you wish to attempt it, Payne," said Patton, "I would be the last to stand in your way."

"Then pass it on to those bloody admirals who you're so friendly with." His eyes moved just enough to take in Harry. "Mind, you seem to be able to find companionship in the strangest places. You're so eager to tell how clever you've been, you'll consort with thieves and vagabonds."

"While you," snapped Patton, deliberately looking at the girl, "seem to be confined to the companionship of the bedchamber."

"Give me a decent whore any time," Payne replied, oblivious to the distress this caused the girl. "At least if they rob you they give something in return. Not like damned privateers."

Harry started to rise, but Payne was already walking away, dragging his confused companion behind him, and Ned Griffiths had a hand on his shoulder.

"Pay no attention, Harry," said Griffiths, seeing the glare in his old friend's eye. "I reckon someone at the Admiralty had a sense of humour. They gave him a thirty-two-gun frigate called *Impétueux*."

It was the noise that distracted Harry, not Griffiths's hand, his attempt at humour, or his plea to remain calm. Suddenly the staircase to the upper floor was full of senior officers, all descending, the masses of gold braid fronting their uniforms flashing in the lamplight.

"The meeting is over," said Patton, standing quickly. "Let's see what they've decided."

CHAPTER NINE

"WHAT the devil are you doing here?" demanded Lord Bridport, the moment he spotted Harry Ludlow in the throng.

"Merely curious, my lord," Harry replied, with a smile.

"Then you join a great and pestilent mass, sir," said the admiral next to him, a tall, gaunt-looking man with hollow cheeks, a prominent nose, and bushy, beetle brows. The eyes beneath them flashed angrily as he continued. "It's like being at the centre of a cowpat, the number of flies there are around seeking to dip their feet in fresh shit."

"May I be allowed an introduction, Uncle," said Griffiths, slightly flustered. By the look he'd given Harry when Bridport spoke, he was of the opinion that his friend should have stayed seated at the table. "Captain Ludlow, of the Letter of Marque *Bucephalas*. Harry, my uncle, Admiral Colpoys."

"Tom Ludlow's brat?" demanded Colpoys.

"None other," said Bridport. "And with all the family traits firmly in place, as I recall it."

"You will be pleased to know, Lord Bridport, that the orders you wrote were accepted with alacrity."

That made Bridport frown, bringing the edge of his wig very close to his eyebrows. At their last meeting Harry had practically threatened him, and it was clearly an unpleasant memory. But if he'd intended to allude to that occasion, Colpoys's interruption prevented him.

"You're never a privateer?"

"I am, sir."

"Damned disgrace! A sea scavenger no better than a privy cart labourer. Your poor pa would spin in his grave to hear of such a disgraceful thing."

Harry's eyes now flashed just as much as Colpoys's, and there was no gentility in his voice. "Do all admirals forfeit good manners when they hoist their flag."

"Harry," said Griffiths, looking anxiously at his commander. But Colpoys gave a great booming laugh and turned to Bridport.

"Damn it, you're right, my lord. He's his father's twin for a riposte. I always enjoyed Tom Ludlow's temper."

"That is a singular pleasure, Admiral Colpoys," Bridport responded, as he turned to enter the dining room, "that I can never recall sharing."

Colpoys addressed the retreating back. "That's 'cause you were his equal, sir. I only ever served under him, which given his ways was a damn sight more comfortable."

He gave Harry a last hard look, before turning his attention to Griffiths, his voice dropping to a near whisper. "We have to forgo our dinner, Ned. Call in my barge, then send out a general signal for all delegates from the Spithead squadron to assemble aboard my flagship at four o'clock. Do it in such a way that it can't be seen over in St Helen's."

"May I enquire as to the terms you propose, sir?"

"In time, Ned, in time. If I'm going to miss my victuals I need to line my rib bones with a pint of port. Ludlow, you will join me?"

If it was an invitation, it sounded very like an order, which almost caused Harry to refuse. But he was as eager as Ned Griffiths to know what was on offer to the sailors, which was enough to make him hold back.

"My brother and I already have a table, sir, if you would care to join us."

"Brother," boomed Colpoys, as they entered the taproom. "Is that the one who's a bit of a limner?"

Harry replied quietly, since they were rapidly approaching the table. James wasn't vain as regards his reputation, but to be likened to someone who painted signs for public houses and taverns would certainly make him bridle.

"He's somewhat more than a limner, sir. Though I'm no expert,

I know that his fees are substantial and that he's highly regarded in London society."

"God knows why, Ludlow," Colpoys said, in a loud growl that was supposed to be *sotto voce*. "I saw a picture he did of Lord Mansard at his house in Piccadilly. Far too much light and shade for my liking. Half the subject's face was in shadow, like one of them Dutch peasant women. Not a patch on Beechey, if you was to ask me."

"My brother, James," said Harry, to the figure now standing right in front of the admiral, looking perplexed. "Admiral Colpoys."

"Delighted, sir," replied James, with a slightly bewildered air. Harry hoped he hadn't heard, though he was at a loss to know how he could have failed to do so. His next words confirmed Harry's worst fears. "Did I hear you refer to Beechey?"

Colpoys pulled himself erect. "You did, sir. The finest painter of a likeness in the land, to my mind. Knows where the sun's coming from for a start. I sat for him in '95 and I say that he caught me to the life."

"Really," said James, his lips twitching ever so slightly. "He's repetitious to my mind. I always thought he concentrated on sailors since with all that braid around no one ever bothered to look at the sitter's face. Still, if the prize money doesn't run to Singleton Copley, one must take what one gets."

Colpoys screwed up his face for a sharp reply, then suddenly grinned, exposing a fine set of wooden teeth, as he turned to Harry. "He's a skinny addition to the Ludlow tree, but the tongue is provenance enough."

"Is that an apology, Harry?" asked James.

"Never, sir," boomed Colpoys, in a voice that made those on the edge of the room look towards him. Everyone closer, having heard his earlier remarks, was studiously looking away. His next outburst was clearly designed to take in both sets of customers.

"Admirals never apologize, even to other flag officers. Didn't your pa teach you that! I came for port, Ludlow, and I've little time to spare."

"Of course, Admiral." The servant obviously knew Colpoys, as well as his tastes. He was at Harry's elbow with two pints before he could turn round. Colpoys filled his goblet as soon as the man put it on the table, then swallowed the entire contents in one gulp, smacking his lips loudly when finished.

"Damn it, I needed that. Sharing a table with admirals and the like is worse than a mid's berth." The goblet was full again before he finished speaking and emptied twice more before Griffiths returned.

"Barge is by the Sally Port steps, Uncle."

"Good," replied Colpoys, pulling himself to his feet. He looked at both brothers. "Would you care to join me, gentlemen?"

"To what purpose?" asked James.

The admiral's voice dropped again, since he clearly had no intention of sharing the information with the room. "To witness the end of this damned nonsense."

"The mutiny?"

"What else? I intend to go aboard my flagship, put a question to the crew. And, gentlemen, I also intend to be firm. What transpired at St Helen's this morning will not happen at Spithead."

"Is that wise, Uncle?" whispered Griffiths.

The bushy eyebrows gathered like darkening clouds, as Colpoys's eyes swung round on to his nephew. Harry was almost sure he saw Ned Griffiths quake.

"We have orders to go to sea, reissued by their Lordships this very morning. The wind favours us. I intend to show Bridport that a little firmness will see us a fleet again. I also have another order in my pocket which is a direct command from the Admiralty to tighten up discipline, see that the marines' arms and ammunition are in good order and ready for use, and at the first sign of mutiny to use the most vigorous means to suppress it, as well as to bring the ringleader to a well-deserved punishment. And that, Captain, as you well know, is almost word for word."

"Sir," Griffiths replied, not daring to look his uncle in the eye, "I had that order too. It came to every captain in the fleet. We all were given to understand that Lord Bridport intended to ignore it."

"What he intends and what I do may not coincide."

"I for one would be happy to accompany you, Admiral," said Harry.

"You will forgive me," added James, throwing his brother a despairing look. "After months at sea, I am content to take my pleasure by staying on land. And I lack Harry's predilection for involvement in anything that smacks of trouble."

"So be it," replied Colpoys. He filled his goblet again, then drained it. "Let's be off."

"May I have one minute, sir?" asked Harry.

"One minute, Ludlow, and not a second more. This is the navy, not some damned letter of marque. If you're not at the Sally Port steps in sixty seconds behind me, I'll set off without you."

Harry turned to James as Colpoys swept out of the room.

"Could you write to Arthur and Cantwell's Bank, to tell them we are back home. Cantwell will need to be told to expect the balance of our specie as well as those bonds. And it would likewise do little harm to inform Arthur we've been lucky."

James's face creased with displeasure as Harry mentioned his brother-in-law, Arthur, Lord Drumdryan. Though the enmity that once marked their relationship had diminished, the younger Ludlow could still not bring himself to like his sister's noble Scottish husband.

Harry was heading for the door when he spoke again. "Write to Anne if you must, but just let them know we have safely returned and that we've enjoyed some success."

The admiral's barge lay at the foot of the wooden steps, the crew smart in blue pea-jackets and white duck trousers. If they were mutineers they didn't give any indication. They showed no hint of indiscipline as they sat, looking rigidly forward, oars raised in a neat regimented line. The coxswain was just pushing off as Harry leapt aboard, finding himself a seat in the crowded thwarts. Colpoys had several passengers, all officers, two of them, with whom he was in earnest, whispered conversation, wearing the bright red coats of marines. Ned Griffiths looked miserable, like a man who'd rather be anywhere than aboard the barge.

Once the bows were swung out the oars hit the water with regatta-like precision. The men began to haul, and soon they were shooting away from the steps and out into the Portsmouth Channel. Shallow of draft, they turned to cross the Spit Sand as soon as they'd cleared the fort, passing the sailors' hospital at Haslar on their starboard quarter. That was another deduction made from the common seaman's wage, a contribution to the running of the infirmary, as well the hospital at Greenwich, the first to provide care if they were wounded or sick, the second a place to reside when they retired.

The four ships-of-the-line, well to the seaward side of Admiral Parker's flagship, still lay at anchor, the rest of the fleet just visible at their St Helen's anchorage. Harry, turning his attention from the approaching line-of-battle ships, began to study the barge crew. These men, who rowed the admiral wherever he wanted to go, had to be the steadiest men on the ship. There could be no drunkards or idiots with loose tongues, since any act that brought attention to themselves reflected on the man for whom they laboured. The very idea that such sailors might refuse their duty, under any circumstances, seemed absurd.

Yet with an eye seasoned by so many years at sea Harry could detect something in their bearing that hinted at discontent. Called to put his finger on its exact seat, he would have been hard put to oblige. Perhaps it was the sheer blankness of the expressions, the utter lack of any response to an enquiring stare. It certainly had nothing to do with their rhythm or efficiency in the matter of rowing. Ever since the coxswain had settled on the required pace, they had hauled as a unit, in smooth, distance-eating ease.

London, as they approached, towered over them, a 98-gun three-decker, swinging at single anchor on her buoy. Marines stood by the entry port, as did the watch officer, waiting for their captain and admiral to arrive. The ship was like the barge. It looked normal. So much so that Harry considered fanciful the brooding sense of danger that began to creep over him. Swinging round in a smooth arc, the barge glided alongside. Pipes blew and marine muskets clashed to attention as they came aboard, in a ceremony that Harry Ludlow had not witnessed so closely since he was a midshipman.

Colpoys stood amidships on the maindeck for a moment, looking forward at the rows of mess tables that lay between the housed guns. Each table was occupied by the men of its mess, a group which worked, ate, and slept in close proximity. With a crew of 600 seamen, plus 150 marines and idlers, that meant a lot of tables. Not everyone was on this deck, of course. But a good many hard-bitten seamen and new-pressed landsmen were mixed together. A scene he had witnessed a thousand times, it took several seconds before Harry realized what was missing. Noise. There was no buzz of conversation. They might not be looking at the newly arrived party, but as soon as they'd come through the entry port, all chatter had ceased, and an eerie silence had descended.

"My cabin, Captain Griffiths, if you please. I should be obliged if you would assemble all officers in five minutes."

"Sir," the captain replied, before turning to his first lieutenant, standing right next to him, and repeating the order.

"Would I be permitted to wander, Ned?"

Griffiths replied with a distracted nod. Clearly he was unhappy. The assurance that should attend any captain aboard his own vessel, that air of calm and knowing authority, was quite absent. Harry reckoned that serving Colpoys couldn't be easy. Some admirals were sensible enough to never interfere in the running of the ship, but Colpoys didn't look the type. Being his blood relative would make life doubly difficult, since any hint of disagreement risked a family as well as a professional bond.

Harry made his way towards the companionway, his progress discreetly marked by hundreds of curious eyes. The silence was oppressive only if the person feeling it had witnessed the norm, which was a cacophony of noise that any crowd of boisterous individuals would create. The 'tween decks felt oppressive and threatening rather than spacious. On the upper deck knots of men stood around, wrapped up against the chill north-west breeze, all in earnest discussion, with many an eye glancing south towards their compatriots anchored off St Helen's.

Free to walk where he desired, Harry headed for the quarterdeck. This open space abaft the mainmast was the sole preserve of officers and those they appointed to run the ship. On that clear platform he could look aloft without tripping over some piece of equipment. Not that there was any untidiness. Every fall was flemished and coiled to perfection. Each ball that lay in the garlands by the huge guns was rust-free and freshly blackened. The deck itself was as spotless as any he'd ever seen. *London* was, in all respects bar one, shipshape. But that exception was suspicion, so prevalent it seemed to well up from the very planking.

The midshipman approached him while he was standing beside the great double steering-wheel. It took a moment to catch his attention, since the object of his instructions was lost in some kind of reverie. Harry hadn't stood in such a spot for years. Certainly he'd been aboard capital ships, but rarely here, at the very nerve-centre of control. If he'd commanded a ship of the line this was where he'd have exercised that authority. Thus the midshipman had to repeat his request. It was only then that Harry realized he wasn't some barely breeched youngster at all, but a man well into his middle years, with a rough edge to his voice that hinted at a life which had begun on the lower deck.

"The delegates from the other ships are arrived. Admiral Colpoys requests that you join him, sir, immediately."

"You were before the mast?" asked Harry.

"At one time, sir," the man replied. Stocky, muscular with a weather-beaten ruddy face, he looked past Harry Ludlow with an expression that was instantly recognizable, being the same one of wistful ambition he'd probably had on his own face just moments before. "But with God willing one day I'll stand where you do now."

Harry wanted to ask him how he felt, was dying to know if he was a party to the mutiny. This was the very kind of sailor who might be a delegate. He'd probably started life as a ship's boy, taking blows from any passing tar who fancied passing on some of the pain inflicted by the officers. He'd have been some-one's mate, perhaps a boatswain or a yeoman of the sheets. Sheer grit and determination might have elevated him to an apprentice-ship with the master, so that he could learn first-hand about ship handling and navigation.

Ambition and a kindly officer gave him his present limbo rank of midshipman. How did he feel mixing with youngsters, usually the sons of sailors, their relatives, or minor gentry, in the process of learning their trade? This man knew his inside out. Yet unless fortune provided him with a patron or opportunity he could expire from old age without a change of rank. Very likely, if he was pro-posed, he'd sit and pass his exam for lieutenant. But then what? Would he watch as the offspring of the well connected, with not half his abilities, passed over him to take command of ships and fleets, while he, without the influence to find employment, would be lucky to have control of a coastal merchantman?

"Immediately," the man insisted. "The admiral don't like to be kept waiting."

"Yes," replied Harry with a nod. He moved away, but turned suddenly to look into the midshipman's eyes. "Would I be per-mitted to ask your name?"

"Havergood, sir."

"Then, Mr Havergood, may fortune, or whosoever controls it, favour you. I know how hard promotion can be."

The man smiled for the first time, and his body stiffened slightly as he pulled himself to attention. "Why, thank you kindly, sir."

Again, as he went below, he felt oppressed by the quiet on the upper deck, felt the eyes on his back as he approached the two marine sentries set to guard the entrance to Colpoys's great cabin. They presented smartly, and one leant down to open the door. Harry went through to enter another world. No bare planking here. The floor had carpets, the walls paintings and elaborate sconces for decorative lanterns. The wood of the furniture, where it showed through the assembled officers, shone with the deep patina of years of care.

Colpoys stood in the centre, his gaunt frame slightly bent though he had ample head room. His eyes, under those threatening, bushy brows, swept round the room, taking in each person present.

"Gentlemen. It is time to take back our authority. We were commissioned to lead men, not to defer to them, and that is what we are now going to do."

CHAPTER TEN

"WHAT is the state of the marine armament?" the admiral demanded, fixing a scarlet-coated captain with a frosty stare. Harry had seen him talking to this same officer in his barge, so guessed that the answer to the question, which the admiral knew already, was for the benefit of others.

"Prime, sir. As good as it's ever been."

"And their cast of mind?"

The captain hesitated for a fraction of a second, which robbed his affirmative answer of a great deal of certainty, in reality telling them that though the answer he gave was positive, he really had no idea how they would perform. Colpoys picked it up immediately.

"We shall never know till we put them to the test, will we, gentlemen?"

There was a distinct lack of enthusiasm in the murmured replies. If these officers shared the admiral's determination, they obviously had grave doubts about the workability of what he was proposing to do. Living in greater proximity to the crew, these lieutenants had a much better understanding of their mood than cosseted and cut-off admirals. Griffiths, standing beside his uncle, had no light of battle in his eye. Indeed he looked much older than his years, a rotund figure, distinctly glum.

"Right. I want the marines on the poop, muskets primed, and the men ordered to assemble so that I may address them. Captain Griffiths, your officers will carry side-arms."

"Sir."

Colpoys gave them a last sweeping look before ordering everyone, "Carry on."

They filed out, leaving Harry and the admiral alone. A steward appeared with a fresh bottle of port, which he placed amongst the empties that already lay on the long dining table.

"Drink, Ludlow!" snapped Colpoys, grabbing the full bottle and filling his crystal goblet.

Harry didn't want a drink. There was going to be a showdown, obviously, which might very well be an occasion for a clear head. Then he remembered that he was a mere observer, who would have no effect whatsoever on the outcome. He also detected the slight apprehension in Colpoys's manner. The man wanted companionship, the kind his elevated status debarred him from sharing with the *London*'s officers.

"Pleasure."

Colpoys had already poured it for him, handing it over. He then waited for his servant, who hesitated till he saw the look in his master's eye, to depart. Colpoys's gaze was still on the door as he spoke.

"It's come to a sorry pass, Ludlow, when a man like me has to guard my tongue against eavesdropping by my own steward. Been with me since I was first made post, yet I can't be sure if I lay a plan to take back the ship he won't pass it on to the mutineers."

"Even he's part of the ship's company, sir."

"Nonsense," snapped Colpoys, slamming the crystal goblet down so hard that the stem broke. He held it up for a second, looking at it wistfully. "Damn! That was a gift from the Governor of Jamaica."

The voice changed to the more familiar growl. "Don't believe all you hear, Ludlow. The way folk go on you'd think there wasn't a tar in the fleet who had doubts about this subversion. That ain't so. Most men would return to their duty in an instant if it wasn't for a few malcontents and sea-lawyers."

Having walked across the maindeck, and noticed the silence, Harry wasn't sure he agreed. But he saw no purpose in taking issue with his host. If he believed what he was saying, Colpoys wouldn't be swayed by the opinions of a civilian visitor. And if he didn't, reminding him of the fact would only inflame his very evident anger.

"They threw me off Howe's flagship, you know," Colpoys hissed. "Not just me, but Gardner and Admiral Pole as well. Gave us a dressing-down in the great cabin then hustled us through the entry port as if we were shoddy tradesmen."

"The *Queen Charlotte*," said Harry.

"Damn that fat, gout-ridden old blackguard Howe with his soft sentimental ways." Colpoys's eyes flashed as he threw the broken, empty glass at the bulkhead before filling another. "All this started on his ship. And where is he? Up to his neck in mineral water and gossip at Bath. What's the damned use of being loved by the crews if the bastards won't obey you?"

Harry didn't answer, since there was no point. Colpoys wanted a sounding board, not a conversation. He was working himself up into the state he knew he'd need to confront the sailors.

"They've thrown the officers off the St Helen's ships, and Bridport tells me the insolent sods are set to question if some of them should be removed from their duty permanently. It's always the same, Ludlow. You must be firm, or an inch taken will go to a mile."

The sound of marines assembling came through the planking, loud enough to penetrate Griffiths's cabin, which lay above. Colpoys poured and drained a final glass of port, grabbed his hat, jammed it on his head, and made for the door.

"You may come and observe if you wish."

Colpoys made his way on to the poop, to stand beside Ned Griffiths, both men in front of the line of marines. Harry followed him, passing the row of armed junior officers who stood across the quarterdeck on either side of the wheel. Once he'd ascended the companionway he kept well to the windward side of the poopdeck, which gave him a clear view of everyone, including the crew of the *London* now pushing forward, behind a row of men who must be their delegates, to hear what the admiral had to say to them. This

wasn't achieved without noise, but once they'd assembled they fell
silent, the two groups staring at each other for several seconds.
This was suddenly broken, from aloft, by the rat-a-tat-tat of some
bone player who was so keen to demonstrate his skill that he was
beating out his tattoo at a totally inappropriate time.

One or two heads turned to look south and Harry followed
their gaze. He saw, in the distance, the line of boats heading
towards them from St Helen's. A glance at the admiral showed that
he'd observed them too, and he nodded to Ned Griffiths, who
immediately started to repeat the litany by which all sailors in the
King's navy lived, the Articles of War. Griffiths might be uncomfortable, but he had the voice to carry to the tops. He spoke without
reference to any book or paper, knowing the words off by heart.

Harry knew them too, a set of rules so comprehensive that a
man could face punishment for any number of offences. And where
the law stopped a commander, the articles had enough flexibility
to allow him to exercise his imagination. In the hands of a tyrant
they were a licence to abuse, in those of a good commander the
method by which order and discipline were maintained with the
consent and cooperation of his officers and crew. Each clause was
complete with its punishment, often death, the whole ended with
the final threat that "whosoever shall transgress these Articles, will
answer at their peril to the Lord Commissioners of the Admiralty."

Griffiths looked away from the sea of faces below to glance
south. Colpoys had never shifted his gaze, checking on the progress
of the boats which were eating up the distance. Anyone looking
at them, and seeing the red flags that they flew, could have no
doubt as to their purpose. They were manned by the mutineers of
the eight ships which lay at St Helen's. Having secured their own
vessels, they were coming north to ensure that their compatriots
at Spithead joined with them.

"Men," shouted Colpoys, stepping in front of his nephew,
"do you have any knowledge of what happened at St Helen's this
morning?"

Several men, braver than the rest, shouted out a clear "no."
But most shook their heads then turned to their nearest compan-

ions to seek enlightenment. Colpoys looked at Griffiths and smiled, a look which held as he asked another question.

"And have you, after the events of the past days, any grievances remaining?"

As they again responded negatively, Harry was left to wonder if Colpoys was being honest or indulging in deliberate dissimulation. By asking that he avoided alluding to complaints which might have arisen since the original revolt, the kind of injustices that the men approaching in the boats would no doubt enumerate.

"I thought that to be the case," said Colpoys. "In fact I was sure of it. You will now oblige me by going below, and leaving the deck to the officers."

The mass of the crew obeyed immediately, reacting like the sheep they were to a direct command. Nothing better demonstrated how difficult this mutiny must have been to organize: the vast majority of the men involved would have had to be cajoled into even the most minor disobedience. The bones, which had fallen silent as the admiral spoke, rattled out again, this time at a frantic rhythm, as though the player was angry. But that didn't stop the flow of men on the companionways, and within a minute only a couple of dozen sailors, plus what he assumed were the delegates, who'd crowded forward in the bows, were left. Colpoys had his eye on them, his brows lowered as he no doubt contemplated issuing some form of punishment. Suddenly he shrugged, as though they were of no account.

"Captain, I want the lower deck guns run in and the port-lids closed, with junior lieutenants and a pair of marines on hand to ensure they stay that way. Hatches to be put in place and all entries to the upper deck sealed off. If those men in the bows won't go below, hem them in on the forepeak. On no account are those bastards from St Helen's to get aboard this ship. If we can keep the pestilence of their opinions from our men, then we might keep *London* loyal."

"How far do you intend to go, Uncle?" asked Griffiths nervously.

"Just do it, Ned!" snarled Colpoys. He growled again as his

nephew leant over the rail to give his orders. "And do it yourself."

Griffiths's round face, when he looked back at Colpoys, was flushed with embarrassment, since every one of his subordinates had heard the rebuke. Shoulders hunched, he made his way down the steps from the poop. Colpoys stomped over to the starboard rail, demanded a telescope, and even though he could see them with the naked eye fixed it on the approaching boats. Harry moved across the line of the marines to join him.

"Damn it! That bastard Valentine Joyce is there."

"Who is he?"

"He was, I'm told, a good able seaman, Ludlow, attentive to his duty. Some fool rated him quartermaster's mate and now he's the most seditious bastard in the fleet. He's one of the delegates from *Royal George* and to my mind a leading light of the mutiny. He was one of the sods that shoved me off *Queen Charlotte*."

Colpoys was swinging his telescope around, searching the faces and reeling off the names of the delegates, all the time cursing as he regaled Harry with the humiliations he'd suffered at the hands of these men. "Can you imagine it, Ludlow, having to sit in Howe's own cabin, and to have to listen to these pigs tell us, admirals all, what they would and would not accept? One of them, Riley, is forward there now with the other vermin, the quartermaster of this very ship. Damn it, if I'd had a pistol I'm not sure but I would have discharged it at them. But never fear, sense will prevail. I marked the sods, names, rating, and ship. I'll see them at the yardarm, each and every one a-dangling, if it's the last thing I do."

"They're heading for *Marlborough*," said Harry, pointing to the boats which had swung round to approach the first ship-of-the-line in their path.

"Damn them!" He spun round and shouted, "Bover, get a signal aloft to Captain Deacon to secure his ship."

The young lieutenant this was addressed to pulled himself to attention. "With respect, sir, the signalling officers are down below guarding the port-lids."

Colpoys nearly screamed at him. "Then use the book yourself, Bover. Christ Almighty, man, you're the first lieutenant."

Bover turned to the other naval officers, still spread across the quarterdeck, all older than him, and issued a string of orders. That produced the signal book, but it also engendered a degree of confusion. They'd all used the thing before, and run the flags up the mast. But not for years. The actual mechanics of signalling lay beneath the dignity of any man who'd been promoted from the most junior station. Colpoys couldn't contain his impatience at the delay.

"Run up *'Repel boarders,'* for the love of Christ."

They were too late. Whatever was happening on the upper deck of *Marlborough,* no attempt was made to resist the delegates coming aboard. Several minutes passed, then the sound of cheering floated across the water. Harry was sure he could hear Colpoys grinding his wooden teeth in frustration. The delegates' boats pulled away from the entry port to allow the captain's barge to come alongside.

"God in heaven," hissed Colpoys, "I never dreamed I'd live to see this."

The stream of officers, led by the captain, came through the entry port and stepped down into the barge. Each one who passed from the darkened interior into the light was greeted by loud, sustained booing. Harry turned to look at Ned Griffiths, his round face anxious, standing beside him.

"That will be our fate too, Harry," he whispered. "We'll be slung off our own ship, just like Deacon."

As the barge pulled away from the ship, the *Marlborough*'s shrouds and yards were filled with cheering sailors. But they weren't just there to celebrate. They were loosing sails, so that the ship could be got under way. Not all the noise was coming across the water. Below their feet the crew of *London,* who must have heard even if they'd been prevented from seeing, started to push on the closed hatches, yelling to be set free. The boats from St Helen's that had surrounded the *Marlborough* were now heading for them.

CHAPTER ELEVEN

HARRY leant over the side. The arc of the tumblehome made it hard to see, but he suspected that at least some of the lower port-lids had been opened.

"Captain Griffiths," said Colpoys, making his way down to the quarterdeck, "I want the marines to put a salvo into the water in front of those boats. Get the swine to sheer off. If they don't oblige, aim for those damned delegates with the second round."

The orders were repeated to the marine officers, who stood alongside the party on the poop, just as the first of the spikes securing one of the hatches was broken off. The rest would follow, and men would begin to pour on to the deck, easily overwhelming the few defenders. Harry could hear the marine officer issuing ever more frantic orders to his men, and looking back saw the first of their muskets clatter to the deck. Several more followed, the owners deserting the poop to go forward to the bows.

Following their progress he spotted what was happening at the same time as the premier, Bover. The men who'd remained in the bows had cut free the breechings on one of the forward cannon, and were heaving it round to aim at the quarterdeck. He'd promised himself not to interfere, but that was a threat too far and he yelled a frantic warning.

"Do I have permission to fire on our own mutineers, Admiral?" shouted Bover.

"Yes, Lieutenant," replied Colpoys, glaring at his nephew. Clearly, the admiral thought the request should be coming from that quarter. "You do have my permission, and an order from the Admiralty as well."

What happened in the next few minutes was as confused as

any battle Harry had engaged in. The rest of the marines, called to the starboard poopdeck rail, might have retained their weapons, but they'd refused to budge, which left their officers screaming useless imprecations at them. Men were now squeezing through the gap in the hatches on to the deck, some stopping to extract the last spikes and open them completely, the rest making for the bows to get behind the cannon.

Clearly, despite the presence of marines and officers, the men had taken control below. A gangplank shot out from the *London*'s entry port, with men yelling that the first delegates' boat should come alongside. Only two of the marines tried to interfere, their shots wild and ineffective. Colpoys was now standing amidships in front of the wheel, his nephew beside him. His voice was calm and measured, and directed at the first lieutenant.

"Mr Bover. You will oblige me by retaking possession of that cannon from the mutineers. I need hardly remind you that aimed at us, it is decisive." The marine captain was next. "Livingston, your marines to secure and replace the hatches."

"They won't obey, sir."

"Issue the orders, Mr Livingston."

The marine complied, only to see the remainder of his men, save the two who fired into the sea, drop their weapons and rush down the companionway to join the sailors. They passed Bover, who was lining up the rest of his officers, and some of the younger midshipmen. Looking closely at the crowd in the bows, Harry saw that other mids, including the man he'd spoken to earlier, Midshipman Havergood, stood amongst the mutineers, yelling just as lustily as their lower deck comrades, calling out for Colpoys to surrender the ship.

The crash of gunfire as the officers and the remaining marines opened up rent the air, and brought an immediate response from the hatchways. Clearly the armoury had been unlocked and the seamen had pistols. The two marines who'd stayed at their posts lowered their muskets and put in a second volley. Harry, who'd ducked behind the rail, saw Havergood spin and drop as a ball took him. Bover had rushed forward and fired into the crowd, clearly unable to hear Griffiths, who'd stepped in front of his uncle, yelling at him to cease fire. Bover discharged a second pistol right into the mass of bodies in the hatchway, then rushed towards the cannon in the forecastle. But none of the other officers followed him. He turned to fall back but he'd gone too far and was isolated.

Ned Griffiths was now screaming at his uncle. "Order them to cease fire, sir. We have but two marines to aid us."

There was no gunfire now, but plenty of noise as officers and men traded loud insults, while others called for retribution. Several seamen had seized Bover and were manhandling him towards another group on the larboard gangway, who'd got hold of a rope and were quickly fashioning a noose. Seeing this, Ned Griffiths started forward but his uncle grabbed him and pulled him back.

"I must rescue him," Griffiths yelled.

"They'll hang you with him. Get everyone up on the poop and what guns we have available reloaded."

That was a command that required no repetition. Every officer knew that they risked the rope. In a mutiny in which no one had received so much as a scratch they had been the first to spill blood, perhaps enough to turn these well-behaved and loyal seamen into a screaming mob. As soon as he reached the poop, Harry approached Colpoys. Bover by this time had the rope round his neck and a party was assembling behind him with the clear aim of hauling him aloft.

"Let me go forward, sir, and plead for his release."

"What good can you do, Ludlow?"

"I can do no harm, and as a civilian I think I am safer than anyone in uniform. Can I say that he was not responsible since he was acting under your orders?"

"Harry," said Griffiths, anxiously. But Colpoys had held up his hand to silence him. A second that felt like an hour passed before the admiral nodded, proof that he knew the potential consequences of that message. There was a very good chance that they might hang him in the premier's place.

Harry looked over the side again, to confirm that the delegates' boats were alongside. He didn't run, not wishing to create any alarm. He walked slowly down the companionway steps, on to the empty quarterdeck, then forward towards the waist. The gangways that lined both sides were crowded. He stepped over the rail that delineated the point which no seaman could cross without express orders, moved forward to the netting, there to ensure that no one fell into the central section of the upper deck, and, stopping, called out to the men holding Bover.

"I have come to plead with you to release your prisoner."

"That bastard murdered at least one of our number," said the man nearest him, a pock-marked individual who jerked the noose he was holding. "And he has certainly maimed another, I reckon."

"The lieutenant was only obeying Admiral Colpoys's orders."

"Then that's good reason to string him up, I say," shouted a voice from the rear. The bone player was in there somewhere and he rattled off a quick tattoo, as if he agreed with the sentiment. At a sudden commotion at the rear the crowd parted, and several men pushed through with great difficulty to surround the hanging party.

"Let him go," said the tallest of their number, a fair-haired and handsome fellow dressed in petty officer fashion.

"It's none of your concern, Joyce. This is the *London,* not the *George.*"

"Where's Riley?" Joyce demanded.

"Here." Another man pushed his way through. He was older than Joyce, similarly dressed in a long kerseymere waistcoat and good breeches. Another followed, younger and fitter, with a long, greased pigtail, decorated in the fashion used by the ship's élite, the topmen.

"You should be putting a stop to this, not me," snapped Joyce. Harry noticed other seamen easing their way into position, so that the men holding the ropes were isolated from their fellow Londons. "You know what'll happen if we spill so much as one drop of blood."

"Bit late for that," growled Riley, stepping back and waving. A space cleared, to reveal Midshipman Havergood's inert body. "He's dead already."

"The admiral ordered him to use force," Harry shouted.

"Leave me to my fate, Joyce," said Bover.

"Never in life," the delegate replied.

"You know him?" demanded the pock-marked fellow with the noose.

"We served on another ship together," replied Joyce, taking hold of the rope himself. "And I know him to be a kindly officer, one who was no friend to either the rope's end, the cat, or the greedy, robbin' bastard who was purser."

He stepped back slightly so that he could address everyone. "What man here has had a flogging of Lieutenant Bover that he didn't richly deserve? He's a man that only thieves need to fear."

The crowd started to murmur, half for their premier, half against. Harry called out, hoping that what he said would help rather than hinder Joyce. He'd acted spontaneously to save Bover's life. Yet given a brief time to think he could see that his action had been more profound than that. Everything he'd heard about the mutiny and the delegates gave Harry Ludlow cause to admire them.

They'd taken on an uncaring government and a group of superiors many of whom would have hung them if they could. Only solidarity and strict discipline had kept them from such a fate. But blood had been spilt now, and that could alter everything. If they retaliated by taking Lieutenant Bover's life the mutiny might fall apart, and every delegate who'd sat in the cabin of the *Queen Charlotte* would end up where Colpoys wanted them, hanging from the yardarm.

"Can you not admire the bravery of a man who came at you all, hundreds of men, with no thought for his own safety, obeying his admiral's orders? Is he not the very best kind of man to serve under?"

"Who are you, sir?" asked Joyce.

"A private citizen, Mr Joyce, who admires the navy, and none more so than the common seamen."

Harry saw one man press forward to whisper in Joyce's ear. He wasn't sure, but he thought he recognized the face as someone who'd been a ship's boy on *Barfleur*. Whatever he said must have been flattering, since Joyce's tone was quite friendly. And now he had a name.

"Then I thank you for it, Mr Ludlow." Joyce turned to face his mutineers. "And he has the right of it. But I, for one, am a man to trust the law. Let Bover appear before a magistrate. If he says he's guilty, then justice will be done by those with the power vested in them to apply it. That, brothers, is not us."

"The law won't touch him," said the noose-holder.

Joyce put a hand on his arm taking a firm grip. "You may be right, friend. But as sure as this ship is made of wood, the law will have us if we harm him."

Voices were raised on both sides, the less seamanlike men calling for summary justice, while those who looked like proper tars, with their pigtails and ruddy faces, were in favour of backing Joyce. For several minutes there was no knowing which way they would swing, but eventually the cautious element prevailed.

"Let Colpoys confirm," someone shouted, a cry that was taken up by dozens of throats. Joyce held up his hand for silence, but it was ignored. Then it began to die away, and Harry heard the footsteps on the deck behind him. He didn't turn round because he didn't have to.

"I gave him his orders," said Colpoys, coming to stand beside him. "And if he hadn't obeyed them I'd have had him stripped of his commission."

"Then you should stand in his place," shouted the hangman. "You're a damned bloody scoundrel."

Harry had to fight not to smile at the response to that, especially amongst the older hands. Trained all their days to deference, they held admirals as akin to gods. To hear one so traduced flew in the face of a lifetime's habit. The man holding the rope was roundly cursed for his cheek and one old fellow got close and berated him to his face.

"How dare you talk to the admiral like that, you low-life swab!"

"Admiral Colpoys had his orders too," shouted Harry. "Let him explain them to you."

He turned to the older man, praying he had the wit to see that if they could save Bover by pleading a case of orders then they could do so for every officer on the ship, including himself, by using the instructions which had come down from the Admiralty. There was a moment when the idea of pleading seemed so distasteful that Colpoys couldn't do it. And when he did finally speak his voice had a crack in it that the men took for remorse, but which Harry knew to be strain.

"I had written instructions to fire on any mutineers. Had I disobeyed, I would have been shot on my own quarterdeck, like Admiral Byng."

"I must ask you, Admiral," said Joyce, again holding up his hand to quieten his comrades, who were far from convinced, "if this is the plain truth?"

Harry heard the old man suck in his breath. To him it was the final insult, to have his word and honour questioned by a man he considered vermin. He was working himself up to a furious bellow. Harry spoke before he had a chance.

"The orders are in writing." Then, as another bout of shouting and disagreement took hold of the crew, he whispered to Colpoys. "For God's sake, sir, keep your temper. If you want to live, indulge Joyce. If they hang you, or Bover, they will have to kill us all. Help him save us."

The long hiss of released breath that came from the old man convinced Harry that he had succeeded. Colpoys waited till the noise had died down. "I have those very instructions in my cabin. You may elect two men to accompany me to fetch them."

"They are in your pocket," whispered Harry.

"I know," Colpoys replied, equally softly. "But time may help calm the malcontents."

"I'll go," said Joyce, "but only if you remove this rope from Mr Bover's neck."

"Me too," said another sailor, stepping forward.

"Huddleston," said Colpoys, "delegate from *Queen Charlotte*."

"I wish I had a pistol," said Harry.

"In God's name, why?"

"I don't trust the man on the rope with Joyce gone. A gun would be just the thing to stop him having his hanging."

"Damn it, Ludlow," Colpoys growled, "you're madder than your damned father."

Harry only heard later how Colpoys had delayed matters, pretending to search his desk for a good five minutes before producing the orders from his coat pocket. In the meantime those on deck with a less bloodthirsty nature had a chance to work on the hotheads, so that by the time the trio returned, to stand over the waist, matters had definitely swung towards a peaceful outcome.

"He must face the law," said Joyce, pointing to Bover, that after he read out the Admiralty order. "That is only right."

Colpoys nodded, reluctantly, as Harry spoke. "I didn't know Midshipman Havergood, Mr Joyce. We exchanged but a few words an hour ago. But he was, like me, a sailor. If you will permit me, once the coroner has passed his body, I would be happy to pay for a decent Christian burial."

"Why, that is a most noble thing to offer, sir," said Huddleston.

"I accept," replied Joyce, looking at him strangely, "and I say to the whole of the fleet that they are welcome to attend."

"You propose to let the men ashore," barked Colpoys, having also given Harry an odd look.

Joyce, in the process of patting Harry gratefully on the back, grinned at him. "Do you think they'll run, Admiral? Pardoned men, who have just won the greatest victory in their entire life?"

CHAPTER TWELVE

"**THE NOTION** of a grand funeral with thousands of grieving tars weeping into their pigtails may appeal to you, Harry, but it does nothing for me. Quite the reverse."

The brothers were eating a late supper in Mistress Blackett's comfortable sitting room, before a flickering wood fire, having met up again at the Fountain when Harry returned from *London*. How news of what had happened got ashore before he did was a mystery. But it had, and Colpoys had been forced to run the gauntlet of a great deal of hissing and booing outside the Sally Port. That was as nothing to his reception at the hotel, where Bridport had made perfectly plain the depth of his disapproval. Oddly, Lieutenant Bover was spared from the general opprobrium, though he had been confined until a coroner's court could be convened. Midshipman Havergood, at Harry's bidding and expense, was at this very moment being prepared for his interment.

"I suggested a decent burial, not a spectacle. That was Joyce's idea, a way of rubbing salt in Colpoys's wounds. Not that the old boy requires it. He'll need a pipe of port to get to sleep this night. Did you write to Arthur?"

"I did, and to Cantwell. I took the liberty of asking him to contact your prize agent so that we could get accurate figures for the entire cruise, with the caveat that the American Treasury bonds have a degree of speculation in their value and what coins remain will have to be checked for debasement. I also sent word to Cheyne Court so that Pender's children will know he's safe returned."

Harry looked wistfully over his brother's shoulder as soon as Cheyne Court was mentioned. James didn't know what plans he laid for a future with Hyacinthe Feraud, but it would be fair to speculate that the family home figured in them quite largely.

"He'll thank you for that," Harry replied, before recovering himself. "By the way, speaking of Pender, where is he?"

"Still visiting, I think. No doubt he's ensconced in some rookery chewing over old times with the dregs of Portsmouth society."

"I'm heading back to Buckler's Hard in the morning to see what progress has been made with *Bucephalas*. Do you want to come?"

"No, thank you." James looked at Harry in a peculiar way before proceeding. "I wish to say that what I'm about to tell you has nothing to do with your recent behaviour."

Harry grinned. "But you're not coming back to sea with me."

"You guessed."

"Such a sonorous tone, brother."

"I have, as you know, neglected my true calling these last years."

Harry's face changed immediately, from being quite gleeful to totally bereft in a split second. "Not entirely. I can think of at least one very good portrait you've completed."

James had deliberately turned away, and kept talking as though his brother's mood hadn't altered. Nor was he prepared to make any reference of his own to the painting he'd done in New Orleans, at present rolled in a leather carrying case.

"It's not that I don't like wandering the oceans. Quite the opposite. But if I leave things much longer I'll never be employed to do a portrait again. And I'm concerned about my technique. I'm sure when you've been away from the sea for a while things get rusty. Painting is no different."

"I will miss you, James, and so will the men. Now they will just have to make a guess about where we're going and what I intend."

From the first moment James Ludlow had come aboard Harry's ship the crew had sensed that he was a soft touch. The element of self-interest was soon mixed with a genuine liking, since James harboured no airs or graces in the nautical line. Indeed it was his ignorance that provided one priceless asset to men who were endemically curious: he could ask his brother to explain his intentions, a right Harry extended to no other. Primed by the seamen with appropriate questions, he would elicit answers that a sharp ear could latch on to.

"I doubt they need my services now, brother," James replied. "You will not thank me for saying so, but you've become a mite transparent of late. If you see a ship with a British flag you run. Anything else and you attack."

"You've excluded the neutrals."

"I didn't know, in your case, that there were any."

"Are you going to London?"

"Eventually. But I have an acquaintance at Petersfield that I might drop in on. They live near General Murray and his wife. They were after me, offering a commission on our last run ashore."

The door opened and a slip of a girl entered bearing a tray, preceded by Mistress Blackett. James examined her closely, since the flaming fire plus the candles, throwing their light upwards, did nothing to hide her years, nor the scars of what must have been a very rough existence. She wasn't old, but she was a hard woman, perhaps not through inclination but necessity. Yet she could exude kindness, even although it had to it a commercial tinge. She oversaw the clearing of their soup plates, fussed while the girl laid a course of stew and vegetables, then shooed her out of the room.

"Pender has come back to us, carried between two of his old companions." She grinned, which in the light added a devilish hue to her heavily lined and powdered features. "He has a sweet voice, which I never guessed at."

"Drunk?" asked Harry, who'd never guessed at it either.

"As the proverbial lord, Captain Ludlow. I put him into a cot in the attic to sleep it off."

"Thank you."

"It ain't no trouble, sir. Pender was always decent to me. Robbed half the houses in the town, but never this one."

"Will you join us in a glass of wine, madame?" asked James,

lifting up the decanter that lay to one side of the hearth. That produced a simpering noise. She was a lady who'd been called madame many times in her life, but rarely with such gentility.

"Why, I'd be delighted, sir, though I can only stop for a mite since my parlour is full to bursting. And Jack Willett Payne is here, which means things are prone to turn boisterous."

"We've had a brief run-in with the good captain," James replied, his face expressionless. "He's certainly one for forthright opinions."

"He's forthright in all manner of things, sir, and a satyr to boot, especially in the article of virgins. And he will try and lure them away."

Taking a drink, Mary Blackett didn't see the Ludlow brothers exchange rueful glances.

"How long have you known Pender?" asked Harry.

She responded with a raucous laugh, which was magnified uncomfortably in the small room, then took a deep gulp of wine.

"More years than I care to name. I knew him when he was new come to Portsmouth, a callow youth scratching the streets to make a crust. But he was a sweet lad, for all that, and I was happy to take him under my protection. That is, before he came upon his true callin'. There never was such a man for unpickin' locks. It's like he can talk to them. Mind, I was glad he ran for the sea. He got out the window with the law at the door, escaped by a whisker."

"One robbery too many," said James.

"One friend too few. He would never bow the knee, sir. And Portsmouth is no different to any other town of a size. There's folk here who saw it as their patch, an' didn't like it when someone worked on his own account, not, so to speak, giving them their due."

"Do those same people still exist?" asked Harry, with just a hint of anxiety.

"Never fear, sir. The turds that did for Pender are long transported, strung up by the neck or gone to Botany Bay. Not that matters have improved. Shit floats, gentlemen, and it was ever so.

Others have risen to take their place, some of them people that Pender knew well enough. I dare say they are the ones that got him intoxicated. I will not opine for certain that the warrant is laid to rest. But I doubt it is still waiting to be served, so he is safe."

"Did you know his wife?"

"I did, and she was at one time a sweet girl, if a touch over-fond of gin. That's what did for her in the end, if you leave out being poor. The town is full of navy wives in similar straits. Good women, with bairns, who can't get a penny from the Paymaster to feed them. And if they do manage to see a pay warrant, they like as not have to walk to Chatham to cash it in. Captain Jack Willett Payne might curse those tars for mutinous dogs who're taking French gold, and a person in business will not disagree to his face. But it is pure moonshine, sirs, and there's few in Portsmouth who'd disagree with that. The very idea. Why a Jacobin in this town would stick out like a boil on a bear's arse." She stood up, coquettishly touching her dress. "I thank you kindly, but I must be about my occasions, or they'll start rending the furniture to bits."

Harry stood too. "Do I need to look in on Pender?"

"Never. He's sound. And well found enough too, I warrant, sailing with the famous Harry Ludlow."

Harry bowed his head slightly. "Hardly famous, Mistress Blackett."

"More'n you know, sir. Why, I had a lad here this very morning asking if you was in residence, and dying to know if he could have a place on your ship. His face fell when I told him it was laid up."

"I hope you didn't tell him where," said Harry, a sharp note in his voice.

The owner's face creased suddenly, as though she was about to deliver an equally caustic reply. But either good sense or the business variety stopped her, and she forced herself to smile.

"How could I, Captain Ludlow," she lied, "when I ain't got the faintest notion of the answer?"

◆ ◆ ◆

James's letters went off on the early morning coach to London.
With a good road between the naval base and the capital, and regular stops to change horses, his mail, plus all the other post from
Portsmouth, travelled one of the best routes in England, being carried over Putney Hill not long after the light began to fade.
Collected by the postal franchisee at the Angel Inn, behind St
Clement's in the Strand, they were delivered to the various
addresses before eight o'clock in the evening, where the reactions
to the news that Harry Ludlow was home induced a remarkable
result in three locations; the Sheriff's room at the High Courts of
Justice, the city offices of Cantwell's Bank, and most tellingly at
the house Harry had rented in Hanover Square.

"Get me a horse messenger at once," barked Arthur
Drumdryan, his habitual sang-froid completely deserting him as
surely as he'd deserted his guests playing cards in the drawing
room. The startled servant, normally as leisurely as his master,
actually ran from the house, which caused the rest of the staff to
speculate that the French had invaded. Meanwhile Lord
Drumdryan was busy scribbling:

Harry, there is no time for lengthy explanations. Your affairs are
in a tangle, so much so that I cannot guarantee against a warrant
having been already issued to apprehend you for debt still being
in force. Cantwell's Bank is, at this time, insolvent, with the owner
himself enjoying the hospitality of Newgate Gaol. Notwithstanding his own actions he has engaged on your behalf in speculations
that have left you penniless. His response to my challenge on this
matter leads me to suspect that they are nothing short of fraudu-
lent. If you have the freedom, get back to sea and head for the
Downs. I will proceed to Deal and take rooms at the Three Kings.
Contact me there, where I will be able to inform you in detail of
what haste debars me from explaining now.

"Where is that damned messenger?" he shouted, as he sanded and sealed it, his voice echoing off the walls of the spacious hallway when that same shout was repeated within thirty seconds. The noise brought his wife to the head of the stairs, and she leant over the elegant circular banister to enquire what was amiss.

"Government business, my dear," said Arthur, fighting to sound calm. Anne was pregnant again, and she knew nothing of Harry's difficulties. "The usual thing of a man saying he will do something and failing. Normally it is not a matter of urgency, but on this occasion it is. Please rejoin our guests, and I will come as soon as I've got this message away."

His panting servant came through the door as Anne turned to comply. "I've sent a boy to Hanover Mews. The farrier there, Harper, has a lad who engages for this kind of work."

"You should have gone yourself," said Arthur icily. "Get upstairs and make sure Mr Dundas and his good lady are taken care of."

The sound of hoofs covered the clatter of the servant's footwear as he ascended the stairs, and Arthur went out the front door on to the porch. The youthful horseman leant down to take the note, and the coin that went with it.

"Portsmouth," said Arthur, passing both the sealed parchment and a golden guinea. "Can you read, laddie?"

"No, sir."

"What's your name?"

"Ben Harper, sir," he replied, before patting his horse's neck. His eyes gleamed with pride as he continued. "And this is my horse, Lightning, who has raced and won prizes on the Sussex Downs, mostly at Uppark."

Arthur had no interest in either the horse or its exploits.

"The superscription is to a Mr Harry Ludlow, who is staying at a Mistress Blackett's in the town. You will not be able to find it without assistance. The Fountain is the main hostelry, ask there for directions. Hand it only to Captain Ludlow or his brother James. No one else."

"I'll do that, sir."

"And boy, ride that horse till it drops if necessary. I want no delay."

"Lightning won't let you down, sir."

"I'm glad to hear it."

"Is it the mutiny, your honour?" asked the boy, touching his hat and hauling on the reins to turn his horse's head.

"No," said Arthur bitterly, "it's much more important than that."

Mr Frayne, who'd taken over the running of affairs at Cantwell's Bank on behalf of the creditors, read James's note with some interest, then sent straight to the Sheriff's court for a bailiff. Bullen actually arrived from Bow Street within minutes, having set out to visit Frayne of his own volition. He in turn showed Frayne the letter he'd received, adding that it was sound policy to have folks in every seaport in the land who could keep their ears to the ground.

"I have sent off a response that will catch the four of the morning coach to tell my man to keep the quarry in view."

Frayne held up both the letters. "Odd that they came in by the same post, Mr Bullen, wouldn't you say?"

"Not odd, your honour," replied Under-Sheriff Bullen. "I'd be minded to call it fortuitous."

"When will you leave yourself?"

"As soon as duty permits, sir, which should be sometime tomorrow. I've collared many a sailor in my time, and I knows that, barring it being a Sabbath day, when they's immune to being had up, time and tide are the enemy."

CHAPTER THIRTEEN

THE MESSAGE came for Harry very early in the morning, while he was getting dressed, delivered personally by Admiral Parker's flag-lieutenant, Leybourne.

"You will appreciate, Captain Ludlow, that given the present emergency my commanding officer is busy. He would appreciate it if you could find your way to comply with his request, in what will be probably the only time he'll have free today."

"I don't quite understand your reference to the presence of Captain Illingworth."

"He spoke with Admiral Parker late last night. Given what Illingworth said it seemed proper to ask him to attend as well."

The merchant captain had been quick, so much so that Harry wondered if he'd come straight to Portsmouth once he'd landed, without going to London to inform his employers of their loss. And given the shortage of time, what had he done with the remainder of his men?

"I cannot see what possible information I can add to that of Illingworth. After all, he came face to face with this Tressoir fellow. I only saw his ship for the very briefest of moments, and through the mist."

"I was given to understand you had spied the corvette the night before."

"I spied a corvette, Lieutenant. I have no guarantee it was the same one."

Harry was equivocating and both men knew it, just as they knew that a man like Sir Peter Parker would not be inviting him to an early breakfast unless he intended to ask him for something. Given that his brother, Sir William, and his family were being held for ransom in a Normandy port, and that with the mutiny every frigate in the fleet was required for service, it didn't take a genius to work out what turn it would take. The temptation to decline here and now was strong. But that would be seen as a slight, and Admiral Parker was powerful enough to make that unwise. Harry would want to go to sea again, with the same exemptions for his crew he'd enjoyed previously. To make an enemy of any senior officer was foolish. But the admiral commanding at Portsmouth held a special office, very close to that of the First Lord himself.

"I will attend upon Sir Peter within the hour."

"Thank you, sir. And your brother?"

"I think not. He's still asleep. But please be so good as to inform your admiral, Lieutenant, in the strongest possible terms, that I have only just returned from a two-year cruise. I have neither the inclination nor the means to proceed straight back to sea again."

Leybourne pulled a gold watch from his waistcoat pocket and examined it. "If you could be with him in thirty minutes, sir, rather than the hour, I'm sure he'd be extremely indebted to you."

In the event, it took Harry slightly longer, since he had another visitor, Valentine Joyce. He was reluctant to come upstairs, so Harry went down to greet him and took him into Mary Blackett's parlour. The room had a stale smell, a mixture of human perspiration, drink, tobacco, and cheap scent. Joyce had his woollen cap in one hand, and swept the other through his fair hair as they entered, then wrinkled his nose.

"Give me a decent bilge anytime."

The voice, in conversation, was less strident than the day before. Harry took the opportunity to study his features. Much the same height as himself, he had a lankier body. The face, good-looking, also had well-defined bones, with wrinkles around the corners of his blue eyes that denoted a man easily amused.

"If I don't ask you to sit down, Mr Joyce, it's for the care of your health rather than any lack of courtesy. This is a haven for the lowest type of King's officer. I don't doubt the very chairs in here are poxed by being occupied by such people."

"I had to come ashore this morning, Captain Ludlow, and I wanted to take the chance to thank you again for what you're proposing for poor Havergood."

"I spoke with him just before the trouble started. He seemed to me to be a good man. The very best that the service could boast."

"He was. Just as Mr Bover is."

"Yet Havergood was prepared to mutiny," said Harry, trying to disguise the fact that what should have been a statement was actually a question. He saw the petty officer stiffen. "Forgive me, Mr Joyce. I am of a curious nature."

"There's no mystery, Captain Ludlow. The men are fair sick of being treated like pigs, that's all."

Mystery intrigued Harry, since he had never implied that one existed. "Well, let me say how much I admire you all. I know that a man was killed yesterday. But I'm also aware of how close we came to a bloodbath. That man on the rope, as well as those men on the foredeck who'd turned round that gun—had they acted they would have caused just such a thing."

"And ruined us," Joyce replied, looking away. "Which would have played right into the hands of diehards on the Board of Admiralty. Sometimes, Captain, you have more trouble with your own than you do with your enemies."

"Will you be able to maintain it?"

Joyce grinned, proving the provenance of those wrinkles round his eyes. "You won't need to fund me a plot if we don't. They'll throw me to the fish."

Nevertheless, some of the strain Joyce was under showed as he said that, particularly in the clenching of his jaw, and observing that made Harry reluctant to probe further.

"One day, when this is all over, I'd love to know how you achieved it."

There was no need to elaborate. Joyce, who looked him

straight in the eye, knew exactly what he meant. How had they combined and communicated with such effect as to act as one, and to impose enough control so that the hotheads were contained?

"Perhaps, one day, Captain Ludlow, I'll tell you."

Harry responded with a soft laugh. "Why is it that I think not, Mr Joyce, that you will take the secrets of what you have done to the grave?"

Joyce allowed himself the slightest of smiles, as if in confirmation.

"Speaking of that, you must tell me how much I owe for poor Havergood's funeral."

"I asked that the bill be sent here."

"Good."

"I'll bid you good day, Captain Ludlow, and just say again that you have the thanks of every man before the mast in the entire fleet."

"That seems rather excessive."

"It ain't, sir," said Joyce emphatically. "Believe me it ain't. And it has nothing to do with burials. Now, if you don't mind, I'll go out the back way, instead of the front."

"Be my guest," Harry replied.

The hall clock struck the hour as he opened the door, reminding him that he was late for his appointment with Admiral Parker. A minute later, he rushed out of the front door, heading for the dockyard. In doing so he bumped straight into a tall dark man who, for reasons best known to himself, had stepped right out into his path. Physical by nature, and in a hellfire rush, Harry brushed him aside with an apology that lost much force by being aimed away from the victim.

Parker had an air of prosperity, a presence that was immediately apparent to all who came within his orbit, and he knew it. Handsome for his age, though somewhat florid, his dress had an impeccable quality, with those small additions to standard uniform that hinted at a touch of the dandy. This was reinforced by the numerous mirrors that lined his private quarters, multiplied by the number of times he glanced into them to check his appearance. Dark brown eyes, a straight nose, and full red lips were accentuated by the white wig and sparkling linen of his neckcloth. And since he was going out of his way to be charming, the whole effect would have been pleasing to anyone but his present visitor.

"Colpoys is finished, Ludlow," he said. "Damn fool he is too. It might not have been actually stated yet, but if the Channel Fleet returns to duty, his flag won't be sailing with it."

"That seems rather harsh, since, like Lieutenant Bover, he was only acting under what he considered to be firm orders."

"Captain, I would not wish you to mistake me. Given a chance I'd use the rope to decimate the entire fleet complement. One man in ten, sir, as the Romans did with their legions. And if that meant the odd innocent cove being strung up with the guilty, then so be it."

Harry was tempted to say he didn't care about Colpoys, that he was only making conversation; that since neither Illingworth nor Parker had broached the real reason for inviting him along, he was damned if he was going to be the one to do so.

"Now I know you're a bit less of a disciplinarian than I am, what with you financing that funeral for Havergood. And perhaps I am being tactless. But I won't dissemble for the sake of manners, sir, so if what I say offends you, it is my opinion and must stand."

Illingworth, who'd been very silent for such a garrulous soul, finally cut in, no doubt worried that if Parker and Harry became disputatious it would serve all of them ill.

"No doubt there are several different solutions to the present crisis. But what is very apparent is that it creates a dilemma that would not exist in normal times. The navy would have the means to deal with Tressoir."

Parker's handsome face showed a slight trace of anger. Clearly if anyone was going to bring up that subject he intended that it should be him.

"I do hope," said Harry, slowly, "that your flag-lieutenant delivered my message."

"He did," Parker replied.

"Then I fail to see why the subject of Tressoir should be broached."

"You know as well as we do that he has offered to sell back Illingworth's ship and cargo, provided he's paid in gold and the price is reasonable. On top of that he holds for ransom my brother, his wife, their daughter, and a travelling companion, Lady Katherine Fitzgerald. I need someone to find out what his terms are. The East India Company, or their insurers, can deal with ship and cargo, but the human contents are my family responsibility."

"Admiral, you can do that with a cutter. Any midshipman in Portsmouth would jump at the chance to sail to the Bay du Grand Vey and back. And even in a mutiny, you could muster enough hands to sail a ship's boat for a seventy-mile trip that with a good wind and even a cursory knowledge of the Channel currents could be over and done with in three days."

"That's true."

"Then why, pray, am I here?"

Illingworth leant forward with an excited air, the eyes alight in his florid face. "What if opportunity to reverse matters presented itself, Ludlow? The kind that no cutter could hope to take advantage of. The chance to take back the *Lothian* as a prize. That is something that would enhance us all. It would save the admiral money and you'd earn a fortune."

Harry was thinking that it might also save Illingworth's position as an East India Company captain, but he left such a supposition out of his reply. "I have no need of a fortune."

"I know you've been successful in your cruise, Captain. Yet I feel the value of my ship can match that."

Harry was about to ask how he knew. But that was obvious. Everyone aboard *Bucephalas* had that knowledge and sailors were not noted for discretion. Boasting was more in their line, and clearly one or even more, regardless of what they thought of

Harry's investments, had indulged in just that with Illingworth. The merchant captain continued eagerly.

"I've looked at the tide tables for the Carentan coastline, and Admiral Parker has kindly let me consult his charts. Tressoir cannot get my ship up to Isigny for at least two weeks. So he must be lying to, off the coast, in a vulnerable position."

"Illingworth pointed out to me that you have a well-armed ship," added Parker, "plus, of course, a freedom of action denied even to the most zealous naval officer."

"Did he tell you how badly that well-armed ship was damaged, or that, after what happened, I am a touch short-handed to both sail and fight?"

He glared at Illingworth, who had the good grace to flush slightly, since he'd not even enquired after the two men he'd left in Harry's care. But Parker smiled, lifting his handsome head just enough to check its quality in the mirror behind Harry's head. A finger straightened an immaculate eyebrow before he responded.

"Henry Adams and his sons are excellent shipwrights. No doubt you'll be out of Buckler's Hard within the week." Harry felt the stiffness of his face, and knew that he'd failed to hide his surprise. "That was a job for a midshipman, and one that could be accomplished quickly. I knew you couldn't be far away from Portsmouth, since you arrived the morning after Rykert brought you in to St Helen's. Given that you had to find a yard, negotiate the repair, and I presume get some sleep, even with the most favourable wind you could not be more than twenty miles away. So, when Illingworth here outlined the possibility, I instituted a search."

"*Bucephalas* may be gone by now," said Harry, although he didn't believe it. "I had a boat off Gull Island for that very purpose."

Parker only hesitated for a split second, and never once did his face lose that air of superiority which was his abiding trait. Yet still his words carried an air of sudden invention, rather than knowledge.

"Then I'm glad I had no cause to alarm them. It wasn't necessary to actually approach the Beaulieu Estuary." Parker nodded towards Illingworth. "Especially if you acknowledge that a ship with a jury foremast, a spar for a bowsprit, and lacking half her rigging, will be remembered by every fishing boat she passes."

Parker's smile had broadened as he spoke. Clearly the man was very pleased with himself, which made Harry angry. In fact he was so irate that he didn't consider the consequences of deflating his dignity.

"I will say this once, and not repeat it. Even if my ship was whole, and I was penniless, nothing would induce me to oblige you."

"A pity," said Parker, still smiling, and totally unfazed by what was clearly hyperbole. Harry was left feeling foolish for having made such a statement, his only aim to underscore his determination not to become involved. The admiral lifted and rang a small bell, the door opening immediately to reveal his flag-lieutenant. "Can you ask Captain Vosper to come in?"

"Sir."

The alacrity with which the door had been opened worried Harry, having, as it did, a well-rehearsed quality. That was underlined by the speed with which it was repeated, to admit a one-armed captain who had half the side of his face missing, the resulting hollowed-out bones and scar tissue making him look like an ogre.

"Captain Vosper, of the Impressment Service. Allow me to name Captain Harry Ludlow."

Vosper only had one eye that worked. The other was glass, which stayed still while the real one moved. With only half a mouth, his voice had a deliberate, lisping quality as he mouthed, "Delighted."

"As you can understand, Ludlow, with the mutiny in progress, Captain Vosper has been obliged to curtail his normal activities. How many men do you have available, Vosper?"

"Two hundred, sir."

"That many!" exclaimed Parker, with a degree of surprise that unsettled Harry even more.

"They was spread around the counties, but I was ordered to bring them all into the port to help man the guns at the Southsea fort."

"And do your men find that duty congenial?"

"They do not, sir. They're used to being their own masters."

"Tell me, Ludlow, what would you do with two hundred discontented men from the press? Given, as you say, that I would have no trouble manning boats for a short cruise, perhaps I should send half of them off to Buckler's Hard. The rest would, of course, land at Lymington so as to close the road and block any exit."

Harry's face was rigid, as stiff as the piece of parchment Parker picked up between two fingers. He held it out, and the flowing writing was obvious, just like the seal and ribbon that graced the bottom of the page.

"Or," Parker added in a silky tone, the look of admiration as he perused his reflection adding to the finality of his words, "you may accept my offer to extend, in writing, your present exemptions."

"The dirty, blackmailing bastard," Harry growled. "Sitting there smiling all the time he squeezed me."

That had been bad enough to make his blood boil. But worse was that sod Illingworth prattling on about the trip being financially worth the commission, even if they couldn't take his ship back. Harry had without reserve given the merchant captain a piece of his mind when they left the admiral's office.

"I take it that exit by sea is impossible," said James.

Harry shook his head. He didn't know the state of the ship; it could, for all he knew, be heaved over on the bank. At the first hint of a press gang his lads would scatter. They had two choices, to get lost in the New Forest or walk right into the men Vosper landed at Lymington, a port less than five miles away. Then there were the wounded, a dozen men ashore and under the care of the doctor. The fact that two of them were Illingworth's was neither here nor there.

Pender looked up, his bloodshot eyes very obvious in his grey face. When he spoke, the rasping voice was a good two octaves lower than normal.

"What about lying to the bugger? Say you'll do it then leave him to stew."

"Illingworth intends to come with us and handle the actual negotiations for the *Lothian*."

"Makes no odds, Captain," Pender growled, "we can sling him ashore at Deal the same way we did in the Solent. Let him walk back to Portsmouth if he has the need."

"You are in a bilious mood this morning, Pender," said James. "But I rather fear that my brother may have been forced to give the admiral his word."

"Parker would settle for nothing less. And he also hinted that with Lord Spencer in his present mood he could easily have my original exemptions annulled, which would make landing at Deal very tricky even if we could get clear. The liberties of the Cinque Ports only extend to the inner anchorage. And Admiral Duncan, who, Parker was at pains to tell me, is a close personal friend, has a third of his fleet there. Needless to say they are seriously undermanned."

"So discretion is the better part of valour," said James.

"It is a valuable prize, Pender, all ours if we can take her, and ten per cent of the recovery value if Illingworth has to stump up. What do you think the men will say?"

"Seems to me they'll do as you ask 'em, Captain."

"I wish I was as sure as you are."

"Who said I was sure?" Pender rasped. "After your black mood and misery anythin's possible." Seeing the effect that had on his captain made Pender feel a little more benign, and a quick drink of watered-down lime juice took some of the crustiness out of his tone. "Mind, the thing that will worry them most is risking what they already have."

"You're right. There's no point in taking that to Normandy and back. Better if it's ashore with Cantwell's Bank. Could I ask you to take care of that, James?"

"The letter?"

"And the transportation."

"On my own!"

"It's only a packet of papers, James," replied Harry, impatiently.

"Which has a value, albeit long term, in excess of two hundred and fifty thousand pounds. That means I'll have to go straight to London."

"I'm afraid it does, brother. But if my memory of the Portsmouth coach is accurate, I promise you some faces to draw that would make Hogarth and Gillray green with envy."

Mary Blackett knocked and entered without waiting to be invited. "There's a gentleman to see you, Captain Ludlow, a Mr Villiers, and he tells me his visit is of an official nature."

"Is he navy?"

"If he is, he's not uniformed as such. Shall I show him up?"

"No," Harry replied. "I don't have the time to indulge him. Pender, get our dunnage together, plus someone to take it down to the Sally Port, then go ahead and arrange our boat. I need to get hold of some charts, and tell Illingworth that I will require him to bring his steward along." James was looking at his brother in a quizzical way. "Remember, the man's a Guernseyman and speaks the local argot."

CHAPTER FOURTEEN

HARRY stood up, and accompanied by James followed Mary Blackett out of the door. The man called Villiers had his back to the stairs, but turned round as he heard them descend.

"Captain Ludlow," he said, in a voice that was less than friendly.

The tone was replicated in his stony, thin face, the intense dark eyes fixed on Harry's in a most challenging way, though the severity was somewhat spoiled by the drop of mucus on the tip of his nose. Even inside his heavy cloak both brothers could see that he was tall and rangy, with a long neck and prominent adam's apple which bobbed as he spoke.

"And who, sir, are you?" asked James.

The visitor turned to the younger Ludlow, the look still in place. The expression it conveyed was one of outright superiority. James took an instant dislike to him.

"I gave my name to the lady."

"A name conveys nothing," James replied. "But by your manner you impart a great deal."

"Mr Villiers, I believe," said Harry.

"Of Dromana, County Waterford."

The young man looked at them as though this should carry some weight, which led to a long, slightly confused silence, which was eventually broken by a cough from James. Even if Harry didn't know what James was thinking, he knew him to be offended. Indeed, he partly shared that same first impression, but didn't have the time to bait their caller.

"How do you know who I am?" Harry demanded.

"I was at Admiral Parker's this morning. Leybourne pointed you out to me, but was disobliging when I insisted on being admitted to the admiral's quarters so that I could question you."

"Disobliging?"

The face stiffened, making him look even more gaunt. "He does not understand, and therefore will not acknowledge, my function. But that will soon change."

"Mr Villiers, I am in a hellfire hurry to get away. If you would be so good as to state your business, I'd be obliged. Otherwise I will have the unpleasant task of sending you packing."

"I represent the government, Captain. You will accommodate me voluntarily, or by writ. You were aboard *London* yesterday, and I have some questions to ask you concerning that, and your singular attachment to the insurrectionists, made manifest by your intervention on their behalf plus your intention to pay for the funeral of the miscreant who was killed."

"There were a number of people present, Mr Villiers, ask them."

"I need no explanation of the events, Captain, since I have questioned several people, including Admiral Colpoys. He, I must say, was slow to comprehend that your actions, indeed your very presence, might have been less than entirely innocent. But he is of course a sailor, and cannot understand the ramifications of this devilish intrigue."

"What is this buffoon talking about, Harry?" asked James, as Pender, lugging a chest, came down the stairs behind them.

Villiers threw his head back in anger. "I warn you, sir, to guard your tongue. There is a conspiracy afoot in this town, as well as aboard His Majesty's ships. And it is my sworn task to uncover it. If you think that Valentine Joyce's visit here this morning went unnoticed, you are mistaken. Nor did the fact that he came in the front door but exited elsewhere, which he could not have done without permission."

"I bumped into you this morning, outside," said Harry.

"An act which gave Joyce an even better chance to slip away."

Harry grinned. "You should look where you are going, sir."

"Which if I'm not mistaken," added James, "you are just about to do now."

"Have a care. The power I have entitles me to delay, and to question, whomsoever I please."

"But it does not allow you access to Admiral Parker," said Harry, stepping forward. Villiers was blocking the way so Harry gently pushed him aside, an easy task since the man was, for all his height, a featherweight. "Nor does it permit you to delay me."

"I demand that you tell me what you know." His insistence lost all credibility as he fell backwards and the drop of mucus parted company with his nose to land on his collar. His voice rose with a degree of desperation as he continued. "I saw Joyce later, talking with four strangers who turned out to be from the Nore squadron. There are Jacobins at work, both here and there. Your conversations with the delegates have been reported to me, Captain Ludlow, particularly the easy nature of your relationship. That and your subsequent actions place you in their camp, sir, which is nothing more than a nest of sedition."

Harry half turned as he squeezed past. "I am in no one's camp, Mr Villiers. Nor, as far as I can see, is there any Jacobin conspiracy. If the fleet is useless it is because of the people you claim to represent. If you wonder whether I have sympathy with the sailors, let me say unequivocally that I do. But only an idiot would suppose that I had taken part in a conspiracy, if there is one, when I only landed in Portsmouth after the thing had commenced."

"This may be your idiot, Harry," added James, exerting enough pressure to move his brother on.

"I am not convinced, sir," Villiers cried, a new drop of fluid on the end of his nose shaking, threatening to come loose and join its predecessor.

Harry called over his shoulder, "Then that, Mr Villiers, is entirely your affair."

"It is not, sir," Villiers called at the retreating backs. "I await my letters of authority. We will meet again, and in circumstances where you shall be compelled to satisfy me."

"You're blockin' the doorway," growled Pender. Villiers turned and tried to glare at him, but the look he got in return killed that. "It's not only the captain that's in a hurry."

"Where is he going?"

"Why, didn't he tell you?" said Pender, a twinkle in his eye, the depth of his voice adding a conspiratorial air to his words. "He's off to Brest to tell the French it's safe to come out and play."

Leybourne was most obliging in the article of charts and tide tables. They chatted for a while about the local currents, which properly used were an asset to any sailor who knew them. He promised to get a note to Illingworth, informing the merchant captain of the need to fetch along his steward and be on the Hard this evening to wait for the boat that would bring James back to Portsmouth. Then Harry told him about the visit from Villiers.

"I believe you spoke with him this morning."

The flag-lieutenant rolled his eyes slightly. "The man is a damned pest. He's been sent down by someone in London to enquire into the causes of the mutiny."

"Not the Admiralty, I take it?" asked Harry.

"Heavens, no! Claims that his employers are so secret that proof of his authority cannot be provided."

"Then why not send him packing?"

"He is here officially. Lord Spencer confirmed that. When the admirals told the First Lord we had our own people looking into things he made it quite plain that Villiers was to have any assistance he required. So whoever his patron is, it must be someone powerful."

"Why do I get the feeling that you have not complied?"

Leybourne smiled. "We have rendered him every courtesy. But since we have no information ourselves, we can hardly share it with him."

"And if you had," Harry continued, "you'd want to make damn sure you knew where it was going to end up, and to what use it would be put."

"That is a very succinct appraisal of the situation, Captain Ludlow."

Ben Harper came into Portsmouth, a good hour after the Ludlows had left, sitting on top of the midday mail coach, the intended recipient of his letter now well out in the Solent. His horse, Lightning, of which he was so proud, was hobbling around a field near Hindhead, lame from finding a pothole. He himself was bruised where he'd come off, only the way he rolled along the ground saving him from serious injury. As he climbed down he saw the postal agent take the sack of mail from the coachman. That was galling. Lord Drumdryan would have saved himself some money if he'd just used ordinary delivery.

Never having been to Portsmouth before, and hearing what was said in London taverns about the mutiny, he'd feared turmoil. But although there was ample bustle around the front of the Fountain there was none of the mayhem and murder he'd been led to expect. Enquiries for directions to Mistress Blackett's were greeted with derision, with many a ribald comment that a lad his age shouldn't need the services of a bawdy house. In vain he protested that he had a letter to deliver, and the good Samaritan that saved his blushes only did so after he told all and sundry who the letter was for.

"Captain Ludlow, you say, young 'un."

"That's right," Ben replied, looking up into the pock-marked face under the large round hat. "Lord Drumdryan told me to enquire for directions at the Fountain."

"You need ask no more. I will show you where Captain Ludlow is stopping. I got a letter about him myself this very morning. Seems he's come into a bit of good fortune."

"Lord Drumdryan didn't look as though he was passing on good news. Nor did he sound like it. The other is more true. I never in my life saw a man more alarmed."

"News takes folk in different ways. Can you read, lad?"

"No, sir."

"Pity." He pulled a bill from inside his coat, and with a sharp flick of the wrist, opened it so that Ben could see the writing, as well as the list of figures. "If you could read this we could see if they have the same news."

"Mine's sealed," said Ben, holding it up. "So it makes no odds."

"Then you best look after it," the man said, whipping it out of his hand. The youngster's cry of despair was stifled by the way he rammed it into a pocket in Ben's coat, an act which was followed by a cautionary pat. "If you go waving it about in a den of thieves like this, then one of them will have it off you."

The man grinned and pointed straight ahead, pocketing Drumdryan's letter as the boy looked away. "That there is Mistress Blackett's."

Ben Harper's voice was half fearful, half excited. "Is it really a bawdy house?"

"It is, boy. And who knows, Captain Ludlow might just stand you the price of one of the girls. Got to dip your wick some time, I reckon." He laughed as Ben Harper blushed, the sound bouncing off the high walls of the surrounding buildings. "All you need do now is haul on the knocker."

"Would you mind coming with me?" asked Ben.

"Not in the slightest," the man replied, that followed by another laugh. "But only as far as the door."

That made Ben blush, and the older man turned away, the noise of his humour continuing even after he was out of sight. That left Ben Harper alone to confront Mary Blackett. At first she refused to acknowledge that she'd had any guests at all, let alone Captain Harry Ludlow. But at the look on young Ben's face she finally admitted that he'd stayed there.

"But he's gone," she said.

"Gone! Gone where?"

"Back to his ship, where else? Paid for his room and victuals, handsomely an' all, and left at around ten of the clock."

"I have an important letter for him," said Ben. There was desperation in the boy's voice as he asked, "Do you reckon he will be coming back?"

His horse was lame, he was far from home, and he'd failed miserably.

"I'm not sure he is, but his brother will definitely be stopping by tonight, before he takes the coach for London in the morning."

"I was told to give the letter to him if need be."

Mary Blackett was as fond of a virgin as Captain Jack Willett Payne, and she prided herself that she'd rescued several such from a life in the gutter. Country boys fresh to the town, like Pender. She was thinking at that very moment that this London lad might be tender in years, somewhat downcast and nervous, but he was fine-looking, a well set-up young man, with soft blond lashes over gentle blue eyes. And if he didn't need to be rescued, then at least he was in need of comfort.

"Then you'd best come inside, lad. Things'll look brighter after a drop of gin."

"Gin," Ben replied, casting an anxious look at the open door.

"Never been in a place like this, have you?"

"No."

"Then come with me. You'll come to no harm. Why, I intend to look after your well-being myself."

Illingworth was ensconced at the Fountain, two streets away from his steward, Derouac, who'd been left shivering on the Hard, overlooking the inner anchorage of Portsmouth harbour, to keep watch for the return of James Ludlow. The captain of the *Lothian* had in his pocket a note from London regarding the value the East India Company insurers put on his ship. In his hand he held the latest of several drinks. Harry Ludlow had become a subject of much conversation in Portsmouth after the previous day's events, and no one saw himself better placed to dissect the privateer's deeds and actions than a man who'd been his enforced guest and was now his partner in a daring enterprise.

The merchant captain was drunk enough to be boastful. And he was an obliging man by nature, a seeker of harmony rather than confrontation, especially in his cups. This was a trait which had served him well in his professional capacity, ensuring that his passengers to India remembered him fondly and recommended the *Lothian* for the journey home.

Addressing a naval audience that had little desire to hear Harry Ludlow praised, he couldn't help himself. Besides, as he saw it he'd been exposed to an overbearing condescension while aboard *Bucephalas,* and that very afternoon, at the conclusion of the interview with Parker, he'd suffered a bit of a verbal drubbing on the subject of gratitude, with a pointed question about his lack of concern for the wounded men Harry had taken charge of. Smarting from that, as well as the indignity of reimbursing the sermonizer for their care, Illingworth was game enough to list Harry's faults rather than what might be considered his virtues.

Naturally, in diminishing his rescuer he elevated his own abilities, waxing lyrical on the way he had fooled Rykert of the *Amethyst,* adding the rider that Captain Harry Ludlow should have been more grateful for his efforts. The officers he was addressing cared nothing for this, even if he was, in his intoxicated way, rubbishing one of their number. Their interest lay elsewhere. All had heard rumours regarding the success of Harry's cruise. Eager to extract the details, they quizzed him almost as energetically as they plied him with drink.

"He's made a mint. One of his crew told me he'd bought half of America, and that the government of that benighted spot might well have crumbled but for his intervention." Illingworth took a long swallow, then gave his audience a knowing look. "Strange thing for a true-born Englishman to do, don't you think, with the Americans more friends to France than they are to us. Strikes me, with what happened on the *London,* that Mr Harry Ludlow is not as sound in the political line as he should be."

That was followed by growls of agreement, plus a greater arching in Villiers's back as he heard that sentiment receive grunts of assent. He nearly fell out of his chair as he sought to pick up every word.

"Mind you, it is my opinion that any success he's enjoyed has turned his head. Why, I had to practically force the sound advice I gave him down his throat, and this to avoid his entire crew being pressed."

Villiers, eager to find more evidence of political unsoundness, heard all about Harry's exemptions. Illingworth had, it seemed, with masterly cunning, persuaded him to extend them to the Lothians. He listened even more carefully as the merchant captain outlined their forthcoming mission to recover both his ship and the passengers, one that would take them to the very shores of France.

"If I'd had the price Lloyd's is prepared to pay, I'd be there now. Just as well, since Ludlow needs time to get his ship repaired. James Ludlow ain't coming, which is a pity, since he is more of a gentleman and certainly, by comparison, congenial company. I'd rather sail to Normandy with him than his elder brother."

"Just how successful was his cruise in pounds sterling?" asked one naval captain, eschewing subterfuge and posing a direct enquiry in his eagerness to hear the truth.

Illingworth looked at the questioner, an officer whom he suspected had been slung off his ship, a man who might never find employment in the service again. He touched the side of his nose with a finger, then leant forward to impart an amount. Villiers didn't hear what he said, but he did hear the response of all those at the table, a very profound sucking in of collective breath.

"I hope he chokes on it," said one of the naval officers. "Damned privateers are all thieves."

"I just hope his ship is repaired, sir," said Illingworth. "I have no mind to be kept hanging about on the Hard for half the night."

Villiers considered himself an expert in the art of subtle eavesdropping. Yet he didn't notice that he wasn't alone. There was a stocky, dark-looking man with a pock-marked face, sipping port. He too was close enough to hear what Illingworth was saying, and anyone looking at him hard enough would have noticed the way he arched his body backwards.

He pulled a letter from his pocket, opened it, and began to read. The smile seemed to indicate that what he'd read and what he heard added up to something that pleased him.

CHAPTER FIFTEEN

GOLD obviously spoke loudly at Buckler's Hard, where Adams's men had excelled themselves in the speed of their repairs. The quay was lined with the stores from the hold of Harry's ship, and *Bucephalas,* having been hauled over to show where Spanish shot had wounded her below the waterline, was now upright again, with a stretch of New Forest oak replacing the damaged timbers, the join covered by a fresh sheet of copper. Now she was alongside a great barge, waiting for a new foretopmast to be stepped in, the stump of the old one having been plucked out just before the party from Portsmouth had arrived. Another team of men were working to slot home the bowsprit, yet more employed in repairing some of the more obvious damage to the bulwarks.

"The tropics never was good for a ship's bottom," said Balthazar Adams dolefully. "Copper-sheathed notwithstanding. And there's little to be achieved in one tide. To be put to rights the hull needs a proper scrape, and that can only be done in dry dock."

"I never intended that you should make it anything other than seaworthy, Mr Adams, and repair those parts of the upperworks where we'd suffered badly. What I must ask you now, is this: can that undertaking be completed any quicker than you originally proposed? It would aid me to save a day."

"Why the hellfire haste, Captain Ludlow?"

"Opportunity, sir," Harry replied. "That and a desire to get home."

It was only partly true. The Beaulieu Estuary had turned from a safe haven into a trap. He didn't believe that Admiral Parker would go back on his word, but then neither did he entirely discount the possibility. Stranger things had happened in his life, when events outside his own control had thrown relative calm into complete turmoil.

Crossing the Solent his imagination had supplied any number of reasons why things might change. Tressoir, sailing his tub of a corvette with the *Lothian* in company, had to pass through a very crowded stretch of water, one in which other British letters of marque operated. On top of that, sloops and frigates of the Royal Navy cruised the area. They could easily encounter other navy vessels, setting out or returning from the duties which took them to every corner of the globe. Outward bound, or returning, they'd not pass up the chance to take back a fat East Indiaman as prize.

Sir William Parker and his family could at this very moment be warming their toes before the fire of some south coast inn. And if that was the case, and his admiral brother learnt it to be so, Harry could find the *Royal William*'s boats barring his exit from the Beaulieu, while the Lymington road was blocked by Vosper. Then the letter Sir Peter had given him to extend his exemptions stating the reason that he was employed on navy business would be worthless.

His first task was to get the proceeds of his cruise out of the hold, into a boat, and back to Portsmouth, so James could take it on to London. Even although it looked like nothing special, just a large oilskin pouch, its arrival on deck showed just how much gossip it had created. What should have been kept in confidence was common knowledge. There was hardly a soul in Buckler's Hard, it seemed, who didn't know what the pouch contained.

"Loose tongues," Harry said to James, observing the way the work slowed, as the locals, trying to look unconcerned, watched him go over the side. "Sailors do love telling a tall tale. And I've little doubt that there are young girls here, as well as married women, who've been promised a life of ease in the American hinterland in return for their favours."

Balthazar Adams was watching too, his face a mixture of longing and relief. Once the boat carrying it and James began to drop downriver, he cursed it as much as his Christianity would allow.

"It was like having Satan beneath our feet, sir," he said to Harry. "And I know that despite my best efforts the tentacles of sin have spread through the village."

"How long before the ship can sail?"

"Some time tomorrow forenoon, God willing, though you will know as well as the Almighty what can go amiss when stepping masts. But things look set to go fair, and the Lord be thanked, I say."

"You've done well, Mr Adams."

The look the yard owner gave him was less than friendly, an indication that he wished he'd never agreed to the repair in the first place, and over the next few hours, through words and hints, he let Harry know why. Visitors were rare at Buckler's Hard, never numbering more than the people necessary to take delivery of a finished vessel. Harry's numerous crew, with their deep-sea ways and tales of wealth and exotic places, had turned every female head in the place, not to mention a few atop the shoulders of the younger men. Fathers and husbands were displeased. Trouble was brewing, and the only way to cap it was to get the ship, and the crew, out of the estuary.

With the exception of the wounded, Harry was happy to oblige; it had little or nothing to do with Parker's request and everything to do with his own nature. He hated to be idle and that was exaggerated by his sailors' wish to be free of the shore. Added to that was the prospect of action. He would have scoffed at anyone who hinted that what lay ahead excited him. But it did. Having been cajoled into sailing for Normandy he could not completely ignore the possible outcome. And for a man to whom the taking of a prize was the staff of life the idea of capturing the *Lothian* acted as a powerful spur to his imagination.

So he harried his men to restow the holds and refill the water casks. Then followed a hurried visit to the injured men, each one of his own receiving a promise that he would return to pick them up. Next he went to see Lord Montagu's steward at Beaulieu House, and on being granted permission, he sent parties out to cut and collect wood from the abundant New Forest. Fresh meat and vegetables were available, and could be bought from the surrounding countryside. Likewise beer, which in the absence of lime was useful as an antiscorbutic. No one complained, or asked their captain why he was preparing for what looked like another cruise. They knew his nature, as well as their trade, and were aware that Harry Ludlow would never put to sea unless fully provisioned.

Villiers was there that evening to observe James Ludlow arrive back in Portsmouth, coming in through the narrows as the last of the light began to fade in the west. But his presence at the actual time of landing was more fortuitous, given that half his attention was centred on the possible arrival of a messenger at the Fountain. Trying to look innocent, he listened as James exchanged a few words with Illingworth, now completely drunk, before the steward lowered his master and his sea-chest into Harry's boat. The cutter headed back out past the Round Tower, Illingworth singing at the top of his voice.

James Ludlow stood for a moment toying with the oilskin pouch in his hand, looking first this way and that before moving off, which forced Villiers into the shadows. Once James had passed him he followed, far enough behind to remain unseen. Confident that the Ludlows were in some way connected to the mutiny, following the younger brother made good sense, but he also needed to keep an eye out for that special message from London, which might contain papers of authorization, as well as news from Chatham.

Sure of his quarry's destination as he walked towards the Sally Port, Villiers slipped back to the Fountain to check whether anything had arrived. This took longer than normal, the town being full of sailors, men normally trapped on their ships. Every tavern was full to bursting, with singing, drunken tars spilling on to the roadway; this being the very thing he had come to Portsmouth to suppress it annoyed him greatly. "Which I could have done," he hissed, talking to himself, "if only those navy boneheads had assisted me."

Disappointed in the article of his messenger he retraced his steps, catching immediate sight of his quarry. Ludlow had been dawdling, seemingly interested in the crowds overflowing on to the roadway. Suddenly, as he passed the last of the taverns, he stepped out, heading into the gathering gloom towards Mill Quay and Portsmouth Point. The government agent began to catch him up, then abruptly slowed. This sudden increase in pace revealed another man following James Ludlow. Thickset, wearing a round hat, he was in no hurry, content to maintain his distance. Villiers felt his pulse begin to race. In his imagination he saw himself coming upon both those ahead of him, in secret conclave, discussing ways to bring down the government and install a Jacobin terror, a conspiracy that he would contain and squash through brilliant timing and doglike tenacity.

The rewards would be enormous. The King would want to have him to a levee at Windsor, perhaps just to ask him how he'd been so clever, or to confer an honour commensurate with the service he'd rendered the nation. Admirals, instead of ignoring him, would defer, and listen patiently while he explained to them what they must look out for in the way of seditious behaviour.

It was galling therefore when the second man, once James turned into Broad Street, peeled off down a narrow lane and disappeared, leaving the government agent with the dilemma of which one to follow. The streets became busier again, even fuller of rollicking tars than the inns around the dockyard. Seeing James pass through the crowd outside the bawdy house and enter the door without turning round, he set off after the second man, and after a fruitless twenty minutes spent searching various byways came to the conclusion that he had lost him.

"Damn," he said to himself angrily, before the embarrassment caused by swearing made him feel contrite. Then an image floated into his mind. His blood raced, and he punched his palm. "The oilskin pouch!"

How easy it was. James Ludlow didn't actually have to meet anyone. All he had to do was drop the information he was carrying at an agreed spot on the route. The man following could then pick it up.

Harry had lanterns all over the ship, so that his crew could continue reeving the replacement rigging well after the sun had gone down. The breeze, the same wind that would have wafted the Channel Fleet to Brest, was still blowing. But it could turn any time and gust strong enough to bottle him up in the Beaulieu. Thanks to Adams and the expert shipwright's eye he possessed, the stepping of the mast had gone like clockwork, and since the upper sections were already cut, planed, and chamfered, and the cheeks trimmed, fitting had proceeded rapidly. With the foremast cap fitted he'd seen a chance that he could get away at first light, and despite Balthazar Adams's complaints that Harry's men would get in the way of his they'd been set to work.

"Pender, take a boat and drop down to Gull Island. Find our guard boat and take them to the north channel of the estuary. If the cutter returns from Portsmouth keep Captain Illingworth with you. We'll pick you all up on the way out."

One watch was still toiling throughout the ship as they cast off, the topmen aloft thumping at the stiff canvas of the new sails, the seamen on deck hauling hard to sheet them home; waisters sweeping away the last shavings that littered the deck while Willerby the cook and Tom Biggins, his assistant and part-time manger man, struggled to get the last of the pigs and chickens down below. It looked like bedlam but Harry could see the beginnings of order, and knew that by the time they made the estuary and had Lepe on their larboard quarter, they'd be a ship again.

Pender, and a very irate Illingworth, were waiting for them at the mouth of the river. But Harry had no time for the merchant captain's temper, or what seemed like a serious hangover. Nor did he wish to intervene in what appeared to be instant animosity between Pender and the steward which broke out as soon as the man, Derouac, began to lord it in Harry's cabin, insisting that he knew how to treat quality better than a creature who should, judging by his manners, be before the mast.

Cautious to the last, he declined to sail back along the north and east of the Isle of Wight through the still mutinous fleet. Instead he put up his helm to head south-west, his yards braced round to take the north-westerly wind on his weather quarter, heading for the open sea beyond the coastal forts at Hurst and Norton. Noon saw them off the Needles, stark white megaliths battered by creamy spume. It also saw *Bucephalas* shipshape and, even if she was still trailing Caribbean weed on her hull, near as dangerous a predator as she'd ever been.

By that time Pender had been on the quarterdeck a dozen times. He wasn't the type to whine, but Illingworth's steward had driven him very close. "If you don't get that ugly interferin' bastard out of my road, Capt'n, he might go out into the water through the pantry scuttle."

Derouac not only had an unfortunate manner, he was really ill-served by nature in the physical line: small, with an imperious look in a face that was yellowing and cratered, with two little black eyes in the middle. Pender had nicknamed him "Frogspawn," and Harry had to admit it suited the Guernseyman well.

"The lads are missing Mr James, your honour," Pender added, once he'd calmed down a bit. "There's not one of them that has the faintest notion of where we're heading, and no means of finding out that will satisfy. The ship don't feel right, what with him not aboard."

Harry felt a pang of sadness himself, since James had become as much a fixture of his deck these last years as the ship's bell. He also knew what Pender was implying, that James would have sorted out the cabin, to his servant's satisfaction, in no time. But he declined to be drawn, responding only to the first part of what Pender had said.

"Then you must act in my brother's place, Pender. Tell them

we're headed for Normandy. And by the way, you may also pass on to them that I miss him too."

James had been let in by the maid and informed that her mistress had taken to her bedroom, in the way of communication that indicated that the lady was not alone, which was confirmed by the faint noises coming through the thick panels of the connecting door. Contemplating the notion of going downstairs to Mary Blackett's parlour, he was bewildered when he heard the knock on the landing door. He was even more surprised to open it and find the snotty-nosed fellow who'd called on Harry that morning.

"I come on official business," said Villiers, nasally, adding a loud sniff that failed in its primary duty.

James gave him a wry smile. "What a worker bee you are, sir. Toiling from dawn till dusk, indeed. Is there so much sedition about?"

Villiers threw his shoulders back, the dark eyes flashing as he growled at his quarry. "Perhaps that would be a question you should answer, sir."

"Me?"

"Who else?"

James threw up his hands in mock despair. "I am undone, I see it now."

Villiers, lacking a sense of humour, or any hint of irony, was about to take these words at face value when he saw the twinkle in James's eyes.

"I will not be trifled with, Ludlow."

"Mr Ludlow to you, sir," James replied firmly.

"I followed you from the landing steps on the Hard."

"You did what?"

"A neat way to pass intelligence."

"There's no risk of your doing that, Villiers."

Tall as he was, that barb went right over his head. "I demand to know what that oilskin pouch contained, plus the identity of the man you left it for."

James laughed. "What man?"

"The fellow who followed you, of course," Villiers replied, impatiently. "I didn't see him at first, but he was there all right, dogging your footsteps, waiting for you to pass him the information. Surely you don't deny it?"

"I do," James replied, "and I'm prepared to prove it. Not, I hasten to add, because you demand it. But you are so stupid, Mr Villiers, that I fancy you will spend all night on this landing, and be knocking on my door again at dawn if I do not."

James spun on his heel, slipped through the door, and returned in a matter of seconds, the heavy oilskin pouch in his hand.

"The contents . . ."

"Are private," James growled. "Now be so good as to go away and leave me in peace."

CHAPTER SIXTEEN

IN THESE waters, with the prevailing westerly holding steady, Harry had little to fear from French capital ships. Locked up well to the south in Brest, they needed the wind to swing into the east, one that would blow the patrolling British frigates out to sea so that they could escape their Breton harbour. The English Channel was well named: the power of Britannia ruled supreme. That no enemy force should threaten such a vital strait was a staple of British tactical policy which had been adhered to with near religious zeal since the defeat of the Spanish Armada.

Not that the sea was empty. This stretch of water was one of the busiest in the world, the artery by which Britain, whose whole power and influence was based on maritime trade, fed the nation's mercantile interests. That in turn provided the profits that allowed her to subsidize the Continental powers, and their armies, to fight the French on land. It was also the avenue by which neutral vessels, from the Hanseatic ports, Scandinavia, and Russia, could make their home ports, the presence of the British navy protecting them from French corsairs.

Many ships, including British vessels, sheered away from the course he was sailing. From their crosstrees they would see he was armed and dangerous. The flag he flew might identify him as a friend, but that was no guarantee that close to he wouldn't haul down his colours, and replace them with the bloody Tricolour. He too had his lookouts on edge, keen to avoid any British warships, anxious to spare himself the indignity of being hauled aboard some armed cutter by a newly promoted lieutenant, obliged to explain himself like some recalcitrant schoolboy to an officer determined to show that the navy was superior in every way to any freebooter.

And there was always the faint chance that a French frigate might have slipped out of Brest on a raiding mission.

He was steering for the Îles de St. Aubin, a pair of rocky outcrops that sat slightly to the west of the Baie du Grand Vey. The great arc of the Carentan peninsula, swinging north, afforded some protection to these waters from anything but the very worst Atlantic storms; though with variable strong currents, which altered completely throughout every tide, the coastline, especially the long beaches to the west of the Roches de Grandcamp, had their fair share of wrecks. If Illingworth was right, they expected to find the *Lothian* anchored in the Baie du Grand Vey, in seven-fathom water.

Tressoir wouldn't get too close to the actual estuary of the two rivers, tidal up to a point some eight miles inland. Les Roches de Grandcamp formed the western edge of that estuary, a wild rugged shore of half-submerged rocks that could be fatal if the wind blew strong enough to drag a ship from its mooring.

The most potent factor in all their calculations was the prodigious rise and fall of the tide levels and the subsequent effect on the river. Low, they barely provided room under the keel for a decked longboat. According to the tables Illingworth had borrowed from the navy, only flood level, or very near it, would allow something as big as an East Indiaman to be warped upriver. And given the distance, and the limited time that it would stay at peak, such a ship required a following wind if it was not to find itself stranded halfway, tipped on to its side at such an angle that the next incoming current would submerge the lower decks.

"That, I believe, is the real reason he wishes to trade with us," said Illingworth. "He has either to ship my cargo up to Isigny in boats or risk the whole venture, and his profits, on a fluke of wind."

Harry, who had the St. Aubin Islands square in his telescope, nodded absent-mindedly. Two high bluffs, at this distance they were like a pair of ships with all sails set. His guest had advanced this same opinion a dozen times; it was one he didn't entirely share, but good manners demanded a response. And Illingworth had been obliging since coming aboard, showing a proper sense this time of the hierarchy that being on *Bucephalas* imposed. Harry Ludlow was the captain, so on their way to their destination all decisions lay with him. This being the case, Harry replied in an amiable way.

"It's a curious place to base yourself for privateering. I can't see much point in seeking prizes if you can only get them to a safe berth at best twice a month. And who in a place like this is he going to sell the hulls to? He'd be better operating out of the mouth of the Loire. That gives him an easy place to sell his goods and there's dozens of merchants in the port of Nantes who'd buy the vessel."

"I dare say that the Jacobins levy a duty on private captures, hull and cargo. Perhaps Tressoir wishes to avoid that charge."

"He'd still be better off than selling it back to Lloyd's. My knowledge of what's going on in France is limited, Illingworth, but I can't believe luxuries are cheaper there than they are in Britain. And given their losses in ships, I should think deep-sea bottoms are at a premium."

"Do you suspect a trap?"

Illingworth hadn't advanced that notion before, though it had occurred to Harry. Worse, the merchant captain had a loud carrying voice, which he did nothing to temper, even though several of the crew were close by. Harry noticed their heads jerk up in alarm at such a notion.

"No. Not unless your friend Tressoir knew about the fleet mutiny."

"He is not, Captain Ludlow, my friend," Illingworth replied, with a rare note of asperity.

Harry had noticed in the last three days' sailing that the merchant captain, either by nature or inclination, tried very hard to be liked. It was somehow pleasing to have him react for once like a normal human being, instead of for ever playing the diplomat. Such behaviour made the man hard to pin down though, so speculation remained about how to proceed when they met

Tressoir. Strictly speaking, any notion of taking the *Lothian* back by force should be Illingworth's province, but every time they discussed it, he was at pains to assure Harry that he would abide by whatever he thought best.

Harry smiled as he replied, to take the sting out of his unwelcome allusion. "Given that Sir William Parker boasted of his connections, in issuing an invitation to trade Tressoir's virtually asking for a warship of some kind to reconnoitre his base. Common sense would tell him that before negotiating any British admiral worth his salt would examine the possibility of rescuing the captives by force."

"Not to mention the value of my ship!"

That turned Harry's smile into a full grin. Admiral Parker would crave prize money as well as the next man. It was a fair reflection of the state the country had been reduced to by the mutiny that he'd been forced to offer such an opportunity to a privateer rather than send one of his own client officers to snap it up, which went some way to compensating for the way it had been foisted on him.

"I can see something poking up from the top of the rocks, your honour," the lookout called down, "though the gulls are making it hard to pick out. Could be a flagstaff, or maybe it's a ship's maintopgallant."

Harry ran for the shrouds, the ropes that exerted lateral control on the masts and provided the avenue by which the men who set and trimmed the sails made their way to their stations. Getting aloft quickly was a matter of great pride to the topmen, commonly held to be the cream of the crew. Their captain, not one to be outdone, was determined to show that he could still beat any sailor aboard to the crosstrees, 120 feet above the deck. He shot up to the top, a wide platform that provided in turn a secure leverage on the topmast shrouds. There was a lubbers' hole for the less nimble, but Harry ignored it, throwing himself on to the futtock shrouds, attached to the outer rim of the top, continuing his climb leaning backwards at 45 degrees. Above the top the rigging was narrower and steeper, and Illingworth, who hadn't been aloft himself for years, found himself forced to admire the brisk way Harry made it to the top, where his lookout had been placed.

"You'll pick it up on the rise, your honour," said the sailor, pointing towards the islands as the bows dipped, carrying the two men so far forward on the swell that they looked down not to a planked deck, but to the grey-green water running along the side of the ship. "To the seaward side of the peak."

Harry followed the lookout's finger as the bows lifted, the motion much exaggerated by their height. With a sheer face set against the incoming Atlantic, the biggest outcrop, the aptly named Île du Large, was diamond shaped. Harry's charts showed a tiny bay at the south-western end, opposite the much smaller Île du Tertre. As an anchorage it left a lot to be desired, since the tidal race through the narrows, at certain times of the year, would be truly fierce.

But if Tressoir was moored there, waiting for the flood to take him up to Isigny, it had one priceless asset: it protected him from any sudden descent by an armed enemy. A man with a telescope on the peak of du Large would have spied *Bucephalas* over an hour ago, before Harry's lookout had picked up the first hint of the islands. No wonder Tressoir wasn't worried about British warships. Any notion of a frigate springing a surprise was foolish as long as the weather stayed clear. Tressoir would be waiting for them, ready to run for the Seine Estuary if he sensed danger.

Any doubt that it was a flagstaff was removed as *Bucephalas* breasted the next wave. Tressoir had not only hoisted some kind of pennant, he was loosening his topsails, a wise precaution given that he had no idea who was approaching. Harry cupped his hands and shouted down to his passenger.

"Time to break out the truce flag, I think, Captain Illingworth."

This instruction had really been delivered to Pender, who'd already brought the two flags on deck, one the East India Company ensign, the other plain white. Dreaver stood by the loaded signal gun and as soon as they broke out aloft he pulled the lanyard, sending a loud boom, and a puff of white smoke to windward. The sound must have carried, since it was immediately matched by a cannon from the top of the island, which sent a hundred thousand gulls into panicky flight.

"Pender," said Harry, now back on deck. "Get the ship cleared for action below, and have the gunner prepare charges. Do nothing on deck, since that will be observed."

"Is that necessary?" asked Illingworth. But Harry had walked to the rail, so hadn't heard him.

It was Pender who replied, his face split with a wide grin, the snow-white teeth lighting up his weather-beaten face.

"If they've got a signal gun all the way up that rock, your honour, this ain't no temporary base. Capt'n's being cautious, which is only right considering he don't know what's laying ahead. It don't do to get caught with your breeches down, Mr Illingworth, in either clear weather or fog."

Harry had no intention of taking his ship right into the narrows. For one thing, common sense allied to prudence dictated that he run out his guns, regardless of the way it could be misinterpreted. And even if it was possible to guarantee Tressoir's peaceful nature, Harry had no knowledge of the best place to anchor. The charts showed deep water in mid-channel, but were vague as to the way it shelved nearer the shoreline. So he luffed up to windward of the islands, put a boat over the side, instructed Dreaver to sail round to the eastern, lee shore and, taking care with the tide, to box the compass and wait for him.

They needed boatcloaks in the cutter, though the weather wasn't rough. But the swell was substantial, and in such a small boat that inevitably meant they shipped a certain amount of cold green seawater. With the tide rising their progress was swift, the oars only needed for steering, especially as they entered the narrows between the two islands and the current increased markedly.

The *Lothian* was anchored in what had to be deep water, right under a steep escarpment, sheltered from the westerly wind by the bulk of the island. There was no sign of Tressoir's small corvette. With a shallower draught, she could easily be upriver in Isigny.

It wasn't an anchorage Harry would have chosen. This part of the world was very prone to stormy weather, and given a gale of wind this sound could very easily change from its present benign nature to an absolute death trap. He reasoned that the main part of the lookout's job, atop the cliff, was to keep a weather eye out not for the enemy but for squalls.

The wind dropped as they rowed into the lee of the cliffs, but the tidal flow increased. To Harry's left lay the small bay that he had seen on the chart, a thin strand of white sand barely enough to support the few fishing huts that lay along its edge. Behind them the land rose steeply, black threatening rocks, with ledges here and there for a climbing man to rest. Whoever occupied the place had planted gorse bushes to shelter each piece of flat ground, and Harry suspected that behind them lay small vegetable plots. The countless gulls that occupied the seaward side of the island were muted here, enough to hear the piercing cries of individuals, swooping for food to the rock-blackened waters.

As they closed with the East Indiaman, Harry glanced at Illingworth, noticing that his eyes were slightly moist. That had nothing to do with spume and everything to do with emotion. Every sailor, regardless of how garrulous or pompous, felt for his ship. The ruddy-faced merchant captain had sailed to India and back in his ship a dozen times, had spent more time in her cabin than he had in his own family home. She was a segment of his being, just as *Bucephalas* was part of Harry's. No landsman could understand that feeling, not even James, who'd spent a long time at sea.

"She's a beauty, Captain Illingworth."

"Ain't she just, Ludlow," he rasped in reply, "ain't she just. A fine sailer going large, and not too bad on a bowline. A sound vessel that has never let me down. There might be a bit of Hooghly mud on her keel, but that would be my wandering mind, and a crew trying to shake off the pox as much as the drink they've consumed. I will not have any man say that *Lothian* is crank."

"Who would dare!" Harry said, wondering what fellow sailor had so offended Illingworth by making that very remark. It was a commonplace of seafarers as well that whatever faults their ship had they were blind to them. "Let us hope you can get her back, and prove it to be true."

"I hope that blackguard has shown proper respect for my furniture."

Harry had to hide the temptation to laugh, and so did Pender. They were rowing, unarmed and unprotected, into the unknown. Furniture, however valuable, seemed an odd thing to be concerned about.

"Steer for her lee, Pender, it might be easier to get aboard with our dignity intact."

They swept round the stern, under a heavy cable that ran to the shore, several pairs of eyes on the poopdeck following them; silent, unsmiling, definitely unfriendly. Under the counter, they passed beneath the stern casements that formed the rear of Illingworth's cabin. Suddenly one was flung open to reveal the faces of two young women, their eyes excited. Harry had a fleeting impression of the closest, mainly the auburn colour of her abundant hair. Then a voice, faint, firm, and deeply masculine admonished them, ordering that the casements be shut.

"That was, without any doubt at all, Sir William Parker," groaned Illingworth. "No hearty greeting of a rescuer from that source. Stiff ain't the word for his sort."

"He must have been a trying companion on the voyage home."

"Very," sighed Illingworth, his diplomacy slipping. "Just as any man who is never wrong is prone to be."

The faces on the lee rail were less threatening, with one or two actual smiles visible. The gangway was open, and side ropes lined either side of the ladder. Pender hooked and pulled the cutter close, he and one of the oarsmen holding it against the side so that it rose and fell on the swell. Harry pointed to the way aboard, indicating that Illingworth should precede him. The older man hesitated for a fraction of a second, took a deep breath, and obliged. He was standing, hat off, abundant grey and ginger hair blowing in the breeze, when Harry joined him on the deck.

"Allow me to present to you Captain Harry Ludlow," said Illingworth, "who has kindly undertaken to escort me here. Captain Ludlow, this is the man who took my ship, M. Auguste de Tressoir."

This was addressed to a tall man who in turn removed his own hat and bowed. He had a sharp but handsome face, lively eyes and an engaging, lopsided smile which feature slipped quickly, to be replaced by a quizzical expression.

"I had a long look at your ship as she sailed by the western approach, Captain. A fine vessel, though she is not a naval warship?"

"No, Monsieur. I am a private individual. Admiral Parker asked me to transport Captain Illingworth as a favour to a busy fleet."

"I see you have some very new wood about the forward bulwarks." Harry nodded, and Tressoir continued, his expression now concerned. "Then something tells me that we might have met before."

Harry replied in a friendly tone, since he saw no point in being bitter. "We have, Monsieur, and I am open enough to admit that you bested me. But I would also add that should we meet again, in clear weather, you'd not enjoy the advantage a second time."

"I thought I did more damage than that I observed a few minutes ago."

"You did, Monsieur," said Harry, producing a sudden, full smile. "Especially, it has to be said, to my pride."

Tressoir responded well to that, clearly amused, as his lopsided smile reappeared. Then he adopted an expression of mock sadness. "Pride, Captain. That is something that takes a great deal longer to repair than mere planking."

CHAPTER SEVENTEEN

HARRY'S senses were not dulled by this exchange of pleasantries. There were many things to see: the guns that the Frenchman had run out, probably when *Bucephalas* had first been sighted on the horizon, the loosed topsails and the axes by the hawse-hole ready to cut the cables for a quick getaway. But most of all that unless Tressoir had a host of seamen below, the *Lothian* had only the minimum crew to sail her.

Had the rest of his crew stayed aboard his corvette, preferring the delights of Isigny-sur-Mer to the discomfort of this exposed anchorage? Harry's nerves were tingling with anticipation, so much so that he wished he was not standing right before his late adversary. He was frightened that he would fidget, worried that even if he mastered himself Tressoir might pick up from his manner some hint of his thoughts.

The Frenchman was vulnerable and with the deep keel of the Indiaman, in no position to alter matters. He'd moored here out of necessity, using the channel despite its manifest disadvantages. To then send off his own ship and most of the men was sheer folly: it robbed him of the ability to defend the straits or to fight off any predator who, favoured by good fortune, could block his route to the Vire Estuary. Harry's mind was racing with possibilities, and several moments passed before he realized that the Frenchman was talking to him. "Sorry," he said, quickly.

Tressoir smiled again, much to Harry's annoyance, in a way that seemed to imply that he could read his thoughts. "I asked, Captain Ludlow, if you would object to meeting the passengers that we took with the ship."

"Why would I object to that?"

"You are here to bargain, are you not? It strikes me that sentiment, which could very well enter into your calculations, would hardly aid your purpose."

"You are mistaken, Monsieur de Tressoir, I am merely here as a supernumerary. It is to Captain Illingworth that you must look for terms, and he has already met Sir William and his party." Then Harry remembered the moist-eyed way the merchant captain had looked at his ship, and silently chastised himself for his haste in replying. "But I am, of course, to be consulted regarding any offer price for the *Lothian* herself."

Tressoir must have guessed that was a lie by the way that Illingworth, with an absence of subtlety, shot his fellow emissary a questioning look. Harry realized that because the merchant captain had deferred to him on the journey, they'd never actually talked of the method by which a decision to attack would be made. Now their adversary knew that, since the pause between that look and Illingworth actually speaking was so slow it approximated to instructions sent through the post.

"Yes. Captain Ludlow has the ear of the East India Company directors," Illingworth waffled, waving his arms to cover his confusion. "But Admiral Parker was adamant that I come for his family, since I know them well."

Tressoir threw back his head and laughed out loud. "Did the good admiral think I might substitute them?"

"Of course not!" snapped Illingworth, as aware as anyone of the illogicality.

"Rest assured that I was not even tempted. Though I find Sir William's daughter and her companion delightful, the gentleman himself is a little oppressive."

"His wife, I trust, is well?"

"Yes, though you'd hardly know it since she says very little. I have left them in my . . . sorry, your cabin, Captain, where there is also a good dinner waiting. I suggest that we eat first, before conducting business."

Illingworth looked at Harry, to check that he agreed, and when he nodded they followed Tressoir towards the spacious area under the poopdeck. Tressoir afforded them no chance to speak privately as they passed through the forward section, the table set with good china and crystal that Illingworth could not help inspecting, it being his own property. The Frenchman stood aside as he entered the rear, day cabin, to show the assembled party their visitors. The girls, even more attractive whole than they had been through the window, were desperately trying not to fiddle. Lady Parker curtsied slightly. Only Sir William seemed in control, his angular face wearing an expression of undeniable hauteur.

"Well, Illingworth. You took your time in returning to your duty."

"I hardly think less than a week a lifetime, sir."

Harry was sure that Parker actually curled his lip when he responded. "I suggest you try confinement, Captain, before you advance any theories on that score. Meanwhile, I will be obliged if you will do the decent thing and introduce this other fellow."

Illingworth opened his mouth to do so, but Harry cut him off.

"This fellow, sir, to whom you so offhandedly refer, has come over seventy-odd miles to effect your release. But as a free agent, under no obligation to anything other than my own notion of duty, I am quite capable of upping my helm and going straight back home."

Sir William turned away, his head lifting to create a noble and troubled profile against the light coming through the casements. "Naturally you have my gratitude, sir."

It was Harry's turn to be cut off, since what Sir William had proffered was the very opposite of thanks. He acted like a man complimenting his servant for doing a good job burnishing his boots. This was certainly an occasion to have James in tow. He had a readier wit than his elder brother, and would have punctured Parker in an instant. Harry sought desperately for the words James would have employed, while Illingworth, his ruddy face an even deeper hue, had his hands up to stop him from saying anything.

"This is Captain Harry Ludlow, Sir William, and I do assure you he is a man of parts. Your brother, Sir Peter, engaged him personally as being both by birth and temperament most suited to the task."

Parker turned back slowly, to examine Harry more closely, as if birth or breeding was a commodity that could be worn on the breast. Harry himself was only aware of Tressoir's silent mirth. The Frenchman was watching him closely, and with the pained look on the faces of the three females it capped his anger. If he couldn't manufacture his brother's wit, he could at least, as he had done on more than one occasion in his life, borrow his manners. James, when exposed to intolerable condescension, generally adopted a tone of studied languor to demolish an adversary.

"That is so, Sir William. I'm not to be engaged to rescue any old Tom, Dick, or Harry. I confine myself, in the Good Samaritan line, to persons of quality, sir."

The redhead's chest started to heave inside her cream dress, the pale face turning puce as she tried to contain her laughter, proof, to Harry, that he had done better than he'd expected. Illingworth looked like the other two women, pained. Harry was racking his brain for a riposte to the inevitable blast of anger. None of them, not even the man's wife, a much put-upon creature judging by her mouselike demeanour, suspected that Sir William would do as he did, which was to take Harry's words at face value.

"Then my brother has shown rare sensitivity, sir, in choosing you. Perhaps his service in such a rough trade as the navy has not coarsened him as much as I suspected. Though I confess the name Ludlow does not register with me as anything other than a fortified town on the Welsh marches. There was, of course, a low-born Cromwellian general so styled."

As a way of putting Harry in his place, it would have been perfect, especially since he was a direct descendant of that same General Ludlow. But the expression on Sir William's face was one of enquiry, not triumph.

"Allow me to name the ladies," said Illingworth quickly. "Lady

Parker, her daughter Caroline, and her companion Lady Katherine Fitzgerald."

The bobbing curtsies of the trio identified them, which established that the girl with the round face and full figure was Sir William's offspring. The redhead, who was quite a beauty, didn't look much like a lady, since she was still trying to control her giggles.

"Lady Katherine is a blood relation of the Duke of Leinster," said Sir William, his head slipping sideways to indicate to all that they should be impressed.

"Then I am honoured," Harry replied, with a slight bow. Lady Katherine, who had sparkling green eyes and a trace of freckles showing through her powder, pulled a face which implied that the subject was as regular as it was tedious.

"Indeed," added Sir William, "you will be aware that Leinster is Ireland's premier dukedom. That is why I consented to allow her to travel with us. One cannot be too careful when initiating one's daughter to society."

"Now that the introductions are complete," said Tressoir, even more amused than before by the legion of raised eyebrows, "I suggest that we repair to the dining cabin. My cook has gone to some trouble over the dishes we'll consume. Too much delay will only annoy the poor man."

"Delighted, Monsieur le Vicomte," said Parker, with a warmth that he'd signally failed to show to his rescuers. "And I look forward to another demonstration of his culinary expertise. Not that I ever doubted that a table kept by a man of your noble antecedents would be anything other than superb."

"You're in rough trade for a nobleman," said Harry.

Tressoir nodded. But Harry had clearly touched a sore point, since the Frenchman allowed his anger to show. "The times we live in rather constrict my choice of employment, Captain."

Any lingering doubt about being in the presence of a boring snob was laid to rest over the meal. Harry, listening to Parker castigate the entire Company structure in India, from the governor-general down to the meanest clerk, was very thankful that whatever happened his exposure to the man would be brief. Boiled down to its essentials, it translated into a long wail about his own excellent advice being continually ignored, while other, lesser brains, without breeding or good manners, were indulged. Had Sir William not been too close to Illingworth Harry would have leant over to put to the merchant captain the proposal that they leave him behind. Judging by the discreet looks of ennui that were thrown in his direction by the females, the idea was not his alone.

Only Tressoir was able to interrupt this litany. He seemed to find silencing Sir William effortless, the Englishman falling mute every time his captor opened his mouth to speak. And in the man's sycophantic responses to his conversation, and his constant use of the title, he managed to let both Harry and Illingworth know just how lucky they were to be entertained by such a host. A brother of the present Comte de Thury Harcourt, who was with the allied armies in Coblenz, Tressoir came from one of the oldest families in Normandy. Sir William was at pains to point out that the line had been noble when the Conqueror left his patrimony to do battle with King Harold.

He was also, due to his boastful nature, the main source for details of Tressoir's recent background, one which went some way to explaining why he chose to operate from such a backwater. Normandy had an isolated quality and a strong feudal tradition that made it difficult for the Jacobins to enforce their edicts. Auguste's father, trapped by his duties at Versailles, had been a benign landlord, held in some esteem by both his tenants and the peasantry. It had not saved him from the guillotine, but his tenants had tarred and feathered the commissioners sent from the Committee of Public Safety to sequester his properties.

With too much of France to subdue, revenge had been postponed beyond the life of Robespierre. Under the new ruling élite, merely being of elevated birth was not an automatic death sentence. But with his elder brother serving the Comte d'Artois, the late King Louis's untrustworthy brother, Auguste was at some risk of attainder. It was one thing to be noble, quite another to have a blood relative actively engaged in fighting the Revolution and prepared, like Artois himself, to become an ally of France's enemies. Unable to lay their hands on the head of the family, the neck of a younger brother might serve just as well to satisfy Madame Guillotine.

Hence his determination to stay in the part of the world where loyalty to his bloodline protected him. Parker, embarrassing in the way he praised the family's courage, positively simpered when Tressoir cut across his sycophancy to counter the Parker flattery with a welcome dose of modesty. No one else was blessed with the same rights. Sir William's daughter, Caroline, tried hard. She seemed to Harry like a girl who craved enjoyment, with a ready laugh, often muted by a stern glance from her father. But every time she changed the subject, and Tressoir chose not to speak, she was overborne by her suffocating parent who, in condemning all and sundry, sought to heap praise on himself. His two admiral brothers would, he contended, have fared better, like everyone else in authority, had they only listened to his excellent advice.

"I cannot fathom what they could have done better, Sir William," said Harry. "They are both senior flag officers, and serving ones at that."

"Something a man achieves by mere survival, sir."

"Rank, yes, Sir William. But employment is another matter."

Judging by the sharp response, Harry had obviously touched a nerve by alluding to that. "I could not begin to tell you how much of my own influence was squandered in that direction. In aiding my brothers I have put a check on my own advancement."

"A great loss to the nation, no doubt," Harry replied, deliberately looking at the one person at the table who he knew would appreciate his sally.

He was quite taken with the way that Lady Katherine responded; she required a napkin to disguise it. Then he felt a deep frisson of guilt, and conjured up in his mind the beautiful, dark-skinned face of Hyacinthe Feraud, which induced a degree of misery, a return of the black dog that had plagued him on the journey home. He realized that in the bustle of the last few days he hadn't thought of her at all. How could he attempt to amuse Lady Katherine when such a memory was so fresh in his mind? Now it was Harry who needed a napkin to hide his emotions, though fortunately for him this went unnoticed since Sir William prattled on.

"My parents," he continued, "were misguided in allowing them to enter the service in the first place, Ludlow. Having done so, they have failed to gain the kind of distinction which raises a man above the herd."

"I don't follow," Harry responded hoarsely, having coughed to clear his throat.

"Have they won a battle?" demanded Parker, as though such a thing was easy, and commonplace. "Look at Rodney and Hood, and that other fellow, the royal bastard, Howe. And what do we hear as we land at Gibraltar? Jervis, who is certainly no gentleman, has won a fleet action that will gain him an earldom. That is achievement, sir, and I dare say any relatives they have are in receipt of the benefits. Me? Despite a huge effort, I have nothing."

That was just too outrageous, and a clear indication that he was sitting eating delicious food with a man armoured against ridicule. With some difficulty he shut his ears to the continuing tirade, cutting out Illingworth's feeble attempts to lighten the atmosphere. Instead, to block out the memories that were plaguing him once more, he turned his mind to what he'd observed so far that day, and the possibilities that had emerged because Tressoir had left himself exposed.

In one way Sir William's dominance of the conversation helped, since his long silence barely registered. Within minutes he was calculating tides, times, and numbers, trying to decide whether an assault with boats would be better than bringing his ship in close. On balance he favoured using *Bucephalas,* for two very good reasons: the firepower she could bring to bear, and because boats meant boarding, and if Tressoir spotted their approach and cut his cables they might find themselves in the open sea, where it was no task for an under-strength crew. But there was no way Tressoir could best Harry in a ship-to-ship contest, even if he chose to run. Sailing or fighting, *Lothian* was no match for *Bucephalas*. In open water, or in this constricted channel, short-handed with a well-armed ship alongside, and no chance to escape, Tressoir would be obliged to surrender, quite possibly without a shot being fired. He might try to use his prisoners as hostages, but Harry was prepared to risk that, sure he'd have the upper hand.

"I sent upriver for some ice yesterday," said Tressoir. "So we shall have flavoured iced cream as a dessert, served with a well-chilled champagne."

"Splendid, Monsieur le Vicomte!"

"And then, Sir William, I must ask you and your family to withdraw, so that our visitors and I may discuss terms."

"That, sir, is something for which I wish to be present."

"No!" replied Tressoir, without gentility. "You will not be."

Parker was stung enough to respond in a like manner. "Why the devil not?"

The Frenchman hesitated where he should have given a robust reply. He looked to be on the verge of telling Parker the truth: that his presence, plus his overweening vanity, would make any conclusion impossible; that the really valuable commodity was the ship and its cargo, and that he and his family had been used as pawns, bait to ensure someone came to trade for the ship. But good manners won out over the truth.

"How could a gentleman bargain for his own person? It would, Sir William, be too demeaning."

Parker was actually lost for words, his hand waving as uselessly as his trembling lower lip. "I was thinking to act on behalf of my family," he spluttered.

"Never fear, sir," said Illingworth, proving how easy he found it to play the diplomat. "The thought is paramount in our considerations."

Harry was thinking that once more Tressoir had exposed himself, partly through allowing Parker to recount his history, but more by the way he'd hesitated. The Frenchman needed to deal. Given his rank and relatives, plus the threat he faced from an unfriendly government, he had nowhere else to sell his goods. He would be forced to take whatever price was offered, and since he wanted to stall the negotiations Harry was determined to propose as his opening offer one he'd be bound to refuse.

CHAPTER EIGHTEEN

DISCUSSING terms with Tressoir was going to be a trying business, especially since he and Illingworth were never left alone to sort out the approach. And if he suspected that Harry Ludlow knew his difficulties he certainly didn't behave that way, pitching his first requirement well over the actual value of the ship and its cargo by demanding a fully armed and rigged frigate.

"At that price, I might even be prepared to let the passengers go."

"I'm not surprised," replied Harry. "Indeed, I'd expect half Normandy for that price. Nor is it one that any admiral could agree to, since that would leave you in prime position to prosper by harrying British trade. Parker would be impeached."

Tressoir smiled, slightly. "Nevertheless, it is what I want. And a swift conclusion would be welcome. Even in these troubled times, I find holding people for ransom uncomfortable."

"Perhaps," Harry responded, "not entirely commensurate with the status of an aristocrat and a gentleman?"

Tressoir wasn't offended. He bowed his head slowly in acknowledgement. Harry was about to follow that up by asking for their release regardless when Illingworth, evidently impatient to proceed, spoke across him.

"You originally demanded gold. The insurers have advised me to proceed on that basis, and gave me a figure."

"Which I advised them was way too much," said Harry, quickly.

Illingworth paused, caught off-guard. He'd discussed the value put on the *Lothian* with Harry Ludlow, and heard him agree that it was fair. Yet he also knew that Tressoir had altered his demand, so he chose to remain silent, and nodded for Harry to proceed.

"I am curious, Captain Ludlow," said Tressoir, a wicked gleam in his eye. "Just how much power do you have in these matters?"

Illingworth adopted a bland expression as the Frenchman's gaze shifted to him, which he maintained throughout Harry's response.

"I can veto anything if I so choose, since I command the ship that brought Captain Illingworth here. Now, let us be sensible. You have nowhere to sell your captures but back to the rightful owners."

"That is a very large assumption."

"But an accurate one. We could sit here all day, haggling like Arab traders to narrow the gap between our respective positions, which would leave us the unenviable task of rowing back to my ship, in darkness, on an ebb tide. But after such an excellent dinner I find such a notion too exhausting. So I propose that a little honesty might serve us all very well."

Tressoir was looking hard at Harry, in a way which made him feel slightly uncomfortable. It was the same expression that he had worn on deck, the one that indicated he could see right through to whatever he was thinking. Oddly enough, Harry did want that very thing, but wished to reserve the thoughts behind his behaviour to himself.

"Honesty, Captain Ludlow?"

"Yes!"

"If I might be permitted to speak," said Illingworth, hands raised as if he wanted to control a debate in danger of becoming acrimonious.

"I'd rather hear from your companion," replied Tressoir, his voice, for the first time, hard and unfriendly. "I believe he was about to expound the truth."

"You know your situation better than I, Monsieur."

"That is certainly a fact."

"I propose that for the sum of twenty-five thousand pounds

sterling you hand over both the *Lothian* and her passengers, along with any personal possessions they carry, and leave Captain Illingworth and me to sort out our respective portions of the total." Tressoir, whose face had originally clouded with anger, suddenly laughed out loud as Harry continued. "Perhaps we could meet again tomorrow, so that you have time to think about it."

"The answer is no!"

"Till tomorrow," Harry repeated emphatically, as he got to his feet. "Now with your permission, I will say good day to Sir William and his family."

The Frenchman still seemed amused rather than offended, though Harry wondered if the man was acting. "Don't tell him what you have offered me. He thinks he's worth more than that all on his own."

"I apologize for that, Captain Illingworth," said Harry, as their boat pulled away from the side of the Indiaman. This time the current was against them, strong and steady, the strain of the long pull soon showing in the faces of the boat crew. Behind them the sun was sinking towards the western horizon, silhouetting the two islands, with a sliver of moon already well up in the east.

"You left me high and dry, sir," Illingworth growled from inside the folds of his boatcloak, "though so did that damned Frenchman with his demand for a frigate."

"A curious request," Harry replied.

"And nonsensical, for the very reasons you pointed out. The man is a menace in a leaky corvette, imagine what he'd be with a frigate at his disposal."

"Lethal."

"But I think that a higher offer would have made him more amenable. Not even the most devious Calcutta trader would have proposed such a derisory opening sum. He was bound to refuse."

Seeing Harry smile at that produced a questioning look from Illingworth, then one that tried to convey that he'd known all along what was afoot. "Of course, it was deliberate?"

"Certainly. Even with his evident problems, your ship is worth ten times that sum."

"What do you propose?"

"I should have thought, Captain Illingworth, that you of all people would guess, since it is one of the prime reasons for my being here."

The silence that followed that question was clear evidence that Illingworth wasn't sure what he wanted. Part him of him must crave retaking his ship, while another section would shudder to think of his precious *Lothian* suffering damage. When he replied his voice had none of its usual carrying power. "You intend to make an attempt at recapture."

"Tressoir has made it all but irresistible. He has sent his own ship away, so you must have observed that he's undermanned. I doubt he has enough crew to handle your guns, and we can observe any help he might expect long before it can get near him."

"That channel is narrow, and I will wager it's more dangerous than the benign creature we saw today. Even calm, it is not a place I'd sail into without proper soundings."

"Which is why I intend to drive him out into the open sea. You admire your ship, but know as well as I do that she can't outsail *Bucephalas*."

"The Parker family?"

"He is uncomfortable with the notion of hostages."

"Sir William Parker thinks him a gentleman."

"I must say I do, as well," replied Harry, "though it has nothing to do with a slavish regard for titles. He handled Sir William with consummate skill, when it would have been very easy, and must have been exceedingly tempting, to cause offence. I've met a few insufferable people in my time, Captain Illingworth, but Parker beats the band. I wouldn't pay a brass farthing to get him back."

"I doubt that his brothers have any regard for him. It is more likely that their interest in his safe return is financial rather than familial."

"Tell me, Captain Illingworth, given all the alternatives, how would you go about recapturing your ship?"

Illingworth held up a hand, palm visible in the fading light. "I will not be drawn, sir. I have suffered too much in that area already. The taking of prizes is your profession and your affair."

Harry grinned at him, thinking again that his first impression of the merchant captain had been wrong. After they'd had words outside Admiral Parker's office Harry had felt, even more strongly, that the man was pompous and overfond of his own voice. But the sea had brought out the sailor in him, giving them some common territory to discuss that was neither personal nor contentious. His confusion regarding an attack, given his profession, was hardly surprising. Harry Ludlow had spent half his life making such decisions, Illingworth most of his praying to avoid them. And while talking to Tressoir he'd had the good grace, once he perceived that Harry and the Frenchman had a different, albeit mysterious agenda, to stay silent. Now, though he might say he refused to be drawn, his comments showed a firm grasp of essentials.

"I agree with you about the channel, but I will sail into it if I have to. But I'm hoping that Tressoir, because of the sum we offered, will guess my intentions and try what has to be his only hope."

"Which is to flee."

"Yes. And preferably to get to open water before I realize that he's unmoored. The tides in the morning watch will be advantageous, and it will still be dark till around seven. By stealing a march on me he might just think they can put enough sea between us to make the Seine Estuary before I can overhaul him." Harry heard Pender call to the sweating, grunting oarsmen, and the cutter swung round to get into the lee of his ship. "And to give him good cause to do just that, I intend to get to windward of St. Aubin so he has a clear avenue in which to sneak away."

"Surely he will have worked all this out for himself?" said Illingworth, as they entered Harry's cabin.

Willerby, who'd seen them coming, had cooked them a light supper, with a hot rum punch to warm them after their time in the boat, and the sound of Pender and Derouac bickering about the right way to serve it emanated from the pantry. Clearly, judging by the stony atmosphere when it arrived, tempers were still as hot as the drinks.

"If he has any brains he will," Harry replied, when Illingworth repeated his observation. He continued, having taken a grateful sip of the rum punch, "But what alternative does he have? If he stays where he is, I'll take him at first light."

"Not tonight?"

"Never. If I'm taking *Bucephalas* into that channel it will be very slowly, on a rising tide, and when there is something to see by, with a leadsman in the chains calling out the depth of keel."

Illingworth divested himself of his coat, and sat down and began to eat. Derouac immediately picked it up, brushing it heartily, his face full of concern. Both captains looked at their servants so that they withdrew, leaving the older man free to respond to Harry, pacing at the head of the table, with his mouth full.

"I fear I must remind you of the expertise with which he plied my guns on your first meeting. If he does stay put, I cannot see how you can get within range of those cannon and not suffer damage yourself."

Harry stopped his pacing. "No attack is without risk, and this one is no exception. But even if he inflicts some damage, he will be forced into an artillery duel which he cannot hope to win. And if he's thought about that as we have, he will at this very moment be thinking of the most propitious time, given the wind, tide, and darkness, to cut his cable."

He grabbed a slice of the pie that had arrived with the drink and made for the cabin door. "Which is why I must get the ship under way. I want Tressoir to see us tacking to windward, opening the door for him to make good his escape."

On deck, he called all hands. Pender emerged from below eating a slice of the same pie.

"I'm sorry to interrupt your supper, Pender."

"The only thing you're interruptin', Capt'n, is me strangling Frog-spawn."

"Then why don't you leave him to a job for which he's well suited. You have enough to do without looking after the needs of me and a guest."

"You're not suggesting that I give way to that little bugger?"

"No, Pender," Harry replied with a sigh. "I reassure myself with the thought that he'll be gone soon."

"One way or the other," Pender growled. Harry laughed.

It had been a rare sound these last few months, and the response told him just how much the atmosphere on deck had been restored. He even ignored Flowers rattling on his bones. With such a ship, and a willing crew, Tressoir didn't have an earthly hope of avoiding surrender.

"I want to beat to windward, and with plenty of noise. We'll go south of the island so that whatever moonlight we have will silhouette any ship to the north. As soon as we're under way, set some of the men to clear for action, and get everybody to make a racket when they rig the nettings and lay out the charges we need for the guns."

"What are we about to do, your honour?"

"We're about to draw our fox."

"Saving your presence, sir."

James looked up from his writing, glad of the respite since he'd written about a dozen letters to friends, acquaintances, and potential clients to say he'd returned.

"Are you the messenger?"

"You knew I was coming?"

James pointed to the pile of letters. "I asked for you."

"Then you know about this," said the boy, holding out a piece of paper. James took it from him and opened it up. The list of figures meant nothing to him as he read it, nor did what the boy said next. "I had the letter, but then I met this man who offered to show me where you and your brother was residing. I didn't know what he'd done till I went to my pocket to fetch it just now."

"What are you on about?"

"The letter."

"What letter?" James demanded, the discomfort in his writing hand making him more crusty than usual.

"The one Lord Drumdryan gave me to bring to you."

"Lord Drumdryan sent a letter?" Ben Harper nodded. "What did it say?"

"I don't know, your honour," Ben pleaded, "it was sealed."

James looked hard at the boy, then seeing him cringe, he closed his eyes and leant back in his chair. "Tell me what happened, from the very beginning. Take your time, and leave nothing out."

CHAPTER NINETEEN

THE BLIND spot created by the looming bulk of the Île du Tertre was Harry's main concern, that and the paucity of light from the thin strip of the new moon. With the run of the tide reversed, it was unlikely that Tressoir would make a break now. But since the wind was still in the west it was a possibility that had to be accepted. If he tacked right round to windward there would be a gap during which Tressoir could get out into open water without being observed. Yet to stay to the south-east of the islands presented the Frenchman with too little sea room. Could the alternative offer him too much? It all came down to sailing qualities, of *Bucephalas* set against the merchantman. At least he had the *Lothian*'s captain aboard, willing, with reservations, hesitations, and numerous caveats, to tell Harry the true worth of his vessel.

"You must hold in your mind," Illingworth concluded, "that she's been to Calcutta and back twice without a scrape, and the Indian Ocean is no more of a friend to a hull than the Caribbean."

"Then that makes us even," Harry replied, as they lost sight of the eastern exit to the channel. "Pender, a party into the cutter if you please, with a couple of flares. Tell them to keep an eye on that strait and signal the moment they see a bowsprit. They're to hold position with oars, and on no account hoist a sail."

"Will they not be seen from the top of the big rock regardless?"

"We'll lower the men to larboard on the next tack, and hope the lookout has his eyes fixed on our top hamper. There's not much light and they will be against the black of the sea. If they do spot Tressoir coming out tell them to try and fetch his wake, so we can pick them up. If they miss us, they're to make for the small bay between the islands. If he doesn't emerge, and they hear gunfire, head for the same spot."

"Aye, aye, Captain."

Harry gave the necessary orders as soon as Pender had the party gathered, and as the ship's bowsprit swung round on a north-westerly course they hauled the cutter alongside and had it loaded before the manoeuvre was complete. Each tack would take them a bit further to windward, and he fully expected to see those flares aloft, alerting him to the fact that Tressoir had run, at some point when he was well to the west of the islands, at the turn of the tide.

There was nothing more he could do for at least two hours; even with the leeway to aid him progress was slow. But Harry, pacing the windward side of the quarterdeck, wasn't lost in idle speculation. Having sailed these waters before, he knew only too well how quickly the weather could change. He kept a constant watch on the dim light around the new moon, as the clouds slipped across, measuring their speed and density for the smallest hint of an alteration. The wind speed gauge was fairly steady, the odd stronger gust making it whistle as it slowed his forward progress.

At one point, lost in thought, he conjured up the image of his brother. If James had been here on deck he would have been posing questions, with certain members of the crew always sure to be in earshot to pick up the answers and relay them to the rest of the hands so they knew exactly what was planned. Their curiosity wouldn't be dimmed, but the channel of information was no longer present. That idea made him smile. But at the same time he realized that he missed his brother just as much as they did. In the years since he first took James to sea he had come to appreciate the fact that talking to someone he could trust helped him to think.

The tide reached slack well before he completed his westing, and still there was no sign of a flare. He had a night glass trained on the channel when the flow turned easterly, though he could see precious little, the high rocks cutting out any hope of light penetrating the shadows. The chill night air, which he'd withstood without too much discomfort, began to pierce his thick boatcloak, seemingly in strict correlation to his falling spirits. Tressoir hadn't moved, which meant one of two things: he'd not comprehended the nuances of Harry's derisory offer; or he had understood them only too well, and decided that if he was going to lose anyway he would go down fighting in a spot of his own choosing.

By the time the first hint of grey touched the eastern sky Harry was frozen to the marrow. He called to Pender to breakfast the hands, with an extra tot of rum to warm them, and returned to his cabin to stand and thaw out before the stove. As arranged he woke Illingworth, who posed the obvious question as soon as he realized the time.

"No. Tressoir has not obliged us."

"So we attack him *in situ*."

"Yes."

Illingworth coughed loudly and looked at the floor as he spoke, in a determined effort to avoid contact with his host. "Forgive me for alluding to something strictly outside my province."

"Your late passengers?"

The merchant captain raised his head and nodded, his unbrushed hair sprayed out in the dim lantern light, seeming to double the size of his head. "He may well parade them on deck, and challenge you to fire your cannon."

"I doubt he'll do that. At the very least he'll keep them below."

"You have no assurance of that, Captain Ludlow. He may not be the man you think he is. I am bound to ask: if that is the case, what happens then?"

"You and I will be obliged to carry on negotiating, and we will be back where we started. Neither further forward, nor further back."

Illingworth knew that to be untrue, just as Harry did himself. Tressoir would have called their bluff. Once used, and acknowledged valuable, negotiation would swiftly turn to surrender. Far from Tressoir having no cards to play, he would be holding all the aces.

"I suggest you eat something, Captain Illingworth, and don some clean linen. If I have judged my man right, we are going to have a battle."

Harry changed his own shirt, a common precaution against infection from a bullet, then put on a plain, dark blue coat that would not stand out in the early morning light. Pender, fed, had come to fetch his weapons.

"I want two reliable men in the chains, Pender. We're going to drift in rather than sail, and once we get between those islands we'll have precious little in the way of wind to get us out again. In fact, we will probably be obliged to go right through."

"Would it not be better to pay the man, Capt'n? After all, it ain't our coin, nor our relatives."

"If we take her, Pender, she's our prize."

"Something we need like rats in the breadroom."

"I need a party ready to drop anchor," Harry continued, as if Pender hadn't spoken, "with a cable attached that can run to the starboard gunroom port and act as a spring. We want some holding ground so that we can swing round broadside on. Once we've done that he'll have to strike. There is no way he can outgun us once the carronades come into play."

These guns, short 32-pound smashers, had proved to be Harry Ludlow's secret weapon on more than one occasion. Normally a cannon confined to use by the navy, few of his enemies expected to see them mounted on a privateer. They fired a huge ball over a short range, iron shot which could smash through the side oak planking of anything but a ship of the line. Not that he intended to fire them into the *Lothian*. But the sight of a ball that size, hitting water in between, should be enough to convince Tressoir that his situation was hopeless, a prelude to him having to haul down his flag.

"Do I have your permission to tell the men what you intend?" asked Pender, making little attempt to hide his continuing annoyance.

He'd expected the Frenchman to run as well, and was perfectly prepared for a fight in the open sea, where all the advantage lay with *Bucephalas*. But sailing into that channel wasn't the same thing at all. Clearly, to him, this was risk to no purpose. Harry's question in response was posed in an amused tone, but underneath his casual demeanour he was anxious. "Do you think they might decline to follow me?"

"They ain't got the sense," Pender snapped.

"And you?"

"You ain't goin' to start on me bein' shy again, are you? I just thought the lads should know what's what."

Harry grinned, with relief as much as anything. "No James, and Captain Illingworth not well enough known to plug. I don't want a fight, Pender. But I must look as though I'm bent on one to persuade that Frenchman to surrender. So we must go in there as though we mean business, everything ready, guns double shotted, and plenty of smoke from the slow match wafting about the decks."

Pender persisted. "We don't need this, Capt'n."

"What! A prize worth a quarter of a million pounds sterling, and the undying gratitude of one of the senior admirals in England?"

Pender just shook his head slowly, eyes on the deck. "Are we going back to Portsmouth when this is done?"

"No, Pender. We will pick up our men from Buckler's Hard, then make for the Downs and home. And when we get there the share of the money that my brother took to London will be waiting for the crew, in good English coin that they can dispose of as they wish."

Pender looked him in the eye. "That's the first time you've ever opened right up, Capt'n, about what you intend. And that includes to your own brother. Can I put forward the notion that you try it another time?"

That amused Harry. Pender, who was as close to him as anyone, surely knew how much he was prone to sudden improvisation, which he always sought to disguise when events unfolded as a deep-laid plan. "My friend, this is one of the few times I actually know what it is I'm doing."

The sky had lightened by the time he made it back to the deck. Not adequate to see everything clearly, but enough to set a course for the St. Aubin channel. He called for the change of course, and sent the topmen aloft to take in sail. Even fighting under topsails, he'd be approaching at speed. The breeze was coming straight over the stern now, with the flow of the current increasing as it was sucked through the narrows. Raising his telescope he looked straight ahead, over the bowsprit. What he saw surprised him enough for Captain Illingworth to notice.

"Tressoir's paid out his cable," said Harry, "and dropped a stern anchor. The *Lothian* is now blocking the eastern entrance to the channel."

"Which means he intends to fight."

"It can only be a bluff," Harry replied. "He's counting on my being overcautious and heaving to."

"Would that not be the best course?"

Harry dropped the telescope, and the look he gave the merchant captain had all the venom that he'd been exposed to on first acquaintance. No one questioned Harry on his own deck, friend, brother, or guest. Pender, seeing the look, hooked Illingworth's arm and led him away towards the taffrail.

"Best leave Captain Ludlow to con the ship, your honour. You'll find he's a more tolerant soul if you do. Perhaps, if you have the time to spare, you could teach that steward of yours that it's bad manners to go interfering in another's pantry."

The wind increased as well as the current as it rose in velocity to speed through the gap between the towering black rocks. Tressoir had run out his guns, and had manned as many as he could. Harry suddenly swept his telescope round, to search the open western sea, but it was empty. Surely the men he'd left in the boat would have the sense to fire off their flares if they'd seen any help coming from the Normandy shore.

"Leadsmen!" he shouted, then an order to ease the braces to spill some of the wind.

The litany began, as each man cast forward with the lead weight, each line longer than the depth of the keel. They plucked it up as the ship passed over, to swing it forward again to land well in front of the prow. And at each completed cast they'd shout, "No bottom on this line!"

Harry was wondering if there was a connecting bar between the two islands, with Tressoir on the other side of it. Yet looking at the water, now picking up the low orange sunlight, he saw it flow smooth, with no change of colour or speed to indicate an underwater obstruction. The feeling he had that something was wrong had no rational basis, so he repeated to himself what he'd said to Illingworth. *He's bluffing.*

"No bottom on this line."

"Pender, get the anchor party standing by. If the water's that deep we'll have to pay it out early. Let it go as soon as we enter the narrows. I'll steer closer to that bay. If there is sand on that, there's likely to be sand on the bottom too."

He could see the smoke on the *Lothian*'s deck now, the black wisps from the slow match drifting into the air, to be whipped away towards the orange ball of the rising sun by the breeze.

"I take it your guns have flintlocks, Captain Illingworth?"

"They do."

Illingworth's voice sounded slightly peevish. Clearly he was wounded by Harry's attitude. The merchant captain wasn't to know that the glare he'd received would have been the lot of anyone who'd questioned him at such a moment. Deliberately, Harry set his voice to sound friendly.

"Then Tressoir knows his trade. He has slow match lit as a precaution against their failure."

"Then it is his own, sir, since I had none aboard."

"If you'd care to join me by the wheel, Captain, I would have no objection."

"I am content to remain here, sir, out of your way."

"So be it," Harry replied. But his response was drowned out by the splash of the anchor hitting the water. The familiar smell of the cable running over wet wood, smoking despite that, filled his nostrils. The time it took to reach the bottom seemed an eternity, and removed any fear he had about running aground. The party on the spring were hauling their hawser towards the stern, where it would be looped below to the capstan. Once in place, hauling on it would swing *Bucephalas* round, the ropes forming a triangle, with the anchor cable the point and the ship the base. And once that happened all his starboard guns, loaded and run out, would be facing the enemy.

"I need a speaking trumpet, Pender," he said, "to call on him to strike his flag."

"Aye, aye, Captain," Pender replied, as the anchor cable began to straighten, evidence that he'd found good holding ground.

"Let her run a bit more!" he shouted. "I want to get good and close."

"He's got men ashore, Capt'n," shouted Pender, pointing to several heads sticking up over the gorse bushes that provided a windbreak for every piece of level ground. Some of them had muskets, which they were training on the British ship. Harry responded by holding up a finger to feel the stiffening breeze. Not even a marksman could achieve much using a musket at over a hundred yards, especially with such windage.

Time stood still, a seeming age which was in fact no more than a few minutes. Harry, as the cable went slack, gave the order to put a brake on the anchor cable, and a simultaneous one for the men at the stern to secure the spring, with the crews of the starboard carronades to be released from other duties and told to stand by, aiming their shot into the sea.

"Let fly the topsails!"

Gently, as the anchor bit into good holding ground, *Bucephalas* slowed, until with the anchor cable rising out of the water, she came to a halt. The sound of the tidal flow running by her hull was mixed with that of the creaking cables as they took the strain. Down below, men pushed on the capstan to bring in the spring. Slowly the ship spun broadside on and Harry, lifting his telescope, looked right ahead to where Tressoir stood on *Lothian*'s quarterdeck.

"Pender, get the men up from below and man the guns. Topmen, get out of the rigging in case he fires off a warning salvo."

Harry stepped forward and raised the speaking trumpet, at the very moment that Tressoir did the same. The Frenchman beat him to it by a whisker, his voice floating across the two hundred yards of bright water that separated the ships.

"You said, Captain Ludlow, that should we meet again I would not be able to beat you."

"And any small amount of sense will show you that I was right. I am now going to demonstrate the lethal nature of my firepower."

He nodded to the carronade gun captains, who pulled their lanyards at the same time. The two guns roared out a spit of orange flame and black smoke, shooting backwards on the fixed rails of their carriages. The balls hit the water some twenty-five yards from the *Lothian*'s larboard side, sending up twin founts of water that, with the wind, was carried across the merchantman's deck to drench everyone aboard.

"And I, in turn, must do likewise," Tressoir shouted, as the last of the white water fell back into the sea.

CHAPTER TWENTY

THE CRASH of gunfire seemed to come from all around the ship. Every man aboard threw himself to the deck. Fired from fixed platforms, at short range, the chain-shot from the land-based guns ripped through the upper rigging, cutting sails, slicing ropes, and smashing spars in a maelstrom that made Harry wonder if he'd been attacked by a ship-of-the-line. The gorse bushes he'd seen had no innocent purpose. Every one was a gun emplacement, each cannon fully manned by what could only be the bulk of Tressoir's corvette crew.

In the lull between their first salvo and the second, Tressoir opened up with canister from the *Lothian*, small deadly iron balls that scythed across Harry's deck. As well as maiming and killing it kept heads down. Harry, on his knees, was stunned into silence, as all around him parts of his rigging was falling, some into the sea, but even more on to the netting above his head. The gunners at least had stayed at their posts to respond, and standing up to check their target they caught the full blast of Tressoir's fusillade. Men were spinning away from the side, only two of his guns firing off their shot.

"Axes!" Harry shouted, getting to his feet. Pender had anticipated the command and grabbed a pair of topmen to help him cut the cable. "Dreaver, Fellows, get another axe and help Pender. Price, Hillyard, get below and release that damned spring. And never mind what damage it might do, just get it loose."

They were in mortal danger, in truth defenceless against these reloaded cannon. It was no mass salvo now. Each gun was carefully aimed, some at the base of the masts and those with a better angle at the join between the sternpost and the rudder, where the

metal pintles and gudgeons held the coppered rudder assembly to
the ship. If they lost that they couldn't steer. But no action Harry
or his crew could take would do much to distract the gunners
enough from their tasks. Only escape would save them, and for
some reason the Frenchmen had themselves provided the lifeline.

Deadly as their attentions might be it was a mistake to fire
their guns individually. Harry, running for the wheel, miraculously
intact, knew that well. If they'd kept to their devastating salvos,
even badly aimed, he would have been forced to strike, just to
avoid the annihilation of the crew. But under this sporadic bom-
bardment he could begin to sort some order out of the terrible
chaos. And given a chance to draw breath, discipline told. These
men had sailed and fought together for two years. During that
time, hardly a day went by at sea without Harry Ludlow ordering an hour's practice on the guns. The dividend of such training
now came to the fore as each unhurt or unoccupied member of
his crew went where they could be of some use.

The wounded gunners were replaced and the undischarged
cannon now fired. Ignoring what was happening elsewhere, a section of the crew had gone to man the bow and stern chasers, firing
them high at the platforms containing Tressoir's cannon. And
because they were practised they were good, sensible enough without any orders to drag their own canister out of the magazine and
return to their enemies a dose of their own medicine. On deck
Harry, ignoring everything that flew or dropped past him, walked
along to calm the gunners, an anxious eye on Pender and his men,
swinging their axes by the starboard hawse-hole.

"One salvo for those sods on the East Indiaman!" he yelled.
"Carronades to sweep the quarterdeck clear. Then reload, and as
the ship swings take every one of those emplacements on which-
ever side the guns are loaded. Let the bastards have a taste of real
gunnery."

They were ready, crouched down behind the bulwarks,
impervious, like Harry, to what was going on around them,
which included roundshot, musket balls, canister, deadly shards

of splintered wood, and the writhing bodies of their own wounded mates. Harry raised his arm, looked to the last spot where he'd seen Tressoir, now invisible through the smoke, and bellowed, "Fire!"

This was no rippling broadside, with one gun preceding the next, but the complete thing, and the recoil made the ship's timbers groan with the strain. The anchor cable went at the same time, and the ship swung round, bows pointing towards the *Lothian*, the stern still attached to the spring. The gun crews rushed across the littered deck and manned the starboard guns, fingers eagerly pointing to those of their enemy they thought they could hit. Harry was still looking at where their last volley had gone. As the smoke cleared he saw that the very piece of wood that had sheltered the *Lothian*'s quarterdeck had gone. He opened his mouth to yell in triumph when the musket ball took him across the back.

He fell forward, more from the force of the blow than any pain, landing once more on his knees, this time fighting for breath. Two of his men abandoned their gun, grabbed him, and hauled him aft towards the wheel, their captain screaming at them to belay and get back to their posts. Pender, amidships, hacking at some fallen rigging with his axe, saw what was happening, and ran to assist. By the time he arrived Harry had got hold of the wheel and was trying desperately to haul himself upright.

"Get back on your damned guns, or we'll all die."

"Capt'n," said Pender, taking his arm to support him.

"Forget me!" Harry gasped, for the first time feeling the searing pain of his wound and the warm blood running under the waistband of his breeches. "Just fight the way you always do. You don't need me."

"Carrick," said Pender to one of the gunners, at the same time as he was examining Harry's back, "get below to the cockpit and fetch up the biggest bandage you can find."

Harry was hunched over the wheel, clutching the spokes to try to stay upright. He heard the ripping sound as Pender tore the ragged remains of his blue coat. That was followed by the linen shirt as well as his servant's yell for a bucket of sea water.

"It's mostly a flesh wound, I think, but deep enough to show your bones. You're bleeding bad."

"To hell with it, Pender."

"How do we get out of here, Capt'n?"

Harry raised his head, to look aloft at what he had left in the way of topsails. It was precious little, certainly not enough to take them out on the wind that was blowing through the channel, and unquestionable death for any topman who went aloft to attempt it.

"Drift," Harry croaked. The pain was intense now, his control of his limbs uncoordinated. "We must get close to the *Lothian*. That will make them cautious with their fire. Stern or bows, but not amidships, with the bowsprit right on one of Tressoir's cables."

"Cut the cable?" Harry just nodded. "We're drifting already, Capt'n. The spring is gone."

Harry wasn't listening, he was too busy thinking. "Fire every gun on the ship at it. If that fails board *Lothian* with axes and cut it. But break the damn thing."

"Bandage, Pender."

"Thanks, Carrick. Hold the captain upright while I bind it round."

Harry's protests that seeing to his needs was a waste of time were ignored. The men he led were carrying out their duties, doing what needed to be done without any help from him or Pender. But that could alter at any second, and without a word being exchanged they all accepted they would need Harry Ludlow upright and in command if they were going to get out of this scrape alive.

"It will only slow the bleeding," Pender whispered in his ear, as he tied the knot. "It'll take a needle and thread to stop it proper."

"Rum!"

Harry lifted his head at that word, to see the one-legged

Willerby standing there with a tankard, as calm as a day on the green, as if there were no shots nor shells, not to mention blocks, pulleys, and shards of wood, flying in all directions. Two of his guns were hit at once, though with luck only on the wood of the trucks, but it was enough to slew them uselessly sideways, their splinters adding deep cuts to bodies smashed by moving metal. The whole of the deck was covered in blood, and most of the guns that could still fire were doing so with reduced crews. The loss, in men and firepower, was ruinous.

"Get off the deck, Willerby."

"This rum will help set you up, Capt'n. Very least it'll ease the pain."

Harry, even wounded, knew better than to argue with Willerby. He grabbed it and drained it down, gasping at the strength of the mixture. "Now get below. The men will need you more than they need me after this is over."

Willerby grinned and ducked down the companionway like a man with two good legs. "The old rum never fails a sailor."

Bucephalas was drifting crabwise, the current carrying her towards *Lothian*. The fire from the East Indiaman was infrequent now, while that from the shore had lessened considerably as the guns on the privateer's deck engaged in individual duels. But someone was in command, and had the means to signal his desires, since the shore-based cannon ceased their duelling and started to fire in unison. Even with fewer guns it was like the first salvo, deadly in the sheer quantity of shot that came aboard. But this time the target was moving—not much, but enough to make the victims of this renewed barrage feel that at least they had a chance.

Harry could hear the men coming to the quarterdeck to report, each one talking to Pender rather than himself, a sorry litany of more men wounded and guns rendered useless. He was looking to larboard. Over the shattered bulwarks he could see the outline of the *Lothian* clearly now, still square on and blocking the channel. He tried to move the wheel but he lacked the strength.

"Pender, help me. Get her rudder round so that she's bows on."

"Can't be done, your honour. Rudder's near shot away. You can see the top part hanging off. Not even the relieving tackles have any purchase."

"Then get me on to the guns. I'll aim the damn things myself."

There were only four cannon left. The rest were dismounted or smashed, including one of the carronades. Even those that had survived were surrounded by dead or wounded men, not one cannon able to muster a complete crew.

"Who's loaded?" Pender called, a cry to which two of the captains responded. He helped Harry to the nearest gun, taking the rammer himself to heave it round on instruction so that it was pointing well forward, aimed at the *Lothian*'s stern cable. "Any men spare," Harry gasped, "load the rest of the cannon. This is likely to take more than one shot."

Harry was kneeling, peering through the gun port, calling for inch changes to the aim and elevation. Satisfied, and ignoring the pain, he stood up, swaying back and forth as he pulled the lanyard. Pender dropped the rammer and leapt forward as he did so, and was just in time to save Harry's legs from being smashed by the recoil of a ton of metal. Eyes screwed up in pain, his captain didn't see how close he came to success, with a spout of water shooting up right at the point were the cable sank beneath the water.

"Carronade's ready, Capt'n," said a voice in his ear. They helped him to it. But this time, with a fixed carriage, there was no way of levering to change the aim. Only the drift of the ship could aid him and something in the current obliged. As *Bucephalas* swung slightly, Harry fell backwards, pulling on the flintlock as he did do. The gun roared out and the great 32-pound ball shot forth, smashing the stern and slicing through the cable in the luckiest shot of Harry Ludlow's life.

The effect on *Lothian* was immediate. Reduced to one cable, the current pushed her sharply towards the northern shore. Her shot was ill-timed and badly aimed, inflicting little damage. She wasn't quite out of the way and *Bucephalas* crashed into her stern, taking off what little remained of the fancy gold decoration that had adorned the area around the casement windows.

Muskets had been placed around *Bucephalas*'s deck when they'd cleared for action, with balls and powder. These were now discharged *en masse* at the enemy ship, just enough to stop the Frenchmen's attempt to grapple the British ship fast to them with irons and prevent her escape. The gunfire from the shore had all but died away, although the odd cannon shot was still being exchanged between the ships. Smoke was billowing around, only to be whipped away by the wind, and Harry, with eyes that were going out of focus, saw Tressoir by the mainmast. The Frenchman was looking right at him. He didn't know, in the haze, half smoke, half approaching delirium, if what he saw was right. But it seemed to his fevered brain that the bastard who'd nearly destroyed both him and his ship had on his face that very superior smile.

"Give me a pistol," Harry croaked, as *Bucephalas* ground past.

"There's no point, Capt'n," Pender replied, grabbing hold of him as gently as he could. The bandage untidily wrapped around his upper body was soaked with blood, and judging by Pender's previous sight of the wound if Harry Ludlow didn't get attention he could bleed to death. "You've got to come below and get stitched up."

With a final groan of strained wood the ships broke free of each other, *Bucephalas* drifting out into the open sea, still carried on the current. Pender and two sailors took their captain below, and as they helped Harry towards the companionway he could hear his ship being restored to order: some housing the functioning guns and lashing off the damaged to stop them trundling around the deck as it began to cant with the swell, topmen going aloft to rig some sails that would put some way on the ship, waisters were working with axes and knives to cut free the damaged rigging, and someone, probably the carpenter, had sensibly put men to working the pumps. Screams rose above all the other noises as men who'd been wounded were finally shifted from where they lay.

Harry suddenly stopped and pulled himself up to his full height. "Where's Captain Illingworth?"

One of his supporters pointed towards the taffrail right above the sternpost, which was smashed to bits. What was left standing seemed to be covered in blood.

"He was placed right by there, after you and he had words, exposed to the first dose of roundshot."

"Dead?" asked Harry.

"Carried below," the man replied. "Though I reckon a canvas sack is what he's got comin', with that wound."

CHAPTER TWENTY-ONE

HARRY had never sailed with a surgeon on his books, his experience of the breed being that they were to a man drunken sots who killed more than they cured: when they'd fought these last five years James had run the cockpit and dealt with the bloody aftermath of action. But as he lay face down, with Pender working on his back, he knew that he needed a surgeon now, and not just for himself.

All around him in the faint glim from the candlelight, men were in pain, some so deep in shock that they merely stared at the low deckbeams above their heads while their shipmates tended to their needs. Others screamed and begged for relief, the rum administered by Willerby seeming to add to their fears and suffering rather than placating them. The smell, a mixture of blood, wounded flesh, sweat, and involuntary human waste, was so overpowering that Harry Ludlow, whose own back was covered with rum, thought he would expire from it rather than his wound.

"It's the best I can manage," said Pender, leaning forward so that Harry could see his strained face out of the corner of his eye. "But the ball has lodged in the flesh of your right shoulder, very close to a bone from what I can see, and I don't have the skill to try and dig it out."

"Illingworth?"

"Tom Biggins and Frog-spawn are tending to him, right now."

"What's our position?"

"We're still driftin' on the current, about five miles to the east of them islands. I've got boats out to keep her head steady and we've managed to keep well to the north of some nasty-looking cliffs off our starboard quarter."

"What about Tressoir?"

"Still where he was, as far as I can see."

"Help me up," Harry croaked.

"You'd best not. That stitchin' ain't too secure."

"Just do it!"

Getting Harry to his feet wasn't helped by the narrow confines of the crowded cockpit. The deckbeams were so low that he had to adopt a painful crouch till they reached the companionway that led up to the upper deck. Standing fully upright nearly did for him, and it was only by a supreme effort that he managed to hang on to consciousness. Every step of the steep ladder was a struggle, with Pender behind able to offer only limited help.

"We could stretcher you out," he said, not in the least surprised when the response to that suggestion was somewhere between a grunt and a growl.

They did make it eventually, and Pender could get beside his captain to take his weight. Not that looping Harry's left arm over his shoulder was achieved without more suffering, but at least the pain was confined to the side of his back which was merely cut. Once in the cabin, Harry leant his head against the wooden bulkhead, his fists clenched as he sought to stay conscious.

"What's the state of the ship?"

"Bad, your honour. We've taken more punishment than she can truly bear, though we were lucky below the waterline."

"The angle of fire was too high."

"Aye. But we don't have a single upper mast standing, and what's left of the rudder is only being worked by ropes running through the gunroom port. God help us if we meet a gale."

"I need a coat, Pender."

"I don't suppose there's any use me arguing?"

"None," Harry replied, his eyes tight shut. "I need to see for myself."

"Why didn't that French bastard come after us?"

"He doesn't have to, with the damage he's inflicted. And remember most of his men were ashore on the guns. Besides, he has, I hope, his own casualties to deal with."

"Can I suggest a cloak instead of a coat, Capt'n? If you try to get a jacket on you'll pass out."

Harry pushed himself off the bulkhead and turned round, nodding as he did so. The pain across his back was a dull, constant ache but each movement of his right shoulder was agony.

"Have we got the making of a sling?" he asked. "I need to keep this arm still."

They cheered him when he came on deck, which made their depressed captain wonder if they were witless fools. Now, after he'd been nearly destroyed, he could see all of the signals he should have picked up before sailing into that channel. Tressoir's confidence, that slight smile which seemed to mock him; the Frenchman's lack of outright anger at the offer Harry had made. He'd guessed to the letter what his opponent would do, and had just been waiting for him to fall into his already baited trap.

But cheers, however ill deserved, had to be acknowledged. His first task was to check, to his own satisfaction, that the ship was in no immediate danger of running aground on the Normandy shore, faint, low-lying, but a hazy danger some three miles to the south. He then made his way around the scarred deck, Pender at his side, to talk to what remained of his weary crew, so that encouraged they could return *Bucephalas* to a state fit to get them all safely home. It would be quite a task.

"You need a chair, Captain," said Pender, softly in his ear, as Harry staggered slightly.

"No!"

"I won't take that. Seeing you has given the lads heart. If you fall down, which you are bound to do if you try to stay on your feet, it will reverse it. You will sit down or walk this deck unaided."

Forced to nod, and angry at his own weakness, Harry nevertheless favoured Pender with a grim smile, a crooking of the lips that was a mixture of rueful acquiescence as much as regard.

"Remember, I'm still the captain."

Seated, Harry finally got round to asking the question he'd

been putting off since he came on deck. When Pender related the bill for his folly, he dropped his head forward on to his chest.

"Fourteen killed and another ten serious with wounds. There's about four of the crew who ain't carrying some form of hurt, being it from the scraping of a ball, bruising, or a cut and they are all in the boats holding the ship's head straight. There's barely enough men left to sail the barky."

"Have what warrants there are report to me."

One by one the men Harry called "warrants," a nickname carried over from his navy days, detailed the damage. It was a sorry tale of wood smashed, both mast and bulwarks; guns dismounted and useless; sails tattered and the yards shot from their slings; blocks gone over the side and their ropes cut to ribbons. Yet while gunner, sailmaker, and carpenter detailed all this the steps necessary to put some of it right were already in place and beginning to take effect. They would have some canvas aloft, using spars lashed together to rig jury masts. A scrap of the same would do for a headsail and the driver's boom that ran from the stump of the mizzen had survived.

"The rudder is hangin' by a single pintle. We can't steer on sails alone and we'll never make any headway into the wind without that working proper."

"It's not just fashioning a bit of a sternpost, it's the ironwork," said the carpenter, a tiny man called Shilling, known to all, because of his stunted appearance, as Farthing. "There are no gudgeons or pintles for the top part 'less we make them. But that means setting up the anvil and a charcoal brazier. I don't fancy trying that on this here swell so we'd need to find somewhere calm so's we can work. Meantime, if you're prepared to cut some holes in the stern below your cabin we can improve on the jury rig we've made up to work it."

Farthing went on to describe how and where they'd rig the pulleys in his cabin, taking the ropes from the rudder and running them forward to either side of the capstan. That could then be used as a temporary steering gear, with the ropes lashed off if it needed to be used for another purpose. Translated that meant if you needed to hoist sails, you couldn't steer, and vice versa.

"That way," Farthing continued, "we can get as much purchase on the thing as we need, in a way that no amount of relieving tackles would manage. I can put a small spar up on top so that the man on deck can see which way the rudder is pointing, which will aid in whatever sail plan we manage to get aloft."

Harry replied, his head bent, and supported by the fingers of his good hand, "Set a party to do that, then set up the brazier over wetted sailcloth, hanging free of the deck with some chain. That way the swell won't tip it over."

"It'll take time to heat up, even with bellows."

"Then get started," said Harry, looking up. The sky had been overcast, except for a strip over the eastern horizon, but was clearing, the voluminous clouds thinning and changing shape, opening up to show a trace of blue sky, and presaging an alteration in the weather. Hard to be sure, but the wind seemed to be swinging slightly to the north, which if it continued would drop the temperature, produce a bright blue clear sky, and, for them, a contrary wind. But that same breeze would provide something to sail by, unless it blew a gale, at least enough to get him out of the long Normandy bay into deep water past the Cap de La Hogue.

He needed a port. A friendly one, if possible, but the enemy shore would have to suffice if the weather turned foul. Life as a prisoner didn't appeal, but it was a lot better than drowning, which would be their certain fate if the sea got up seriously. He wouldn't know what his options were until he tried the ship out, saw how she manoeuvred. And on top of that, given the pain he was in and the blood he'd lost, could he stay conscious long enough to make a judgement? The orders he issued were passed softly to Pender, and he, knowing how exhausted the men were, passed them on in as a gentle a voice as he could.

"Cast off from the boats and stand by to tack."

Bucephalas came round very slowly, lying practically dead in the water at the point where the bows turned into both the wind and the leeway. The need to shift sails to compensate was made a hundred times more difficult because of the lack of the rigging to do so. The ship fell off twice before Harry abandoned any further attempt. He knew from memory where they stood, relative to the Banc de Cardonnet, a spit of sand very like the Goodwins, so he used both the boats and the temporary rudder assembly to steer a few degrees south for the lee of that. There, in waters made less forceful by the sandbank, they tried the same manoeuvre with greater success.

Now the danger was reversed, with the tide full and about to turn he had to get to the north-west of that same bank to avoid drifting aground. Progress, using boats as well as what they had aloft, was agonizingly slow. All the while, amidships, the banging and shaping of metal over the anvil acted as spur to their efforts. Hanging over the shattered taffrail, men were working to repair the top section of the sternpost so that when the metal connections were ready there would be something in place to attach them to. Another two planks were waiting, ready to be fished either side of the damaged rudder so that the whole thing would be connected.

The difficult decision to make was at what point he could safely heave to and carry out work that might take hours to complete. Harry had unwittingly fallen into a deep slumber, despite the pain he felt and the noise of metallurgy amidships. All around him men worked to get enough ropes reeved to work the scraps of sail. Hard-cases they might be, but they were true sailors, who had been afloat since they were boys. Once their tasks were allotted few further commands were necessary.

The banging on the anvil had abated and Farthing was now at the stern, supervising the repair. Pender, conning the ship, was, like every man aboard, looking aft even as they worked. Which meant that Tressoir, in the *Lothian,* had cleared the eastern entrance to the channel between the Îles de St. Aubin before anyone aboard spotted him. The cry that followed when they did brought Harry awake in an instant, and his scream of agony as he tried to move underlined this new peril.

"Why now?" snapped Pender, angrily.

"Who knows?" Harry replied, his words coming in gasps. To him it seemed just another example of Tressoir's ability to anticipate everything he would do. "Perhaps he preferred to leave us to carry out the repairs, rather than burden his own crew."

Painfully, and with Pender holding his left elbow, Harry got to his feet. "Get the boats in and let her head drop round to the north-east. We'll have to try and run."

"To where?" asked Pender, the posing of the question in such a loud voice testimony to his feelings of near despair.

"Darkness," said Harry, wearily. "It's the only hope we have."

For a crew already close to collapse from their forced exertions, the rest of the day was cruel indeed. Nothing really worked aboard *Bucephalas,* and men were scarce, so every task was a test of stamina as well as sheer brute strength. Half the sails they tried aloft on jury yards, in the hope of even a minuscule increase in speed, were blown out or broke the temporary bindings. And all the while Farthing worked on, occasionally finding he needed to return to brazier and anvil, to make tiny adjustments to his metalwork, which had to be an exact fit to his rough-hewn timber.

Tressoir gained on them steadily, but Harry reckoned that his pace was insufficient to overhaul them before dark. The question he couldn't answer was how badly the Frenchman wanted to take him. If it was paramount he'd seek to pursue even after the light faded. If not, he'd haul his wind as night fell and head back to his anchorage.

With an insight that comes only occasionally, even to the best trained mind, Harry was sure he'd discerned Tressoir's needs. The corvette he had sailed in originally was too crank for the task he'd set himself. The man needed a better vessel to be an effective privateer. But with his relationship to the Revolutionary government he could not purchase one. He'd set the trap that Harry had stumbled into for a ship, the frigate he'd asked for when the negotiations opened.

The lack of damage to Harry's hull was nothing to do with the angle of fire from the shore-based cannon. It was deliberate. So Tressoir had the means to repair any ship that wasn't seriously holed, and the vessel he was now pursuing, put to rights, was perfect for privateering in the English Channel. That didn't explain why he hadn't come out sooner. But by his failure to strike and subsequent escape Harry had already confounded Tressoir's initial plan, so the Frenchman was now engaged in an action for which he hadn't anticipated the need.

If Harry was right it would mean a continued pursuit, the harrying of a ship unable to manoeuvre, even if it took several days to bring her to. And if he thought capture impossible Tressoir would go for a kill. Sinking *Bucephalas* or running her aground wouldn't be ideal, but he'd risk that. The one thing he didn't want, should Harry elude him, was that they should know in England of his snare in the St. Aubin channel. In time of war *Bucephalas*'s failure to return, could be put down to any number of causes. So he'd rather see his enemies sunk and drowning, just so that they could not interfere with the possibility that another ship, perhaps the frigate he craved, would be sent from Portsmouth to take up the negotiations.

"Pender. Get the wounded stretchered on to the deck, and enough canvas rigged as an awning to keep them from expiring of cold." He could see, even out of the corner of his eye, the penetrating look he was receiving from his servant. "Let everyone know that we might have to abandon ship and take to the boats, so one by one they should go below and fetch any possessions they wish to take along."

CHAPTER TWENTY-TWO

"THERE'S a pair of visitors to see you," said Ben Harper, his head hanging low. He seemed to be looking at the adjoining door to the bedchamber, and James assumed his behaviour to be shyness and embarrassment at what he'd got up to with Mary Blackett.

"And one of them be a sheriff's man," Ben added, his head sinking lower.

"What can a tipstaff want with me?"

James dressed quickly, and remained standing to greet such a person. The tipstaff was a big man made bigger by the coat he wore, so thick he was almost squat in appearance. Behind him stood a pock-marked fellow wearing a round hat, who was pointing his finger at the occupant of the room.

"This is Mr James Ludlow, the brother of the man you're after."

"There's no reward for brothers, mate. That only applies to principals laid by the heels."

"What if he satisfies?"

"That'll be the day."

"But . . ."

"Wait outside, Marsh," said the tipstaff, shutting the door.

"Why have you called upon me?" asked James.

Carefully, the sheriff's man explained. The fellow outside, Marsh, was a man who worked for a bounty, be it taking up thieves or tipping the wink to a sheriff regarding the whereabouts of certain persons. His own name was Bullen, he was an undersheriff at the Old Street Court in the City of London, and he had a writ to take up a gentleman by the name of Harry Ludlow for failure to comply with an outstanding debt.

"Debt!" barked James, his habitual easy manner evaporating at the suggestion.

Bullen tapped the large staff on the wooden floorboards, light catching the embossed head in the shape of a crown that earned him his nickname.

"The sum is a mere five thousand pounds, a trifle given what your brother has in the way of property. Not worth a night in Newgate for such a middling sum."

James had to sit down when the full enormity of what had happened was explained to him. He had no actual idea of how much money Harry was worth; that was something they'd never needed to discuss. But his holdings, in government stocks and the like, had been substantial. These were deposited with Cantwell, famed for his probity. That and all his other property was watched over by their brother-in-law, Arthur Drumdryan, much to James's chagrin. No wonder he hadn't heard from Cantwell. But did Arthur's silence mean he too was implicated? Much as James disliked him, he had to suppress that thought. Arthur might be many unpleasant things, but he was scrupulously honest.

Trying to evaluate the depth of the losses, James realized they were enormous. There was the money that Harry had inherited from their father and the steady income he received from his farm tenants, all dwarfed by the profits he'd made from cruising as a privateer.

"What happened to Cantwell's Bank?"

Bullen snorted, missing the point of the question. "How could a man like that fall for such a scheme?"

"I'm sorry," said James, "I have only just returned after two years away. I need to know why the bank failed."

Bullen smacked his lips, then eyed the half-empty port bottle and the other chair. James, taking the hint, invited him to sit down, filled the empty glass, then rang the bell to order another bottle. Bullen teased him till the next drink arrived, and really only opened up on the third bottle.

"Some projector offered to sell him the treasures of Italy. As you know, the Jacobins have been sacking the Lombardy plain, which they say is the richest seam of gold and jewels in the Christian world." Bullen's face darkened as he looked at the floor. "Trust the Papists to hoard such stuff. If it was anyone else but Jacobins that had relieved them of it I would invoke divine justice. But a good God, a Protestant God, would not line the pockets of heathens even at the expense of Papist heretics. Why, he might as well give it to the infidel."

James tried to ask a question, not the least interested in differing religions, but received, in reply, a compelling glare. Bullen was going to tell this tale at his own pace, and no other, drinking liberal quantities of wine as he did so. And what a sorry tale it was, one that proved there wasn't a man born, regardless of his personal rectitude, who could not be dunned out of his money by a silver tongue.

In this case it was a fellow in the guise of a recently arrived French émigré officer who claimed he'd been at the right-hand side of the terror of the Italians, a young general called Bonaparte. What he offered Cantwell, for the right sum in gold, was the treasures of half the monasteries of the Po Valley, religious artifacts of precious metal and stones beyond price.

"And he supplied samples, too. Jewelled crucifixes and the like, studded with gems, as well as scraps from illuminated manuscripts."

"How do you know all this?"

"Cantwell's been bleating from his own little bit of Newgate."

"He's in gaol!"

"Man can't meet his obligations," Bullen replied testily, "where else is he to reside? He's telling all and sundry how he's been robbed, and that if the likes of my good self would care to chase the miscreants, instead of innocent victims like himself, then he could satisfy every creditor he has."

Bullen sniffed, finished his tankard of port, and lifted the third empty bottle. James, determined to extract more for the price of another, just stared back at him. Yet his mind was working on a different level. He felt a touch of elation mixed with guilt as he recalled that due to a disagreement he'd moved his own funds to the safer vaults of Baring's Bank. And the third thought mixed in with that was less welcome, being the nature of those American Treasury bonds.

He'd advised caution on Harry when his brother had explained they were only redeemable at source, three thousand miles away from home. That was significant enough to begin with. But with this news it took on the proportions of a disaster.

Bullen picked up the bottle and tipped it, even though he knew it was empty, a look of innocent surprise on his square face.

"When the rumour got out that he was in difficulties he was doomed. Every depositor was at the door a-hammering to get their monies out. No bank can stand that, regardless of how well it's run." Bullen shook his head at the folly of his fellow humans. "Which is why, sir, I never trust my own humble stipend to their greedy hands. I've collared too many bankers in my time to trust the breed. And I know, whatever they say, that they has monies tucked away, even if they are in gaol. Just let the turmoil subside, then they settle their pressing debts, and walk off to a life of ease and comfort."

"Another bottle?" said James. He suspected that Bullen had invented the last statement, but necessity meant he'd have to follow it up, and that was something that could not be achieved without the means to lubricate the under-sheriff's throat.

"I don't know that I should, your honour," Bullen replied, this said in the way that people employ when they fully expect their feeble protest to be ignored.

James rang the bell, then walked on to the landing to call down. Marsh was still outside the door, his pock-marked face set in a scowl that looked habitual.

"You're a thief-taker, I'm told."

"I am that," Marsh replied, in a voice that exactly matched

the face, low in the throat, rumbling, and very unfriendly.

"Who found it necessary to follow me last night after I came ashore?"

"Had to make sure I could direct Mr Bullen to the right abode, didn't I."

James was thinking how amusing it would be to put Villiers on to this fellow's tail, Marsh's reaction adding spice to the image, when Ben Harper arrived with the fresh port bottle. The way the boy looked at Marsh was singular indeed.

"Is this the man who stole my brother-in-law's letter?"

"Can't be sure, your honour," Ben replied, unconvincingly.

"What are you afraid of?"

"He's not afraid of anything," Marsh growled.

Ben took the opportunity to rush back down the stairs, leaving James staring malevolently at the thief-taker. "What have you said to frighten the boy?"

Marsh gave him what passed for a smile. "Not a thing, mate."

"You have a letter belonging to me," said James, holding out his hand.

Marsh looked at the bottle. "Best not keep Mr Bullen waiting for his port. A lack of a drink makes him ten times as fierce."

There was little point in the staring contest that followed, so James re-entered the room and handed Bullen his port. His loquaciousness grew ten-fold, and while he was informative about Cantwell and his troubles he felt the need to range far and wide regarding the state of the nation. James was treated to chapter and verse about the troubled climate of public finance, the unpopularity of taxes and paper money, a weariness with the war and the way it was affecting prosperity, and finally the opinion that every mutineer in the fleet who didn't kiss the deck in abject supplication should be strung up from the nearest yardarm.

"For we are a seafaring nation, Mr Ludlow. And that is as plain a fact as the nose on your face. Those devils can be replaced to a man, and that by honest Englishmen who could learn to sail their vessels in no more than a long hour. Two days of hard practice, sir, and they'd be up the Goulet burning every French ship that threatened these shores."

James tried to keep him to the subject of Cantwell, and any possible hidden monies, but failed. And as he consumed more port, it became even harder. Bullen was drunk, and James suspected that he and Marsh had consumed a certain amount of ale before coming on. Finally he got back to the subject for which he'd called, and the news that Harry Ludlow was back at sea and not waiting somewhere, so full of remorse for a life ill-spent that he was begging to be arrested, brought forth the true nature of the sheriff's man.

"Am I being trifled with, sir?" he demanded, pulling a writ from his pocket and waving it under James's nose. "Do you seek to ply me with port while your damned brother makes a getaway?"

"He's been at sea these last two days, Mr Bullen. And he set sail thinking, indeed knowing, he was still a wealthy man."

"Pride before a fall, sir. Which is what I see all the time." Bullen tried to look cunning, but being inebriated looked like a low comedian. "And where, pray, will he make his landfall when he returns?"

"I've no idea, Mr Bullen," said James standing up. "And what makes you think for an instant that if I knew I would tell you?"

Bullen was on his feet suddenly, swaying slightly, his staff of office waving to and fro under James's nose. "Don't attempt liberties with the law, sir, or you may find yourself in a place of confinement, your only companions rats and the steady drip of water from the moss-covered walls."

James responded with a yawn. "One cannot be confined for silence, Mr Tipstaff, nor terrified by the threats of an overripe imagination. My brother is not here, I do not know where he is, nor when he will come back. And since you have no business with me, I will bid you good day, sir."

Bullen looked set to continue the argument, his countenance exceedingly belligerent, which forced James to administer the *coup de grâce.*

"And since I have been robbed myself, by that villain on the landing who calls himself a thief-taker, I feel disinclined to indulge your bad habits. If you refuse to depart I will get the owner of this establishment to present you with a bill for the wine you've consumed."

"Damn you, sir, for a rogue."

"What a pleasure it would be, should you fail to satisfy the bill, to see one of your own type on your heels, waving a writ for an unpaid debt under your nose."

Bullen's eyes expanded then, but even full of drink he could reason that to argue further was futile. He spun on his heel and barged out of the door, past a confused Marsh, stomping down the stairs, shouting at the top of his voice about gents now being paupers soon. He stopped at the foot to deliver his valedictory threat.

"I will not be gainsaid, not by you or any other thieving rascal. Happen one day the name I'll be after is James Ludlow, not Harry, and if that be the case, rest assured I'll not be gentle when I take hold of your collar. Come along, Marsh. If you want to earn your fee, there's work to be done."

James sat down as soon as he was alone, deflated more by what Bullen had said about Cantwell than the useless, drunken threats, and running over the consequences of this loss. Half that money traded in America belonged to the crew, and now it seemed that Harry lacked the means to repay them. And very likely, as a condition of his licence to sail as a privateer, there was a percentage of the profits from the voyage due to the government.

The soft cough at the door had to be repeated several times before he noticed. Lifting his head, he saw Ben in the doorway, with fine blond hair and long, soft lashes making him look almost theatrically sheepish.

"Saving your presence, your honour, Mistress Blackett sent me to see that you was all right, what with that man shouting all them things."

"All right?" James responded, with a sour laugh. "No, Ben, I'm not. And neither are you. Why did you lie just now?"

"I'm sorry, sir," the boy bleated, "but you should have heard what he threatened me with. Said he could get me transported by a flick of his little finger."

"You lost a letter, Ben. My brother, it seems, has lost a fortune. Tell me, what was Lord Drumdryan's mood when he gave you the note for my brother?"

"High," Ben replied, "like he was angry about something."

"Was he? Then I think I now know what his letter contained." James shook his head slowly. "I need to find him."

"He's in London, your honour."

"Is he, Ben? Then why no word from him? I've written, clearly in ignorance of how matters stand, yet he hasn't replied, and this from a man who sent a special messenger by horse, so acute was the need to warn us. Wherever he is, he cannot be in London or I would have heard from him by now."

"That's a fact."

"I want you to rent a horse, Ben."

"Sir."

"Ride back to London, find out where Lord Drumdryan is, then either get him to come to me, or I will go to him. But find out where he is and ride back and tell me."

"Can I look in on Lightning, your honour?"

"Who?"

"My own horse, who's lame at Hindhead, eating grass paid for by Lord Drumdryan's guinea."

James was glaring at the boy, who clearly had no idea of the enormity of what had happened in the past couple of days. But then few did, and as he sat down to write an updated missive to his brother-in-law, exposed to such a crestfallen face, he couldn't help but relent.

"You may stop for a minute, Ben. But no more."

CHAPTER TWENTY-THREE

HARRY slept for four hours with *Bucephalas* running in a wallowing, lubberly fashion before the dying breaths of the westerly wind. Pender shook him gently awake as soon as the situation became critical. Getting from his cabin to the deck took an age. His limbs had stiffened and his wounds ached even more than they had in daylight. The sky had cleared completely as night fell, and the breeze, still light, shifted northerly. It was the worst thing imaginable; even though there wasn't much of a moon the sky was full of stars, and on a relatively calm sea the reflection made hiding from Tressoir impossible. And given the ship's condition there was no way of outsailing the Frenchman. The temporary rudder was in place, but with the *Lothian* plainly visible no more than two miles distant, it only seemed to prolong the agony.

"Time to lighten the ship," said Harry, looking along a deck lined with bodies that had yet to be sewn in canvas. The wounded were on the forecastle, most asleep, but some groaning in agony. "If we can spare the men, I'd like to bury the dead."

"Them that can sit up, can sew," Pender replied.

The guns, whole and in pieces, were first to go over the side. With no yardarms to speak of, and lacking time to rig a temporary davit, they had to be eased through the damaged bulwarks on a rope to the capstan, only released when they were below the curve of the hull. There was an unseen bonus in this; without splashes the enemy would not know what they were about. More men were down below, their first task to smash in the water butts so that the pumps could jet the contents over the side. Once the guns were gone the shot followed, manhandled in a chain from the holds below to the nearest lee gunport, then barrels of everything from salt beef to iron nails, each one setting up a small phos-phorescent splash as it went over the side.

Harry made adjustments to the sails that helped, allowing him to stay ahead of Tressoir for an extra hour or two. But the French-man was still gaining, and without really striving, judging by the sails he had aloft. Racking his brains, Harry could think of no way to evade capture, the only possibility, a slim one, being to take to the boats in the hope that their pursuer would be satisfied with the ship. Even then, they would have to split up, since a cut-ter, or a launch boasting only a single sail, would soon find themselves overhauled by a determined East Indiaman. The jolly boat, if they used it, would have to be towed.

Timing was the key. If he could lash off the wheel to keep *Bucephalas* running on while he got the boats away on a differ-ent course, Tressoir would, he reckoned, go after the ship. But to sail south, on the wind and the tide, would only land them back in the great bight of the Normandy coast, a place where they could be hemmed in so comprehensively that only going ashore, and then abandoning the wounded, would ensure escape. Going north, tacking or wearing to make any headway, and they'd be just as vulnerable. Only a gap so great as to make pursuit questionable would stop the Frenchman from trying to take them too.

The dead were sewn in their sacks, roundshot at their feet, the final thread of each shroud running through their noses to ensure they were truly gone. Of necessity there was little ceremony attending their disposal; Harry said a collective prayer from mem-ory as they were slid over the side. Having supervised that, a very subdued Pender came aft.

"Boats are alongside, Captain, and I've got a sling rigged that will be able to take the stretchers."

"Good. Anyone who can manage without one must make him-self as comfortable as he can in the boats. Try to get those that can't into the jolly boat. Sails might not be enough. We may have to row hard, and we'll never manage that with half a dozen stretch-ers laid across the thwarts."

"What are the odds, Capt'n?" asked Pender.

Harry replied knowing it was a valid point. If taking the wounded jeopardized the rest they should be left. Tressoir had shown no signs of an excessively bloodthirsty nature, and would probably take good care of them. But they were his crew, and he was damned if he was going to lose them. Giving up his ship was bad enough, without handing over good men, some of whom he sailed with from the very beginning of the war.

"He won't come after us until he's taken the ship, perhaps not then if we can put some distance between us." He slapped the ship's timbers hard, which sent a jarring, almost welcome pain across his back. "I'm sure this is what he's after."

Pender looked at him for several seconds. "And what about you?"

"I'll survive, Pender, never you fear. I have to, since I intend to take *Bucephalas* back from the bastard."

The smile was no more than starlight on white teeth, but it cheered Harry to see it, just as much as the words that followed.

"Then I pity the poor sod. He don't know just how much trouble he's in."

Harry began to laugh, but the pain caused by his heaving chest soon put an end to that. Pender was gone, shouting out the orders to get ready to abandon ship, exchanging a glare with Derouac as they passed each other. The steward looked even more like his nickname in this light, and he hunched his shoulder as he approached Harry, making himself look even smaller.

"My captain is not up to being shifted into a boat."

"He'll be safer there."

"With respect," Derouac replied, hunching even more and rubbing his hands in supplication, "I cannot agree. The wounds he has will prove deadly if he is not kept in a stable condition. And since he is my responsibility, I take leave to ask that I be allowed to decide."

"The ship may sink."

"My service in the cabin, sir, has not stopped me from a

knowledge of pumping. The hull, I suspect, is sound."

"Very well. Tressoir will take the ship. Just hope that he does not wish to revenge himself on Captain Illingworth for our attack."

"You forget, sir, that I have met him. Though I have not had the honour to serve him even a simple meal, I suspect him to be a gentleman."

"Very well, you may tell Pender."

"If you will permit, Captain Ludlow," said Derouac, pulling back his shoulders, "I would prefer you to do that."

Harry held the wheel in his good hand, his heart heavy as he contemplated what he must do. The temptation to sink the ship so that Tressoir couldn't take possession was hard to resist. It wouldn't serve, since she was the only chance of freedom for the crew, but to give her up to another pair of hands was hard, and in his mind he recalled every action he had taken her into, remembering how the way she handled had confounded his enemies more often than any tactical skill he possessed.

"You should be here now, James," he said to himself, looking around at what damage he could see, "to draw this."

"Boats loaded, Capt'n," called Pender. "I put the chest in the cutter, underneath a stretcher."

"Illingworth?"

"Frog-spawn has had him taken to your cabin."

"Good," Harry said. The lump in his throat made his voice sound strange. "Now I need you to help me lash off the wheel."

Pender came a few feet further aft to help, then taking Harry's arm led him to the side. There the sling that had been used for the stretchers awaited him, the last load. It was an ignominious way to depart, but with only one good arm he had no choice. The three men who'd stayed aboard for the purpose, Pender, Jubilee, and Tom Biggins, hoisted him out over the black water, and lowered him gently into the bobbing cutter. As soon as he was by the tiller, Pender and his party joined.

No one said a word as Pender cast off, to join the already departed launch and jolly boat. Even the hoisting of the sails was undertaken in total silence, evidence that the captain wasn't the only one affected by what they were being forced to do. But once they'd cleared the ship many an anxious eye was aimed at their pursuer, in case the Frenchman should alter course. He didn't, and they could still see both ships when the drifting *Bucephalas* was finally overhauled.

"I hope one of the bastards drops a candle in the magazine," growled the gunner. "I left enough powder on the floor to start a right good blaze."

"Never mind that," Pender replied. "Just worry that the sod don't put a prize crew aboard and set off after us."

Harry looked up at the mass of the Milky Way, so dense it was almost like a cloud. The whole sky was full of stars, but one, to the north, shone brighter than the rest. He put the tiller round till the prow was aimed right at it, and ordered Pender to keep it there.

Dawn, grey and overcast, found the little flotilla in line ahead, the jolly boat struggling as, being towed, it shipped more water than its larger consorts. Everyone was cold, hungry and uncomfortable, with the wounded, including Harry, suffering from the cramped conditions. The wind was increasing, promising even more discomfort as the size of the swell increased. At the top of each rise, those who were awake searched the horizon eagerly for any sign of a sail, most, though they wouldn't openly admit it, not caring whether it was friend or foe.

Harry was using a small compass to steer, an imperfect instrument, the main purpose of which was to put him 15° east of magnetic north. Kept steady it would provide a guaranteed marker by which they could find their way home. Sailing north, he knew he couldn't miss the south coast of England, his preferred landmark Beachy Head. Once spotted that would allow him to bear up for the Downs.

He dredged his memory to recall how the tides ran, though he lacked the chronometer which would allow him to use Dover as the fixed point in time. But the way the sea flowed back and forth in this confined stretch of water allowed for a margin of error. Judged right the north-westerly wind would hold him to his chosen course, the very worst that could happen would be a sight of the French coast. That mattered little, since the Channel current, still strong from ebbing through the Dover Strait, would take him back out into the open sea, whence he could haul round to reach his destination.

As long as the wind wasn't dead foul, when that tide turned it would carry him up to a point where he could contend with the variable flows and breezes around the South Foreland then reach the southern tip of the Goodwin Sands.

The sea was too fickle an element. The wind shifted slightly overnight to the south-west, gusting rather than blowing steadily, which engendered the weary business of tacking and wearing. In the darkness Harry hauled in his sails, and attached a line to the launch so that contact wouldn't be lost, a rope light enough to break under pressure, so that they were no threat to stability. Little movement was possible in any of the boats, and once dawn came again changing direction was difficult, a discomfort which bore heavily on the wounded. Two more men died, burial immediate upon the discovery of their demise. Pender had loaded as much water as he could, but still Harry insisted on strict rationing, well aware that the weather could easily change and drive them away from the safety of land rather than towards it.

They made their landfall within three days, having, from their low elevation, not sighted a single sail. Then, with the wind right abaft, and the current in their favour, progress became both more comfortable and swift. Numerous boats appeared as they got closer to the Dover Straits, mostly cutters but some ketches, there to meet the incoming merchantmen and trade for goods that could later be smuggled ashore. Once they'd ascertained that Harry's trio were nothing to do with the excise they ignored them. Closer inshore were the pilots from places as far apart as Hastings and Ramsgate, sent out by the harbour-masters to entice captains into their various anchorages to boost the port revenue. One or two of these looked set to exchange a word, but Harry steered away from them and they let him be.

Soon they spied the huge bluff of white cliffs that rose out of the sea south of Dover. Then, after the port itself, the depression to the north that stood between the town and the steep escarpments of St Margaret's Bay. The swell eased as they entered the southern end of the biggest anchorage on the east coast. The Downs ran from just off St Margaret's all the way up to Pegwell Bay, three miles deep in parts, with the huge bank of the Goodwin Sands providing shelter for an armada of ships, protecting them from anything but the most severe weather.

They steered through the mass of shipping, including Admiral Duncan's line-of-battle ships; the twin Tudor castles, shaped like royal roses, of Walmer and Deal, standing watch over the great strand of shingle where Julius Caesar had landed nearly two thousand years before. This was home to a lot of the men in the boat, as well as some of those they'd buried at sea. Harry, once he'd seen a doctor, and had his wounds properly dressed, would have the heartbreaking task of telling women and children that their husbands and fathers had perished because of his blind stupidity.

"Steer past the jetty, Pender," he said, "and run us in upshore of the Three Kings."

Pender did as he was asked, the other two boats in his wake, calling to some of the local hovellers to help him get the wounded out, before rolling the boats further up the beach. Harry insisted that he was the last attended to, with a messenger sent ahead to the Three Kings to fetch medical help. In ten minutes half the folk in Deal knew that Harry Ludlow was home, that he'd lost his ship, and that in his two-year absence something like half his crew had perished.

But that was nothing new to the people of a seafaring town; parents, wives, and children who saw men depart each day of their lives with no knowledge of when, if ever, they'd return. The sea was cruel enough without a war to fight, even here when the wind blew strong from the north-east, and vessels dragged their anchors. Pulling fifty bodies out of the spume after a gale, some from ships, others from the boats that tried to help them, was too common-place for long despair. So those that came to see him lifted ashore were sympathetic rather than angry. One of them was his brother-in-law, Lord Drumdryan.

"What are you doing here?" Harry asked him, struggling, and failing, after so much time spent sitting, to stand upright.

Arthur Drumdryan looked down into Harry's drawn face, saw the way that Pender was supporting him, and knew this was not the time to tell him that every penny he owned had gone down with Cantwell's Bank; that as soon as the courts were informed that he had landed, which would be just as quick in Deal as in Portsmouth, there would be a tipstaff calling on him for payment of his outstanding debts.

"Coincidence, Harry," Arthur replied.

James responded to Arthur's note, arriving at the Three Kings from Cheyne Court within two hours of Harry coming ashore. In the meantime, his brother-in-law, using a variety of coins from the chest Pender handed over to him, had sent the most seriously dam-aged off to the local hospital, a charitable institution built for the purpose of treating sailors; organized food and a change of cloth-ing for those well enough to stand, and arranged for a carter to transport them to the family home, having sent instructions ahead to prepare for their arrival.

"The physician examined him," he said, as James entered the smoky, panelled room which overlooked the busy anchorage. Among the locals and the sailors who occupied the place, rough men bred to the sea, Arthur, in his old-fashioned cream silk coat and elegant white wig, looked totally out of place. He and James didn't get on, a mutual dislike that was of long standing, but the circumstances precluded any outward show of animosity.

"How bad is he?" James asked.

"The wound is serious, but not threatening without infection.

He took a ball across the back, which seared the skin and then lodged itself close to the blade in his right shoulder."

"Is Pender with him?"

Arthur nodded. "Fell sound asleep in a chair as soon as Harry was laid on the bed."

The surgeon, his coat covered in a thick layer of dried blood, came into the room. Spying the pair by the great fire in the hearth, he walked over to join them, turning and lifting his coat to warm his hams.

"He passed out when I went into his skin for the ball." James shuddered as the surgeon continued, his mind filled with the notion of the long probe and the following pincers entering his own flesh. "He'll sleep for an age, since he had a lot of rum to dull the pain."

"But he will be well again, soon?"

"Oh, yes. Whoever stitched him up in the first place was ham-fisted enough, but they washed the wound with ardent spirits, and took care to remove the cloth that had adhered to the gore, so it was clean. I've re-sewn him properly. I wouldn't be surprised if he's up and about in a day or two, stiff mind you, and in pain. But he'll be well recovered inside the month."

"Did he speak?" asked Arthur.

"Not much. Said he'd been a fool, and that I should hurry since he had to get back to Normandy and retake his ship. I'll look in on him tomorrow and check his dressings for bleeding."

"Thank you," said James.

"So," said the surgeon, pushing himself up on to his toes as his buttocks were scorched. "All that remains is my fee for today."

Arthur and James looked at each other. Neither had said any-thing about Harry's losses to a soul in Deal. Yet it was obvious by that remark that everyone knew. Harry Ludlow had been one of the richest men in the area. Just to have him as a client was con-sidered a reward. He was a man who was billed for any service rendered, and not hurriedly. It was Arthur who replied, his man-ner cold enough to chill the heat from the flaming, crackling logs.

"I think that can wait until you've finished with the patient."

◆ ◆ ◆

Pender finished his tale as darkness fell, the light from the lanterns throwing shadows across his face.

"Capt'n blames himself. Says he should have known it was a trap. But no one else saw it that way, and that Frog set it so well a nervous badger would have walked straight in."

"Harry told the surgeon he intends to get the ship back," said James.

"Don't see how he can, 'less he has half the navy to help him. And then, given the condition she was in, she'd need a tow to get back to England. He'd be better off forgetting her and buyin' another."

James opened his mouth to speak, but hesitated for a second as Arthur shot him a warning glance. That made him bridle. It was typical of Arthur Drumdryan, with his snobbish ways and old-fashioned opinions, his "Versailles manner" James called it, to see Pender as no more than a servant, instead of what he was, a friend and confidant.

"I think Pender should be told."

"And I think not," Arthur answered, his eyes arched and commanding, in a way that James recalled with no pleasure from his childhood.

"Saving your presence," said Pender, looking at both of them. He was well aware of the nature of their relationship, and wise enough to see that whatever truce had been brokered was about to break down. "Is what you're going to tell me likely to see me expire?"

"No," James replied.

He smiled, that full grin which James knew so well, one that lit up his whole face. "Then I dare say it will keep till the captain's up on his feet again."

He was up on several pillows when he heard the sorry tale from his relations.

"I am forced to ask, Arthur, why, when you had the power

to do so, you didn't prevent this happening."

Lord Drumdryan reached into his silk coat and produced a piece of parchment. "I was forestalled by this."

Harry winced as he tried to sit forward to receive it, and fell back helplessly. "What is it?"

"A letter you signed some two years ago, Harry. I don't know if you recall the time when you suspected me of playing ducks and drakes with your money."

Harry remembered it only too well, it being another occasion when his hot temperament had led him to a false conclusion. "Have I not apologized enough for that?"

"You have, and I take no pleasure in reminding you. But, Harry, you didn't alter this."

"What is it?" asked James, with evident impatience.

Arthur held it open, as Harry turned his head away, proof that he at least no longer needed to be told.

"It is an instruction, James, in writing, giving Cantwell control of Harry's account. Neither you, nor he, saw fit to mention it to me. And at no time did the bank ever treat me in any way different to the manner they'd employed before. That is, until, on hearing of Cantwell's difficulties, I tried to withdraw your money."

"I forgot all about the damn thing," said Harry.

"And I didn't know it existed," added James, softly.

"You will need to mortgage property," Arthur continued, seemingly oblivious to the pain he was causing. "Otherwise you will join that fool of a banker in Newgate."

"Harry, are you sure those bonds you bought in America have no value."

"Of course they have a value," snapped Arthur. "But only if you are willing to let them go at a usurious discount. What I am proposing is that Harry borrows money on his property, which will allow him the time to redeem them for their full value and clear his debts."

"Are you incapable of explanation without hectoring, Arthur?" James demanded.

"Only when I'm faced with bovine incomprehension."

"Please," said Harry, holding up a hand that looked as weak as his voice had sounded.

"I'm sorry," said James, quickly, glaring at his brother-in-law. "Fate has played you a rotten hand."

"It's not fate, James. It is the same run of luck that has followed me all the way from New Orleans." The single laugh that followed was soft and humourless. "Imagine if I'd brought Hyacinthe back to this."

Arthur, clearly confused, looked as if he was about to ask Harry what he was talking about. James waved a hand, stood up, and opened the door, making it perfectly plain that it was not a subject to pursue. "We'll leave you be for a while."

"Yes," Harry replied, in a weary, listless voice that his brother-in-law had never heard him use before.

CHAPTER TWENTY-FOUR

PENDER laughed, which echoed off the panelled hallway of Cheyne Court and made James wonder if anything could depress the man. They were heading for one of the barns, which had been turned into a temporary shelter for the crew. Harry was in the house, ordered to his bed by the surgeon. Just as well, since James had decided that if anyone was going to tell the men of what had been lost it would be him.

Pender had agreed, adding, "He's got enough on his plate, what with all those papers he's having to sign. And it don't take a genius to work out what he's up to."

"But I'd like you there."

"I can't think why," he'd replied, which is what had made him laugh. "The lads never lost faith in you, the way they did in the captain."

James wondered if Pender knew just how much Harry was borrowing. Not content to settle his own debts, he was raising everything he could for the men, insisting that it could be between three and six months before his affairs were in order. The dependants of those who had died, or were so badly wounded they'd never get to sea again, would take priority. But Harry was determined that no single member of his crew should suffer for what he saw as his own stubborn stupidity.

The house he was walking round now might well have to be sold. Not that James was bothered. He'd never really cared for the place, a red-brick pile from the reign of Queen Anne that had all the inherent problems of an old property. People might praise the proportions, and wax lyrical about the colour of the brickwork in a setting sun. But to James's mind it was draughty, with an awkward and cramped interior layout. More than that, it was the house in which he'd grown up.

That turned his mind to Arthur, whose presence and interference during that upbringing had sown the seeds of their mutual antipathy. It was he who'd arranged matters with various lenders. Having gained a minor sinecure in the government he was using his proximity to Henry Dundas to exert maximum pressure for good terms.

"I take it you're not going to tell me," said Pender.

"What?" James responded, dragged back from his musings on childhood, houses, and felonies.

"How deep the captain is in," Pender continued. "I don't care for myself, but my nippers reside in this house. The way you was walkin' so slow, and lookin' at it just now, had farewell written all over."

"It won't come to that," James replied, hoping that he was right. He nodded towards the nearby barn, dark brown, wooden, and with a steep-pitched roof. "And as for my dilatory pace, I'm just trying to put off what I must do."

Crossing the driveway their boots crunched noisily on the gravel, with James leaning close to hear what Pender was saying about the various members of the crew. He stopped talking as they entered the barn, the sound of Flowers whistling and playing his bones ceasing abruptly and the eyes of everyone present quickly on them. They might not know the details, but every sailor present had an inkling that something was amiss. The loss of the ship, and their comrades, as well as Harry being wounded, was bound to put a dampener on things. But they could smell, as all sailors could, that there was a deeper reason for the air of misery that filled the house and grounds of Cheyne Court.

And they listened in silence. Not that James was fooled by that. If they had any opinion, it wouldn't be expressed while he was present. They'd wait till he'd left, so that they could speculate freely about the truth, or otherwise, of what he was saying. It was odd, the way that these men, many of whom would seek

him out to talk to him on board ship, were now looking at him
with deep suspicion.

"But you will be paid what is owed to you. My brother asked
me to tell you that."

"How?" asked Flowers. He'd probably spoken as a reaction,
but given his habit of talking out of the corner of his mouth it
looked and sounded like doubt, which produced an explosive reaction from Pender, who was a good friend of the speaker.

"You swab," he shouted, his fists clenching. "You take leave
to doubt Harry Ludlow?"

"No one's doubting him, Pious," said Flowers, hastily.

"It sounds like it to me," Pender growled, the ferocious look
that accompanied that ranging round every face. "Barring a few
weeks when he weren't himself, none of you have ever cruised
with a better captain."

"Pious," pleaded Flowers, holding up his hand.

"You lot wouldn't have a seat in your ducks if'n it weren't
for him."

"I'm trying to agree with you, for Christ's sake," Flowers
shouted, that being followed by a murmur of assent from the rest
of the hands.

"Good," Pender replied, though he looked far from mollified.
He turned on his heel and walked out of the barn, followed by
James, who was surprised, when Pender turned round, to see him
grinning. "That made them think, eh!"

"What would I do without you?" said James.

Harry couldn't remain in bed, regardless of what the surgeon said,
so he was up and about within two days. The confines of the house
did nothing for his mood either. He needed air, with a wind off
the sea, to think properly. At around the same time as James
arrived back in London a stiff Harry Ludlow alighted from a shay
outside the Three Kings in Deal. After a brisk tot of brandy, no
doubt local contraband, he set off to walk along the strand of
shingle beach to the tiny fishing village of Kingsdown.

His thoughts ranged far and wide over a life that had seen more than its fair share of trouble, and would be difficult again. There was little self-pity in this. Harry was too honest to do anything other than admit that he'd brought most of his misfortunes on his own head. But now it was different. The cushion of his inherited wealth was being stripped away, and he was going to feel, as most men did, the chill consequences of making an error.

The arrangements he'd made in New York were not as easily redeemable as he'd made out, fairly obvious to anyone who thought about it. If a government was so short of hard cash that it would enter into such a transaction then it would hardly be awash with the means to satisfy his demands. Even if they were, it was a long two-way crossing, one which suffered all the dangers inherent in sea travel. In his own ship he'd have felt reasonably secure, but in another vessel, even a fast mail packet, the risks of carrying such an amount of money were great indeed.

But he could see no other way to pay off his borrowings. And once that had been achieved he would no longer be in the position of commanding wealth he'd previously enjoyed. Harry had no trade but the sea, no way of repairing the fortune he was losing other than by privateering. But now, once he'd settled with the crew, he'd be hard put to raise the money to purchase another ship.

Looking to his left he could see plenty of those merchant ships destined for every part of the globe. Perhaps he'd be reduced to that, offering his services to another ship-owner for the twin purposes of making a living and indulging in his love of the life.

He passed many people between Deal and Walmer Castles, more when he tired of walking on shingle and moved inland to the road. Acknowledging some, in the way that one does when passing a stranger, he ignored more, and might not have noticed the tall figure in the black Garrick coat if the man hadn't stopped some twenty feet away. The act made Harry look up, his first thought being that the heavy coat was odd dress for such a mild day.

"You," said Villiers, pointing to Harry as though he was about to shout, "Stop thief!"

Harry looked up at the round stone walls of Walmer Castle, his eye drawn by the flag at the staff. The device, of the three sleeping lions, was familiar; it was the insignia of the Lord Warden of the Cinque Ports and meant that the holder of the office was in residence. That sinecure office was held by the King's First Lord of the Treasury, William Pitt.

"You will oblige me, Mr Villiers, by ceasing to point."

"What are you doing in Deal, sir?" he demanded, looking at the white sling which held Harry's arm as though that in itself was a cause for suspicion.

"I live here, you fool," Harry replied, flicking his good hand towards the fluttering flag above the castle, "as does your master, from time to time."

"Master!" Villiers barked.

Even at this distance and in this weather, Harry could see that he had the usual drop of mucus on the end of his long nose. Despite the fact that Villiers was still pointing at him in the most insulting way, it made him smile.

"Just because you are dense yourself, Villiers, does not mean others share your affliction. You claimed great authority in Portsmouth. I doubt that it comes much higher than that which can be derived from Billy Pitt."

Villiers's mouth moved like that of a fish in a tank. But he couldn't speak. As a man who wanted to be taken seriously, he couldn't deny it. Yet he craved secrecy and must do so. The dilemma produced by those twin aims floored him.

"It is no concern of mine, Mr Villiers, who employs you. And if no one asks me, I will not volunteer the connection. Now, if you will excuse me."

Harry had already begun to move past Villiers, about to bid him good day, when the thought came to him, one of those ideas which seems to spring to mind whole, as though it had been there all along, lying dormant, just waiting for the right set of circumstances to raise it up. So compelling was it that he stopped right beside the government agent, lips very close to the man's ear.

"How certain are you, Mr Villiers, that there are outside forces at work amongst the sailors of the fleet?"

"Absolutely, sir. And I defy anyone to tell me, however well disposed they are, that such men could formulate a plan without such assistance. It would require genius, sir, and having observed the species of late, nothing leads me to suspect that commodity is abundant in admirals, let alone the lower deck." Villiers wiped the drop from the end of his nose with a large handkerchief before continuing. "I grant you had a case at Spithead, but if you knew what was happening at the Nore you would soon change your tune."

"I had heard that matters are more confused there."

"Confused," trumpeted Villiers, in a way that a man might use talking to a complete fool. But Harry kept the lid on his temper. "There are Jacobins on the Medway, sir, and there's no question of that. The mutiny has spread while the man who leads them has given himself the title of President, and threatened to blockade the capital unless his demands are met."

"And those demands are?"

"Proof, if proof were needed."

"That really doesn't tell me very much, Mr Villiers."

"It tells you everything," Villiers answered adding, to Harry's confusion, "Their ultimatums are not designed to bring about eventual harmony. They are merely an excuse to maintain riot and unlawful assembly. A hint that they will be satisfied leads to an immediate increase in terms."

Harry flicked a glance at the grey stone walls of Walmer Castle. "And just how desperate is the need to prove that this is the work of outside agencies?"

Villiers knew Harry was talking about William Pitt, and the actions he would have to take to settle matters. England could do without a standing army, even survive the loss of allies. But the fleet was everything, the one weapon that made the country safe. Without it, there would be no alternative to ignominious peace.

"The necessity can hardly be overstated, Captain Ludlow.

Imagine that you hold the supreme political office in the land, called upon to make far-reaching decisions. Yet you are also required to make concessions to an unseen enemy, without ever being sure that having done so their demands will not increase."

Villiers had told him more than he should in that reply, but that suited Harry. He wasn't sure if the man was right or wrong. But the really encouraging thing was that both Villiers and his master were in the same position, one that must be turning increasingly uncomfortable as matters deteriorated at the Nore anchorage.

"What you lack, sir," said Harry, "is an intimate knowledge of the navy and the way it operates." Villiers, thinking Harry was putting him in his place again, opened his mouth to argue. But Harry kept talking. "And the officers you could ask have, as you have doubtless observed, their own agenda to pursue."

"What are you driving at, Captain Ludlow?" asked Villiers suspiciously.

"I was wondering," Harry replied, "if you'd like some help."

"I shall introduce you to my uncle William," said Villiers, softly. "But you must let me do the talking."

The sound was magnified by the stone walls of the castle keep, which they'd entered by merely pushing at the door. There were no guards, not even a lock, which on a shore barely 25 miles from the nearest Frenchman was, for the leader of his nation's war effort, singularly lax.

They made their way through to the rear of the castle, and out over a narrow wooden bridge to the huge gardens at the rear. Several people were working, but spotting Pitt was easy. First there was the slight, tall frame, familiar from a hundred satirical drawings. Then he was attired as a gentleman thought a bucolic peasant should dress himself. But the smock was too clean, the breeches too well tailored, half-covered by soft leather boots, and the large straw hat, new and bright, was wasted, since there was no strong sun from which to demand protection. The rest of the people, barring one lady in similar headgear, were truly of that class, and it showed in the threadbare nature, as well as the greyness of their garments.

"Uncle William?"

Pitt pulled himself upright and turned to face Villiers, removing the hat as he did so and mopping his high brow. His thin, greying hair was made to look sparser by perspiration, but he fixed his nephew with steady blue eyes that only lacked real force due to the heavy pouches of a drinker underneath them.

"I thought you'd gone."

"I came across someone who may be of great assistance to us."

Harry was watching Pitt closely, and saw the flash of impatience that crossed his face. But he was then distracted by the woman, tall, willowy, and sharp-faced, not a beauty but pleasant enough, who had the same eyes as Pitt but with a much steelier quality.

"This is Captain Harry Ludlow."

"From Chillenden?" Pitt asked, sharply.

Harry nodded, and Villiers turned to the woman. "And this is another cousin of mine, Lady Hester Stanhope."

The curtsy was slight enough to register, without in any way being deep enough to denote respect. Harry, forced because of his wound to do no more than bow his head, noted that she wore an apron, stained with greenery and dirt, as were her hands, both signs of someone who was a serious gardener.

"We are near neighbours, sir," said Pitt, "and have been for several years. I see you are carrying a wound."

"Most of which I have spent at sea, sir," Harry replied, sticking to the first part of what Pitt had said. Discussion of his wound and how he'd been shot would not be helpful. "Had I been in residence at the same time as you, I can assure you we would have met before this."

"I have been to your house, a most elegant establishment, as the guest of your brother-in-law." He turned to the lady to explain. "Drumdryan, the fellow who works under Dundas."

She just nodded, and fixed Harry with a direct look as Pitt continued. "He has been very kind in his support for the ministry, Captain Ludlow, while making it very plain that he acts only as he thinks you would wish."

Harry didn't care how Arthur exercised the power that control of two parliamentary seats gave him as long as he had his exemptions. But it would be tactless to say so.

"I think you can count on my continuing good wishes."

Villiers cut in, talking rapidly, explaining about Harry, without once even alluding to the fact that he'd suspected him, a gabbling performance that took in Spithead, the Nore, Paris, London, and the Board of Admiralty in a confusing jumbled order. Harry was watching Pitt's face, which registered a look compounded of boredom, exasperation, and distance, which to any other speaker would have screamed uninterest. Not Villiers. He chattered on as though this was the subject dearest to his uncle's heart. But when Harry turned to glance at Lady Hester Stanhope he saw there a concentration so deep that she was mouthing some of the words her cousin was using.

"We must use any means that come to our disposal to crush these fiends," she said suddenly, her voice harsh and rather manly. "You do agree, William, don't you?"

"Of course, Hester," Pitt replied. It seemed to be without enthusiasm, but Harry wondered if it was a matter of the man's health, it being common knowledge that Pitt was not robust.

"What I need from you, uncle," said Villiers, "is permission to tell Captain Ludlow what we already know."

That cracked the studied veneer by which he'd been holding in his anger, and showed some of the steely nature which had elevated him to his present eminence, and kept him there for over a dozen years. "Know! We don't know anything."

"Precisely," Lady Hester said, pounding one grubby hand into an equally dirt-stained palm. "And it is high time we did."

"But it is plain to me, Ludlow," Pitt continued, his eyes slightly feverish, "that there are demons at work here. The men who man our ships are the salt of the earth. I cannot, and will not, believe that they would mutiny unless they were being misled into doing so."

Harry couldn't argue, even though he did wonder how a man famed for his razor-sharp mind could be so misguided as to the true nature of his sailors' feelings.

"And we have made concessions," Pitt continued, beginning to pace up and down. "Pardons, extra pay at a time when we are stretched to the limit. But I've told Spencer. No more! Not another penny piece. He may concede what he wishes, as long as it does not cost money."

"Perhaps with Captain Ludlow's help, we may uncover something," said Villiers, looking at him with an air of wonderment that was just as deep as the previous suspicion.

"There will be certain things I require," said Harry, which earned him a glare from Pitt. That was eased when he added, "At no cost to the Treasury, of course."

CHAPTER TWENTY-FIVE

HARRY noticed the difference in atmosphere within an hour of arriving in Sheerness. Home to the widely dispersed North Sea Fleet, and still a major naval station when it came to building and repair, the Nore was rarely a quiet place, even in peacetime. But noise and bustle had increased, if anything to a level greater than anything he'd witnessed at Portsmouth. More worrying, it had a darker tinge to it.

Firstly there was the presence of soldiers, two regiments of militia who'd been brought into the area by a nervous government, their rows of tents outside Queenstown a chilling reminder of what this uprising might degenerate into. More telling was the attitude of the sailors themselves. Certainly they had bands playing and red flags flying as they rowed around the anchorage or paraded through the town. Yet they seemed more intent on trouble, keener to trade insults with the locals rather than win them over to their side.

He did reason that perhaps it was the place itself. Sheerness dockyard was neat enough. Having been entirely built under the careful eye of Samuel Pepys a hundred years previously, as a defence against the Dutch, it was delightfully proportioned. But it was also stuck at the western end of the Isle of Sheppey, surrounded by low-lying country, windswept and barren, with only the hills to the south that formed the valley of the Medway, and the towns of Chatham and Rochester, breaking the monotony of marsh land, bog, and grey Thames water. Britain's premier naval station when Holland had been the chief threat, it had lost some of its glory to Portsmouth and Plymouth, more handily placed to oppose the French.

The journey hadn't helped either, and it wasn't just the flat, tedious landscape, or being rattled around with an aching back in a coach that served to depress the spirit. George Villiers was a tedious companion, a man who talked non-stop and never, ever saw any of his own actions in anything other than the most flattering light. The look in William Pitt's eyes, of patience tested to the limits, was replicated in Harry's as he was forced to listen. Villiers had clearly engineered the creation of this task for himself, the leverage of family connections overcoming his total unsuitability as a confidential agent.

Judging by the tale he was recounting, Villiers was prone to react to any rumour, however slight, dashing hither and thither with little sense of purpose, prepared to pursue the faintest wisp of smoke as though it presaged a blazing fire. Thus, a rumour that emanated from a poor source on the Isle of Wight was tracked down with great fervour just as matters were reaching a climax at the Nore, while his absolutely essential journey from Portsmouth to Plymouth, a hotbed of rebellion, managed to coincide with the moment that Sir Roger Curtis's mutinous squadron arrived in the Solent. Being in the wrong place at the wrong time was clearly his greatest talent.

"Consider that, Captain Ludlow," Villiers continued, his eyes bright with unabashed zeal, "and ask yourself if that is mere coincidence. I fear my enquiries have alarmed those who are at the centre of this conspiracy. They feel the heat of my breath upon their necks."

"Damned uncomfortable," Harry replied, wondering as he did so if his ears could take much more. And Villiers seemed convinced that Harry Ludlow now shared wholeheartedly in the belief and pursuit of his aims. Pitt had been right about knowing nothing. When asked to reveal what he had gleaned from his extended investigations, his companion had told him little he couldn't have picked up for himself, gossiping in a Portsmouth Point tavern.

Villiers rapped his cane on the roof of the coach. "Make for the

Chequers. That is where the scum have foregathered in the past."

"I wonder," said Harry, "if my servant and I could alight here?"

"Why?" Villiers replied, looking out into the busy streets of the town that had grown up around the yellowing outer wall of the dockyard.

"Secrecy," Harry answered, trying to imbue the word with as much drama as he could muster. "If, as you say, you are known, then my arriving in the same coach will alert those men to our shared mission. Go to the Chequers by all means, but do not attempt to stay there. Leave that to me."

It was too easy. That was obvious by the glow in Villiers's eyes. "That is a clever touch, Captain Ludlow. I see we think as one. By merely being here, I may flush them out. Force them to break cover."

"While I pursue the running fox. Take a room at the Flagstaff, if not there then the Tudor Arms. It would be best if we communicate through my servant, rather than meet face to face."

The speed with which that glow died, to be replaced by a look of petulance, was startling, even if it was becoming familiar. It was the look of a particularly indulged child.

"Am I to do nothing, then?"

"You will have a purpose, in carrying to Admiral Buckner that letter from your uncle."

Pitt had sent written instructions to old "Papa" Buckner, the admiral at the Nore, to provide his nephew with a craft suitable to his needs—a most nebulous request, since the purpose wasn't stated. This had allowed Harry to outline the vessel he required for his own designs, as well as encouraging Villiers in his desire not to tell Buckner face to face what it was for; this on the grounds, so dear to the agent's heart, that no one, even a vice-admiral of the white, could be trusted.

Villiers put his hand inside his cloak and fingered the letter, which he carried next to his heart, his expression now full of concern. Having been exposed to a flag officer, one who'd treated him with disdain, the prospect of bearding another was clearly worrying.

"I do hope the old man will not be difficult, like Sir Peter Parker."

"Why should he be? Buckner has ships in abundance. What he lacks is the men to sail them. You will have the pleasure of telling him that in such an area, George Villiers, without so much as a day's sea service, is more favoured. If there's a blush going it will be on his face, not yours."

The appeal to his vanity, as it had since they'd met outside Walmer Castle, didn't fail. His thin chest puffed out slightly, shaking the drop of clear fluid that seemed so much part of his nose.

"I need only, of course, remind him of who I am."

Harry patted Villiers on the arm, aware that he would have to outline the arguments this young man could use, without in any way lecturing him on the subject.

"He'd be a fool to take liberties with a man with your impeccable connections. I would not wish you to be rude to such a distinguished officer, but an allusion to the removal of his present posting may work wonders. Serving officers are prone to forget who appoints the First Lord of the Admiralty. Spencer has enough on his plate without getting into a scrape with your uncle. You must tell him you require a sloop with decent armament, that is not some hog in need of repair, and you must be firm."

The cane hit the roof again, the command to stop instantly obeyed. "Pender, Flowers, get our dunnage off the roof."

"Aye, aye, Capt'n."

Harry opened the door to alight as both men jumped down. Villiers grabbed him by his good arm to restrain him. "How shall we communicate?"

"I told you. Through Pender. And if we need to meet he will have the details of somewhere secure. A day or two here should suffice, then when my crew arrive we can take ship to look at matters elsewhere."

Villiers stuck out his hand, his chestnut-coloured eyes wide and excited. "Good luck, Captain Ludlow."

"Thank you," Harry replied, the relief he felt at getting away from Villiers passing for a shared enthusiasm. Moving stiffly, he eased his arm out from the sling and stuffed it in his pocket, feeling that it would make him too conspicuous.

"Where to, your honour?" Pender asked, having heaved Harry's sea-chest on to his shoulders.

"Anywhere," Harry replied in a soft weary voice, well covered by Villiers's cane banging on the coach roof to restart it. "Just get me away from that man."

Pender had a wicked look in his eye as he whispered his response. "Now is that the way to talk about your new friend?"

"I know my luck hasn't been of the best lately, Pender, but do you not think this must be the nadir of my fortunes?"

"I'll answer that," said Pender, more seriously, "when you get round to telling me what we're about."

Having not been separated from George Villiers since the meeting with Pitt, Harry'd had no chance to inform Pender, or to test the sudden inspiration that had assailed him outside Walmer Castle against that most necessary benchmark, a Devil's advocate. Pender, with Flowers ahead clearing a path, played that part to perfection, forcing Harry to think hard about how he was going to turn what was at best a sliver of opportunity into something that would meet his objective.

"There's not a soul born, Capt'n, who could take what you've got now and turn it into something useful. Long shots is one thing. And how the hell you're going to manage to be off the Vire Estuary when the May tide is right beats me."

Like most ideas, it had seemed easier when inspiration had struck than it did subsequently examined. But there was one thing Harry Ludlow was sure of. He had no means at present of getting a ship, and without that he was hamstrung. Even Pender agreed with that.

"Let Villiers do that one thing, Pender, and suddenly the odds will be halved."

"Move over, there!"

The shout had cleared the street. Deep in thought and conversation, they'd paid scant attention to the increasing noise of music being played behind them. Flowers had dropped back when he heard, so that the man who uttered the warning found himself faced with a trio blocking his route.

"Are you deaf, you swabs?!"

Flowers was well known for liking a scrap, and since he was only carrying a ditty-bag, he stepped forward in challenge. The man he faced, in striped trousers and a leather waistcoat, was a sailor to his fingertips. Wiry but strong, his face was weatherbeaten from years at sea, the pigtail long and intricate, sewn with coloured threads that told all who knew the navy that here was a first-rate topman.

"You mind your lip," said Flowers, his voice raised to be heard over the sound of the following band.

The topman put his hands on his hips. "That's rich, mate. You can't hardly watch yours since it seems to be somewhere under your ear."

Harry grabbed Flowers before he could throw a punch, dragging him to one side to join Pender. There was an exchange of curses that concluded when the topman told them why they were being ordered to clear the route. "It don't do to get in the way of the President of the Nore Delegates, mates. You might find yourself being trampled over."

"Happen I'd do the tramplin', friend," spat Flowers.

The topman just laughed, then hurried on to clear away any other recalcitrant folk. Pender put the sea-chest down and stood on it, so he could get a better view. Harry put one foot on it and eased his good shoulder on to the wall behind him. From that vantage point they had a good view of the approaching procession, a slightly military affair in that one man led from the front, while ranks of his companions, many of them with red and pink ribbons sewn into their hats, followed along.

The leader, a dark-complexioned fellow, with heavy black eyebrows, looked straight ahead, acknowledging neither the cheers or insults with which he was assailed. Not so his consorts, who threatened to lash out at anyone who had the temerity to disparage their cause. This was the mutiny in all its glory, and looking into the eyes of the men leading it, Harry had that first inkling of a darker purpose than anything he'd seen in the Channel Fleet.

"Who's that, mate?" Pender asked a man beneath him.

The look he got for that question was one that might have been bestowed on a village idiot, or a man from the moon.

"Where you been, mate, with your head up your arse? That there is the high and mighty President Richard Parker."

"He's not an admiral, is he?" asked Pender. "Because he shares a last name with one or two."

"No, mate. But that's not to say he don't carry on like one. They've been outside the Commissioner's house all morning, demanding this, that and the other from old Buckner." A hollow unpleasant laugh followed. "Not that it's done them a rate of good, the bastard refused to meet with them."

"President Parker," said Harry, softly.

"President, my backside," said the local man. "He's nothing but a jumped-up nobody. Hasn't been here more'n a few weeks, the cocky bastard."

The parade passed, and Harry, Pender, and Flowers fell in alongside their talkative informant. They heard that Parker had once been a midshipman, disrated for insubordination; after years of trying and failing to make a crust he had been taken up for debt, using the twenty-guinea bounty he received on joining to pay that off.

"You don't like him?" Harry asked.

"No I don't. An' I'll tell you why. You ain't got to look too far to see soldiers in this town. Nor the nose of a hound to smell. There's going to be trouble, and when it goes off, who's to say those red-coated swine will know who to shoot at, and who to leave alone?"

"How do you know so much about Parker?"

"He's the talk of the place. I'm surprised they don't post a bulletin when he goes for a piss."

Judging by the looks and growls that had greeted Parker, and were even now following in his wake, neither he nor the mutiny was popular, in stark contrast to the way the inhabitants of Portsmouth had universally supported the tars. His informant was still talking, cursing and swearing as he castigated President Parker for getting above himself.

"Did you see the look in his eye as he went past? Like he was talking to bloody God."

"Will they be going to the Chequers?"

"They will. There to drink themselves into more bravado, like working out one or two other demands to give to 'Papa' Buckner."

"Let's step out a bit," said Harry, and the trio did so, leaving their source, still mouthing imprecations, behind them.

Getting a room at the Chequers proved simple. Though the seamen were using it as shore headquarters, none actually stayed there, instead going back to their ships each night. In the main taproom someone had set up a long table, one side occupied by some dozen men, clearly the delegates. Richard Parker sat at the centre, while the other side of the table was clear.

"Looks like the Last Supper to me," said Pender.

"An unfortunate reference," Harry replied. "Especially for the man in the middle. All we need to spot is Judas."

Flowers spotted the man he'd argued with amongst the crowd close to the table, which produced a snarl. "They're an ugly bunch, an' no error."

"I need a wet," said Pender.

"Me too," Harry replied, raising his hand in a vain attempt to attract the attention of the girls serving at table. "Might be best if I go to the hatchway."

He stood up and pushed his way through the throng, knots

of men who looked at him suspiciously over their pipes and tankards. He was just about to shout an order through the hatch when the room suddenly went quiet, every voice dying, the only sound left some tuneless whistling accompanied by the playing of bones.

"Flowers," said Harry to himself, a fact which was confirmed as the crowd behind him moved enough to give him a view of the table which Pender had chosen. Every eye was on it, as one of the delegates rose and approached Flowers's back. He leant forward and spoke to him quietly, and Harry's crewman stopped his rattling abruptly. Whatever had been said induced the same reaction as had occurred in the Sheerness street. Flowers was swinging round to argue when Pender grabbed him and hauled hard enough on his arm to pull him backwards.

The voice from the table was loud, with a clear West Country burr, even though some of the words seemed to be Scottish. "Play on, laddie. And if your rhythm is any good, then we'll get a fiddler to give you a wee bit of accompaniment."

The man who'd talked to Flowers stepped back quickly, turning to grin at Richard Parker. His words followed as he made his way back to the table. "It's all right for you, Parker. But I can't hear myself think when those things are in play."

"They're fine in the company of a bit of string, man." He made an expansive gesture, and a fiddler started right away. "There you go, stranger, now give us a right good rattle."

Flowers looked set to refuse. Again it was Pender who intervened, probably to tell him that outnumbered as they were this was no place to go standing on pride. Harry used the continuing silence to order three tankards of ale, then, hooking them into his one good hand, slipped back through the crowd as the fiddler struck up. Everyone in the room it seemed was watching Flowers as he resumed his rattling on the carved bones. The flat parts cracked together, and once he'd got the crowd's attention he began bouncing them off his hands, arms, thighs, and occasionally his shoulders to produce a rhythmic background to the fiddler's tune.

"What happened there?" Harry asked when he could finally get to the table and sit down, grateful to distribute the ale. Flowers and the fiddler finished, to loud applause from Parker but a muted response from everyone else. He started to explain, until Harry stopped him by telling him that he'd seen everything. "I just wondered what he said to you."

"The second thing he told me was I could get my throat cut for letting fly with these," Flowers replied, holding up the intricately carved bones, his face angry. "What he said afore that I couldn't make out."

"What do you mean?"

"He whispered a bit in my ear, but I couldn't get what it was. Sounded foreign."

"What kind of foreign?" asked Pender.

"Difficult to say, mate. But it weren't unlike that little sod you calls Frog-spawn, when his temper is on the go."

Harry took a sip of his drink. "What happens to Derouac when he's annoyed?"

It was Pender who replied, all his dislike of the man evident in his voice. "He curses in that heathen French tongue that all those island sods use."

CHAPTER TWENTY-SIX

THE MOVEMENTS were subtle, but to men with senses acutely tuned to danger they were obvious. Without exchanging a word the trio at the table knew that their exit from the Chequers was barred. Harry sipped his ale, trying to look unconcerned while he sought to make sense of what had happened. The gathering had been upset by Flowers playing his bones. Parker, perhaps wiser than the rest of his fellow mutineers, had sought to make light of it. But others had done the opposite, reacting in a very obvious way to an event which should have passed unnoticed.

There was a genuine frisson as Harry stood up, a stiffening of limbs that spelt danger. As he sauntered towards the centre of the room, instead of the door to the street, they eased slightly. Conversation, which had become muted, continued but all eyes were on him, even if many a head was turned at an odd angle. Many of the papers strewn across the table had writing on them already, proposals perhaps that had been started and abandoned. He turned one round, grabbed a quill, and wrote quickly on the bottom. Then tearing off the piece he moved to the centre, in front of Richard Parker, and slid it across to him. He was back at the table before the President of the Delegates picked it up.

He could almost feel the men willing their leader to read what Harry had written out loud. But Parker, having looked at it, merely folded it and put it in his pocket, ignoring the anger that caused. The tension was just about to explode when the door burst open and a messenger entered, waving the paper he was carrying in an excitable way.

"A refusal, mates," he cried. "Spencer intends to post a bulletin to say that he will not meet with us."

His words acted like a match to dry tinder. Suddenly Harry, Pender, and Flowers seemed forgotten as a bitter cry burst forth from the assembled seamen. Richard Parker was on his feet, shouting to the men who'd crowded round the doorway to part and let the messenger through to the table. He, still waving his paper, was surrounded by angry, questioning faces. Eventually he reached the middle of the room, and slammed the poster he was carrying on to the table with a resounding thud.

That brought silence, which fell just as quickly as the earlier irate shouting had erupted. Parker leant forward, picked up the letter, and opening it began to read, his thick black eyebrows pressed together in concentration. Occasionally he would look up, stare at one or two faces for a second, then go back to his perusal. After what seemed an age he finished, and passed it to his nearest neighbour, his black eyes sweeping the room as he opened his mouth to speak.

"Well, shipmates," he said, "it seems that our generous offer to treat with the government has met with a refusal. We are still included in the Spithead pardon, as well as all the other articles of pay and conditions, and are even offered a dispensation of our own, for acts carried out since matters were settled at Portsmouth. But that does not extend to acts carried out subsequently."

"Shore leave?" someone yelled.

"Is denied to us, as well as a better distribution of prize money."

"Why did those bastards come down from London if'n they ain't going to talk to us, face to face?"

Parker slowly shook his head. That response set up a cacophony of noise, as suggestions rained down on the men at the table, these ranging from hanging a couple of the worst officers, to taking the ships into the Medway Estuary and bombarding Chatham. Parker had his hands out, palms down, in an effort to calm the men before him, but his gesture was having no effect whatsoever. Pender leant forward, close to Harry's ear, so that he could be heard.

"Seems to me that the tail is wagging the dog here, your honour, for all he is styled President of the Delegates."

"There's little control, that's for certain."

"Can I ask," said Flowers, and this time speaking out of the corner of his mouth was more appropriate, "what did you write to that sod?"

"Just a name, Flowers."

"Will it get us out of here whole?" asked Pender.

"We could go now, Pious," said Flowers. "They're all too busy with their laments."

Pender responded gravely. "I wouldn't try it, mate. I think if you was to attempt to get up on your pegs, you'd see that there's still a fair number who care what we do."

"Stay still, Flowers," Harry snapped, as the man looked set to test the theory.

"Whatever you say, Capt'n," he replied. Flowers sat back, and picked up his empty tankard, peering into it. Harry grinned and waved to a passing girl, ordering three refills.

"So what do we do?" asked Pender.

"We sit still, and we wait," Harry replied, the grin staying on his face so that all who cared to look could see it. He was thinking about that slow shake of the head that Richard Parker had given, again relating it to what he'd witnessed at Spithead. There the men had admirals treating with them. The First Lord had come to Portsmouth, as he had to the Nore, not of course to parley, but to be on hand so that the officers, in conclave with the delegates, could refer to him immediately the sailors' grievances. The impression here was that the mutineers had demanded more, and had been rebuffed.

The question was, did this firmness of purpose being applied at the Nore, this refusal by the Admiralty to bow to pressure and meet the Delegates in force, augur well or ill? Harry had no way of knowing. But he did suspect that not returning to their duty on the Spithead terms had put Parker and his men beyond the pale. And the whole of Sheerness seemed to be in a state of near riot, which further undermined them. At no time in Portsmouth had the delegates there allowed such loose behaviour.

Parker, all passion spent, had managed to restore some order to the meeting. He was now trying to tell the assembly that the Admiralty had issued no threats, and while they had called for the men to return to their allegiance, they had not added to that a warning of any retribution. That Admiral Buckner and the senior Nore officers like Captain Mosse were still available, willing to meet the delegates at a place of their choosing.

Each one of these statements was greeted by howls of protest, mostly cries of "Spencer" repeated like a chant. Passions were rising and the girls serving drinks were having to move swiftly to keep up with demand. It did occur to Harry, and looking at Pender it had obviously entered his head too, that they might be made victims of this outrage. But as unpleasant a prospect as that was, they were still hemmed in, and unless they wished to try and fight their way out, there was nothing that could be done about it.

"We shall respond hard, lads," Parker shouted, "and let them know that we are not cowed."

More suggestions followed, several of which suggested the removal of "Papa" Buckner's balls. Parker was yelling at the top of his voice trying to get them to pay attention, a distinct air of desperation in his behaviour.

"Take to the streets, mates. Let them hear the sound of our fifes and drums, so that Spencer in his tower, and those bullocks in their camp, know we'll not be awed by their guns. March around the town so that those who side with the oppressor can run to their masters and tell them that the mutiny holds."

"Fuck the parades," called a voice. "It's time to show 'em what's what. I say we take over them gunboats sitting in Sheerness dock."

"If you do that," Parker shouted, "you might as well send in a declaration of war."

"We need to defend ourselves," called another voice. "Don't tell me you trust those bastards, President Parker. Why, I bet this very minute they're lining up ships to come and take us over."

"No, I don't trust them. And any man that knows me will grasp that. Trust Spencer, who will see an innocent man damned rather than set up fair rules to live by? But I see no future in fighting them, and that ain't nothing to do with numbers. There's not a man here that is not loyal to King and country, willing to go out and trounce the Hollanders if they poke their noses out of the Texel. We want grievances redressed, not wholesale riot. Is there any man here who truly wants that? Us against the whole nation with the French and Dutch just waiting to sail up to the Pool of London itself?

"There's more'n one kind of tyranny, lads. But even if you think wrong the laws we are subject to, they are still adhered to by all, high or low." Parker's hand shot out, sweeping from the east to the south. "That ain't the case over yonder, where the bloody guillotine rules."

"Then how in the name of hell will we get them to talk?" asked one of the men beside the President.

Harry had been wondering how Parker had got himself the title, plus the leadership of these men. And as he spoke at least one reason emerged. He was on the defensive, yet still impressive in the way he exhorted his fellow mutineers regarding the justness of their cause. His eyes shone and he spoke with easy facility, clearly more at home with zealotry and peace-making than any kind of violent action.

"By being as brothers, that's how. There's no need for a shot or a shell in the face of common purpose. All we need do is look these men square, as equals, which in the eyes of God and humanity we are. Our cause is just, our hearts are pure and right is on our side. No man, from the highest to the lowest in the land, can stand before such a notion, and remain unmoved."

It worked, the more violent members of the group overborne by those more placidly inclined. His propositions, regarding marches and the like, repeated, were taken up with loud approval. Tankards were drained, while others were concealed under coats

to be taken along. Men began to file out of the door of the Chequers, to gather in the streets, their yells to each other loud enough
to penetrate the walls. Left inside, surrounded by these muted cries,
were Parker and half a dozen sailors, all sat on the far side of the
long table. Apart from their leader they had the demeanour of
fearful men rather than firebrands. Parker kept that zealous glow
in his eye until the last man departed, then sat down heavily, as
though exhausted. He looked across to where Harry sat, pulling
the piece of paper from his pocket to be perused. Then the President stood up, and, watched by his companions, he walked slowly
across to the trio at the table.

"Mr Parker," said Harry, standing up.

"There's cryptology in this," Parker replied, holding up the
paper.

"Pender, Flowers," said Harry, without taking his eyes off
Parker. "I think you're free to leave the table now."

Parker responded with the faintest of nods, and the two sailors
left quickly. Harry held out a hand to indicate that the President
should sit down, an offer which was declined.

"Valentine Joyce did not send you here."

"No, he didn't."

The scrap of paper was held up under Harry's nose. "Yet you
feel free to use his name."

"I cannot think he would mind."

Parker's heavy black eyebrows lowered menacingly. "That
depends on the purpose."

"It's well intentioned, as is Joyce himself."

"We've never met, but I have been so informed on more than
one occasion."

"Why did my man playing the bones cause such an upset?"

The expression changed immediately to one of bewildered
enquiry. "Who said he upset anyone?"

"Just about everyone in the room, Mr Parker, except you. I
don't think that we could have moved safely from this table while
that rabble was within these walls."

"You're dreaming."

"I'm not prone to that."

"Who are you?"

"Harry Ludlow."

"Navy?"

"Once. Now a privateer."

"Are you spying on us?"

"Would I say 'yes' if I was?" The paper was under Harry's nose again. "I met Joyce in Portsmouth, the day they had that business on the *London*. You will have heard of that."

Parker nodded. "We've spilt no blood here, to speak of, barring that from some of our own."

Harry jerked his head to the fading sound of the marching band. "How long will that continue?"

"Till the high and mighty give way."

"And what if they don't?"

Passion returned to Parker's face then. He slapped his hand on the table. "They must. Otherwise they will live to regret it. They might see blood running in rivers."

"Is that what you wish?" asked Harry gently.

"Don't be daft, man," Parker spat.

"But you might not be able to stop it?"

The President was about to respond to that with a vehement denial. But before he could speak he looked Harry in the eye, and that killed the words in his mouth. When he spoke, his passion had evaporated. "We will win."

"No doubt, Mr Parker, you feel that in your bones."

"What did Joyce tell you?" Parker asked, suddenly suspicious.

Harry was tempted to speculate, but he had no information to make even half a convincing impression, so he told the truth. By sitting down himself he forced Parker to do likewise. He explained about the Colpoys and Havergood incident, his own part in that affair, and his offer to pay for the burial.

"They had quite a fête that day," said Parker, "a long procession of mourners, but as nothing compared to the day Howe came down with the power to grant their wishes."

"You were there?"

"No. But some of our lads went down to confer. They stayed long enough to meet up with old Howe, and brought back the terms the Spithead lads had settled for."

"Ones which you have still to accept."

That brought another heavy slap to the surface of the table. "We demanded more!"

Harry was running the conversations he'd had with Villiers through his mind, a slow process since there had been so much of it. But the man's uncle was First Lord of the Treasury, the King's first minister, ultimately the person who would decide what terms he would offer to the mutineers. Pitt had said little that was encouraging and Villiers had been quite vehement that the government wouldn't budge.

The Admiralty had been undermined at Portsmouth, but they had not been humiliated, partly due to the good sense of people like Bridport. And Black Dick Howe had consented to take upon himself the opprobrium of the actual capitulation, not to save their faces, but because he thought it right and proper. But many a powerful voice had been raised calling the whole thing an error. Such people, having lost one battle, would be disinclined to lose another, and Parker and his men had played into their hands.

Those troops camped outside were not there by coincidence. They were a sign that compromise was not a consideration. It was a moot point as to whether Lord Spencer should meet with Parker and his fellow delegates. He hadn't met with Joyce. But then he hadn't been asked to. Here in the Nore he had, refusing point blank to even consider it, in a quite offensive way, from what Harry could gather. The meeting here had gone Parker's way by a narrow margin, the power of his oratory the determining factor. But if Spencer stayed obdurate, the siren voices would gain ground, and eventually they would take over the mutiny. Added together, what he knew and what he suspected presaged not a harmonious meeting of minds, rather bloodshed on a grand scale.

Harry moved his shoulder slightly, to ease the dull ache. "Mr Parker, would it anger you if I gave you some advice?"

For the first time the President smiled, and it made quite a difference to Harry's impression of him. The habitual frown made him look ill-tempered by nature. The opposite showed that behind that was a warmer creature, one to whom men might have responded naturally, without being swayed by the power of his speech.

"I have to take the advice of every man at the Nore, from Admiral Buckner down to the meanest ship's boy. I cannot, in conscience, deny you the same right."

Harry hesitated, aware that he had to be careful. He couldn't just tell Parker that less than twenty-four hours before he'd been in the company of Billy Pitt, nor that the Prime Minister's nephew was here in Sheerness, determined to prove that there was a Jacobin conspiracy at the root of all the trouble. Parker's smile had slipped a little as he picked up the confusion in Harry's manner.

"I'm sorry, Parker. I'm not quite sure where to begin."

The smile returned in even greater strength. "Then that separates you from the mass, and no mistake. It seems that every man I meet knows the beginning, middle, and end of everything."

"You will lose here." Parker sat back abruptly, his face shocked, as Harry continued. "Everything that could be won was gained at Spithead. The Admiralty got a bloody nose there. They'll not stand to take another."

"You speak with an air of authority, sir."

"If I do, it is because of my personal certainty, not any inside information about the workings of the Admiralty mind. There are soldiers here, and too few ships to threaten the security of the nation."

"We sit across the throat of London!"

"That is the worst card you can play, Mr Parker. Hardly a voice in the country was raised against the Channel Fleet mutiny. The mass of the populace supported it not only because it was just, but because they knew that the least sniff of a Frenchman poking his nose out of Brest would have seen the fleet back at sea. That, for all your protestations of loyalty to the King, has not been promulgated here. Instead you threaten London. That smacks not of righteous mutiny, but of revolution, and you will find yourselves tarred as Jacobins if you attempt it."

"There are no Jacobins here," Parker barked, so loud that the others in the room, still at the long table, who'd been studiously avoiding looking in their direction, were forced to do so.

"There are those who will not believe that," Harry responded quietly. "And if you're not wary you will by your actions hand them the right to brand you so and be believed. You must look for another avenue to pursue redress, and bring what is happening here to an end."

"Me?" said Parker, suddenly weary.

"Who else?"

That produced a bitter laugh. "You overrate my powers."

"If you, Mr Parker, and the people at the table, do not control this mutiny, who does? How will you convince the outside world that there is no conspiracy?"

Suddenly Parker was alert again, and wary. "How do I know that you are who you say? You could be a government spy, sent to sow the seeds of disunity amongst us."

"I could be, but I'm not."

"And how, pray, can I be certain of that?"

"If you wish, you may communicate with Valentine Joyce. I think he would be willing to vouch for me."

"That's an easy thing to say, Mr Ludlow," Richard Parker replied, his habitual frown now firmly back in place, "but not so easy to do."

"Why not?"

"The Channel Fleet weighed for Brest, and is at sea as we speak. And that fact was known to everyone who had any contact with the Admiralty telegraph."

CHAPTER TWENTY-SEVEN

"WELL, Mr Villiers, a man would not have to be a charitable soul to say, without fear of contradiction, that you've excelled yourself."

As Harry said these words, Pender was standing, hands on hips, a look of utter disbelief on his face. Flowers had turned away to look across the great estuary of the Thames towards Essex, so that his captain would not see him laughing. The ship lying by the quay at Faversham, which went by the name of the *Good Intent,* was the cause of this hidden mirth.

"I was firm with Buckner," Villiers replied, as usual completely missing the fact that Harry was being ironic, almost unbelievable given the expression on his face. "He tried to fob me off, but I said that I would sit in his office until Doomsday unless he complied with my uncle's request."

"And this is the result?"

Villiers must have picked up some of the displeasure Harry felt in the way that was said. For once his voice lacked that irritating tone of complete certainty.

"You said you required a sloop, victualled and armed. Admiral Buckner was most careful, once he realized my station, to quiz me regarding the vessel I needed. I demanded no more, nor no less, than what you asked for."

The temptation to shout at him, to call him a fool, was almost irresistible, yet it had to be smothered: Buckner must have realized after one or two simple questions that Villiers knew nothing at all about ships. He certainly had no notion of the naval habit of calling anything that couldn't be classified in any other category as a sloop, this so that they could be rated as King's ships and given to young officers as their first command.

Fore-and-aft rigged, with a square topsail, she was shaped something like an old-fashioned Dutch *boier,* a short-haul merchant vessel, with the foremast stepped well forward and the mizzen poking out of the poop. She was elderly, but well maintained, cared for by a couple of retired seamen, who through boredom or application had kept the well dry, the ship painted, her deck planking clean, with ropes and rigging taut and all the blocks properly greased, waiting for the day when some youngster, well connected and on a fast route to promotion, would be allotted the hull as a step on his road to high rank. Every admiral with a shore posting had vessels like this, part of the patronage they could bestow on the offspring of people of influence, extracting a high price for the act, since the men put in command of them were never ever to be exposed to danger. Rumour had it that some of them never even took their vessels to sea.

The armament consisted of six 4-pounder cannon, old well-worn guns that would probably roll out the ball if depressed to fire low, the top of their touch-holes worn into saucers by decades of use. Broad in the beam, *Good Intent* looked seaworthy enough for a pleasant day's cruising in estuary waters, but Harry guessed that in the open sea, in any kind of swell, she would wallow like the devil, threatening to tip out her masts by the extent of her pitch and roll. She'd float in storm weather, but with a degree of discomfort that would churn the steadiest stomach. And as a fighting vessel, *Good Intent* would fall victim to any half-determined midshipman in a leaking, armed cutter.

But what could he say to Villiers? The strain that his face was being forced to bear in this exercise in self-control was acute, his jaw so taut that it was actually trembling. He'd seen the youngster react to criticism already, and the thought of inflicting more was not inspiring. In fact, Villiers was so petulant that any hint that he'd been practised on by Buckner would infuriate him. Not enough to send him back to the admiral's chambers to complain. Instead he'd probably stalk off in a huff, a prospect Harry could not yet be sure was welcome.

"I thought you said your luck was set to change, Capt'n."

"Clearly, Pender, the road to hell is paved with good intent," Harry replied quietly as, followed by his two sailors, he strode down the gangplank. One of the elderly seamen, who'd been working forward at splicing some rope, stood up as they came on deck, walking forward with a belligerent look in his eye.

"I don't see no sign saying we're receiving," he said.

Harry was about to be emollient, not yet knowing if he was going to sail this vessel out of Faversham or leave it, and the man who'd acquired it, here to rot. If he decided to take it to sea, the old tar could be a useful ally. All ships had a personality, even this one, and this caretaker sailor would know all about the *Good Intent*'s ways, how she handled, and if she possessed any good points of sailing, what they were. But none of those considerations applied to Villiers, who stopped on the gangplank and adopted a haughty expression.

"Mind your tongue, man."

Harry saw the old sailor roll the piece of rope he was holding round his gnarled fist, the look in his eye leaving no doubt that he intended to use it as a whip. As he knotted his fists, ready to retaliate, he felt a sharp stab of pain across his upper back. "Did Admiral Buckner send anyone down to advise you?" he asked.

"No, he did not."

"Then that is a pity."

"Come, Captain Ludlow," Villiers called, "we are not about to spend our time arguing with this lowly creature, are we? He must quit the ship forthwith."

Pender stepped forward smartly as the hand went back, and got too close for the old man to take a swing. "Pay no heed to him. We are here for the ship, with written orders."

"What good are written orders to a man who lacks reading?"

"It's a damn sight better than a clip on the ear, which is what you'll get if you lift that rope."

"Ahoy, there!"

Everyone aboard turned in reaction to the shout, to see an almost comically theatrical figure heading along the quay. He was as broad as he was tall, with one leg which when walking exaggerated his rolling gait. Cheery and red-faced, and buttoned up in a uniform coat that dated from the American war, he looked like the living model for a Staffordshire jug.

"Lieutenant Aherne," he cried, waving a set of papers above his head. "Which one of you is Mr Villiers?"

"I am."

He'd reached the gangplank by then. "Then I have here the documents handing the ship over to you, which will, of course, have to be signed."

Harry turned to the old sailor, who'd now been joined by his fellow caretaker. Both looked very peeved indeed, hardly surprising since the arrival of Aherne meant that their cosy livelihood was about to evaporate.

"May we be allowed use of the cabin?"

"Don't see no purpose in refusing," the newcomer growled. "But I hope you have it in mind to see to those that will find themselves deprived."

Pender leant forward, pressing some tobacco into a waiting hand. "See that young fellow, old 'un, on the gangplank. If'n you tell him he needs to pay you to get off the ship, he won't know if you're right or wrong."

Age might have affected their limbs, but it had no effect whatever on their wits. Palming the tobacco, they slipped past Pender, Harry, and Flowers and were grovelling to Villiers before five seconds had elapsed. A double act, one took up speaking as the other left off. There was much about being tired after a journey, and being in need of both a seat and a wet. Villiers was gently pulled on to the deck and ushered towards the cabin door as if he was visiting royalty.

The formalities were swift, and to Harry's mind entirely satisfactory. Villiers was signing for the *Good Intent*, not him, which was just as well given the caveats that Buckner's clerks had inserted, which meant that any stores consumed would be replaced at premium rates, while any damage sustained to hull or rigging was to be put right at the lessee's expense, the work undertaken by a shipwright of the admiral's choosing. Cheery-faced Aherne was just the fellow to sell this to a man like Villiers. He'd spotted Harry for a sailor right away, and tried very hard to exclude him from the arrangements. Villiers, showing more sense than usual, had sought his advice, though he'd been careful to couch his request in the terms of a precautionary second opinion.

Harry read the documents transferring the ship with the same care he would have used if his own signature was required. Not that he would have obliged, since he knew too much about the ways of admirals to fall for such a trap. Buckner was prevaricating, giving in to Villiers with the wrong ship on usurious terms, expecting a flat refusal followed by a long gavotte in which each side negotiated for the proper kind of ship until either Villiers gave up or the admiral ran out of excuses.

Aherne was watching him closely. Harry suspected the man, a half-pay officer who had guile in abundance behind that rosy round face, was wondering why he hadn't thrown the document back at him, half read. But Harry was caught on the horns of a dilemma. With all the variables in what he was trying to achieve there was one absolute, and that was the timing of the May tides on the River Vire. Not that the *Good Intent* needed deep water. It was the ships he wanted to take that required water under the keel to get downriver to the sea.

Harry smiled to himself, an act which had Aherne leaning forward ready to counter his objections. But the amusement was internal, as he conjured up an image of himself leading his men against Tressoir in such a vessel. What had happened to *Bucephalas* would pale by comparison to the drubbing he'd receive in this tub. In fact, the very idea was risible. But against that, *Good Intent* was a bird in the hand. He didn't know Buckner. But the old admiral was probably a dab hand at procrastination, well able to string out matters for a month. And that was a period of grace that Harry simply didn't have.

"I think this is very fair, Mr Villiers," he said suddenly.

Aherne covered his surprise with a loud cough, using that as an excuse to turn his head away. By the time he looked back he had reddened even more, but the expression was fish-faced, one of bland acceptance that all was well with the world. Harry looked him right in the eye, wanting the old lieutenant to know that he was aware of what was afoot; that poor Villiers would probably never be free of the trouble engendered by signing these transfer papers. By the time Buckner was finished enforcing the clauses of this agreement, Villiers and his uncle would have provided the admiral with enough funds to build and victual a crack frigate.

"I thought so myself, of course, Captain Ludlow," said Villiers, confidently, "but it is a fool who does not ask for an unbiased endorsement from someone professionally qualified."

Aherne had to struggle then to keep his face straight, and as the young man bent to write his signature, Harry gave him a long slow wink. That brought, from the recipient, a sudden burst of haste as he gathered up the papers, a desire to be out of the way, signature appended before such good fortune was withdrawn.

"Gentlemen, I bid you good day," he said, before rushing out of the cabin, his wooden peg stomping heavily as he sought to move with the required speed.

"Well, Captain Ludlow," Villiers exclaimed, "we have done a good day's work here, have we not? We are in possession of a fine ship, and . . ."

The young man stopped, hands in the air, since he had no actual notion of what exactly to say next. He had a ship without a crew, and no real knowledge of what purpose it was to serve. Harry had been deliberately vague about that, hinting mightily that it was essential without actually underlining the reasons.

"We must make haste, sir," said Harry, leaning forward. "Time, tide, and conspiracy wait for no man."

"Of course," Villiers replied, without the least understanding of why he was agreeing.

"I told you that a sailor would see things a landsman would miss."

Villiers suddenly looked very eager. "You did indeed, Captain. Am I to understand that you have found something out?"

"I spoke with William Parker."

"You did what?" the young man demanded, his colour rising. "You actually had words with that seditious scoundrel?"

Harry, well aware that he was playing a deep game with Villiers, was nevertheless totally nonplussed by that response.

"How else am I to find out what is going on?"

"What if your suspicions are disclosed, sir? The whole nature of my enquiries could be put at risk."

There was no dealing with Villiers's idiocy. It was as if the conversation they'd had that morning had never taken place. But to remind him of that was unwise. Better for Harry's purposes to continue to humour him, and weave a conspiratorial web that would have him operating, not at his own whim, but at that of the man he was talking to.

"What did Admiral Buckner have to say in that regard?"

"He agreed with my conclusions, of course," replied Villiers dismissively. "Which was gratifying. I think it was that argument, and the way I said we were going to lay the culprits by the heels, that made him so malleable in the matter of the ship. Certainly Lord Spencer was for the case. He actually said we'd be the saviours of the nation."

"We?!" Harry demanded, while on another plane he wondered about the tone in which Spencer had said it. "Did you mention my name?"

"No!" snapped Villiers unconvincingly. Then, like Harry, faced with a difficulty, he abruptly changed the subject. "What did you glean from Parker?"

Harry had been thinking about this ever since Pender had returned to the Chequers with "orders" to proceed to Faversham.

Being away from the Nore before Harry, did Villiers know what had happened that afternoon? If he didn't then Harry should tell him, but that risked an outburst of indignation and an immediate return to the rapidly deteriorating seat of the mutiny.

Despite Parker's pleading, the men who'd set out to parade had failed to control the more ardent spirits in their midst. The gunboats in Sheerness harbour had been seized, and as Harry had left, he'd seen them, and the ships that the mutineers controlled, being manoeuvred into a wide defensive arc that would prove difficult to breach. Sitting in the Chequers, he'd also observed the effect of this act on Parker and his fellow delegates, the despair that such behaviour had engendered.

That was deepened as more and more news came in. Several ships were lukewarm in their adherence to the cause, most notably the *San Fiorenzo* and the *Clyde*. They were still flying white flags instead of red, and the impression Harry had was that they would have severed their support if they hadn't been under the guns of several 100-gunners, most noticeably Parker's ship, the *Sandwich*, plus the vessel of a fiery delegate called Gregory, the *Inflexible*.

The President, after a further doleful talk with Harry, had gone off on his own to plead with Spencer for an interview, partly to warn the First Lord that a failure to treat the mutineers as human beings was dangerous, and secondly to plead for a swift acknowledgement of some grievance so that the delegates would have a lever to persuade the waverers to return to their duty. Despite the peremptory nature of Villiers's demand that he join him, Harry had waited till Parker returned, dejected, having been ignored by both Spencer and Buckner, both of whom had, as soon as he left, withdrawn to Rochester for their own safety.

Parker's parting words to Harry had stayed with him, as the downcast delegates prepared themselves to be rowed back to ships in which they would not be entirely welcome.

"We will not be done down by this, Mr Ludlow. We will bring these people to their senses, and see this action succeed, you mark my word."

Harry had smiled at him, thinking him wrong but within limits hoping he was right. He couldn't help comparing him to his namesake, the Sir William Parker who was Tressoir's enforced guest. And in the balance he placed the mutineer well above that pompous oaf.

Not to tell Villiers all this was dangerous, since he was bound to find out about the events that had taken place, if not Parker's reaction to them. Added to that there was a trace of guilt, a feeling that he should stay in Sheerness and try to help. It was Pender, sensing the mood, who'd scotched that idea, pointing out to his captain in no uncertain terms that the only thing they could possibly achieve at the Nore was trouble for themselves. No thanks at all if the men returned to their duty, or a share of the ropes that would be liberally used if this mutiny was put down.

Villiers was looking at him, impatiently waiting for him to respond. Harry apologized, which cleared his mind for the sudden inspiration that followed. "I was gathering my thoughts, indeed getting ready to offer you an apology."

"What for?"

"I blush to recall to you our first meeting in Portsmouth." It was Villiers's face that went red at the memory. "You were then in pursuit of Valentine Joyce."

"Him and the rest of his rogues."

"And I, foolishly, told you that you were wrong."

"And you're now about to inform me that I was right all along?"

Harry tutted slightly, and shrugged his shoulders. "Not in a way that would please a judge."

"That is not what we require."

"Parker said certain things when I mentioned Joyce that made me think we might build a case."

"What things?"

"Hints, only." Harry could see impatience building in Villiers and moved to head it off. "You see, Parker thinks himself a very clever fellow. But sitting before him, I wondered what questions you would put to him, and whether in answering them he would be as sharp as he thought."

"He's not, is he?" said Villiers eagerly.

"No. But then neither is he entirely a fool. That is why I use the word 'hints.' You must agree that if there is a conspiracy . . ."

"We have agreed that!"

Harry carried on as if he hadn't been interrupted. "Then there has to be some form of communication between Spithead and the Nore."

"Go on."

"Well, Mr Villiers, I think if we can establish that, we will be halfway to determining the whole nature of the web that joins them."

"This is all very misleading, Captain Ludlow."

Harry smiled. "Only because I have not yet had a chance to put the suspicions Parker raised in my mind as questions to Valentine Joyce."

Villiers wasn't slow to see the implications. In effect he would be sidelined. "I think I should put the questions, don't you?"

"Let me talk to him first, then you will be able to do that very thing, armed with enough to break his resolve."

"There's only one problem, Captain Ludlow. Unless I'm very much mistaken he's at sea. Admiral Buckner told me, in passing, that the Channel Fleet weighed for Brest this morning."

"Then that is where we must go," replied Harry with a grin, leaning over to slap the bulkhead, "and due to your good efforts here we have the very vessel."

CHAPTER TWENTY-EIGHT

"I'D BE a mite happier, Capt'n, if you told me what it is you have in mind."

Harry turned slowly, to favour his back, and to ensure that Villiers had not returned. But he was still below, trying and failing to overcome a severe bout of seasickness, which given they were still well inside the Thames Estuary indicated his capacities as a sailor.

Pender's question, and his use of "happier," brought home to Harry just how dejected he was. Compared to *Bucephalas* the *Good Intent* was a dog, the idea that it might exhilarate risible. The anticipation he'd had so often at sea was entirely absent. Perhaps if James had been here, ready to exercise his savage wit on Villiers or on the boat, he'd have helped to lift Harry's spirits. But he wasn't, and the boredom of conning this vessel, slow and crank, allowed him to indulge in a depressing feast of unhappy memories.

On the forecastle, Flowers and the two elderly caretakers, having trimmed the sails the way Harry wanted them, were talking over old times. Adding to Harry's annoyance, all three had a proficiency at playing the bones, each taking it in turn, discussing, as if it were a science, the best way to grip them so as to produce the sharpest and most rhythmic crack. Animal bones were being compared with great fish bones, one of the oldsters loudly adamant that there was nothing better for the task than the jaw of a decent-sized shark.

The *Good Intent* was crawling along, bows pitching into every little trough, under courses only, as she tacked into a gentle east wind. Having sailed these waters as a youth, taking soundings in the decked longboat belonging to his father's ship, Harry had no need of an estuary pilot. But he did have need of some speed. They'd left Faversham at dawn, and here they were, midway through the afternoon, off the port of Whitstable, the long shallow bay full of the tiny boats of the oyster fishers.

"What I have in mind?" Harry replied eventually. "I wish I knew, Pender. I know what I want to do, but it's very much one step at a time. Let's just get to the Downs first."

"A bit more aloft wouldn't hurt," Pender moaned.

The two old sailors who looked after the ship had jumped at the chance to stay aboard for the trip round the North Foreland to Deal, ribbing each other about how they'd use the money Villiers had offered to create merry hell in a town famous for the level of available debauchery. Conversationally, both men had shed their years, and returned to the creatures they once were, deepwater tars desperate to get ashore and take their pleasures. But that didn't apply to their ability to get aloft and set sail, or haul heartily on a rope, which meant a limit to what Harry, Pender, and Flowers could do.

"I just hope you're not planning to try and take back our ship in this."

"It's all we've got," Harry sighed.

"Christ, Capt'n," Pender spluttered, looking to the gods for support, "is this one you get a chance to volunteer for?"

Harry laughed, expecting that if he went Pender would be right behind him. It wasn't something he thought he deserved, but it helped to lift some of the gloom which had overcome him since he'd guyed Villiers.

"Strikes me," Pender continued, suddenly serious, "if we can't surprise that Tressoir bastard we'll get a hiding anyway. And that can only be done by getting up the river faster than the news that we're about. In this thing they'll know in Paris."

"Any suggestions you have will be most welcome."

"And what are we goin' to do about him down below? He's
not about to take kindly to a cutting-out venture when he thinks
we're going after the Channel Fleet."

Pender was about to continue when he caught the expression
on Harry's face, that look in his captain's eye denoting that the
brain was at work. He stayed quiet when Harry started speaking,
aware that he was thinking out loud.

"You said it and you're right. We have to get upriver before
he knows we're there, preferably when he doesn't think we're coming. How would you defend against that? A lookout on St. Aubin
means that no warship can get close enough to the estuary in clear
weather without Tressoir being warned, even in foul weather. He'll
have a positive age to get ready to defend against them at Isigny."

"Not that sod, your honour," Pender snapped, not caring if
he was breaking Harry's train of thought. "He'll have something
well before, a surprise set before you get anywhere near our ship.
He out-thought you the last time and you've got to guard against
him doing the very same thing again."

"Which means, Pender, we have to conjure up a surprise for
him, instead of him landing one on us."

"Well, if we arrive in the *Good Intent* he'll be so surprised
he's like to faint."

Harry grinned, although there had been little humour in Pender's remark. "That's right. What he won't do is feel threatened."

"No," Pender replied, giving his captain a hard look. "That
will be me!"

"Take the wheel," said Harry softly.

When Pender obliged he went to the rail and started to pace
up and down, head on his chest. No great distance was covered
in this, since none was available. Every time a change of tack was
needed he joined Flowers and Pender, leaving one of the two caretakers on the wheel. But as soon as the task was complete, he
resumed his pacing. As the tide began to ebb, so the *Good Intent*
found a bit more speed.

In some senses, he could hardly have been on a better river

to indulge such thoughts. Though the Thames was huge compared to the River Vire, the tidal nature was very similar, with the fresh water flowing from inland, denied easy egress, rising and falling well over twelve feet even upstream of London Bridge. The Vire, and its tributary, the Aure, would enjoy the same effect. The brig sailed on past Herne Bay and Margate, with Harry only surfacing from his musings when they were abreast of Foreness Point.

They altered course, and retrimmed the sails to take the wind on her larboard quarter, sailed south-west past Ramsgate Roads, then luffed up to run through the Brake channel between the white cliffs and the northern point of the Goodwin Sands. Pender was watching Harry carefully. He knew him very well indeed, and reckoned he could rate the progress of the scheming that was going on by the number of lines on his captain's forehead. It was with mixed feelings that he saw them clear, until by the time they entered the Deal roadstead Harry Ludlow was smiling, with not a crease to be seen on his brow.

"So, Capt'n. What's the answer?"

"You provided the clue, Pender, when you said that we had to get upriver before he knew we're about."

"And how do we do that?"

"Centipedes," Harry replied.

"What the hell are they?"

"Something our good friend Tressoir will not have taken precautions against." Harry lifted his head to look at the great anchorage, ten miles of tethered ships. "They only exist in one part of the world, friend. And as luck would have it, we are at this very moment sailing right into it."

Pitt had left Walmer Castle to return to London, but Lady Hester Stanhope was still in residence, engaged, as she continued to be while inviting them to dinner, in her task of turning the draughty castle into a decent home, and the gardens into something that would complement it as a residence.

"My cousin receives no income from the Cinque Ports sinecure," she said, her annoyance clear on her face. "So all the funds he is expending are his own."

"Quite a burden," Harry replied. It was well known that Pitt wasn't wealthy, a source of amazement to the honest and amusement to his more venal contemporaries. But that was a family trait. His father had cemented his reputation as the "Great Commoner" by his refusal to act like his contemporaries and milk the public purse. "And I shall not add to that by the need to feed me," he continued. "I fear I must decline your kind invitation. My men will be aboard by now, but there is a great deal to do in the way of loading stores and water. Matters are at such a stand in the nation's affairs that we must make what haste we can."

Villiers cut in, pleading hunger. The green colour he'd had at sea was completely gone, and he was clearly attracted to the idea that he might get a chance to restore to his stomach all the contents it had so unceremoniously chucked through the scuttle. For once Harry was quite brusque, guessing that the lady before him was made of sterner stuff. The words she responded with proved that assumption to be correct.

"How right you are, Captain Ludlow. The needs of the nation must take precedence."

Seeing the crestfallen look on Villiers's face, Harry relented a touch, but soon realized that it was for his own selfish reasons. Pender and Flowers had set out to find crew replacements. He needed time to check that they were numerous and of the right sort: he wanted men who'd been in a man-of-war at some time in their lives, preferably those who were bored by life in the merchant service. There was no actual shortage of hands, this being the place where merchant vessels took on and dropped off their deep-sea crews. Only the minimum of men necessary were taken into the River Thames, awash as it was with prize crews trawling for experienced seamen.

The question remained, would they sail with Harry Ludlow? Because of his need for centipedes, locals had to be avoided, which was a pity, since Harry had always enjoyed a high reputation amongst the Deal seafarers. He longed to know how much his recent losses had dented that standing. His assertion when insisting on itinerants, that only the addled-brained would be willing to serve with him now, brought forth a frown from Pender and laughter from Flowers, the latter at least keen to convince him that recruitment would be easy.

Both men would gild the lily, of course, and recruit on a promise of easy wealth just waiting to be plucked from a Frenchman's grasp, and that under a captain who'd enjoyed great success in the past. The truth, that his luck was fickle, that they'd need exceptionally good fortune, and that men often died in pursuit of riches, would be glossed over. Thankfully, sailors were generally fatalistic types, from their calling prone to sudden expiry from weather and disease, so they were almost to a man easily tempted into adventure.

That seen to, he must make some calls, visits which of necessity Villiers could not share. Leaving him here would satisfy both the gnawing of the young man's stomach and his own need for time free from his gaze.

"That is not anything that need occupy you, Mr Villiers. We shall work through the hours of darkness so that we may weigh at first light. It would be better for our cause if that sharp brain of yours was granted a good night's sleep, something you are unlikely to achieve in a ship taking on provisions."

Gratitude shone from Villiers's face. He hadn't enjoyed their little cruise from Faversham, and even if the *Good Intent* was now at a mooring and relatively stable, he couldn't get aboard without an uncomfortable trip across the anchorage in an open boat, which would without doubt return him to his previous bilious condition.

"I expect to see you by the Admiralty jetty at dawn."

"I shall be there, Captain Ludlow, never fear."

His recruiting officers were as good as their word, and when Harry came back aboard it was to a vessel crowded with over forty men.

The survivors from *Bucephalas* were there, too ashamed of the ship they now sailed to lord it over the two dozen new-comers. But that included three men who'd been wounded, and their keenness to serve after the fiasco in the waters off Normandy cheered him up.

He spoke to each new hand in turn, rejecting the services of four, who lied about navy service or failed to answer his questions in a straightforward manner. There was no room for shiftiness on this trip. He needed men who would obey him absolutely, and blend in easily with the existing crew.

"We've got them here, Capt'n," said Pender, when he came back on deck. "The question is, do we know we'll ever need 'em?"

"I hope we will," Harry replied, going back over the side to his waiting boat. "Anyway, I'll know soon."

"When?"

"The very next time you see me."

Naomi Smith gave Harry a direct look that made him feel very uncomfortable. She had a habit of pushing her cheek out with her tongue before she said something that might be disturbing. Even that could not spoil her looks: slightly pale, cornflower-blue eyes and even features.

"I wondered when I heard you'd returned if you'd bother to call."

Harry had felt distinctly odd since he'd come through the door of the Griffin's Head, as if he was visiting a place that only still existed in his dreams. Sitting opposite Naomi had only added to that. Now, as he heard her utter those words, he was very close to blushing. Having been his lover for years, she knew him too well. He was sure that she would see in his eyes the truth; that only a need of the most desperate kind could have brought him to this place.

"Your brother James came in to tell me you'd had some troubles. How is the wound?"

"Improving by the hour."

"He also hinted that my lease might be mortgaged. Consider-

ing that you were at Cheyne Court on your own, recuperating, I
had expected you to tell me the rights and wrongs of that yourself."

"I'm afraid it has. So has the house. In fact, everything I own.
I'm not the man of parts I once was."

She smiled, the tongue poking her cheek again. "You don't
need money to be a man of parts, Harry Ludlow."

There was a slightly unreal quality in this, talking as a near
stranger to someone with whom you'd been intimate. Harry was
normally the kind of man to avoid entanglements, the life he led
precluding such things. Naomi, a widow and a tenant, had fulfilled a need for several years, seemingly happy in a relationship
that left both parties free from strain. That had come to an end
under the pressure of events, and this was the first real conversation he'd had with her since that parting. Added to that, he had
no idea how much James had told her about his troubles. He
decided that if she didn't mention Hyacinthe Feraud neither would
he, to avoid the need to explain himself, and for the misery explanations would induce.

"That's a very kind thing to say."

She leant across and laid a hand over his, an act which
didn't pass unnoticed by the other taproom customers. "I bear you
no ill will, Harry, I hope you know that."

Something in her eyes made her statement suspect, and Harry
realized that intimacy was a two-way thing, that he knew her just
as well as she knew him. Not that he thought she bore him a
grudge. But he did feel that there was something more behind the
words, something she wanted to say but couldn't.

"I've come to ask you for a favour."

"Then perhaps if I can grant it, you will oblige me with a
favour of your own."

"Which would be?"

Naomi hesitated, clearly debating if she should speak, or force
Harry to do so. "I wondered why, if you needed money, you
didn't offer me the Griffin's Head."

"That would have been a permanent loss to me. Did James not tell you? My problems are temporary. Once I have cashed in my American investments, I intend to pay off all my loans."

James obviously hadn't told her, judging by the look of disappointment that crossed her face. But she composed herself quickly, and looked him directly in the eye.

"What favour is it that you are after?"

"Centipedes."

She was shocked enough to sit back sharply, but sensible enough to keep her voice low. "What makes you think that's something I have in my gift?"

"You're a beautiful woman, Naomi, and that means people notice you. They also talk, and while I'm not one to take cognizance of everything I hear, neither do I shut my ears to what might be on the edge of credibility."

"I don't have any centipedes, Harry, whatever you've heard."

She was involved in smuggling, but to what degree he didn't really know. In this part of the world it was an industry not an occasional indulgence, and as the owner of an inn on one of the routes to Canterbury and London she knew everybody who mattered.

"No. But I dare say you know where they are kept hidden."

Her first instinct was denial, but the words died in her throat when she saw Harry's smile. There was no use pretending to him. He knew better. Her own late husband had been a smuggler. He would know she had spirits in her cellar and cloth in her loft that had come ashore without being taxed. And how many meetings had taken place in this very room at which scarce luxury goods had been ordered by the London vendors, cut off by the war from their French suppliers?

There were dozens of vessels engaged in the trade. But the supreme vessel of the smuggling art, so successful they were actually banned by the authorities, was the centipede, a 24-oared rowing galley so fast that it could make the journey to the French coast, on a calm night, in just over two hours. They were particularly prized for carrying gold, which was worth twice as much in France as it was in England. One trip could net a fortune, as long as the men making it could get in past the excise the contraband their gold had purchased.

"I don't suppose there's much point in my asking why you want them?"

"None," Harry replied, kindly.

"I know who has the use of them, if the name will help."

"It won't. I want the boats, and I doubt the people who own them would be willing to lend them out."

"You could offer to buy them, pay the money to build new ones."

"I don't have the means. So I will need to borrow them."

"That could get you killed, Harry," she said anxiously.

"A chance I'm prepared to take." It was Harry's turn to lay his hand on hers, which added knowing nods to the expressions of the curious onlookers. "And you have nothing to fear, Naomi. Who would ever guess that I would come here, to see you, in order to ask you that?"

"My lease?"

"The freehold of the Griffin's Head will be my gift to you, with access to the road, if the task for which I want the boats is successful."

There were no guards on the Church of St Leonard's, Upper Deal, even though the boats, judged to be priceless for what they could achieve, lay inside. For those who knew the location, the local smugglers, were in the main to be respected. If they couldn't command respect they worked through fear and intimidation, practising on the local excisemen as well as the populace. The Cinque Ports magistrates, blood relatives or business associates, needed no such strictures: unless the government engaged in one of its periodic crackdowns they represented the law, so the smugglers operated with near impunity.

But precautions still had to be taken. So the galleys, wide

enough for two men to sit together, and with a low freeboard, were stood upright behind giant decorated screens at the back of the church, their twenty-four oars lashed inside. Entering the building proved no problem to Pender, but moving the screens silently was really difficult. The smugglers had to get the boats down, out, and into the water in record time, and the double doors of the church, why they were there in the first place, worked in Harry's favour. The local clergy were carefully chosen souls content to take unexcised brandy as a reward for their cooperation, and they would turn a blind eye to such activities.

The street outside was wide enough to swing the boats round, and the road to Deal proper, dotted with silent red-brick farmhouses, presented no difficulty. Likewise the alleys they chose that led to the sea were amongst the broadest in the town. With two dozen men on each, they ran through them, which caused no surprise since it was, if not commonplace, not astonishing. On the shingle they tipped the boats on to their keels and ran them down into the water, the men jumping into them as soon as they floated and grabbing the oars to propel them out to sea.

The *Good Intent* was at single anchor, sails loosely furled ready to be dropped. The centipedes were lashed to each other then tied on to the boat davits, as the majority of Harry's scratch crew worked frantically on the capstan to get her over the anchor. Harry was at the gangway, handing the two caretakers a letter, and pressing enough coins into their hands to mollify them, urging them into the jolly boat.

"I don't care how much you drink tonight, or how many whores you try to bed. But be at the Admiralty jetty at first light. Mr Villiers will be there. Give him this."

"This is extra labour," said one.

"Worth more than the money he promised us," added the other.

"Take my word for it. When he reads the letter, he'll shower you with gold coins."

"Anchor's aweigh, your honour," said Pender, softly.

Harry's push was gentle, but still enough to persuade the two old sailors he was serious. Grumbling for the sake of appearances they obliged him, and by the time they'd got their oars in the rowlocks and turned towards the long strand of shingle beach the anchor was clear of the water, catted, and fished, and the *Good Intent* had dropped her sails to take the wind.

"Just what did you put in that letter, your honour?"

"I told Villiers that he would expire from seasickness if he spent too much time in a ship."

"You could have the right of it there," Pender replied, with a shake of the head. "But he's still not going to be pleased."

"But I've left him a worthy task to perform."

"What's that?"

"You know that Billy Pitt burnt all the boats on Deal beach a few years back."

"He hates a smuggler and that's no error."

"Well, I told him he could ingratiate himself with his uncle in our absence if he was to launch a thorough search of the town of Deal for banned smuggling boats known as centipedes. I've told him to pay particular attention to St Leonard's Church, in Upper Deal."

"That's goin' to please him even less, Capt'n, especially since what he'll be huntin' is tied to our davits."

"But that's the whole point, Pender. I live near here, and I don't think it will be long before it's known who's pinched them. So I've left information with a reliable source, to let on to the Deal smugglers, that in order to avoid their valuable galleys being taken and burned I have shipped them out of the town for a while."

CHAPTER TWENTY-NINE

IF ADMIRAL Parker was surprised to have Harry Ludlow calling on him again, his visitor was shocked when having been kept waiting for nearly an hour he entered the office and found Derouac, Illingworth's steward, sitting there, his cratered yellowing skin making him look more like frog-spawn than ever.

"I didn't think to see you here, Ludlow," Parker said, his eyes wandering to a looking-glass to make sure his facial expression was stern enough. "I should have thought you'd be brought to the blush by presenting yourself before me again."

Harry didn't want to be there. Time was exceedingly precious, and never was the old saw that it and tide would wait for no man more apt. But brother-in-law Arthur, clearing up every loose end from the previous unsuccessful mission, had written to Sir Peter Parker to recount the details of that failure. There was no way Harry could sail to Normandy without knowing what steps the admiral had taken since. Not trusting to a correspondent who could be as dilatory as he liked, Harry had been forced to come to Portsmouth in person.

And what a depressing journey it had been, in a ship more crank than any he'd ever known: three whole days from Deal to Chichester Harbour, and a two-hour journey in a hired shay over a poorly maintained road. The only consolation was that most of that trip would have been necessary in any case, since the currents in the Channel favoured an approach to the French coast from well west of the Dover Strait. So in truth he only risked losing one day. But he was in a hurry. More than that, he was in no mood to accept Parker's condescension.

"I'm even more surprised to see Derouac occupying one of

your chairs," Harry replied, "when I haven't even had the courtesy of a similar offer."

The steward shot to his feet, as though sitting in the presence of such an elevated personage had been a gross breach of trust.

"M. Tressoir has sent me as an emissary, Captain, to discuss the terms for the release of the passengers, our ship and its cargo."

"So he's still willing to bargain?"

"That is no longer any of Captain Ludlow's concern," snapped Parker, as Derouac opened his mouth to reply.

"It most certainly is, sir. Lord Drumdryan sent you word that Tressoir has taken my ship as well."

Parker sat forward, paused to check posture and countenance, then growled at Harry. "And this fellow has obliged me with something you failed to. He's told me how it happened, and hearing the details, sir, I can comprehend your reluctance to recount such folly."

Harry had no desire to reprise all that so he turned to the crouching Derouac. "How is Captain Illingworth?"

"The wounds were grave, as you know. But when I left he was recovering well, able to take light soup."

It was Parker who'd gone red, annoyed at the way Harry had ignored him to make his enquiry. The strain of holding his voice normal was obvious, as he sought to regain control.

"Derouac is not gifted in the description of sea battles. But then, given such a pathetic display as you put on between the Aubins, he barely needs to be. I might hardly add that you seriously exceeded your brief."

"I used my judgement, Admiral Parker! And I would point out to you that I have paid a higher price for my mistake than you. Considering you coerced me into going to Normandy in the first place, I hold you partly responsible for the loss of my vessel."

"I sent you to negotiate, sir, and to fight only if the situation was propitious. You declined to do the former in any meaningful way, and failed ignominiously at the latter."

"I also lost a ship."

Parker sat back again, his expression smug. "If you are look-ing for recompense here, Ludlow, you will whistle for it."

Harry was desperate to know what Parker had done. Now that the Spithead mutiny was settled, he certainly had the power and the means to dispatch a frigate. If he had, then Harry's options would be severely curtailed, if not scuppered altogether, but he also knew that a direct enquiry wouldn't necessarily produce an hon-est answer, so he tried to pose his request in an oblique manner.

"I expected nothing less. My sole purpose in coming here was to ask for what assistance I can expect in my attempt to get it back myself?"

"Get it back, man? After Tressoir gave you such a drubbing! Are you a glutton for punishment?"

"No, Admiral Parker. I am a privateer without a hull."

"Then long may you stay that way," Parker barked. "As a breed you're pestilential, so will be no loss, to my way of thinking."

"So, having attempted to rescue your family from captivity, I have no call whatsoever upon your good offices."

That sent Parker into even more of a temper. "Good offices, sir? It's a wonder they are still alive. How dare you fire round-shot into a vessel that harbours my relatives?!"

Harry matched Parker, the primary purpose of his visit sub-merged under his increasing indignation, voice rising so that those in the ante-room looked at each other in alarm.

"With a brother as pompous as Sir William, I should have been encouraged. Must I remind you that he is there because of his own boasting? You need have no fear of him suffering from roundshot. He has a head empty enough to accommodate any number of 12-pounder balls without pain."

Parker came half out of his chair. "You will get out of here, Ludlow, before I call for a file of marines to eject you."

Harry, partially recovering himself, gestured to Derouac who, faced with these two battling sailors, had shrunk back into his seat.

"I came here to find out what steps you'd taken, if any, to

communicate with Tressoir. I will not depart until I have been apprised of them, as well as the state of the defences at Isigny. If I cannot look to you to make up my loss, then I must do something on my own."

"You will stay away from the Normandy coastline, Ludlow, do you hear?"

"That is not something you can command, Admiral Parker."

"Is it not?"

"No."

"And how, pray, do you intend to get there?"

Harry was just about to bark, "By ship, you damn fool," when Parker, in the act of regaining his chair, turned to another mirror, the triumphal look in his eye immediately duplicated. To tell him about the *Good Intent* would be suicidal. The Channel Fleet might be gone but Parker had plenty of smaller ships at his disposal. Given the sailing qualities of Buckner's vessel there would be precious little need to send a swift sloop to catch him. A water hoy with a decent officer could achieve that before he'd managed to clear Hayling Island.

Happy with his appearance, the admiral turned back to look at his angry visitor, who was forcing himself, with great difficulty, to appear humble.

"You must help me," Harry said, the need to contain his resentment making his voice sound properly tense and servile.

Parker squared his shoulders and replied calmly, all need for anger spent. "I will not, sir, out of either duty or inclination. Now be so good as to get out of my presence."

Derouac wasn't allowed to even make it back to his lodgings. Pender and Flowers, when they appeared either side of him, didn't need to explain what they were about, the look in their eyes quite sufficient to persuade the Guernseyman that he was in the last hour of his life on earth. The hands that took him were gentle enough, and he was round the corner, lying, moaning softly, on the floor of Harry's coach, before a minute had passed. As soon as the door closed they set off for the return journey to Chichester Harbour.

"You will now tell me, Derouac, what message you brought back from Normandy."

"I was told to divulge that to no one."

"If you'd rather have Pender in here asking the questions, and not me, I'll be happy to oblige."

That started a gabbling account that only made complete sense when he was finished. The message he'd carried was simple enough, a repeat of the demand to trade for both the *Lothian* and the hostages, with this time no threat of violence.

"When does Admiral Parker expect to see you again?" Harry demanded, jabbing Derouac with his foot.

"I don't know. He told me to go back to my lodgings and wait."

"What are his plans?"

"He didn't tell me." That earned him another jab with the foot, one that encouraged him to continue. "He intends to send an emissary, but not until the last week of the month, when the tides are low. That will convince Tressoir that there is no danger of his being attacked a second time. All he wants is the hostages. He cares nothing for the ships."

"Good!"

Harry had to fight to keep the sense of relief out of his voice. If Parker had no ship off the Baie du Grand Vey, and no intention of yet sending one, then all he had to do was get the *Good Intent* there in time for the next high tide. That brought forth a silent prayer. They'd need a benign wind, and luck with the currents: failure meant the next opportunity was the first week of June.

"What are you going to do with me?"

"You have nothing to fear, Derouac," Harry said, adopting a friendly tone, then leaning forward to pat the steward's shoulder.

"Then you will set me free?" he wailed.

"No."

"Then where are you taking me?"

"Where else would we take such a faithful servant? You're going back to Normandy, to see your master."

They got to sea on the morning ebb, and sailed south, on a gentle north-westerly breeze, Harry busy working out the times of the tidal flows so that he could employ them to maximum advantage. When free from that, and the needs of the *Good Intent*, he interrogated Derouac relentlessly, seeking to find out what defences Tressoir had mounted. It was like drawing teeth, made worse by the ample time that the ship provided, yawing and wallowing. Only the first question was answered with alacrity, the information being that the Frenchman's corvette was called *l'Hyène*.

Slowly, using charts, drawings, cutlery, and crockery, as well as threats of violence from Pender, a picture began to emerge of the area around Isigny-sur-Mer, the watercourse that led up to it, and the precautions that had been taken against an attack. Tressoir had told the steward personally, in a message for Admiral Parker, that a boat was kept permanently at a location called the Point de Grouin looking out for a signal warning of any danger, probably from the highest point on les Îles de St. Aubin.

Taking a break, Harry consulted his charts. The Baie du Grand Vey was a wide estuary up to the point where the two main rivers diverged. To the east lay les Roches de Grandcamp, to the west a long spit of sand that pointed north, both well covered at high tide, exposed at low. The Point de Grouin was at the head of the bay, where it narrowed to form the deep-water channel that led up the River Vire. Some two miles upriver the watercourse split again, at the confluence of the Aure and the Vire: a long way to row just to deliver a warning. This provoked the question of what other defences this messenger was meant to alert.

Derouac showed more assurance at that point, since his knowledge of the local argot had served him well. He'd overheard some of Tressoir's men talking about a boom laid no more than a quarter of a mile from the wharves at Isigny. Set in stakes and hauled taut by mules, it lay at the point where the effect of water rising in the tidal basin petered out. Even taut, Harry reasoned it unlikely to hinder the centipedes, with their shallow hulls drawing little water.

The last thing Derouac had pointed out to him worried Harry more: a battery of cannon being set up on the northern bank, probably the very guns the Frenchman had used at Aubin. This was constructed at a point where the Aure narrowed between the only two pieces of raised ground for miles, if you excluded the town itself.

"By rights, he should have cannon on both banks," said Harry, which earned a shrug from the steward. "Tell me about the ships."

Lothian, with cargo and passengers intact, lay beside the harbour wall, in deep fresh water, no more than thirty yards from the nearest inhabited buildings, in the same state as he'd last seen her. *Bucephalas* was further upriver, at the far end of the town near the high stone bridge, berthed inside Tressoir's corvette, which was acting as an exterior platform while Harry's ship underwent repairs. Their progress proved the least difficult questions Derouac had to contend with. He might be a steward, but as he'd pointed out to Harry on another occasion he'd served a long time at sea. Her upperworks had been repaired, but the yards and masts had yet to be replaced. More importantly she was still without guns.

"Are you sure of this?"

"I am," Derouac replied firmly, showing a confidence which had up till then been rare. "I walked the entire length of that very quay the day that M. de Tressoir put me in my boat, and we both agreed that your ship was a long way from being ready for sea."

"What about the *Lothian*'s guns? Are they still aboard?"

"No. They have been taken ashore, and are lying on the quayside downriver of the ship."

"So when you left the only armed vessel was *l'Hyène?*"

"I think so," Derouac replied, suddenly lacking conviction again. Then he looked Harry square in the eye and puffed out his chest. "No, Captain Ludlow, I am certain."

"And she was at the very far end of the quay?"

"Yes."

"Now," said Harry, "tell me about the fortifications around Isigny itself."

"Captain," the steward wailed, "I saw nothing of them."

"You'd be amazed at what you can observe if you think about it, Derouac, believe me. Look what you've managed already."

CHAPTER THIRTY

PENDER spun the wheel a touch, to compensate for the ship falling off the wind. "Remember what that Frog did before, your honour. I've said it afore, and I'll say it again, he's a tricky bastard."

Harry paced back and forth in front of Pender. A persistent feeling was nagging at the back of his mind, but for the life of him he couldn't put his finger on it.

"Don't worry, Pender, I'm not going to underestimate him this time."

"Good!"

"He sent Derouac to see Admiral Parker, so while the tides are high he'll be on the lookout for a warship. The thought of us coming back for *Bucephalas* will never occur to him."

"He'll know the *Good Intent* is there."

"That can't be avoided. No ship, even a crack frigate, could get past those sentinels on the Aubins. And if they stand off till it's dark the only wind that would get them to the estuary in time to launch an attack would make it impossible to get out again. No, if it was a ship attack, they'd go in well aware that he knew they were coming."

"So tide or no tide, the only way to surprise him is to use ships' boats."

"Yes."

"An' that don't need no warship, any old tub would do."

"True," Harry replied, a slight touch of asperity evident in his tone. He hated to be interrogated, no matter who was doing the enquiring, especially when he was trying to think himself. "There'll be some system of alarm, starting with St. Aubin, that means he can get his men into position before any boats arrive upriver."

"If he's got any sense he wouldn't wait. If'n I was him I'd go on alert the minute I sniffed a threat."

"Ships must pass through the channel all the time, Pender," Harry snapped. "He can't go on the alert every time his lookouts spy a merchant vessel. You're right when you say our presence will be noted, but surely, in a tub like the *Good Intent,* that will be precautionary. He'll not do anything until he has more cause, and he certainly wouldn't man his defences at Isigny, a good ten miles away, unless he was absolutely sure he was facing an imminent assault."

Pender smiled, not in the least fazed by Harry's show of temper. "Strikes me, Capt'n, that you'd act different. And what you've just said, as well as the way it was spoke, would be what your brother James reckons as guesswork."

"I wish he was here, Pender, just to help me sort out my thinking."

"I'm game to stand in as best I can."

"You deserve more than that, friend," Harry sighed. "Part of me is surprised that you're still around to listen. I don't think I've treated you in recent times in a way that's merited it."

"You ain't," Pender replied, with a snap of impatience in his own voice. "But that, I hope and pray, is behind you."

Harry didn't want to labour that point, since to do so would only revive unpleasant memories. He knew, deep down, that Pender was lukewarm about the whole business, and this conversation was proof. Pender would have followed him anywhere; he'd come with his captain out of loyalty not because he thought he was in the right.

"Let's say first, I'm bothered as to why you're doin' it." The raised eyebrows were met with an intense stare, as Pender continued. "Seems to me that the best place we could be heading is back to New York."

"Tressoir has my ship," said Harry, in a soft, but firm voice.

They couldn't look at each other then, neither willing to intimate what they both suspected, that *Bucephalas* was a talisman, and only a means to an end. Harry Ludlow needed a success, something to bring back his self-esteem, a stroke so bold that perhaps he could erase the past year from his memory. And not just that. Being in Portsmouth in the midst of mutiny, and seeing how stupid the authorities had been to let it happen at all, had revived conflicting emotions about his own life; a joy that he wasn't subjected to the discipline of naval life, mixed with a feeling that perhaps, if he'd still been serving, his presence could have made a difference. But that, to Pender's certain knowledge, was a conversation not even James Ludlow could have with his brother. So his surprise when Harry did partially open up was substantial.

"I have a feeling: if I just go back to America, and trade in those bonds, then I'll never go to sea again." He had to turn his head away then, so that Pender wouldn't see his face and observe the misery he felt as everything he'd tried to blot from his thinking came flooding back.

"I can't see that happening," Pender responded, guardedly.

"I'll have the funds to buy a ship. But will I have the heart?" This time Pender stayed silent, as Harry continued hoarsely, "I can't blame you for being concerned. But I would say that we've got this far, which, much as I hoped, I'd never have believed possible outside Walmer Castle."

"Perhaps your luck is on the turn."

Harry didn't want to mention luck lest he tempt Providence. "James says I have a habit of making presumptions sound like certainties, that I give the impression of knowing more than I really do."

"That would be hard to dispute."

Fighting to control his features, Harry looked Pender in the eye again. "Yet you know as well as I do that in any fight a great deal has to be left to chance. I could sit here and list possibilities, things that would guarantee we'd fail, that you haven't even thought of. Like the precautions he might well take to raise the alarm. Fire beacons, for instance. Horse messengers. Signal cannon."

"What if it rains," Pender asked, "or blows a gale? Guns and flame would be useless."

As he formed the words of his reply, Harry's thinking crystallized. Standing in for James, Pender had done better than either of them could have hoped. Once examined, the solution became obvious. How did a man like Derouac, who possessed no military ability at all, know so much? Why tell him about guard boats and let him overhear discussions of cannon positions and booms? Why take him for a stroll along the quay just before you load him into a boat? Had he been fed the information, manoeuvred into absorbing detail for a dual purpose? The Frenchman didn't know his enemy, and any attempt to question the brother would be pointless. Was Sir Peter Parker bold or cautious, would he attack or negotiate? Had Tressoir been clever enough to provide sufficient detail to deter a careful man, yet been cautious enough to show only so much in case he was bent on attack?

Pender was looking at him, still waiting for an answer to his question, curious why his captain suddenly looked so pleased with himself.

"Something tells me that we won't find any one of those things."

"Why?"

"I'll tell you after I've had another session with Derouac."

"You said that Captain Illingworth was still in a bad way when you left Isigny, but he was fit enough to hold a conversation?"

"Yes."

"Did Tressoir talk with him?"

Derouac's little brown eyes narrowed, and he pursed his lips in disapproval. "I told you, Captain, he is a gentleman. And so naturally he came to converse with my master, to ensure that all his needs were met."

"Did he mention, in this conversation, the value of the *Lothian* or of the hostages?"

The lips pressed together even more before Derouac replied,

"That would be a base thing to bring up with a wounded man."

"So our gentleman sent you seventy miles in an open boat to carry a message to Admiral Parker, when he had, in a sickbed, someone who could have answered his most pressing question." Harry watched the confusion on the steward's face for a second or two, before adding, "I've never known such nobility. When did he offer to trade for the *Lothian,* Derouac? Was it before Sir William told Tressoir who his relatives were, or after?"

Harry returned to the deck, his mind racing. "I bet you the value of the *Lothian* he's prepared another trap."

"I can't say that I'm jolted by that notion," Pender replied.

Harry's heels dug in to the planking with increasing force as he explained his reasoning. It had all started with Sir William and his big mouth, and in some sense it had continued with that. He wanted a proper ship, preferably a frigate, though he'd never thought that Parker might trade him one. If the Royal Navy was famous for anything it was its love of a fight, and that's what he planned for. So he set up the snare at St. Aubin, which only back-fired because of a mutiny he knew nothing about.

"He didn't do too bad," said Pender. "I seem to recall he won, hands down."

Harry pretended not to hear. "What do we really know about him? Our Frenchman says he's at loggerheads with the government in Paris. What evidence do we have for that except his own words? None! He says he's a nobleman. I grant you he has an air about him, but is that the truth or another furbelow? The one thing we do know about him is that he's a devious sod. I think everything he told Derouac, or allowed him to see, was deliberate, bait on the line. It's the way he likes to fight, by showing a false picture. Only this time the habit could work against him."

"Please God!" said Pender, with some passion.

"I'll take a wager that there's no cannon on the northern shore of the Aure River. And that the boom Derouac talked about is designed to snare any ship that's gone upriver, rather than preventing it getting there. Tressoir is prepared to negotiate or be attacked, just like he was at St. Aubin. And if it's the latter, he expects someone who isn't wise to his ways. He feels secure, able to fight anybody on his own patch."

Harry could see, every time he turned, the way Pender was looking at him, willing himself to believe but not entirely convinced. "Examine what he did in the past. He set up two situations in which he fought on his own terms, by creating a false image. I admit he fooled me on both occasions. But I do believe it was a trap most captains with an ounce of aggression would have fallen into. He's trying the same again. Only he's expecting the navy, not us, and we've crossed swords with him before. We know his ways."

"That's pushin' it a bit, your honour."

"Pender, I think we have the means to best him. For once we have a surprise for him, instead of the other way round. Even if he thinks the *Good Intent* a threat, he has no knowledge of who's aboard." Harry looked at him, a wry grin on his face. "I can't promise success, no one ever can. And don't think I haven't thought what would happen if I lose again. I know that going after those ships is risky, but then that's the same as everything I've done in my life. But I also know something that applies to everyone, including Tressoir: too rigid a plan is as dangerous as no plan at all. We have the means to knock him off his stroke, and once we've done that he will be on the defensive. I think we'll succeed in doing that by the speed of our approach."

"And after?"

"Then it's down to the fortunes of war. But I have a feeling in my bones, given that I know what he's about, that this time I'm going to beat him." Harry took a deep breath, and looked Pender right in the eye. "This is nothing to do with anything I said to you before, but if you don't wish to come, I'll understand."

Pender's face didn't change at all, but his voice was tight with suppressed anger. "You think with them centipedes, even if he is preparing a surprise, we can get to him before he's ready?"

Harry breathed out very slowly. "They can move twice as fast as any cutter. According to Derouac that's what we'll find in the head of the estuary, a boat that I think has been instructed to run ahead of any raiding party, or a ship, and draw them in. But they won't be able to do that against centipedes."

"And when we get upriver?"

"That practically everything Derouac was allowed to see will be altered."

Pender wasn't finished with his Devil's advocacy. "All we need now is the men to row the sods. All boats are different, and since you're relying on speed, that's important. None of the lads we took aboard are Deal locals. And if some of our crew ever manned one it's so long ago they'll have forgotten how."

"Don't worry, we'll get in plenty of practice. The rate that the *Good Intent* travels leaves a lot of time for training." Harry shook his head slowly, but he couldn't keep the repressed excitement out of his voice. Pender knew it to be the Harry Ludlow of old, which induced a set of mixed feelings he did his best to hide. In that kind of mood, he was never going to be deflected.

"We'd best get started," he said, "one boat at a time."

Harry was pacing again, heels hitting the deck with regular thuds. "We can't man them both fully and leave enough men to watch over the ship. So we'll put ten of the better rowers in the smaller crew."

"Captain," Pender interrupted, determined to nail the last conundrum. "You said that about plans bein' too set. What will you do if there is no guard boat?"

"Improvise!"

If Tressoir had a lookout on the top of les Îles de St. Aubin, Harry prayed he would be mystified by what he saw. The *Good Intent* sailing by was surely no threat to anyone. A squat-looking two-masted merchantman of a type they'd be unlikely to recognize, perhaps too small and unsuitable for bearing much in the way of cargo, struggling, even with a following wind, to make any great easting. Nor would what she was towing seem dangerous, though the idea of a ship at sea pulling a small barge behind it was certainly singular. The two centipedes, too big to be hauled on board, were lashed together with a tarpaulin over both, so that they looked like one flat-bottomed vessel.

Harry, flying a French flag and a La Rochelle pennant, had steered well to the west of the islands, shaving Barfleur, so that his approach to the channel that ran between the St. Aubin islands and the Baie du Grand Vey ran parallel with the arc of the Normandy coastline. This gave him half a day of a strong, making current, and was the common route for a merchant ship. It dispensed with the need to navigate or raise a mass of canvas aloft, as well as lessening the risk from the dangers posed by enemy cruisers. The decks were untidy, in the way of merchant ships, with the majority of his men confined below as long as the daylight lasted. No attempt was made to examine the Île du Large to see if they were being observed, since to do that would only make anyone on top suspicious.

The tension on board was so palpable it could have been cut with a knife, and Harry Ludlow was as prone to the effects of that as anyone. He longed to do something, even to run up the foremast rigging, instead of just standing by the wheel, his skin itching with that feeling of being observed. He knew fretting wouldn't bring darkness any quicker but that didn't stop his agitation. This became acute as they opened the Baie du Grand Vey early in the afternoon, close to the height of the tide. The whole estuary of the two rivers was well on the way to being at flood, just a few centimetres short of the previous day's level.

There was nevertheless a certain amount of admiration for what he suspected Tressoir had contrived. Instead of keeping his men indefinitely at maximum alert so that even a seemingly innocent trading vessel became a hazard demanding a response, he'd allowed the majority of them the comfort of staying in the town. Most captains would have had their ship beating back and forth off the estuary, wearing out wood, canvas, and the men's patience, so as not to be caught unawares.

It was the Aubins which gave him that option, of course, and the lookouts there, the day before, at the very height of the early May tide, must have been screwed up in anticipation. Harry hoped they would now relax somewhat. Would they see the way Willerby was throwing their filth over the side as normal, instead of a careful ploy designed to show the rate of the various currents as they washed around the estuary? He watched each piece of flotsam carefully, any sudden change of direction as it drifted towards land an eddy that denoted either a submerged rock or the tip of a sandbank. This stretch of coastline hadn't been surveyed since the outbreak of the war, so the charts were inaccurate. The rocks were constants, but the flow of silt from inland changed the shape of the sandbars over time.

The rest of the afternoon seemed to last an eternity as the *Good Intent* wallowed on under a blue sky full of high, billowing clouds. Her sailing qualities, a disadvantage in a fight, were now an asset, especially when the tide turned as they came abreast of the eastern edge of les Roches de Grandcamp. The increasing ebb practically killed any forward progress, so that the decision to anchor, inshore of the tip of le Banc du Cardonnet, in good holding ground, looked natural.

Evening came, then darkness. The night sky was the same high clouds, with occasional long patches of moonlight. When they disappeared, nothing would be seen other than a set of lanterns fore and aft, to light the deck and warn against collision. Even through a telescope they would appear from the islands, now nearly five miles distant, as mere pinpricks.

All the weaponry was already loaded in the centipedes, flares, muskets, grenades, pikes, and cutlasses, laid out along the middle of the boats ready for use. With the moon and stars obscured by a huge cloud, the men took their allotted stations. With Pender, Dreaver, and himself he had a total strength of forty-seven men, many less than Tressoir could muster, in a situation in which a numerical advantage would, by a less sanguine mind, have been considered essential.

But Harry Ludlow's spirits couldn't have been higher as they cast off from the blind side of the ship. Both boats maintained an easy pace back towards the river mouth, Harry having set a shaded lantern showing just a slit in the stern of his boat so that Dreaver could follow. He could hear him faintly, calling out the pace that they'd practised in open water.

With the tide low and falling, the sea was breaking over the base of les Roches de Grandcamp, giving them an aural then a visual fix. The spits of sand that projected out from the estuary, the Bancs du Grandcamp, were exposed at low water and presented the greatest hazard. To avoid sticking on them, they had to proceed slowly, Harry's plan to stay well to the north until he was sure he was off the main channel, then turn south and pick up speed.

Pender was casting a lead, instructed not to call out depths unless the water shoaled sharply. On a mainly cloudy night there could be no dead reckoning, only informed guesswork. Harry had triangulated the return, calculating the strokes they'd need to close the distance and counting them off as the oars struck. But the leeway was an unknown addition. So it was with his heart in his mouth that he gave the signal, two sharp flashes of the lantern, that turned both galleys due south. Next came the order to row, followed by him calling out the increasing pace of the strokes.

The centipedes were up to maximum speed within a minute, moving at such a pace that the sweat Harry had on his brow cooled rapidly. They were committed now. Despite Derouac's information and Harry's confidence they were entering the unknown, the area of any conflict in which whatever the plan laid, however careful the preparation, events inevitably took their own course.

CHAPTER THIRTY-ONE

THE SKY cleared almost as soon as the oars started to bite, giving Harry a chance to fix his position and alter course to put both boats in the centre of the rapidly widening yet twisting channel. But it also lit up the whole seascape with that singular light that made any object, sandbank or boat, look like a black mark on a dappled silver screen. He had no doubt that if the St. Aubin lookouts were awake they'd see him, especially as the oar strokes of such large galleys threw up great quantities of sparkling water.

They weren't as alert as they should have been. It was several minutes before the fire started to flicker on top of l'Îles du Large, the red glow at the base spreading rapidly as the flames took hold in the dry wood. Once he'd seen it, Harry turned away. Staring at the fire would serve little purpose. Any danger that threatened them now lay up ahead, not behind.

"Boat!" called Pender, softly, as they approached solid earth, and the River Vire, at the Point de Grouin.

"Where away?"

"Right ahead and pulling, though not flat out."

Harry's heart lifted. For all his apparent certainty he'd had his doubts, and several anxious minutes had been spent staring at the looming bulk of the eastern shore, the fear acute that he might see another flicker of flame. There was nothing, just the boat they'd anticipated, pulling enough to stay ahead.

"They're laying to with the oars now, Capt'n," Pender called. "I think they've just guessed they're in the shit."

This was the point at which the centipedes proved their worth. The guard detail was in a cutter, with every reason to suppose that faced at best with a group of similar boats, loaded with men and equipment, they could stay well ahead if not actually outrun their foes. But no one would have calculated for the smuggling galleys of Deal, which ate up the distance between them. With the need for silence now gone, Harry was free to shout his orders.

"Dreaver, steer to larboard of him. When you have just overhauled, if he's still going upriver, ship your oars and ram the bastard."

Harry's boat was closing on the starboard side, presenting quite a dilemma to the men he was pursuing. If they had guns they'd need to stop rowing to discharge them, yet to do nothing when they were being overhauled, would see them taken. Once they got within range both the centipedes could ship a pair of oars, so that the rowers could take up muskets. The loss of speed with a galley at full tilt in the sheltered water of the inner estuary was unnoticeable.

Not so the French cutter. Whoever commanded it had finally acknowledged that if he couldn't run he'd have to fight. When the centipedes were within a hundred yards of their quarry oars were shipped completely, the man on the tiller swinging the boat across the channel to bar Harry's route while his companions fumbled with a variety of weapons.

"Dreaver, ignore them. Steer to go round with as much clear water as you can manage."

Harry, alongside Pender in the prow of his own boat, had his flints out, bent over to light the entire fuse on a grenade. A musket ball whipped past his ear, passing out over the counter and missing the men straining on the oars behind him. He threw the round casing as soon as the fire took hold, ignoring the pain in his shoulder, deliberately aiming it so that it would fly over the heads of Tressoir's men and land in the water behind them. The last thing he wanted was the kind of loud explosion, ten times that of a musket, whose sound might carry for miles on a calm night.

But the sight of the long, spluttering fuse, arcing over their heads, achieved its purpose. The Frenchmen ducked in fear, and threw their boat off whatever course they'd been steering. The grenade landed in the water harmlessly, the fuse fizzling out. Then, as the men in the guard boat raised their heads again, the two muskets in Harry's boat let fly. Even on the calm estuary water it was going to be difficult to hit anything, but their captain didn't care. Once he'd got past that boat, these men and their task would be redundant. He'd be upriver of them, rowing at almost twice their speed, closing on an enemy who had no idea he was approaching. The element of surprise, which Tressoir had used to such devastating effect, was now in the hands of Harry Ludlow.

Even the fact that the men in the guard boat were shooting at them was a positive thing, especially since their aim was wide. The sooner they expended their limited stock of powder and balls, far away from the town, the better. Harry even had his own crewmen firing over the stern to keep the return fire coming, long after it could serve any other purpose. But best of all the men in the cutter, soon realizing that they couldn't catch their prey, gave up the chase, and their boat shrank to a speck in the moonlight, solitary and silent in the middle of the channel.

The cloud cover swept over them again, plunging the scene into darkness. Harry had come level with the second galley, and the last sight he'd had of the shore showed a straight channel with deep water over a hundred yards wide. That would only increase as the tide made, so having instructed both helmsmen to keep their tillers steady he relaxed for the first time since they'd sighted the St. Aubin islands that morning.

Etched in his mind was the drawing that Derouac, under endless prompting, had sketched for him, showing the long stone quay on one side of the river, running all the way from the very edge of Isigny to the stone bridge which lay below the slight incline that led up into the town itself. The quay was lined with chandlers' warehouses and shops, their occupants living above their premises. The town itself had an old Norman citadel, which he thought had fallen into disuse.

The cloud cover broke several times, making it easy to bear to the left so as to hold to the centre of the River Vire. Within the

half-hour Harry spotted the point where the River Vire was joined
by the Aure, running east to west, and turning into it the centipedes entered a much narrower channel. They were approaching
the point Derouac had identified as the location of the boom over
the river, the obstacle which would hinder both *Bucephalas* and
Lothian, should they succeed in bringing them downriver. Harry
had issued his orders regarding this before they'd left the *Good
Intent,* and since there was no evidence of any obstruction mid-
channel Dreaver took his boat close inshore on the northern bank,
while Harry did likewise to the south.

Again the Deal galleys had an advantage. They had to be
rowed quickly over the Goodwins at low tide then run up a shingle beach within seconds of their landfall, so they'd been built with
as shallow a draught as possible and this allowed both of them
to get right inshore, with a pike trailing in the water in an attempt
to find the boom. Pender, watching the northern bank, nudged
Harry, who turned to see the lantern Dreaver had unshaded for
the second time. Quietly, he called to his men, who swung the galley across the river, and rowed very gently to join their companions,
all of whom, except Dreaver, were crowded into the stern.

"A ship's anchor cable," whispered Dreaver, as Harry came
alongside. "About twelve inches, I reckon. We've lifted it over the
prow."

"Can it be cut?"

"Being wet don't help," Dreaver replied, "and it's near to sinking us by the head already. It'd be best to get at it on the bank."

"Right," Harry replied, stepping over the counter from his
own boat. "Pender, back downriver about fifty yards, close enough
to see our signal. Keep an eye out for that guardboat, just to make
sure they aren't in our wake."

The boat backed off, drifting out into the midstream.

"Where's Jubilee and that saw?" Harry whispered.

"Here," the squat Pole replied. Harry, in borrowing the carpenter's biggest saw, had chosen him as one of the strongest
men on the ship. An axe might be quicker but it was noisier, and

without any clear idea of how close Tressoir's men might be, a saw was a just precaution. "Right, bring another pair of men to hold the cable while you cut it."

Cutlass aloft, Harry went over the side followed by the three men, gasping at the shock of the cold water as it came up to his chest. Wading forward, he touched the thick, slimy cable, using it as a guide to get him ashore. He could feel his feet sinking into the mud, especially if he stood still, and he whispered to those behind him to keep moving.

The riverbank was steep and slippery, difficult to climb without making a sound. And the rope, which hadn't dried out from the soaking it'd received earlier that day, was no help. It was either cut it here or find a spot up or downriver where they could climb on to the bank.

"Get your shoulders under the cable and try and lift it level. Jubilee, you will have to cut above your head. You can use both hands once you get a few strands in."

Having shoved their weapons into the soft earth of the bank the three stood in line, ducking even further into the freezing river; Harry could feel his limbs going numb as the cold penetrated them, and then the jarring pain in his shoulders as he started to lift. Jubilee, could only get his head above the water, and was having no end of trouble finding secure footing. But the saw was in action, with a rasp Harry thought must be audible a long way off.

With the water gurgling past right by his ear, and the sound of Jubilee sawing, hearing the noise from the riverbank was nothing short of a miracle. It was only because one person was complaining that it carried. Harry patted the others in turn, his mouth close to each ear as he commanded silence. He pulled his cutlass from the bank and waded slowly over to Jubilee. "I need to get on to your shoulders."

The Pole just grunted in reply, handed the saw to one of the others, and stepped backwards so his spine was against the sloping earth. Harry lifted one foot, which Jubilee guided to his other hand, under water, like a sling, then grabbed Jubilee's shoulder with his one free hand and tried to jump. The soft mud gave way beneath his feet, and the drag of the water slowed him even further, completely negating his efforts. The second try was no more successful than the first, the panic when he saw the waving lanterns on the riverbank doing nothing to aid him.

Jubilee had either seen that too or sensed Harry's alarm. He sank beneath the rippling water, his forearms locking themselves around his captain's knees. Harry went upwards as if he was on one end of a children's seesaw, easily able to reach out and take hold of one of the thicker overhanging branches. The Pole had now got one hand under his foot and was lifting him still, high enough to get a foothold where the angle of the bank lessened.

He needed the tangled undergrowth to hide him and hold him there as he sought that lantern again. It was difficult to tell, but he thought he could distinguish three voices, one still complaining, another peremptory, in command, the third with a joking lilt, as though the owner was baiting his companions. The lantern flashed again as it swung in an arc, unnecessarily since the clouds broke completely, bathing the whole area in moonlight. They were twenty yards away, three hunched figures by a huge pile driven into the earth, the cable wrapped round it as securely as the Gordian knot.

"Make way, Capt'n," came the soft voice from behind him, as Harry saw one of the men put the lantern on the cable. He prayed that if his men had let it go the thing had ceased to move. But even from this distance he could see the outline of the square glass change as it dipped, following the rope as it slid slowly down to the bottom.

"Have you got your cutlass?" Harry demanded.

"Aye! And my knife."

Harry recognized Flowers's voice. He grabbed the man's shirt, pulling him level. "Three men, straight ahead, armed, and they've got to die. If they don't we will."

"Bugger," the sailor replied softly, but it was a comment without much in the way of feeling.

"Ready?"

Flowers patted Harry on the back rather than reply. Both stood up, still hidden by the thick undergrowth, and started to move forward, which caused all three sentinels to look up in alarm.

"Mes amis, aidez-moi, en le nom de Dieu."

That made them hesitate just enough to allow Harry and Flowers on to the level ground, dry and firm above the high-water mark, close to the edge of the undergrowth. All three Frenchmen had their weapons extended, but only one had a pistol. There being no way to surprise them, they walked out into the clearing, dripping wet, the silver blades of their weapons shining in the moonlight.

As soon as the pistol holder raised his weapon Flowers threw his blade, forcing him to fire off hastily and upsetting his aim. Harry was already three paces in front, sword extended, crouched low, his eye fixed firmly on his nearest opponent. Flowers was right behind, having rolled in one swift movement from his feet, on to his back, then upright again. If the man with the pistol had aimed, the ball flew harmlessly over Flowers's body.

Harry's sweeping blade was checked as it swung down. He hauled it backwards, the sound of metal on metal rasping in his ears. For the first time in a week he could really feel the whole of his wound, was aware that the strength he relied on was not available, and that the advantage lay with his opponent. He jumped back, to avoid not his thrust but the one from the side as the third Frenchman tried to skewer him.

Harry wanted to go forward, well aware that in a fight momentum was ninety per cent of success. But he lacked his usual strength, and with Flowers fully engaged he had two opponents. His sword swung left and right as he parried one deadly thrust after another, each forcing him back another half pace to the bushes that lined the bank until he felt them press into his back.

Despair was alien to his nature yet he knew that these two Frenchmen, quite indifferent swordsmen, were getting the better of him, while Flowers, a vague image in the corner of his eye, was having a real battle with the pistol holder, presumably the leader of this trio of guards. And in the back of his mind, he realized that fortune had brought them to the wrong side of the river. If the cable was tied off here then the means to raise it to a capstan or a pair of mules lay on the other side.

"Flowers, back in the water!" he shouted, his voice rising above the din of clanging metal.

The noise behind him as the bush parted nearly gave him heart failure until he saw half a dozen of his men push through, led by a soaking-wet Dreaver. The Frenchmen only saw them emerge a split second before Harry, the look in their eyes changing from impending triumph to present fear. They tried to disengage, but Harry was going forward now, holding them to their task of defence until his men could overwhelm and disarm them.

Flowers got his opponent without assistance, his cutlass sweeping across the leader's neck just as help arrived. A second Frenchman went down as Dreaver came in from Harry's left side, his sword blade going right through the soft part of his gut to the ribcage. Harry himself got the third one with his guard on the side of the head. "Back to the boats, quick," he gasped.

"The cable?" asked Dreaver.

That stopped him in his tracks. The boom uncut left a problem for the future, but if Tressoir got his men into position well in time and sat waiting for them to arrive, there might not be one at all. It was a classic example of the kind of situation that Harry had mentioned to Pender, and though he tried to avoid thinking of the word luck, he couldn't avoid it. He had to make a snap decision, trusting to that and nothing else.

"We'll have to leave it. We're on the wrong bank for the Isigny quay. It's likely that there's another party over the river and they will have heard the pistol shots. We've got to get up to the town before they do."

Dreaver and his men had almost cut a path through the undergrowth. As soon as he saw the river Harry jumped right over the head of Jubilee, who was sawing away under water, to what avail

Harry couldn't see. A body arrived beside him, landing flat in the cold water and sending up a huge splash, with Flowers's voice calling out that he wasn't dead.

It took Harry a moment to realize that this was the Frenchman he'd clubbed, thrown after him. If he'd been unconscious before he hit the water the chill brought him round, and Harry had to press his sword to his neck to stop him from screaming. The call to Jubilee to belay was instantly obeyed as the entire party waded out to the centipede, the Frenchman persuaded to get into the boat as an alternative to having his throat cut.

"Flash Pender, someone," Harry snapped, "and get on those oars."

The prisoner was thrown down into the centre of the boat as the men obeyed, and the galley was in motion with Dreaver calling out the pace within half a minute. Pender had come alongside, his face anxious in the moonlight, until he saw that his captain was safe. What Harry told him was garbled, but it was enough to have him growling at his own crew, calling for every ounce of effort.

"Fetch me that Frog," said Harry, once his breath had returned to normal.

At the first question, the Frenchman shook his head. Harry hit him hard across the face, part of the strength of the blow caused by his own frustration at his own stupidity. He should have seen if he was alive, not Flowers. As the victim fell forward he grabbed his hair and put him over the side. Hauled out as his heels began to kick, he was told in no uncertain terms that he would be drowned unless he answered the questions. And Harry meant it. He was not prepared to sacrifice the fate of his men on any sentimental finer feelings. His eyes told the prisoner that he would die, and as Harry pressed him, he began to mumble and nod.

"*L'Hyène* is moored downriver now, with a spring on her hawse to swing her out into the middle of the river." More questions followed, with Harry passing on what the Frenchman was saying to the crew. "*Bucephalas* has her masts stepped, and half her rigging in place, but no guns aboard. They are downriver on the stone quay, just astern of *Lothian*."

His soft voice was drowned out by the first boom of cannon shot, the great whoosh of its passing and a fount of water thirty feet high. All hope of surprise evaporated. But even in an anxious frame of mind, with a mountain still to climb, Harry realized that this time he'd read Tressoir right.

"Put your backs into it, lads!" Harry yelled. "Speed is our only hope."

CHAPTER THIRTY-TWO

HARRY had even more cause to rejoice, as nearly every shot landed well astern of the galleys because the gunners, levering their pieces round, constantly misjudged their speed. Whatever training they'd had in firing these light cannon had evidently been based on much slower vessels, and the triangulation required to place a deflection shot in the path of their target was beyond them.

With the waters of the River Aure boiling in their wake, the centipedes raced through the zone of maximum danger, the French prisoner slung out to sink or swim as best he could. The oarsmen were working against the flow now, without the aid of rising tidal water, but that had only a marginal effect on their progress. Surprise had gone as far as the town of Isigny was concerned; the boom of the cannon must have awakened every Frenchman for miles around. But there was just the chance that Tressoir would be denied the luxury of time. Whatever his skills he was no superman, and like any other commander he needed a clear period to get all his defences properly manned, by men settled and prepared to do battle.

Harry had taken the tiller on his boat, aiming it across the river until he was close to Pender. Above the crash of gunfire he shouted what he'd learned from the prisoner, as well as his instructions about their next move. Praying that what he had been told was no lie he got his boat ahead of its consort and steered as close as he dared to the northern bank.

The fire behind them had fallen away as the boats raced out of the arc of the batteries. Ahead, right across the stream, Harry could just make out the rigging of *l'Hyène* against the night sky, and that was only because he was looking for it. Nothing else showed, no lights from open gunports or even a lantern above decks, a testimony to the discipline of Tressoir's men, that same steadiness that had made the trap at St. Aubin so deadly.

But this time Harry knew of their presence, knew they were waiting for the command to raise the gunports and pour a devastating salvo of roundshot low into the centre of the channel, where any enemy advancing on the town would be. But the centipedes weren't there. They were pressed against the riverbank, their shallow draught allowing them to brush the very undergrowth that hung over the gurgling waters of the River Aure.

In order to achieve maximum surprise, Tressoir let off his first salvo a second before he fired off a flare. Harry saw the gunports go up, the black side of the ship turning into a dozen squares of faint light. They soon disappeared behind the orange glow of the discharge, and the great clouds of billowing smoke which belched from the muzzles. The flare burst overhead to show the whole centre of the channel a boiling mass of broken water as the roundshot, fired from a minimum elevation, bounced over the water. The sight made Harry bless the return of his good fortune. If he'd been stronger he might have killed the man he'd taken prisoner, and if he had the two boats would have rowed right into that maelstrom of certain destruction.

The flare lit up more than the river. It revealed the entire hull and upperworks of Tressoir's floating battery and showed Harry that he was no more than twenty yards from the end of the stone quay. The shouting, magnified by the confined space between decks, floated down to them as the men aboard *l'Hyène* reloaded. Harry imagined he could hear the rammers slamming into both deck and carriages, to lever the guns round to aim at the boats. But they could only heave them around as far as the gunport allowed, no great problem when a ship was at sea, but hopeless for one tied firmly to a spring, and by the time they were ready to fire the targets were gone, inside that area of safety. Harry and his men were soon on the quay and he yelled for a few to stay behind and get the boats further up the quayside.

Tressoir had discharged another flare so that he could see what was happening, but all he did was reveal to the raiding party the line of guns ranged along the quay, ready to fire across the front of *l'Hyène* in the unlikely event that any boats coming upriver survived the original salvos. The gunners were poised over their pieces, ready to let fly. The one thing they were not ready to do was suddenly take up weapons and repel a furious attack on their flank.

Harry, steadying his party, lined up those with muskets and delivered a fairly disciplined fusillade that broke whatever resolve they had. Tressoir had hauled men from his guns for the same purpose, and the raiding party was treated to a dose of its own medicine, though delivered at a greater range and therefore less deadly. Some of his men were hit, but Harry had no time to think about that. Yelling the order to charge, he raced for the nearest gun, pistol out and cutlass waving above his head. The gunners on the first cannon, already suffering the most from musket fire, broke and ran, which spread to all the others. More tellingly, not one of them had the wit to discharge their weapons before they abandoned them.

"Pender," Harry yelled, "get as many men as you can on the guns!"

He had no need to say more. Pender knew who to call on and what the target was. As Harry took half the men on to the last cannon, chasing the gunner up the quay, he detailed a gun crew for the first, personally taking the handspike to lever it round as Flowers, with the aid of Jubilee, lifted the cascabel and rammed in the elevating wedge. Peppered by musket and pistol fire there was no time for careful aiming, but the French ship presented such a big target that it was scarcely necessary. As he pulled the lanyard to fire the flintlock his gun crew were on the second weapon.

At close range, using *Lothian*'s guns, and shooting into a stationary target that could not reply with its own main armament, the effect was overwhelming. The shot smashed into Tressoir's hull, ripping the edge out of one of the gunports as it burst through to mangle anyone in the way on deck. Harry, having cleared the other gunners, was on the last cannon. The Frenchman's stern had been left without deadlights and the ball did even more damage as it flew the length of the ship smashing off deadly splinters no flesh could withstand.

"Axes!" Harry yelled, above the screams from wounded Frenchmen.

Only a few obeyed. Most, men from his long-serving crew, stayed on the guns, going through the loading routine as though not exposed to retaliation. It was what their captain had trained them for over two years for, the swabbing, loading, and aiming of guns so well rehearsed that it was automatic. It was also quick, even if the odd member of the gun crews spun away with a wound. Pender was the first to discharge again, sending his ball into the piece of l'Hyène he'd wounded previously, the clang of metal on metal hinting he'd hit the gun. In the dying light of the last flare they could see what they'd achieved. The whole side of the corvette was a mess of broken timber. The gunports were no squares of light now, instead they were ragged outlines of broken wood.

Pender, realizing that the men on board had ceased to return fire, called out for grenades, to be lobbed for the holes in the side in an attempt not only to kill the crew, but also to set the vessel alight. Meanwhile Harry, with his party, was hacking at the upriver cable that acted as a spring to hold the ship in place.

The next flare showed Tressoir himself, standing on his quarterdeck, calmly lining up his men so that the next volley of musket fire would do some damage. His hand was raised, pointing at Harry Ludlow and the party hacking at the bollard and the cable. Pender, who'd just lit a grenade, rushed up the quayside, yelling to Harry and his men to take cover. He threw it as they dived in all directions to avoid the fusillade. The grenade flew in a long arc, the fuse spluttering in the night sky. It exploded in mid-air, above the heads of the Frenchmen, who'd been forced to duck themselves when they saw it coming.

Harry and his men didn't wait. They were on their feet hacking again as soon as the musket balls flew past. More grenades were arcing over *l'Hyène*'s side, bursting on deck and setting fire to the dry ship's timbers. The cable, under strain from the river current, parted with a crack, whipping across the water like an angry snake. Harry was at his gun again, in the company of his party, frantically reloading as *l'Hyène* swung slowly but inexorably side-on to the quay, to smash into the stonework. Only half the guns were manned, but the fire they poured into the hull, at an even closer range, was the most telling yet. So close to the target, the fiery wad followed the balls, setting fire to everything combustible on a deck that the Frenchmen had abandoned.

Harry Ludlow was levering round his cannon point at the bollard holding the second cable. The crack as the metal ball hit the iron-hooped wood no more than a few feet from the muzzle drowned out every other sound. The bollard blew apart, metal and wood shooting upwards and outwards, some striking the ship's hull with such force they deeply embedded themselves. The cap took a Frenchman's head off just as he aimed a pistol, the shattered skull and wood rising on a fount of blood. The end of the cable tipped over into the river, and the released *l'Hyène* drifted on the current, grinding down the quay, jagged pieces of smashed timber ripping off, until the flow took her out from the side towards the midstream.

Harry's yell had them abandon both guns and revenge. He was here for *Bucephalas* first and foremost, with the *Lothian* if he could get her, his main worry that any guards left in the ships would fire them both before he could get aboard. Tressoir, and the fate of his corvette, had limited interest.

There was no return fire now, since every Frenchman was either fighting the blaze or working furiously to get an anchor over the side to moor the ship. And that presented a problem. If *l'Hyène* wasn't destroyed by fire, she'd be armed and across their path as they tried to make their way downriver. The damage to her hull made no difference in these waters. Indeed, it was quite possible that she could be brought under control sufficiently to be brought up, by warping if necessary, to bombard them. Harry began to castigate himself for blowing apart that bollard, then realized that he'd had no choice, since even after taking casualties Tressoir probably had more men available to fight than he did.

"Flowers," said Harry, stopping so suddenly that Pender cannoned into him. "Take a party and stay with the guns. Heave one round and keep up a steady fire downriver, just in case they anchor, or try to come back in boats. If they do, and those bastards show any sign of trying to get ashore, tip the whole battery into the river."

"Aye, aye, Capt'n."

It was odd how quickly silence descended and the smoke cleared. Apart from the glow of fire from Tressoir's ship, still drifting down the Aure, it was as though no fight had taken place. If any of the inhabitants of Isigny were curious they were not about to poke their noses out of window or door to have a look. Indeed Harry rather suspected that at the first gunshot they'd abandoned hearth and hob for the safety of the dilapidated citadel. The silence didn't last long. Flowers had set up one of the cannon, and his first shot boomed out, sending a ball into the river that threw up a great spout of silver water.

By the time the party came abreast of the *Lothian* it was pitch dark again, only a faint glim of light on the edge of a billowing cloud serving to show the outline of the darkened ship.

"There has to be some kind of guard, surely?" said Harry, as he reached the bottom of the gangplank.

"Happen they's run," Pender replied, following his captain gingerly as he made his way up on to the deck, any noise they might make covered by Flowers's second salvo.

Even in this constant current, once the sound of that shot died away, the ship creaked and groaned slightly. But that was the only sound Harry could hear. He fought the temptation to pass straight on to *Bucephalas*. An armed party aboard was a threat that must be dealt with before he could go aboard his own ship. Slowly, he and Pender crept towards the poop, passing into total darkness as they approached Illingworth's cabin door.

Placing an ear next to it, Harry could detect no sound. Slowly he took hold of the lever and pushed it down, Pender behind him with raised pistols in both hands. As soon as it was free he pushed it and jumped backwards, only to be greeted by a dark and deserted corridor. There was no alternative to making their way down past the chartroom and Derouac's quarters to the main cabin door, which yielded just as easily to the touch.

"Is anyone there?" said Harry softly, as he pressed his body back against the hallway bulkhead, feeling extremely foolish, since this was no game of hide and seek but a risky venture in which a man had only to fire a pistol at the narrow doorway to be almost certain of doing mortal damage.

"We are here," came a female voice.

"I told you to be quiet!"

There was no mistaking the peremptory tone of Sir William Parker's irate response. Judging by the lilt in the other voice it was that of the travelling companion, Lady Katherine Fitzgerald.

"Are there any guards aboard?"

"None," the girl answered.

The gun on the quay spoke again, the orange glow from the discharge silhouetting several figures, that followed by a lantern, which threw out a burst of proper light as Sir William unshaded it, flooding the cabin. Harry, tense as he was, nearly laughed. The entire group of captives, barring Illingworth, were sitting around in a semicircle as though attending a musical interlude at a party. The merchant captain was lying across the foot-lockers, the white bandages that covered his torso picking up more light than that which shone on the others.

"Ludlow!" said Parker, standing up. "I might have guessed it was you."

The note of anger threw Harry for a moment, and robbed his response of any force. "If you guessed, why are you sitting in the dark?"

"To avoid detection, of course." He turned to glare at Lady Katherine Fitzgerald. "Which we might have achieved if this young lady had done what she was told."

"Forgive me, Sir William, I don't follow."

"That does not surprise me, sir, since you could scarcely be classed as a gentleman."

"Sir William," Harry barked, his eyes blazing. "Have you ever been clipped around the ear with the barrel of a pistol?"

The older man wasn't frightened, puffing his chest out in indignation. "How dare you, sir."

"He's given his parole, Captain Ludlow," said Illingworth. His voice was weak and his face had lost all the high colour that Harry remembered. "And being Sir William, he believes he should stick to it."

Harry walked straight past Parker, to kneel by Illingworth. His hair was much more grey now than red. But the eyes showed some fire, as though the vital spark of his being was intact.

"Then Sir William is, as we always suspected, a damned fool."

"I heard that, Ludlow!"

Flowers fired a fourth time, but still Harry was sure he heard the sound of repressed female laughter, though he chose to ignore both that and the butt of it. "Do you feel well enough to con the ship, if I give you some men to help unmoor her?"

"Tressoir?"

"Is beaten," Harry lied. "Now we must get *Lothian* ready so that when the tide peaks you can steer her out into the estuary."

"You'll do no such thing, Ludlow. Did you not hear what Captain Illingworth has said? I have given M. de Tressoir my parole."

Harry shot to his feet, so quickly that Parker was forced to take a step back. "I don't care what you gave him. This ship, and you, are sailing out of here, and if I have to tie you to a mast to achieve that then so be it."

"My honour—"

"Is as stupid as the man who claims it," Harry shouted, a remark that produced an anxious look from Lady Parker and an outright giggle from the two girls. "I am telling you what to do, and if it doesn't sit with what you call your honour you may blame me."

Parker raised his head, to look at a point over Harry's shoulder, one hand on his breast. "I shall, sir, I most certainly shall."

"Pender, help Captain Illingworth to his feet. I think the air of hypocrisy in here might be bad for his condition."

Harry was gone before Parker could respond, and one look at Pender's face was enough to make the old man back out of the way. Tenderly, Pender helped Illingworth to his feet, asking one of the ladies to fetch his coat. The young red-haired girl with the green eyes obliged, favouring him with a conspiratorial smile as she did so.

"Just make sure that old sod don't lock the cabin door behind us," Pender said softly. "We ain't got the margin of time to hack it down."

Harry found the rest of his crew gathered alongside *Bucephalas*'s hull, not one of them having dared to go aboard before their captain. He made his way up the gangplank with the care he'd shown aboard *Lothian*, unable to believe that Tressoir had been so confident of his defences that he hadn't bothered to man either ship with even an anchor watch.

The smell of fresh-cut wood rose to his nostrils, and as he groped his way around the deck he was sure he could feel the places where new timber had replaced old. The deck was untidy, full of shavings and carpenter's tools. Gently, the ship rocked, as the current sped up or slowed down enough to move her. Harry felt that familiar sensation in his chest as the deck moved under his feet, the feeling of affection for a ship that was impossible to relate to a landsman.

Bucephalas was alive; in a mess, but still a ship. And then as he looked aloft, the cloud cover broke, to show a complete set of masts, fore, main, mizzen with driver gaff and boom, and traces of rigging already in place. Flowers let fly again, which dragged him back to reality, and the mammoth task he still faced if they were to get out of this place in one piece.

"Right, lads," he called over the side, "get aboard and see what needs to be done to take her to sea!"

CHAPTER THIRTY-THREE

THERE WAS a mass of things requiring attention and very little time available to do them. Downriver, the tide would be at flood within five hours and that would be the only chance Harry would have of getting either his ship or the *Lothian* out into deep water. The alternative was to stay in Isigny for a whole day, at constant risk of a counterattack by Tressoir or the residents of the town, then drop downriver on a tide several inches lower. That was unattractive, to say the least, because he might find himself aground on a sandbank, with no prospect of a tide high enough to float him off for a fortnight. And to cap all that, the less time Tressoir had to adopt measures to stop him the better.

His acute shortage of manpower was another factor in his calculations, since it could only be made worse by delay, but even if it exposed his men to fire he had no alternative but to light as many lanterns as he could find. A quick inspection showed that the rudder assembly had been entirely rebuilt, although despite her masts there were no yards aloft to carry even the minimum of canvas. And when he went below he discovered that Tressoir had obviously raided her sail locker leaving just two bolts of canvas, as well as removing the powder and shot. The realization wasn't long in coming that there would be no time to prepare *Bucephalas* for departure under her own power, and no way of turning her into a fighting ship without an armoury.

Drifting was too dangerous; that left the option of a tow by the *Lothian*. Leaving Pender to tidy things up he went back down the quay to have a quick look. The damage to the larboard bulwarks was still there but his heart lifted somewhat when he saw that her yards were crossed, some with furled sails still rigged.

Before going aboard he decided to find out why Flowers had stopped firing.

"There's not much more'n ten charges left, your honour, an' I didn't want to blaze them off without your say-so."

"Any sign of the enemy?" Harry asked, peering downriver.

"None. From what little I could see they got their fires under control. I reckon, instead of anchorin' right off, he let his ship drift down below that soddin' battery."

"He may have gone even further than that, Flowers."

"How we goin' to deal with them?"

"Let's deal with these first," Harry replied, pointing to the guns on the quay. "We need to get them back aboard the *Lothian*."

"Christ, your honour, we're a bit short of manpower for that sort of thing."

"Leave the one you were using in place, loaded and ready, and get a rope on the rest and haul them up amidships of the Indiaman."

The next hour was a whirlwind of activity. Men too wounded to labour were sent aboard *Bucephalas,* with instructions that those more ambulant should look to their companions. The four who had died were laid out in the forepeak, for burial when and if they got to sea. Guards had to be posted so that no sudden attack could be launched from the town, and a constant watch kept on the river to ward off any danger of a counterattack.

Pender was instructed to make a sea anchor from the available canvas so that *Bucephalas* when towed would hold some strain on the cable and avoid running into the Indiaman's stern. Before the guns were brought alongside, Harry had men smash their way into the small warehouses that lined the quay, to look for powder, shot, and canvas, with strict instructions to confine themselves to the ground floors. The population of Isigny had taken no part in the fight. The last thing he wanted was that by some inadvertent action they should have reason to do so.

Aboard the *Lothian,* also ablaze with lanterns, those who could be spared were hauling out a thick cable to tow his ship while others were reeving a whip from the capstan to the main-yard strong enough to lift first the gun barrels, then the carriages they rested on. Illingworth, ghostly pale, was limping round the ship, checking on various pieces of equipment to ensure that they were in good working order. Seeing him stagger and lean on the rail, Harry had two of his men fetch the captain. Another was sent for a chair so that he could sit by the wheel.

"I would like to be sanguine, Captain Ludlow," he said, rubbing a weary hand across his brow, "but how do you propose to get us out of this predicament?"

"I'll get us out," said Harry, emphatically. "No one would have given us a dog's chance of getting in, but we managed that."

"Would I be allowed to enumerate some of the imponderables?"

"You don't have to, Captain Illingworth. I know what they are. There's a battery of 6-pounders a quarter of a mile downstream, which we have to sail past, and the range is less than the toss of a ship's biscuit."

"With our opponent right behind them, no doubt."

Harry shook his head. "No, he's further downriver, I should think, anchored across the stream like he was when we arrived, hiding behind a cable boom that stretches between the banks."

"That is one imponderable that I knew nothing of," Illingworth replied, with deepening gloom.

Knowing about it didn't help Harry, who had spent some of the time since the battle had ended wondering what he could have done differently. He should have interrogated that Frenchman earlier. Yet if he'd left a party to cut the boom, that would have left him even more short-handed when he attacked. It was tempting to look at what had happened up till now and class it as easy. But that wasn't the case. The margin had been tight, and every man he'd brought on to the quay had taken part in the fight. Happy at last with the word luck, he knew he'd ridden it hard. It hadn't been flawless, but it would have to bear even more strain for a satisfactory conclusion. His shout for Jubilee made Illingworth jump, and sent a flash of pain across his lined face.

"We have to break though it. I am hoping we will be able

to." Jubilee's arrival killed whatever question Illingworth harboured. Harry led him away from the merchant captain, head bent as he quizzed him. Then, sending him back to his duties, he returned to the wheel. "We had a go at sawing through it when we came upriver."

"A go?"

"That was the man with the saw," said Harry, pointing at Jubilee's retreating back. "He reckons he got more than halfway through before he had to abandon the job. Now you know as well as I do, Captain Illingworth, that a strand of rope is only as strong as its weakest part."

"I think we should leave the Parkers here."

"No!"

Illingworth, who'd sunk down in the chair, pulled himself up so that his words would carry some weight. "Captain Ludlow, what you are proposing do to is extremely dangerous. First, you've mentioned that battery, which could easily kill all of us, including my passengers."

"They're no more than 6-pounder cannon. A ship this size will be able to bear the damage. Look at what she's withstood already."

"I cannot share your certainty. And even if you are right, we will be drifting downriver towards a rope boom and an armed enemy with no means of halting our progress. Should *Lothian* be brought to a standstill by that boom, your ship cannot help but run on board my stern. We will then be just as helpless as you were at St. Aubin."

"That is possible, I grant you."

"Then for God's sake leave Sir William and his family here. He is so attached to his honour that he will not blame you. Indeed he'll thank you for it."

"I don't care a toss for Sir William's honour," Harry snapped, "but I do care for my ability to pursue my chosen profession."

"I fail to see the connection, sir."

Harry opened his mouth to explain, but the thought of the complexities of his situation stopped him. "A state of ignorance that you must suffer, Captain, since I have no intention of enlightening you."

"That is not satisfactory to me."

"I have one question to put to you, Captain Illingworth," said Harry softly, crouching down so that his words should not sound in any way threatening. "Will you take the wheel of your ship, or shall I?"

He hesitated a second, looking into Harry's eyes, easily able to see how determined he was. "*Lothian* is mine, sir. I know her ways."

"Thank you," Harry replied, unbuttoning his coat. His back was aching like the very Devil, and he wondered if the pain of his exertions showed in his face the way they did in Illingworth's. "Now if you will forgive me we are a little short of muscle on the capstan. You would oblige me if you would see the guns aboard."

Time stopped them from getting more than three of the artillery pieces on to the upper deck. They were watched by Charlotte Parker and Lady Katherine Fitzgerald, who'd come out of the cabin, probably to get away from Sir William, and, sick of their staring, Harry sent them off to see Pender, to find out how matters were progressing on *Bucephalas*. What he heard when they returned was not entirely satisfactory, though he was impressed by the crisp delivery of Lady Katherine, as well as her command of the technical terminology. The men who'd raided the warehouses had stolen enough canvas. There was no way of cutting and sewing it into a suit of sails, but the decks were clear, the rudder checked, and the sea anchor already in the water.

"Are we going to have another fight, Captain Ludlow?" she asked. Unlike Parker's daughter, there was no trace of alarm in those green eyes as Harry replied in the affirmative. She merely nodded. "Then there will be a possibility of more men wounded?"

"There is a very good chance."

"Then it would be to advantage if we were to prepare bandages and such, and set aside an area for them to be attended to."

"Very much so, Lady Katherine," Harry replied. "I would suggest the orlop deck, which is the one below the lower deck."

There was a slight flash of anger in the eyes, as if what he'd said smacked of condescension, though nothing in her voice matched it. "I know where the orlop is, Captain Ludlow. You seem to forget I have, unfortunately, been on this ship for several months."

Harry was now aching all over, covered in sweat from his exertions on the capstan. Nevertheless he managed an elegant bow, which brought a slight but engaging smile to her lips. For a second their eyes locked.

Charlotte Parker, aware of how long the stare held, was looking at the pair with slight amazement. Harry turned to her and smiled. "You may inform your father that we are about to unmoor the ship. He and Lady Parker would be safer below decks."

"In his mind he is already there, Captain Ludlow, in the bilges indeed, so much have you cast down his spirits."

"Then tell him that I am merely following instructions given to me by your uncle. In order to oblige your father I would have to deny Admiral Parker's wishes, a dangerous thing to do for someone in my occupation."

"Is that the truth, sir?" she asked suspiciously. "If it is, you would have saved him great hardship if you said so earlier."

Katherine Fitzgerald took Miss Parker's arm, to lead her away. "I think then as now Captain Ludlow had other things on his mind, matters that overbore the sensitive subject of your father's pride."

Harry grinned at her, then turned and yelled, "Belay!" in a voice loud enough to have both women scurrying back towards the cabin.

"Captain Illingworth, there are enough men aboard to see to the unmooring. The current should take you out from the bank, but as you will see I have trimmed your yards round to take what little wind we have."

"And *Bucephalas?*"

"Will be at single cable, which my men will slip as soon as

you have some way on the ship, and there is strain on the tow."

"You have set yourself too much of a task, sir." He continued quickly when he observed Harry's frown, "If I am repeating myself in saying that, you must forgive me."

"I think I am committed, Captain Illingworth, so it makes little difference."

"It would pain me to see you killed, sir." Wan and pale as he was, he managed to communicate in his eyes that the sentiments he stated were genuine. But Harry's eyes were just as expressive.

"Then I must wish you good fortune, and express the fond wish to see you again, so that we may toast that most ephemeral commodity."

Harry went to the gangway to join Pender. Dreaver was aboard *Bucephalas* to con the ship, with a couple of men and the walking wounded to help him. Illingworth had been allotted another dozen, the very minimum he could work with, considering that he might get a chance to raise more sail. Four were put into the centipedes, so that they could drift downstream and pick up the survivors from Harry's party. The remainder were on the quayside, armed and ready. A mere seventeen sailors, they had their own task: to attack a gun emplacement that if it hadn't been fortified before would certainly be so now.

"Might I suggest that you use the time available to house at least one of the cannon," said Harry, softly. The merchant captain nodded as Harry repeated his final wish. "Cast off your mooring as soon as you hear the first shot, Captain Illingworth. The very first, pistol, musket, or gun."

The merchant captain nodded once more, and eased his hand out from his side to shake Harry's. He responded gently and made his way down the gangplank. Two of his crew allotted to the *Lothian* were at the bottom, joking with their mates, in the way that men do when seeing friends off to a fight.

"Lads," said Harry quietly, "if that Sir William Parker tries to interfere, clap him in the cable tier to moan at the rats."

He was gone before they could reply, leading his men along

the stone quay, now clear of guns. Those that had not gone aboard the *Lothian* had been tipped into the river. His shoulder ached abominably, after the exertions on the capstan, but he could do nothing to ease it, so it had to be ignored.

The path that led down the riverbank was well worn, having been used frequently in the past by Tressoir's men. At this very moment they could be right ahead, lying in ambush to catch the Englishmen they knew must come. Covering something like half the distance on this trail was a calculated risk, a belief that if they had prepared a trap it would have been laid on the rising ground near their gun emplacements. There they'd have a clear sight of their approaching enemies, plus a safe haven to withdraw to if matters went against them.

The first grey tinge of approaching daylight was touching the sky, oddly deepening the gloom rather than easing it, as it took away what illumination they'd enjoyed from the moon and the stars. Harry, still out front, was gnawing on all the things that could go wrong. He was banking on the hope that Tressoir would not deplete his ship to reinforce these guns. Well placed as they were, they were too light in calibre to sink or stop a large ship floating downriver. They'd been put there to stop ships' boats, and might very well have been turned round by now to blast this track.

But that didn't alter the facts. The Frenchman would know that the only place he could stop Harry Ludlow was at that boom, which would allow him to fire into a stationary target snagged on his rope. Against that, he must be aware that Harry knew about the boom, and so would only come downriver if he had some plan to break it. The only thing Harry could do was to put himself in his enemy's shoes and try to think like him. And that had worked well enough to bring him here.

"Halt," he whispered, holding up his hand, as he felt the ground beneath his feet begin to rise a fraction. "Pender, you and I will go forward, me in the undergrowth on the riverbank, you circling round through those trees on the left."

"Some trees," said Pender softly, nodding towards the stunted growths, gnarled, thin affairs, that were obviously part of an apple orchard.

"The rest of you keep one of us in sight, but don't come forward if they open up with muskets. All we're trying to do right now is fix their position."

The next ten minutes, with the sky getting lighter all the time, were the most nerve-racking in Harry's entire career. There was no way of moving through the bushes in silence: it was as if every twig he broke or leaf he rustled was audible for miles, and to use what little cover there was he had to stay within the deepest thickets. He could see nothing much to his front, his only hope that whoever let fly first would do so excitedly or that Pender might observe them as they revealed themselves and shout a warning.

The bushes ended so abruptly that he jumped back into them in fear, tripping on a root and rolling a quarter of the way back down the incline. Covered in scratches, his shoulders throbbing with pain, he hauled himself back to the clearing which overlooked the river. The guns were gone, the stone walls set up to protect them containing nothing but the detritus of human occupation. He could see the hoof prints where mules or horses had been used to take them away. At the soft footfall behind him he spun round, pistol out.

"Shall I call forward the lads?" said Pender.

"Do that," said Harry, raising his pistol. "And get someone to bring on the galleys."

In the misty morning air the discharge sent up all those birds who listened to these creatures blunder through their habitat. "Tell one or two of them to fire off their weapons as soon as they get here. We wouldn't want Captain Illingworth to entertain any doubts."

"Can I ask just one question, Capt'n?" said Pender, sweeping his musket around the empty emplacement. "Is this a good thing, or a bad thing?"

"That very much depends on Jubilee," Harry replied, enigmatically.

CHAPTER THIRTY-FOUR

THE ASSAULT party were in the centipedes well before the *Lothian* made it out into the channel. Harry had watched the upper rigging anxiously, jerking back and forth as if willing it to move. There was little in the way of a breeze, but slowly, agonizingly, the three masts separated, taking individual form. Then at last the bowsprit cleared the downstream undergrowth, as Illingworth took his ship well out into the channel, way beyond the centre, to give Dreaver some ability to manoeuvre in hauling off *Bucephalas*.

The next part was tricky, for both men conning their ships. Having towed *Bucephalas* out on a short cable it had to be paid out to lessen the risk of a collision, without either ship losing her momentum. The River Aure was far from a fast-flowing stream: a better description would be steady without being entirely gentle. But Illingworth was a very experienced sailor, who'd had to move his ship around many a crowded harbour, and the cone-shaped canvas sea anchor, acting like a drag, stopped Harry's ship, much lighter than the Indiaman, from closing the gap.

"Right, lads," said Harry, softly. "Let's get downriver and see what that bastard has got prepared for us."

The oars bit into the water. There was no haste now, since Harry didn't want to get too far ahead of the ships. Still mulling over the problems he might face, he knew that surprise was impossible. Tressoir would see *Lothian*'s upper poles well before he was in any danger, and would thus have ample time to get his men into position and steady them for their task. The idea that he might rush downstream in the galleys, to try and board, had to be put aside. This was daylight, not night, and the Frenchman had shifted those batteries. What surprise they'd achieved eight hours earlier would not work again. Those gunners would be itching to get their revenge, and would have a better idea of how to lay their pieces to blast these flimsy galleys out of the water.

Really, it all came down to one hope which diminished the more it was gnawed at: that Jubilee had so damaged the boom that it would give way when Illingworth, in a fully laden 800-ton ship, ran on to it. Unless he'd got into a boat and inspected the entire length of the thing Tressoir would have no idea that his main defence had been weakened. And if it went as Harry hoped it would, the surprise would be just as acute as the night before, and the result similar. The problem was what to do if he was wrong.

"Pender," he called. "Come alongside."

His servant obliged, the dark-tanned face fixed with a look of deep curiosity. Having been with Harry Ludlow as long as he had, he knew his propensity for sudden changes of plan, and judging by his captain's expression, this was one of those occasions. Oars were boated in both galleys so that the counters were touching, and as they continued to drift downstream, Harry leant over to whisper so that their conversation would be as private as possible.

"Back upriver to *Bucephalas*. Get a couple of hawsers ready in the bows in case we have to take up the tow with the centipedes. Then get over to *Lothian* and transfer Sir William Parker and the ladies to our ship."

"Captain Illingworth is bound to ask me why, your honour."

"No, Pender. As soon as he hears you ask that, he'll know why. If he can't break through with his weight, I intend to snag that boom on to his ship, fire it, and burn our way through."

"That's a lot of money you'd be chucking away."

"It's that or lose our own ship, Pender," Harry hissed, "which is *not* something I'm prepared to do."

"This should be the other way round, your honour," Pender insisted. "And pride, which is what's at stake here, should be put aside. The Indiaman may not have many guns, but it's got a couple, and it has sails aloft. With our crew aboard it would be a hard nut to crack—too much for a French barky full of holes."

"Burn my own ship under Tressoir's eyes?"

"With *Lothian* as a prize you'll have enough money to buy another, Capt'n. Then you can come and blow the bastard to Kingdom come."

Harry dropped his head to look at the black water of the River Aure. He knew Pender was right, but that didn't make agreement any easier. He'd lost a ship before, and knew that much as he loved his vessels it was an affection that could be transferred. But the loss of pride in finally conceding his ship to Tressoir was hard.

"Ship up ahead, Capt'n," called the man in the bow, "set across the channel at the river join."

Harry moved to the middle of the boat and stood up. *L'Hyène* was where he'd expected it to be, moored head and stern, in tidal water. He could see where the strain lay on the cables, taut downriver and slack at the bows. That would reverse soon as the tide turned. High water was at eleven o'clock, which meant he had less than two hours to not only break through these defences but also make it down to the estuary and get over the sandbanks to the safety of some depth under his keel.

Looking back, he could see that the *Lothian*'s progress was painfully slow. She had few sails to give her way, and was yawing across the channel. While the drag of her tow was checking that, it was also robbing her of pace. There would be little point in hitting that cable just drifting. The more speed Illingworth had the better, massively multiplying the force he could bring to bear, so it would be better to cast off *Bucephalas,* which would continue to drift downriver, albeit more slowly. If the boom was still intact he'd try to steer her away from *Lothian,* haul Tressoir's cable up the side as soon as she touched, and set fire to his ship. Even a soaking wet rope would eventually part in such a conflagration. Once the fire was started there would be nothing Tressoir could do to stop it.

He'd attack *Lothian,* of course, as soon as he saw what Harry was about. But every man he had would be on her by then, perhaps enough to repel his boarders, while the centipedes would still be available for a swift evacuation if things went against them. That would be a defeat, the third one in a row, but he'd fire the East Indiaman before he abandoned her, so Tressoir would watch his prize, as well as the ship he'd hoped to privateer in, burn down to the waterline.

He looked at *Bucephalas* long and hard. Even under bare poles she was his ship, bought brand new, and incorporating several features he'd insisted on. The sacrifice would be enormous, and he searched for alternatives. He tried to recall from the previous night how high the cable had been on the bank compared to the higher water mark created by the tidal surge. Even taut, its own weight would keep it in the water midstream. But what would happen once *Lothian* struck it? The weight of her bows would carry it downstream.

"Pender," he called, "carry out the orders I just gave you regarding the cables, but put them out of the hawse-holes." Seeing the look on his servant's face, he smiled. "Don't worry. I know you're right about *Bucephalas*. But it might make a bit of difference if she arrives on that boom sooner rather than later."

There was a split second's pause, while Pender contemplated asking what Harry was up to. But the look he got convinced him there was no time.

"We're going to get out of here, Pender, take my word on it."

"With one ship?"

Harry grinned at him. "That depends on my luck, friend."

If Illingworth was curious why Harry asked him to cast off his tow he hid it well, aware perhaps that the men on the deck, even if they were few in number, were not really his to command. Besides, in a galley going at full tilt there wasn't much time to converse with a fellow who was still giving orders.

"If you can get up any more speed once you have done that I'd be obliged. I want you to stay in the centre of the channel and hit that cable with as much weight as you can."

Harry was out of earshot before the merchant captain had framed any of the dozen questions he wanted to ask. He gave orders for a party to go below and release the cable, then turned to watch as both galleys streaked towards *Bucephalas*. Pender had reached it first, shipping oars and swinging round, half his crew following him swiftly on to the deck.

But he couldn't watch for long, so didn't see the first rope fly out of the hawse-hole. As soon as his tow cable ran out to splash astern, *Lothian* picked up a fraction of speed, and her main course, though hauled right round, began to take a modicum of wind. Easing the braces increased the speed a little more, especially when Illingworth put up his rudder to steer more towards the northern bank. The half-knot gain he employed to cross over the midstream where the current was strongest, where the yards were bowsed tight again to take maximum advantage of the breeze.

To call it speed was a misnomer of the worst kind. But it was movement and by taking his ship nearer to the southern bank he was able to swing round so that he had more time with the wind playing on his sails. All the while, Flowers, one of Harry Ludlow's men, kept him informed about what lay ahead, relaying information from that curious crescent-shaped face, and talking out of the corner of his mouth as though imparting a secret.

Twice more Illingworth was able to use that manoeuvre, gaining yet another half-knot, now close enough to the enemy to listen to Flowers listing the damage the corvette had sustained. Aware that he was running out of room, he finally looked himself. Ahead, over the bowsprit, Tressoir waited for him. The sides of *l'Hyène* were a mess, with gaping holes where once the Frenchman had housed his guns. And she was low in the water with a steady stream of silver shooting over the side, evidence that at least a proportion of his men were forced to pump ship just to stay afloat.

Looking left and right, the strands of rope, dropping from the riverbank into the water, were easy to see; a hawser thick enough to hold a ship-of-the-line at anchor in a gale, and showing no signs of any damage that he could observe. It was as if his looking at the cable had been the signal Tressoir had been waiting for. He fired off a signal gun, and Illingworth saw the hawser, no doubt attached to an onshore capstan, begin to lift.

"What the hell's the Capt'n about?" said Flowers, who turned to tell Illingworth about the cannon he'd spotted on the riverbank, and in looking past him, had seen *Bucephalas*.

Illingworth spun round as the first shots were fired from Tressoir's new battery position, which forced him to look forward again, to observe the three 6-pounder balls that landed in a pattern right ahead of his bowsprit. The Frenchman was warning him, inviting him to drop anchor and avoid a fight, perhaps determined that such a valuable prize should not suffer any more harm. But he looked back upriver quick enough, not sure that what he had seen the first time was true.

The two centipedes were out ahead of *Bucephalas,* the men in them practically standing up, so great was the strain on the oars. The privateer began to gain on *Lothian,* and the way the oarsmen were struggling that would continue. With no sails to bar his view the figure of Harry Ludlow at the wheel was plain, while Pender was in the bows, yelling at the boats to put in greater effort.

"Cable's nearly right up," said Flowers, forcing Illingworth to look forward again. Only the very centre of the hawser was still submerged, the remainder, now clear, dripping water from long strands of green weed. Illingworth trimmed the wheel, bringing his ship at right angles to the boom. No more guns were fired after that warning salvo, and it was clear that Tressoir intended to let him run into the cable, absolutely sure it would hold even the weight of a laden East Indiaman.

A last glance over his shoulder showed that *Bucephalas* had gained a little more speed. The rowers were still straining like mad, trying to get her to go even faster, with Harry steering to pass by the *Lothian*'s starboard rail: and having overcome the initial inertia, they were having some success, even if it was slight. Those members of Harry's crew he had aboard, even if they had no clue as to what their captain intended, were cheering them on, the galleys now nearly abreast of the *Lothian*'s stern casements.

Illingworth shouted for them to man the braces, to be ready to swing the yards round so that if they broke through he could put up his helm to take the westerly wind over the quarter. He had to grab the wheel hard to stay upright as they hit the cable. There was a crack to starboard at the point where it had been half sawn through—but the boom checked their progress, enough to sway the masts towards the bows with only the preventer stays keeping them in place.

Lothian slowed then stopped completely, her stern beginning to swing in the current, stuck in that momentary hiatus before the weight of the cable on his bows began to push her back. There was only one certainty. With a sinking heart Illingworth realized, as his main course began to blot out his view, that he had managed to break only a few fibres of Tressoir's boom.

The air was full of yells. Pender, now coming abreast, stood in the bows of *Bucephalas* calling for more effort, egged on by the men near the *Lothian*'s starboard rail. The bulk of his own ship denied Illingworth the same view as Harry Ludlow. The thick green slimy cable had been forced clear of the water across its entire length by the weight of his ship. By the bank it now stood several feet in the air. Intrigued by the screams of encouragement coming from Harry's men, he staggered over to the rail, just in time to see both centipedes, still going at full-lick, slide under the raised cable, the ropes coming out of the hawse-holes low enough to allow them to keep the tow.

Pender had leapt from the bows and was now running backwards to join his captain, a wise precaution since the prow of *Bucephalas* was no more than a few feet from Tressoir's thick hawser. The ship hit it at speed and Illingworth looked up, expecting to see all three masts go by the board. Instead there was a mighty crack, louder than any gunshot he'd ever heard, and the hawser parted on the far side of Harry Ludlow's ship like a piece of thin string on a parcel. The singing sound followed as it whipped across the top of the river, his bows forming the fulcrum point for a snaking, cracking, deadly rope, completely out of control.

The guns on the riverbank opened up immediately, only to be silenced as the cable sliced over their heads, at a height that would have decapitated any man who stood up. It killed no one, but

instilled such fear in the gunners that Illingworth could see them
abandoning their pieces to dive for cover, lest that deadly rope
whip back again.

"Flowers," yelled Illingworth, "take a haul on those braces.
Then once they're secured man the guns."

Lothian had already begun to move on the current, but now
able to swing his ship, the effect of the wind on the sails was palpable and immediate. Tressoir opened up with his own ship's
cannon, the few that fired clear evidence of the depletion he had
suffered both in ordnance and manpower. Chunks of the forward
bulwarks flew up in the air and splinters scythed across the foredeck, miraculously doing no harm to any of the crew.

Harry Ludlow had cast off his tow lines and was using the
speed he still had to steer for the main channel. But the boats,
even if the oarsmen must be near exhaustion, were rowing in a
wide arc, to come round on *l'Hyène*'s unprotected side, as though
intent on boarding. Seeing that, Illingworth ported his helm, and
aimed his bowsprit straight at Tressoir. The Frenchman was no
fool. He knew that a ship of that size, with the damage he'd already
suffered, might actually hole him so badly he'd sink. He fired off
a second salvo, more ragged and less effective than the first, then
sent his gunners to the shrouds, to run up and let fall his sails,
while others were at the cables, swinging axes like madmen.

"Stay still, you bastard," Illingworth said to himself, stepping
away from the wheel. The sudden feeling that came over him
caused by tension and his wounds was too much to bear, and he
fell forward on to the deck. Flowers had him taken below, then
grasped the spinning wheel. He'd never conned a ship this size
before. But he was a sailor. With a steady wind coming in from
the west, and a bowsprit that could only be aimed south, there
was not much choice to make.

The course brought him closer to Harry Ludlow and Pender,
standing on the quarterdeck of *Bucephalas,* which was wallowing
gently on the slight river-swell. Flowers let out a whoop, then
grabbed a telescope from the rack, looped an arm round a spoke,

and raised it up. Pender sprung into focus, grinning from ear to ear. But his captain, when Flowers swung the glass to his face, was looking past the *Lothian,* his countenance set hard. Then his lips moved.

Harry Ludlow spent the next two minutes cursing the fact that he had no sails and no guns, each word spat towards an enemy just visible on his shattered quarterdeck.

"One day, friend, I'm going to meet that bastard mid-channel, fully armed and rigged, in clear weather, when he's too far away from home to run."

"You've beaten him, Captain," said Pender, happily.

"Not yet," Harry replied, looking around the near-empty deck, dotted with turpentine barrels that had he failed would have been used to start a fire. He knew just how slim the margin had been, but that did little to dent his frustration. "Only when I've sunk him, or I tow his ship into an English port with my flag over his, will I have beaten him."

It was almost as if Tressoir heard him, and was trying to accept the challenge. He fired off a gun to attract Harry's attention, then raised his hat, and in an extravagant gesture, performed a deep bow.

The rowers in the centipedes had spun round to race back to *Bucephalas* as soon as they saw Tressoir's men in the shrouds. Ropes were attached again, and soon they had her under tow, hard work at first, but one that eased as the tide peaked. Tressoir was in their wake, the same stream of water being pumped over the side. Harry and Pender were watching him anxiously, desperate to see what kind of speed he could muster.

"If we can beat out to sea, Pender, I don't think he will follow us."

"I hope you have the right of it, Capt'n."

"With the kind of water he's shipping in a river, he'd be mad to take *l'Hyène* out into open water."

"I should think he's mad, all right," said Pender with another heartening grin. "You just ruined his whole existence."

CHAPTER THIRTY-FIVE

RYKERT dropped his telescope, rubbed his eyes, then raised it again. It was a theatrical gesture designed to amuse everyone on the *Amethyst*'s quarterdeck, but there was no doubting that what he'd observed was singular.

"Do you recognize the hull, Mr Levenson?" he demanded.

The midshipman, who'd been with the officer of the watch, and had actually fetched the captain from his cabin, was dreading the question, fully expecting that he would be subjected to another bout of ribbing from his fellows for what had happened off St Helen's. He didn't actually want to say the name, but with a direct question from his commanding officer, he could hardly avoid it.

"*Bucephalas*, sir."

"You'd never know her by her sail plan, that's certain. I don't think I've ever seen such a get-up aloft, even on an Arab dhow."

Harry was watching him too, wondering the very same. Rykert had many traits that made him uneasy, but he could not be faulted as a sailor or a disciplinarian. He ran a tight ship, something which had been obvious from his previous visit, when called to explain himself in the company of Illingworth. He knew he'd have to go aboard again, even if the naval officer didn't demand it of him. In some senses that made matters easier. There would be less need for explanation with Rykert than any other King's ship.

"You have a singular way of going about your business, Ludlow," Rykert said, indicating he should sit down. "The last time we met you were short of a bowsprit and foremast, but this is even more remarkable. You look as though you're flying Mother Riley's washing."

Harry wondered how many of his officers Rykert had tried that joke on, since it had a very rehearsed quality. But, though annoyed, he made a great effort to appear to take it in good part, determined to extract what he needed quickly, and be on his way.

"Gimcrack ain't it, Rykert. But I had a little dust-up with that same fellow who did for me in the Channel. He took my ship, and I was obliged to make him give it back again."

"Is this a tale that will last over dinner?"

"It's decent of you to ask," Harry replied, reaching into his coat to pull out a letter, "and I'm happy to give you a swift account. But I am on pressing business, as this will tell you."

Rykert leant over to take the letter, deep suspicion evident in his eyes. That changed to wonder as he read it, those same eyes expanding in amazement.

"How do you do it, Ludlow?" he demanded, waving it. "The first time I haul you up you've got exemptions signed by Dundas. And now you present me with orders that oblige me to leave you be from Sir Peter Parker."

"I offer them only to save time. I'm so short-handed that you'd be exceeding your authority to take a single one of my men."

Rykert drummed his fingers on the edge of his desk, then stood up and walked over to the wine cooler. "I'm not going to let you depart without some kind of explanation, sir. And I suggest we accomplish that over a glass of port."

"Do you know the position of the fleet?"

"Naturally," Rykert replied, as he poured two glasses. "*Amethyst* is one of the patrolling frigates responsible for warning Bridport of any French activity."

"Then we shall agree to a trade. I will tell you how I came to have such an unusual top hamper, if you tell me where I can find *Queen Charlotte*."

Rykert put the stopper back in the decanter and stood still, his back to his visitor. Harry had no doubt what he was thinking: given what had happened at Spithead, and the subsequent events at the Nore, why that particular ship? It underlined to Harry once more just how clever Rykert was, and how careful with his words he would need to be.

"I take it Admiral Bridport's course and speed are not secret."

"No," the naval officer replied, a troubled look in his eye as he returned to sit at his desk, "but then neither are they common knowledge."

Harry picked up Parker's letter. "It does say in here that I'm to be rendered every assistance."

Rykert suddenly looked up, his frown clearing. "And you shall be, Ludlow. Just as long as you are as open with me as I am prepared to be with you."

"Let me tell you about the trouble I had getting my ship back."

Rykert smiled. "I am happy to listen, just as long as you don't depart without telling me the rest."

As Harry explained what had happened with Tressoir, his mind was working on another level. His host was not going to give him the position and course of the fleet unless it was explained to him why it was required. Very likely, Rykert had heard how Harry had become involved in matters aboard *London,* and the way he had financed that lavish funeral. That provided no more than a trace of a suspicious connection. But to a man who prided himself on his razor-sharp mind that was enough to latch on to.

"Damn me, I never heard the like," Rykert said, interrupting the conclusion of Harry's tale as he went to refill the glasses. "And if I didn't know you, I'd say you was making it up."

"My luck was at its very best. As good as Nelson's must have been at St Vincent."

"And then some more, Ludlow. From the sound of it you had all the angels in your corner."

Harry took the glass off him and continued. "Tressoir didn't follow us out to sea, and though *Lothian* scraped the bottom on one occasion we got her out into deep water on the flood. Then it was beg, borrow, and steal in the article of rigging, which is why *Bucephalas* looks so odd, and no end of trouble parcelling out enough of a crew to man three ships."

"And where are the others now?"

"*Lothian,* as my prize, is heading for Portsmouth, with a pleasant surprise for Sir Peter, then to join *Good Intent* which should be on course for the Downs."

"You'll have made a tidy sum, then," his eyes alight, proving that even he, with all his brains, was as excited by prize money as any other sailor.

"I need it, Rykert. My London bank went belly-up while I was away in the Caribbean. The proceeds from the *Lothian* will do no more than clear my debts."

"Sad to hear it, Ludlow," Rykert replied, with very little sincerity. "So! Now we come to the business of the fleet?"

"I need to speak with Admiral Bridport."

"Might I ask why?"

"I won't pretend to you—"

Rykert interrupted him, "That would be unwise."

"—since I'll never get off this ship if I don't."

"Hardly 'never,' but it could take some time."

"What do you think are the chances of another mutiny?"

That stumped him. He didn't want to say yes, but in all conscience, he couldn't say no. Harry took the advantage to continue.

"I have something to say to Admiral Bridport that might help him avoid it."

"And what would that be?"

"At the moment it is nothing more than speculation. I was recently at the Nore, and I had a run in with the leader of the delegates, a fellow called Parker, funnily enough."

"You do get about, Ludlow, don't you?"

Harry, with as much ostentation as he could muster, picked up Sir Peter Parker's instructions. "You will appreciate that what I have to tell Admiral Bridport is confidential."

Rykert had his eyes fixed firmly on the back of the letter, with Harry thinking that he could see the man's mind working. Would an admiral like Sir Peter Parker give *carte blanche* to Harry Ludlow? And why had he used that name, common to two admirals and a mutiny delegate, in that knowing way?

Harry spoke again, pressing home the advantage he'd gained from his host being too clever by half. "Naturally, once I have spoken with Bridport, I will be happy to pass on those same notions to you, that is if he has no objections."

"Do you have charts?" Rykert asked, standing up abruptly.

"Some."

"Then I'll give you a copy of mine."

"Thank you."

"Just be sure to tell Bridport and Sir Peter how eager I was to expedite your journey."

"It will be almost the first thing I say."

"How do you think it will look, Ludlow?" snapped Bridport, as he paced back and forth, a short silhouette against the long line of casement windows. "You come aboard my ship, having arrived amongst the fleet in something that looks like an April Fool's jest, then immediately ask to see Valentine Joyce."

"I didn't have the time to wait until you anchored at Spithead again. The persons I represent bade me chase you here, since they feel the matter to be pressing."

"They're worse than that if the latest dispatch is to be believed." Harry had to bite his tongue, since to ask what that contained would only weaken his case. But fortunately Bridport seemed only too keen to elaborate. "The swine have blockaded London."

The admiral didn't see Harry's face fall. But it did, with the realization that what had been an errand to cover his back might actually turn out to be important. He'd fully expected that the men at the Nore would have come to their senses by now, and that the mutiny would be over.

"Is it successful?"

"Very. And all for something as stupid as shore leave."

"Which was denied at Spithead," Harry replied, just to make conversation while he ordered his thoughts.

"And rightly so, Ludlow. Can you imagine it, men going home every time their ship berthed?! What kind of navy would that be? We'd never get them back again, and as for a bigger share of prize money, I ask you, where is that to come from if not from the pockets of hard-up senior officers?"

That was difficult to swallow, since Harry had rarely met an employed admiral who hadn't made a fortune, including his own father, though that brought back the painful memory that he'd managed to lose everything that same parent had acquired.

"Has there been any violence?"

"Plenty!" Bridport barked, as he stopped and looked down at his feet. "Buckner shut them off from the shore, and any hope of supplies, so they stopped any ships from getting up to the Pool of London. Then there was trouble at Yarmouth. Some fool sent Captain Bligh up there. Imagine sending Breadfruit Bligh to stop a mutiny? He'd already been turfed out of his own ship, the *Director,* at the Nore. He'd not been in Yarmouth for an hour before five of Duncan's line-of-battle ships were *en route* to the Medway."

"What did Admiral Duncan do?"

"What could he do? The Dutch are holed up in the Texel. He's gone to try and keep them there with two ships, God help him."

"What steps are they taking to satisfy the mutineers?"

"There'll be no satisfying them this time, Ludlow. They've partaken of open rebellion, despite what they say about loyalty to the King. Sir Erasmus Gower has a ship-of-the-line at Gravesend, and is preparing to attack downstream."

"One ship."

Bridport wasn't really listening, lost as he was in his own sorry tale. "They fired on *Repulse* when she sought to come back to her duty. And the thought of that sort of action continuing worries me more than anything."

"With Duncan off the Texel, you, and the fleet you command, might be called upon to intervene?"

Bridport sounded very low when he responded to that query, all notion of fiery, warrior rhetoric absent from the reply.

"Will they obey if they are asked, Ludlow? That's the rub. I have stated categorically that I'm against the very idea. But if I'm ordered to do so, I'll be obliged to attempt to obey. We cannot leave these people blockading London, and Billy Pitt and Dundas have said so in no uncertain terms."

"What about Spencer?"

"Just as bellicose. He thinks they rubbed his nose in the ordure at Spithead. He'll not stand for the same thing again."

"These are Admiral Duncan's ships, surely—"

Bridport cut across him. "Pitt maintains that the Dutch are a bigger menace at this moment than the French. Which only goes to show that he might be bright in the political line but he's an ass when it comes to naval strategy."

"But they'll fight the enemy if they come."

"Pitt doesn't believe they will. Not because of the sailors, but because of the agitators he is sure are in their midst."

Harry remained silent, wondering if he should mention his dealings with Pitt. Bridport spun round to face him, the heavily lidded blue eyes boring into his. "Would your seeing Joyce do anything to avoid that?"

"It might," Harry replied, then seeing the disappointment on Bridport's face, he hurriedly added, "It can do no harm, sir, especially if I see him alone."

"Wait on deck."

Harry paced the planking, just by the quarterdeck rail, the subject of much speculation both before the mast and aft. He'd said nothing to anyone but the admiral, but he knew how quickly news spread. The messenger, Bridport's flag-lieutenant, coming towards him, raised the level of curiosity even further.

"The person you've come to see is in the admiral's day cabin."

"Alone?"

"Yes."

Harry went down the companionway, but instead of making his way straight to the door that led aft to Bridport's quarters, he dropped down to the entry port, calling to his boat to come along-side. As arranged, Pender and Flowers came aboard, his servant, seemingly in deep conversation with his captain, covering the quick exchange that took place between Flowers and Harry. Then he asked the officer of the watch if his men could be given a drink and some food, before climbing the companionway and making his way towards the marine sentry that guarded the door to the inner sanctum.

Joyce stood up as he entered, his look half fearful, half curi-ous. "I hope you ain't come to place a rope round my neck?"

"Sit down, Mr Joyce, over here."

Harry pointed towards the foot-lockers underneath the case-ments, well away from all the doors that led off the room. After a quick check to ensure there was no one on the after-gallery that ran round the stern, there for the admiral to take the air in peace, he sat down with him.

"I have no time for lengthy explanation, Mr Joyce. And in truth, pushed, I'd be hard put to justify my being here."

"Then why come?"

"Have you heard how bad things are at the Nore?" Joyce thought for a bit, then nodded, clearly aware that Harry Ludlow knew how news like that would fly round a ship. "Would you like to advance a reason why that is?"

"No, Captain Ludlow, I would not."

"I met Richard Parker."

Joyce was good at controlling himself. Not so much as an eye-lash flickered when the name was used. Harry felt then that he understood what a formidable negotiator this man had been. And he also reckoned that the only thing that would work would be complete honesty. Which is why he found himself doing the talk-ing, and not the man he'd come to see. He explained about the different atmosphere, of the impression that not only were the demands greater, but that the men supposedly running things were doing anything but.

"When I was told at Spithead that there were Jacobins behind the mutiny, I was hard pushed to believe it at first, and after the *London* incident utterly convinced it was untrue. If someone had asked me that question in the Chequers at Sheerness, I wouldn't have been quite so certain."

"There are no Jacobins, Captain Ludlow, take my word for it."

"Then why is it so different?"

"You said yourself they wanted to go one step better than us. It led them too far, that's all."

"That doesn't explain it."

"Poor leadership, then." Harry shook his head slowly, which produced the first slight hint of alarm in Joyce's countenance. "Is my word good enough?"

"Yes," said Harry, reaching into the side pocket of his coat, to fetch out what Flowers had slipped in there by the entry port. Pushing what he held on to the cushioned cover of the locker made Joyce look down, but even in that position Harry could see his eyes widen as he lifted his. "Especially if you explain to me the significance of these."

Joyce stared at the carved set of bones for a full minute without speaking. Harry, likewise, stayed silent, but more because what he'd started out with was a bluff. He had no idea what they meant now, but that they had some importance was obvious by Joyce's reaction.

"I can't tell you."

"What will happen if you're called upon to put down that mutiny?"

"The men won't do it, not to their own, regardless of how daft they've behaved."

"And what happens then?"

"The devil to pay and no pitch hot," Joyce replied softly.

Harry matched the gravity of his tone. "Which will end in open rebellion, something you've fought to avoid since this whole affair started. Even I, much as I sympathize, would be obliged to oppose you."

Joyce looked up, his clear, blue eyes fixing on Harry's.

"When I was aboard the *London*, after Havergood had been shot and just before you arrived, I heard several people playing these. No one else noticed, certainly not Colpoys or Ned Griffiths, being too taken with the risk to their own lives. In the Chequers, at Sheerness, a whole room of noisy sailors was brought to silence by the rattling of these. I have to tell you, Joyce, that I am here because Billy Pitt engaged me to help his nephew, a young man called Villiers."

"You're on their side."

"No. I'm not on anyone's side. But if there are Jacobins or French spies at the Nore, I need to know."

"To what end?"

"Get the bastards out of there so that the men can settle without a bloodbath. That is, if it's not too late."

"Just that?" Joyce asked, the voice as steady as ever, though his jaw was showing some of the strain he was under.

Harry never knew where the inspiration for his next words came from, he just knew he was right. "Richard Parker can't control them the way you did."

Joyce was angry. Harry could see that in his eyes. But he kept his voice level. "It would have been better to be open from the first, Captain Ludlow, instead of pretending Richard Parker hadn't told you."

"But he didn't, Joyce, you did."

"There are no Jacobins, no French agitators."

"I am happy to be convinced," said Harry, slipping the bones back into his pocket.

Another full minute went by before Joyce spoke again. "Everyone wants to see what's not there. Why can't they just accept that the men had grievances so bad that they could take no more? How do you think all this got started?"

"With great difficulty," Harry replied.

Joyce's voice suddenly became full of passion, as the mask of the delegate was dropped to reveal the angry individual underneath. "You don't know the half of it. The fleet weren't happy, but at least the ship's muster rolls were made up of true sailors. Then they brought in the quota men, and they had discontent in their marrow before they ever set foot on a deck. But more'n that, a lot of them were book-learned. I've never met Richard Parker, but I know he was once a midshipman, and that before he was taken up on the quota he was an indebted teacher. He was typical of the sort that came aboard our fleet too."

"Unhappy themselves," said Harry, "and articulate enough to spread discontent."

"I don't know the meaning of that word you just used, but it was just the sort for Parker's type. Soon the whole lower deck of every ship was in ferment, with the Irish especially well prepared for bloody mutiny, though it wasn't long before some doing the stirring realized that not every tar that agreed with them to their face did so in his heart. There was many a man prepared to whisper to the officers."

"So they needed secrecy."

"Yes. That and a way of identifying themselves."

"A rattle of bones."

"Only of a certain rhythm. Once they'd played their beat, they knew it was safe to talk, to exchange the code, even to someone from another ship altogether."

"But that doesn't include you, Mr Joyce. You are neither a quota man nor a bloody revolutionary."

"Do you listen, Captain Ludlow? There are no bloody revolutionaries, and only one or two men who were prepared to spill blood to get their just deserts."

"Were?"

"You can't hide much on a ship, as you know. We, the petty officers, picked up a sniff very early of what was going on."

"And took over the mutiny?"

Joyce didn't respond to the question, he just kept on explaining, now looking at the back of his hand resting on the locker. "It was easy for us. We could meet without arousing suspicion, get ashore and send off petitions and the like. We said to the hotheads we would aid them, did a bit of background talking to the crew we knew were reliable, then when the time came to vote for delegates made sure it was us who got the task, and not the bone players."

"So what about Richard Parker?"

"Sounds to me, him being a quota man himself, that things didn't work out quite the same at the Nore." Joyce looked up, his eyes anxious. "But don't you go getting the notion that those bone players were Jacobins."

Harry described, more fully, what had happened when Flowers had played his bones in the Chequers.

"What's so odd about that?" Joyce snapped. "You know as well as I do that there are dozens of Frenchies serving in the fleet. They are in the main as decent men as you could meet, just like the rest of the men who mutinied, and that includes the Paddies who are blood-sworn United Irishmen."

"Them too?"

"They only wanted justice, and they would have fought any French ship that poked its nose out of Brest. The question I now have to ask you, Captain Ludlow, is, knowing all this, what are you going to do with it?"

"I don't know, Mr Joyce, and that is the complete and honest truth."

"Because I don't want the Navy coming back into our Spithead ships looking for those men. All might look happy on the surface, but six out of ten officers in this fleet are just itching to take revenge. If those sods at the Nore make a mess of things, which God knows they look set to do, then the nooses will be rigged in the Channel Fleet as well as at Sheerness."

"You asked me what I was going to do, Mr Joyce."

"Well?"

"Try and stop it, what else?"

"On your own."

Harry smiled. "I'd love to take you with me, but I doubt that would be wise."

Both men stood up, with Joyce replacing his woollen cap.

"I will say nothing of this to Bridport. But there is one thing you must tell me."

"What?"

"The code that follows the rattle."

Joyce thought for a moment before replying. "I need your word that you'll take it to the grave. Any man coming aboard this one ship, ill-disposed, could hang a round two dozen with that information."

"I swear."

"You play the rhythm, and if the man you're doing it to is one of the original mutineers, he responds with the words, 'Sounds good enough for a purser's death rattle.'"

"You asked that a way be found to avoid your fleet being asked to go to the Nore."

"I did," said Bridport, unhappily. "And if you'll share with me what you found out from Joyce I'd be obliged."

Harry smiled, so much so that it was almost a grin. "The good news, Admiral, is that he had nothing to tell me that I did not already know."

That earned Harry a testy response. "You've failed to enlighten me about that, either."

"What I can say, Admiral Bridport, is that if I can get back to the Thames Estuary in double quick time, I can ease your mind regarding those orders you're afraid to receive. All I ask from you is a loan of some of your best hands, and a chance to raid the *Queen Charlotte*'s cable store and sail locker."

CHAPTER THIRTY-SIX

HARRY felt ridiculously conspicuous standing on the grassy knoll on the eastern tip of the Isle of Grain in his heavy black cloak, as if that article of clothing alone, on a warm June night, made him stand out like a conspirator. To have his hat pulled low and a scarf on as well only made matters worse. He had no idea if the note he'd sent to Richard Parker, in theory banned from any contact with the shore, had reached the beleaguered President of the Nore delegates.

He could see the residue of the mutinous fleet from where he stood, half the ships flying white flags to denote their intention to go over to the Government. The rest, very few now, still sported the red flags of mutiny. Turning to look up the Thames, the vessels that were loyal, or had already deserted the insurrection, were berthed. Lights blazing all over, they were hives of activity so that those downriver should know that their days were numbered, and that official retribution was about to fall on them unless they capitulated.

Harry, in a ship that looked very like its old self, had arrived back in the Downs, having beat up against wind and current to complete the journey from Ushant in ten exhausting days, happy to find both the *Lothian* and the *Good Intent* at anchor. He'd taken care to time his return during the hours of darkness, and in the two hours just before dawn, when the town was at its most somnolent, they'd shipped the centipedes back to their resting place in St Leonard's Church, Harry travelling on to the Griffin's Head so that when Naomi Smith awoke he could tell her the good news.

Any temptation to rest had to be put aside, though he did visit the Three Kings to post letters to Arthur and James and to look in on the convalescent Illingworth to check on his progess. Then he was off to Walmer Castle, heart in mouth and feeling like an errant schoolboy. The relief when he found that neither Villiers nor William Pitt was in residence was tremendous. Lady Hester Stanhope had been as cold as ice as she took the letters he gave her; firstly for leaving her cousin high and dry, and secondly for sending him on a wild-goose chase after the smugglers' galleys. It seemed the entire clerical establishment of upper Deal was threatening to sue the young man for defamation, after he had accused them of engaging in a conspiracy to hide the contrabandiers' boats.

But she thawed somewhat when he told her that he had information that was vital, and would bring the Nore mutiny to a complete and satisfactory end. Harry, standing before her, with Pender looking on, had begun to wonder when he could stop telling lies. Subterfuge was one thing, and he enjoyed the use of it. But ever since he'd met Villiers outside Walmer Castle it seemed he'd done nothing but engage in an increasing mountain of falsehood.

Standing here on the Isle of Grain, another flat expanse very like Sheppey, he felt little different. The news was bad, a fact that was made known to him as soon as he took the *Good Intent* back into her berth at Faversham. It got worse as he travelled to Sheerness. Every person he met seemed eager to tell him how quickly the whole uprising was imploding, a collapse so swift and comprehensive Harry wondered if he'd be in time to achieve anything. Added to that was the frustrating knowledge that he had no clear idea of what he was trying to do.

The soft whistle from Pender told him that Parker was approaching along the track from a beach near Wallend. Looking along in the gathering gloom he was surprised to see that the man was alone. And his general demeanour, shoulders hunched, head on his chest, hands behind his back, spoke volumes for the state of affairs aboard the ships. Harry went down to meet him, well aware that in such a flat, featureless landscape there was little chance of the meeting taking place entirely unobserved.

"Captain Ludlow," said Parker, his voice as feeble as his bearing.

"I had hoped not to witness this," Harry replied, waving his hand over the reaches of the River Thames to include both sets of ships.

"Neither had I, sir. I had every wish to be back at my duty, serving in a navy where men were treated better than cattle."

"I've heard so many tales of what went on, Mr Parker, that it is hard to tell fact from fiction. As we walk, I would be obliged if you gave the true picture."

Parker lifted his head and laughed. His skin had that dark, almost parchment hue of someone with a heavy growth of beard, an impression heightened by dark eyes and heavy brows. In the last of the daylight, as they headed west, he looked slightly demonic.

"You were right, Captain Ludlow. We have lost. Look yonder and you'll see."

"I see white flags over what look like royal standards."

Parker laughed again, but it was a sound that contained a fair measure of despair. "We fired a salute on the King's birthday, did you know that? All to show we were loyal to our sovereign and our people. But they won't be happy unless they hang us all."

"The blockade of London turned the people against you."

"It turned the rich merchants against us. You don't need to read Tom Paine to know that in this country the common people are ignored. Besides, it was that or starve."

"Capt'n," hissed Pender, who was bringing up the rear. Harry and Parker turned to look at him, then followed his pointing finger. They saw the sails break out on a ship of the line, only visible because they were white enough to penetrate the gathering twilight.

"The *Standard*," said Richard Parker, sadly. More tellingly there was no surprise or anger in his voice. Just resignation. "They've been bickering aboard that ship all day."

"It's not unanimous, then?"

"Never in life. There's a battle being raged inside every hull, as some men fight to keep us as we are, against those who are trying to save their necks by surrender. You see, Captain Ludlow, it turns out we were too soft. We should have strung up the worst officers, like Bligh, and sent the rest ashore."

"But you didn't."

"And do you know why? Because if we had decided to take the ships out and hand them over to the French, some men insisted we needed the officers to steer and navigate the damned things. Funny, ain't it, we can't even surrender to the King's enemies, without we need the use of the King's officers."

"I cannot believe you would have done that."

"You're right." Parker pointed to the loyal ships spread upriver, across the channel. "But I don't think they would agree with you. We've had schemes to go to Ireland, others that would take us to the Americas, no one cares much what part, as long as there is wine, women, and warmth. There were even those who thought the best place to impose ourselves was off the Tower of London."

"And you?"

"Knowing what needs to be done, and having the courage to do it, are not often in the same heart."

"That ship is pulling out of the line," Pender called softly.

Parker looked at it for a moment. "I just hope Wallace doesn't keep to his pledge."

"Who is he, and what was the promise?"

"Wallace is the *Standard*'s leading delegate. One of the cleverest of the lot of us, he was. He said he was going to shoot himself, showed me the gun an' all, rather than surrender himself to a naval court."

"Which is what you must do."

Parker looked at him, his dark eyes suddenly unfriendly. "What makes you think I have any power to do anything? Don't be fooled by my title. They might have styled me President, but that wasn't worth an ounce of purser's rations."

"So if you didn't control things, Parker, who did?"

That made the look even more hostile. Harry pulled Flowers's bones from his pocket, hoping that he could reproduce the rhythm he had practised under the owner's supervision. Slipping them between the appropriate fingers and thumb attracted Parker's eyes, which widened slightly, only to open completely, his eyebrows halfway up his forehead, by the time Harry started to play. When Parker didn't respond, Harry added the rest himself.

"Sounds good enough for a purser's death rattle."

"Where did you learn that?!"

Harry opened his mouth to say "Joyce," then shut it again. No point in extending trust where it wasn't necessary, especially to a man who if he didn't escape, or take the route of his fellow delegate Wallace, would soon be in chains.

"Never mind where I learnt those words. It's enough that I have."

"To what purpose?"

"What has the government offered you?"

"Surrender without terms."

"No guarantees about punishment."

Richard Parker spat out his reply. "None!"

"What if I could get you some terms, would that help?"

"How are you going to do that, Captain Ludlow?"

"My brother-in-law works for Henry Dundas. I have asked him to meet me at the Angel in Rochester tonight. I've also had dealings with a nephew of William Pitt. He will be here, if he responds to my summons, first thing tomorrow morning."

"And I thought you might be an honest man," Parker said bitterly.

"I've told more lies in the last three weeks than I have in the rest of my life, Parker. But not one of them has been aimed at doing you, or your mutiny, down. And if it has failed here, in a way that it did not at Spithead, then you and the men you lead must look to your own actions for the cause. My only concern now is to keep a promise I have made to two men, one an admiral, the other a sailor like you. If this does not end peaceably, the next thing you'll see coming upriver are the ships of the Channel Fleet."

"How do you know all this?"

"It makes no odds," Harry barked.

"Keep your voices down," hissed Pender. "You can be heard in Sheerness."

Both men turned round to retrace their steps, Pender stopping to let them by before falling in behind them again. "Accept that I know, Parker, and that my intentions are honourable. There has been enough blood spilt in this mutiny without we add to it with a pitched battle."

"It's come to something when the Spithead lads would fire into the ships of men of their own stamp."

Harry lied again, reassuring himself that it was in a good cause. The last thing he wanted to tell Parker was that the Channel Fleet might do the exact opposite. It would only encourage his resistance.

"Now can you see how far beyond the bounds of sense you have gone?"

"I saw that within the first week," Parker replied wistfully. "Why do you think I went alone, practically on my knees, to see that stuck-up bastard Spencer?"

"Then why didn't you stop it?"

"Because I lacked the power."

"I repeat the earlier question. If you didn't have it, who did?"

"No one. Every delegate was at the mercy of his own associates, blown this way and that by the mood on his own ship. Keeping us from the shore made matters worse, since it allowed the hotheads more sway."

"Are you prepared to name them?"

"No. But if you look 'tween decks on the *Inflexible*, you'd be searching in the right spot for those most committed."

Harry rattled the bones again to bring Parker back to reality.

The President looked at him, his dark brown eyes now misty.

"They won't let us pack it in without exacting retribution."

"Precisely. But if we can minimize that, and get you and some of those in greatest danger away . . ."

"Away where?" Parker hooted, his voice full of disbelief.

"Does it matter?"

"I'll not be a fugitive, Captain Ludlow. Not for what I believe to be deep down a good cause."

"You must, Parker. Everyone knows who you are. If an example is to be made, then you must be it."

The President swung round suddenly, grabbing Harry's arm and jerking it so hard that he brought forth a stab of pain from the now forgotten wound.

"Would they settle for that?"

"What?" asked Harry, pulling his arm free.

"My neck, Ludlow. They can have me, and let the others go free."

Harry suddenly found he was looking at Parker in a new light. He'd discerned, almost from the first time he met him, the fact that he had an inherent lack of stability. It was there now, in his eyes, which shone with near religious fervour.

"Do you realize what you're implying?"

The light died as quickly as it appeared. "Only too well. But you said it. Parker is the name they know. I can't tell how far they want to take their revenge, but I do know this. There will be no clemency for me." He took Harry's arm again, this time more gently. "But let it be only me. Let the President expiate the sin. For if they are let loose, Captain Ludlow, every ship you see, friend or foe, will have men by the dozen swinging from its yards."

"You still haven't told me about the bones," Harry said, praying that what Parker told him, if he spoke at all, would be the same as he'd heard from Valentine Joyce.

"They're the ones who started out to combine. There are men who've been members of Corresponding Societies and the like, and quite a few Irishmen who claimed to be United, though I've never

seen two of that race agree on anything. A lot of the petty officers thought they could control them. I thought so too when I was
elected. They managed it at Spithead, but we botched it here."

"The government thinks there are Jacobins at work."

"Nothing of the sort, though I dare say there's a fair measure
who would subscribe to that if they bided in France. But most are
just sick of living like dogs." Suddenly his voice had more force.
"They aren't bad men, Captain Ludlow. They're good men. And
I only wish I could have led them in the way they deserve."

Harry knew that Parker had corroborated in almost the same
words what Valentine Joyce had told him, which eased his mind
of any lingering doubts he still harboured.

"You're sure you won't run."

"Certain. I have a wife and bairn up in Scotland. Who's to
say they wouldn't be made to suffer in my place?"

Harry never knew what prompted him to say the next words.
Perhaps, even though he felt he didn't really like Parker, he could
admire him. He'd had a tough life, one not cushioned by wealth
or influence; had risen from nowhere, and surely due to some of
his own skill, elevated himself to a position which had caused
admirals to tremble as well as engendering panic in the City of
London. Set the rights and wrongs to one side, and his actions
denoted a remarkable personality. He wasn't as talented as Valentine Joyce, but Harry reasoned that few were.

His own experience in the navy had been cut short because
he had refused to bow the knee to an arbitrary authority, one
much less severe than that endured by people before the mast, so
there was an element of genuine sympathy which was personal;
and now, this one-time midshipman and schoolmaster was offering to take the entire weight of what had gone wrong on to his
own shoulders. That was a courage that Harry Ludlow doubted
he shared.

"I am prepared to help you get away, Parker, if you change
your mind."

Parker, when he turned, had tears running down his cheeks.

He looked back again, towards the last of the mutinous ships. "No, Captain Ludlow, though I thank you kindly. If God has any mercy, he will see my mission complete, and there will be but one noosed rope hanging from the yardarm, and not hundreds."

"I will see what I can do."

"Thank you."

Parker had got back to his boat, which was hauled upon a strand of debris-covered beach. "And if it's any consolation, I never truly thought for one second that there was a single French spy aboard our ships. Sympathizers, yes. Spies, never!"

The President held out his hand. "Then don't go telling anyone about those bones, 'cause it's for sure they'll never believe you."

Pender helped Parker push his boat into the water, and both men watched as he dropped his oars. The sudden rustling sound behind them made Harry freeze, but Pender, equally muffled to diguise himself, spoke softly through his scarf.

"He's been with us since Parker came ashore."

"Any idea who it is?"

"Can't you guess?"

"Not bloody Villiers?" hissed Harry.

"The very same," Pender replied. "He came up on us not long after Parker arrived, and has been tailing us ever since."

"He can't see us."

"There's only one way to stop him, your honour."

Harry sighed. "In the name of God be as gentle as you can."

CHAPTER THIRTY-SEVEN

"**IF IT** was anyone else, Harry, I might be disinclined to believe them. But you have such a nose for crime and the criminal that you may well have the right of it. Though it's unusual for you to parade innocence rather than guilt."

Arthur had secured them a quiet place to talk, and since Rochester was less of a naval port now than in the previous age, the Angel was reasonably under-occupied. He sat, for once looking at home in the dark-panelled Jacobean surroundings of the ancient inn, happy to gently take the rise out of Harry. The question of what he actually did, as an aide to Henry Dundas, had been posed without being answered. But the air of certainty in his conversation led Harry to believe he was more than a mere clerk.

"But," Arthur continued, his voice smooth and far from angry, "do you have any idea of the danger you've exposed yourself to by consorting with such people?"

"I'm used to danger, Arthur," Harry replied without rancour. "Obviously."

"Can you do anything?"

Arthur Drumdryan pushed his fingers together, his eyes firmly fixed on the points. "I can talk to Dundas. Heaven knows everybody wants this business finished as soon as possible. The trouble is that the chair-bound warriors are beginning to sound triumphant already, as though it's all over bar the executions."

"It's that which I'm trying to avoid."

"What's it to you, Harry?"

"Sympathy, Arthur. The fellows at the Nore went too far, I agree. There is a difference between Portsmouth and here. But they had cause. Did you know that the *Sandwich*, where the mutiny started, had twice her normal complement stuffed between the decks, nearly two thousand men? The surgeon even wrote a report about the level of disease which was passed on to Buckner. And still the tenders were arriving, pouring more men from every gaol in the land into a hell worse than the prison at Cold Baths Field. They did nothing, and reaped the whirlwind."

"Everything that was going to be conceded was given away at Spithead, Harry. Admiral Howe told Spencer that he gave the Nore men copies of the agreements. That should have been enough."

Harry responded with something approaching a sigh. "I think they knew that too. Perhaps it was a matter of pride. They needed something from Spencer or Buckner, some small concession, just to feel they weren't riding on the backs of the Channel Fleet."

"That, if I may say so, smacks of sentimentality."

"I don't care, Arthur. I think it happens to be the truth. Richard Parker begged for something like it and Spencer refused. Sadly, Buckner is no Bridport. Things at Spithead could have gone just the same way without the gentle touch of a good commander. Buckner has a heavy hand. It was right to get rid of him."

"They will both lose their commands, nevertheless, regardless of any personal qualities."

Harry looked at his brother-in-law, and saw the certainty in his eyes. "Why Bridport?"

Arthur sat forward, for once reacting with the speed of a normal human being. "He conceded, Harry. He may well, as you have intimated, have been right to do so. But that won't save him. There's Bantry Bay to answer for, as well."

Harry recalled Bridport's depression at the thought of what his fleet might be called upon to perform. "He's a fine sailor, Arthur. He shouldn't be blamed for the French trying to invade Ireland."

Drumdryan had sat back again, his calm demeanour restored. "He will be damned by men who would be seasick dipping their toe in the Thames or the Shannon. But whether we like it or not, they are the ones who will make the decisions."

"Do you make decisions, Arthur?"

"I advise, Harry, that is my sole function. Lord Keith will take Bridport's place, which is why he's been brought to the Nore to replace Buckner for the final chapter."

"He has good connections."

"Few better," Arthur replied. Then he smiled suddenly. "Of course, to be a Scot does him no harm."

"Do you envisage any hope of clemency from a man like him?"

Arthur shrugged. "I do know that those at Gravesend, Sir Erasmus Gower in particular, talk of an assault more than they like the idea of actually engaging in one. If matters were to be at a stand for any length of time . . ." Arthur paused, and looked beyond Harry to the door. "There is a young man with a bandage round his head, and he is looking at you in the most alarming way."

Half turning, Harry knew who it was before he saw Villiers in the flesh. He did indeed have a heavy dressing round his head, one that indicated that Pender's "tap" was understated. Or perhaps, given Villiers penchant for dramatizing everything he did, it was the wrapping that was at fault.

"Captain Ludlow," he said, in an arch tone, his voice strangely nasal.

"Young man," Arthur said smoothly, "you must wipe your nose. You are in danger of dropping mucus on this fine carpet."

Villiers had opened his mouth to continue no doubt, judging by the look in his eye, a verbal blast aimed at his late partner. But Arthur's intervention, and the way it seemed to reduce him to the status of a child, killed the words. Worse, from Villiers's point of view, his nose did indeed drip.

"You suffer from hayfever, sir," Arthur continued. "A most unpleasant affliction."

"Captain Ludlow and I need to speak," said Villiers, recovering a modicum of his composure. "And the matters are concerned with the security of the realm."

"My word," said Arthur. "Then I'd best stay and listen. How could I, in all honour, go to my club without I had some state secrets to give away?"

"This is my brother-in-law, Mr Villiers, the one who dined with your uncle." Harry turned to Arthur. "This young man is nephew to William Pitt."

Arthur was on his feet, only Harry of the two able to see the humour in his manner. "Then you are also nephew to my good friend the Earl of Chatham. Sit down, sir, I beg you, and ease the pressure on that wound."

"I must have words with Captain Ludlow."

"You sound angry," said Arthur.

"With good cause, sir. He has misled me, not once, but twice."

"That, if I may say so, implies a want of application on your part."

"Enough, Arthur," said Harry, seeing Villiers bridle. "Let this young man sit down and castigate me to his heart's content."

"I will not take a seat, sir. You abused my trust most shamefully. I have the unfortunate task of telling my uncle William that I have been taken for a fool."

Arthur cut in, his voice full of concern. "That wound, sir, looks mighty serious."

"I was clubbed last night, while observing that villain Richard Parker. If I had the identity of the man he met, a nest of worms would open up to shake the foundations of the kingdom."

"Describe him!" Arthur demanded.

"It was a pair, Frenchmen without doubt. I could tell by the cut of their cloth. Heavy cloaks, scarves and hats pulled low, and that at this time of year."

"That is hardly a description. What size were they?" Villiers hesitated, a gap which Arthur filled. "Harry, stand up."

When Harry obliged, Arthur pointed to him. "What size were they in relation to Captain Ludlow?"

"Bigger," Villiers replied, without hesitation. "Much bigger."

"Then we must set up a hue and cry, Villiers, for two French giants wrapped in cloaks and scarves."

Even Villiers's thick skin was not proof against that level of irony. He was offended, to Harry's mind with some cause. But

Arthur wasn't finished with him. He still had barbs to play.

"Your uncle William engaged you to this service?"

"He did."

"And you engaged Captain Ludlow?"

"I introduced him," Villiers replied, with telling prevarication.

"To what purpose?"

"To uncover evidence of Jacobin involvement in the mutinies!"

"Question, Mr Villiers. What do you think would make your uncle William happier? To have to go to the King, who is not a well man, and tell him that his fleet is full of sedition, or to pass on to His Majesty that for all the travails of the past two months his subjects are loyal but misguided?"

"The latter, naturally," Villiers replied, seemingly unaware of the degree of turn such a response required. "No right-thinking Englishman would want to add pressure that might affect the King's malaise."

"Then isn't it a reflection of your judgement of character that you have chosen the very man to elicit the facts? My brother-in-law informs me that there is not even a trace of French influence in the fleet, either here or in the Channel."

"What?!"

Harry had watched this exchange with increasing amazement, quite struck with Arthur's ability to turn an argument on its head, then bring it out in exactly the right place.

"It's true, Mr Villiers," Harry added, trying to sound disappointed, as though his hopes had been dashed as much as the youngster's. "As you know, I went to see Valentine Joyce." He paused, waiting to see if Villiers alluded to the Normandy coast. But there was no mention of that, only anticipation at what Joyce might have revealed. "I put to him certain questions, which I outlined to you was my aim. He answered every one to my satisfaction."

"You are wrong, sir," Villiers spluttered, in a sudden show of emotion. He had a new spot of dew on the end of his nose which tended to draw the eye and spoil the effect of this transition.

"I assure you I am not."

Villiers seemed to have recovered himself, as though Arthur's irony and relentless logic, plus Harry's good sense, had never been employed.

"Then I look forward to confounding you. The insurrection collapses as we speak. I have news that four more ships, including the *Agamemnon* and the *Nassau,* have broken with the mutiny. The *Montague, Directory,* and *Lion* have raised white flags."

"The *Sandwich?*" asked Harry.

"There is turmoil there," Villiers replied, his confidence growing, "with a contest for control of the magazine. What matter, she cannot hold out on her own. Every seditious swine in the fleet will run for her or the *Inflexible.* But they are wasting their time. Lord Keith is ready to sail down and smite them. We shall have them before a court and hanging from the yardarm before nightfall."

Arthur coughed, not loudly, but enough to interrupt Villiers's enthusiastic flow, and the words that followed suffered no loss of weight for being spoken softly. "I find myself at a stand. It pains me to remind you, sir, that this is Britain, not France."

"I fail—"

The voice that cut across him was harsh, and much more Scottish in tone than Harry had ever heard it. "I dare say you do, sir, on a regular basis. And the area in which you fail most is that of justice. No man will be hanged that has not been properly tried before a court of law."

Arthur stood up, and walked past Villiers, indicating peremptorily that Harry should follow. "You are a disgrace to your bloodline, Mr Villiers. It will give me no pleasure to pass on that information to both of your uncles."

He was whispering before they got to the door. "Do you want to try something, Harry?"

"Yes!"

"Then you get to Parker, while I get to Gravesend and try to put a check on things."

Harry tugged at his arm to turn Arthur Drumdryan round,

and looked into his pale blue eyes, ignoring the fact that Villiers was following in their wake. "I must ask why."

The thin smile with which Arthur responded was one Harry had rarely seen before, hinting at the true man underneath Arthur's polished exterior. And there was a hiatus as the youngster slid by trying in vain to hear their conversation.

"My grandfather did not support Prince Charles Edward Stuart, Harry. He disagreed with that French-bred pimp both in principle and behaviour. But after Culloden Field, he opened his house to any stranded and starving Jacobite who needed help. Because if the man who led them was a drunken fool, the soldiers were his countrymen."

"And he suffered?"

"He did, Harry. But never fear. Even as rich as I should have been, I would have married your sister for love."

"You should tell James this."

That earned Harry a hollow laugh. "I've been telling James how to behave since he was eight years old, and not once has he listened."

"Villiers?" Harry asked, pointing at the slowly retreating back.

"I will deal with him. Just go."

The panic that was about to explode was very evident throughout the entire anchorage. Boats were flying in all directions, with men calling out to each other, passing messages of desperation or hope, according to their allegiance. Harry and Pender, in a hired wherry, steered straight for the *Sandwich,* still defiantly flying the red flag. But it was obvious as they came alongside that things were far from that simple, and by the time they reached the deck, they discovered just how complicated they were.

Over half the crew, and all the officers, were forward of the waist, spilling down the gangways, gesticulating to the men who occupied the quarterdeck and the poop. One fellow, a huge black, was yelling, indeed chanting, for Richard Parker to be hanged, so loudly that his voice carried over that of everyone. The President was by the wheel, his hands raised in a futile attempt to restore some order. Fortunately the gangway and entry port were neutral, so Harry and Pender had no trouble making their way to the upper deck.

Parker dropped his hands when he saw Harry, and with as discreet a gesture as possible summoned him to join him by the starboard quarterdeck rail. The man was a mess, his thick dark hair awry, eyes wild, and his face black and streaked with soot.

"What have you come for, at a time like this?"

Harry looked forward, his eye on the knot of officers, led by a lieutenant, who had gathered by one of the hatchways.

"I made you an offer yesterday, Parker. It still stands."

"It cannot be."

"We have a boat," said Pender.

"We tried to launch one an hour ago, just to get the most active away. But that was blocked."

"There's always a way, Parker," Harry insisted.

Parker pointed past him. "You see that lieutenant, there, the angry-looking cove with the forehead like an ape. Flatt is his name, which just about sums the bastard up. He's working himself up to fight for control of the ship. I have to stop him."

"How?"

"Watch, Captain Ludlow." He stepped away, then turned round to face him. "I thank you kindly for your concern. But if I don't do what needs to be done, there will be more blood on this deck than any man could imagine."

"You're going to surrender?"

Richard Parker grinned then, and filthy as he was, it was heartening. "I must haul down my flag."

"You will hang. And I have asked. I don't think you'll be alone."

"We will see about that, Captain Ludlow. Meantime, most of those threatened got away to *Inflexible* yesterday. If you can do something for them, I'd be obliged."

Parker moved forward, merely tapping the hand that Harry

held out. He went out to stand in front of the jeering crowd, aware, as Harry and Pender were, that the support at his back was not much more enthusiastic than that in the front.

"Shipmates!"

"Would you believe it," whispered Pender, as the sound of shouting died away. "He's shut the sods up."

"I was elected to lead this challenge, by you, my fellow crewmen. I see before me officers with pistols in their hands, and I don't doubt murder in their hearts. Did you know, brothers, that one of their number offered to do me in, to shoot me for a fee?" He had complete silence now, and so could drop his voice from a shout. "You elected me to be President. I will not give way to these men with their guns. But if you, the men who voted me in, want me to capitulate, then I will do so. If you do not, I will throw Flatt and his friends over the side."

"Hang Richard Parker," shouted the tall black man.

"Shut up, Campbell," a voice answered. But it was no good, the man kept yelling.

"I ordered you flogged, Black Jack Campbell," shouted Parker, "and being the useless shit that you are, you want to see me dead to avenge it."

"Hang Richard Parker!"

Flatt moved then, perhaps sensing that things might go against him. The action seemed to release whatever pent-up emotion was stored in the sailors' breasts, and they all began to yell, some to hold to Parker, but more to support Flatt. The lieutenant's voice, as he made his demands, could barely be heard over the din.

"The keys to the magazine, Parker, if you please. And a return of all the small arms you bear."

Parker shouted at the top of his voice now, calling for three cheers. "And this is to men who have not had their ship taken off them, but have handed it back."

The sound of cheering was in their ears as Harry and Pender pushed their way back down to the entry port, and to their wherry.

CHAPTER THIRTY-EIGHT

THE *Inflexible* was in just as much turmoil as the *Sandwich,* but the balance was very different, so much so that they had great trouble in getting aboard. The split on the upper deck was the same in terms of positions, but the men gathered in the forepeak were few, and there were no officers to lead them. Harry managed to elicit from one of the mutineers that they were still confined, while a discussion was going on in the great cabin to decide whether to string them up or let them loose. Both men pushed their way through the throng, and came face to face with a scared individual guarding the cabin door, who had a forehead so thin that it hardly seemed to exist.

"Nobody gets in here, mate."

"Not even a delegate?" demanded Harry.

"You? I've seen 'em all, and never your face afore."

Harry had the bones out, though the rattle, in the confined space, was far from perfect. "Sounds good enough for a purser's death rattle."

"That's my bit," snarled the guard.

"Open that damned door, you oaf," Harry replied, his voice even more harsh. "If you don't, there's not a man in that cabin who will see tomorrow's dawn."

Still he hesitated. But when Pender pushed past, slipping under his arm, he let them through. The cabin was full of the smoke from a dozen pipes, with anxious-looking sailors sitting around a large table. For men under threat of execution, they were strangely lethargic. One, at the head of the table, did half rise, and Harry recognized the man who'd challenged Flowers when he'd first played his bones in the Chequers.

"What do you want?" he demanded thickly, in heavily accented English.

Harry looked around the cabin, wondering if Joyce and Parker had been right. He'd never seen a bunch of men who could so easily fit the bill as conspirators. But that didn't matter now, since he had no way of establishing the thing one way or the other. He threw the bones on the table, and they slid across to come to rest in front of the delegate.

"Parker sent me."

"Never!" snapped a man right beside Harry's leg, who swung round to show a vicious knife. "Parker wouldn't do that."

"No, mate. But Valentine Joyce might."

That made them sit up and take notice, so much so that Harry was allowed to move round to join the Frenchman who was apparently their leader.

"Parker's surrendered."

"The slimy sod."

"He had no choice," Harry yelled, as the noise began to rise. "And if you want to know, I offered him a chance to get away, yesterday, and leave you all in the lurch."

The French speaker had picked up the bones. After looking at them he tossed them back to Harry. "Play, English."

Harry obliged, adding the passwords as soon as he finished. But the man who'd challenged him wasn't convinced. "You are not one of us."

"No," Harry replied, gesturing vaguely upriver towards London. "But neither am I one of them."

"Then why have you come?"

"To advise you to leave now, while you have the chance." That set up a buzz of conversation, which Harry allowed to continue until it subsided. "You're probably the last ship in the fleet with the red flag still flying. And from what I can see, a good number of the crew want to haul it down. When they find out the *Sandwich* has struck, that number will treble."

"You're very sure of yourself, mate," said a voice through the tobacco smoke.

"That would be because he was right," said Pender, speaking for the first time.

The reply that got earned a stifled laugh. "An' I thought you was just a monkey."

"If you ain't got the brains to see what's what, then you must be too thick to swing in the trees."

"But not too thick to swing on a rope," Harry added. "The men on the deck can surrender without pain. They have a pardon. But you lot will be classed as ringleaders, and you will hang."

Another voice spoke, proving that whatever kind of meeting it was, it was democratic. "So what do you suggest?"

"Run."

"Where to?"

"Anywhere away from here."

"Funny, that," said the French speaker. "We was debating where to take the ship."

"That will need the officers."

"A knife to their throat will suffice," said the man who'd waved the blade.

"Leave the ship, and the officers."

"Don't sound right to me."

"Try to take this ship, and they'll chase you to the ends of the earth. The same goes if you touch a hair on one of those officers' heads."

"You're a fine one and no error!" a voice shouted from the far end of the table. "How the hell are we to get anywhere safe without we has a ship?"

"I'll give you a ship." That produced a gasp or two, but most just looked at him in wonder. "She's no beauty, but she floats well enough. And since no one knows where she lays, she won't be missed."

"Where's that?"

"Faversham," said Harry.

"Why are you doing this?" asked the French speaker. "I for one don't know you."

Harry looked round the table again, peering through the smoke at the suddenly curious faces. "To tell you the truth, I don't know. I just feel in my bones that no good will be served by a spree of hangings. Perhaps you men here have a different agenda from those outside, and always have had."

They stiffened at that, but no one spoke. Harry jerked his thumb back in the direction of the deck. "What they were asking for was no more than their due. But some wanted too much."

"Any other reason?" asked a man with a heavy Irish accent.

"Yes. I met a fellow sailor who told me that you were good men. His name was Valentine Joyce, and he had a fear."

"Which was?"

"That if certain men were taken from the Nore, then the meaning of those bones would become known. They won at Spithead. But if anybody gets wind of an organized conspiracy they will pursue it to the bitter end, and it won't be confined to ships in the Medway."

"How much time have we got?"

"None!" snapped Pender. "If'n I was you, I'd be running for this barky's boats."

Harry had expected trouble in getting hold of the *Inflexible*'s boats, but clearly these men still wielded enough authority to impose themselves. Those who might have stopped them were in the bows, and the boats were lashed to the stern. They ended up with more men than they'd anticipated, as each man who left the cabin seemed to have a friend he wished to take along.

Pender and Harry led the way in their wherry, rowing along in the dark, two lanterns lit bow and stern, innocents out for a night's fishing, with three of the *Inflexible*'s boats unlit and following their wake. There were blockading ships and guard boats out, and at one time Harry was stopped by the crew of a cutter who were speaking a language he guessed to be Russian. While he argued, the men from *Inflexible* stood off, lying low and silent to avoid detection. The loud farewells that Harry made told them it was safe to proceed, steering the course set for them by the lantern.

Harry was having a devil of a time navigating, since the darkness was close to total. He kept running into shallow water then having to heave himself out, an action which forced those following him to back-paddle noisily. Once they were clear of the eastern edge of Sheppey the odd twinkling light from the coastal villages helped him to frame a course for Faversham, heading across to the Kentish shore, where the Swale channel began to narrow.

As soon as he reached the creek that ran up to the harbour he ceased to row, and called softly for the boats to come alongside. Buildings of one sort or another lined the shore, and Luddenham Court, the local mansion, was well lit up, which meant that running aground, not too much of a problem in a boat anyway, was near impossible.

"We left the *Good Intent* back in the hands of two old sailors," he whispered. "They're useless sods, but they are also drinkers, and likely to be asleep. I will take you past her, but I'm not coming aboard. They know me and Pender too well. If we're seen I'll have to flee to France with you."

Harry went on, explaining where they would find charts, what landmarks to look for, and how the ship handled. "Take those two old goats with you. They know every channel and sandbar in the Thames Estuary."

"And what do we do when we get there?" asked the French speaker.

"Send them back with it. Whatever you do, don't try to keep the boat. The navy is bad enough with mutineers and deserters, but take a rated ship of theirs, even a tub, and they'll chase you for ever."

"What," exclaimed one of the Irishmen, "in the name of Jesus, are we going to do when we get there?"

"Without a bloody boat to even fish with," added another.

"Don't fish in anything but a river," Harry said, emphatically, "and an inland one at that. Stay well away from the sea for the rest of your lives. And never, even just to jog your memory, play a set of bones."

Standing on the deck of the *Sandwich,* Harry recalled very clearly the image of the *Good Intent* making her way out into the Thames Estuary, with some of the men he'd helped get away actually waving to him. Had they been as innocent as they seemed, those Inflexibles? Or were they the reason things had turned so bad at the Nore?

Having swung too many ways in so few weeks he was beyond caring. He would probably never know, and if that held true for everyone else, then his promise to Valentine Joyce would be fulfilled. If they were indeed Jacobins, United Irishmen, or avid subscribers to *The Rights of Man* he couldn't be brought to care. At least they weren't here, on this deck.

He looked at the faces around him, most eager. There was some laughter too, as if what they were about to witness amused them. Harry himself could not suppress the odd shiver, though the morning air was anything but cold. A glance at his watch, when he heard the footfalls on the companionway, showed it was well past half-past eight.

Parker emerged on to the quarterdeck, staggering slightly as he saw how many people had come to see him die. Was Harry alone in wondering if he could spot the scaffolding specially erected on the Isle of Grain so that the local populace would not be denied the pleasure of seeing him swing? The parson stepped forward, offering his services in prayer, an overture the prisoner seemed eager to accept.

"Might I be allowed a chair," said Parker, his voice surprisingly strong, "and perhaps a glass of wine?"

You had to admire the man. If this was to be his last public engagement, he was determined to play it properly. He took the wine, which was quickly produced, and once that was consumed he stood up and bowed his head to pray, being joined in this by those who had condemned him.

The words of the prayers were suddenly drowned out by the firing of a gun. Everyone on the deck jumped slightly, except Parker, who continued his prayers as if it was another man facing the rope, not him. Those finished, he offered his hand to Mosse, the captain of the *Sandwich,* the hope that he would accept this as an act of reconciliation stated loudly enough to carry. Then his arms were bound, and the shuffling group of onlookers followed him as he was led to the forecastle.

Harry stayed still, not wishing to be any closer in the final moment. But Parker, turning round, saw him, and produced a sudden smile that made every head turn to see who was so favoured. Having been in the area for several weeks now, his identity and occupation were known. A growl slipped out of several naval throats, and he knew, in their minds, that he was no better than the victim of this judicial revenge.

Parker walked up the scaffold which projected out over the side of the ship. The men who would hang him stood ready, the end of the rope that ran up to the yard in their hands, while the halter was placed around Parker's neck. After a moment to compose himself, he allowed the executioner to place a cap over his head, which was drawn forward to hide his face. But he held up his hands to stop it for a second, and turned to say something to the men who had, so recently, been his shipmates.

The cap was pulled down and the men steadied themselves to pull. Suddenly Parker stepped forward and jumped off the end of the scaffold, jerking as his body weight was arrested by the rope. Harry saw the spasms, as his feet kicked out at the air beneath them. The second gun, which should have been the signal to pull, went off and the crewmen obliged, raising Parker's body well above the deck. But the feet had ceased to jerk and Harry knew that in his own small way Parker had cheated the Royal Navy. He'd managed a final act of defiance, and hung himself.

Reaching into his pocket he took out Flowers's bones, still not sure why he'd brought them along. Walking to the side, he was just about to throw them away when Lieutenant Flatt, who'd been Parker's adversary on this very deck just a few days before, stopped behind him.

"Well, Ludlow, that is an end to all the nonsense."

"Do you think so, Lieutenant?" said Harry, over his shoulder.

"If I were you I'd hurry up and win a fleet action, or posterity will forget you."

Harry turned round and pointed to the body, swaying on the end of the rope. "But they won't forget him, nor the men he led. They, I have to tell you, will live in men's minds for ever."

DAVID DONACHIE is an avowed lover of  naval fiction with a streak of mischief. A best-selling author well-known to European audiences, Donachie—as Tom Connery—is the author of the popular *George Markham of the Marines* novels, also set during the Napoleonic Wars and telling the land and sea adventures of His Majesty's Royal Marines. Under his own name, Donachie is the author of a multi-volume biographical novel about Lord Nelson and Lady Emma Hamilton.

A Scot by birth, he lives in Deal on the Channel coast of England, where he works to keep his inspirations in motion.